What readers have to say about Sheila Jeffries' books

'Stunning. Beautifully written, with an
exquisitely poetic narrative'

'One of those rare books that stays with you
long after you've finished reading it'

'The most heart-warming book I have read in a long time.
I did not want it to end'

'Fabulous read'

'One of the best books I have read. I couldn't put it down'

'Brilliant'

'The prose is simply superb. When the sheer beauty of words
can evoke tears, that's the sign of a gifted writer'

'Of all the books I have bought, this is the best'

'I thought all the characters were brilliant'

'A book to touch your heart'

'Every page was a pleasure to read'

'This novel is sweet and insightful and shows
a good understanding of human emotions'

'Spell binding'

'I thoroughly enjoyed it and the insight into
the afterlife was so interesting'

'Sheila Jeffries is an amazing storyteller'

'A truly unique book, one that I would highly recommend.
I can't wait for her next'

'Deep insight and understanding into the pain and fear many
people live with. I heartily recommend this book to everyone who
is tired of the violence and anger in so many books now'

Also by Sheila Jeffries

Solomon's Tale
Solomon's Kitten
The Boy with no Boots
Timba Comes Home
The Girl by the River

SHEILA JEFFRIES

Born to be Trouble

Cardiff Libraries
www.cardiff.gov.uk/libraries

Llyfrgelloedd Caerdydd
www.caerdydd.gov.uk/llyfrgelloedd

**SIMON &
SCHUSTER**

London · New York · Sydney · Toronto · New Delhi

A CBS COMPANY

First published in Great Britain by Simon & Schuster UK Ltd, 2017
A CBS COMPANY

1 3 5 7 9 10 8 6 4 2

Simon & Schuster UK Ltd
1st Floor
222 Gray's Inn Road
London WC1X 8HB

www.simonandschuster.co.uk

Simon & Schuster Australia, Sydney
Simon & Schuster India, New Delhi

A CIP catalogue record for this book
is available from the British Library

Paperback ISBN: 978-1-4711-5494-2
eBook ISBN: 978-1-4711-5495-9

Typeset in Bembo by M Rules
Printed and bound by CPI Group (UK) Ltd, Croydon, CR0 4YY

To my brilliant cousin, a healer of souls, who passed into spirit on 15 April 2016, and who appears in this book as 'Starlinda'.

Born to be
Trouble

PROLOGUE

1970

Why am I doing this?

Tessa looked down at her silver shoes, the pointed toes peeping out from the ruffles of lace around the hem of her satin dress. She waited on the pavement outside Monterose Church. The March wind surged through the tree tops, but on the lawns the pale green buds of daffodils were stiff and unmoving. *Like aunties*, Tessa thought. The church would be full of them – aunties in their Crimplene suits and portly hats. Watching her. Triumphantly.

It was what they wanted her to do. Conform.

As she waited for her father to ease himself out of the car, Tessa glanced down the road, and imagined herself running, in her silver shoes, her white veil flying, her bouquet of pink roses and freesias discarded in the gutter.

Freddie manoeuvred himself out of the shiny black car. He felt awkward in unfamiliar clothes. Kate had insisted on him

1

wearing a grey top hat. It felt like a cardboard cereal packet on his head, and he hardly dared speak in case he shook it off. He knocked it sideways getting out of the car. 'I'm not wearing this blimin' thing,' he said, at the last minute, and chucked it back into the car.

Tessa gave him a secret smile, and saw his blue eyes twinkle with pride as he looked at her in awe. She didn't care about the hat. *I can't let him down*, she thought, looking up at him adoringly as he took her arm.

'You ready?' he asked.

She nodded. *No*, her mind screamed silently, *I'll never be ready for this!*

'Come on, you're shivering.' Freddie took her arm and walked her slowly down the flagstone path between two rows of yew trees.

The vicar's white robe billowed at the church door. Tessa was glad it was a new, young vicar, not the old Reverend Reminsy who had haunted her childhood. The new vicar had a quiff of boyish dark hair and enthusiastic cheeks. He obviously loved weddings.

Tessa saw him dart inside and nod to the organist. The murmur of voices stilled like water settling, and the stones of the ancient church trembled with the energy of Widor's Toccata. Music had the power to disturb Tessa. *I will not break*, she thought, watching her silver shoes taking her elegantly into church.

Hats and flowers brightened the sombre interior. An unfamiliar fragrance of Pink Camay soap merged with the resident fustiness of old hymn books and candlewax.

Why am I doing this?

Tessa fixed her eyes on her mother who was in the front pew, her bright brown eyes shiny with emotion. Kate's smile lit up the church when she saw her daughter in the fairy-tale dress, walking down the aisle with Freddie.

This is Mum's dream, not mine, Tessa thought. *I've caused her so much worry over the years and she wants me to be happy and settled, and – normal – what she thinks is normal.*

As a teenager, Tessa had been haunted by a vision of her mother leaving. It had flashed into her mind on Kate's birthday when she saw red roses in a vase on the table. 'Freddie gave them to me,' Kate said, her voice warm with joy. 'He knows I love red roses. You smell them.' Tessa had inhaled the fragrance, feeling the cool, pillow-like petals brush her cheek, and in that moment the vision had come. Her mother was leaving. The family were following her coffin into Monterose Church, and it was covered in red roses. The colour seemed darker, the perfume heavier, the sadness an unexplored, fathomless twilight.

Tessa kept the disturbing vision to herself. But Kate had noticed her expression. 'Don't look so gloomy,' she quipped. 'Anyone would think it was a funeral, not a birthday.' And when Tessa stared at her with tears glimmering in her eyes, Kate said, 'For heaven's sake, what's the matter NOW? Why can't you ever behave like a normal person, Tessa?'

It hurt. Every time. But now, after the years of heartbreak, she was walking into church, a bride, a normal person. Despite everything.

3

Tessa was aware of the heads turning to gaze at her, embroidered hankies dabbing tears from powdered cheeks. *It's what they wanted. To see their ugly duckling turn into a swan,* Tessa thought, and imagined the shock it would cause if she turned and fled from the church like an escaping snowflake.

The heavy oak door of the church was closed. Its iron latch clanged into place, and an expectant pause settled over the congregation.

In the moment between moments, a small white dog appeared in the church porch. He sat at the door and barked. His bark echoed in the stone porch, but the door stayed closed, so he stretched his throat and howled.

Tessa heard him, even as the words of the first hymn were being sung lustily by the army of aunties. The spirit of her little dog, Jonti, who had so often warned her of danger, was warning her now, from beyond the grave. She glanced at Freddie. He'd heard it too. His eyes looked startled, then worried.

The satisfied gleam in her mother's eyes brought her back into place and she found herself standing at the altar looking up at Paul. She searched his eyes and saw only hunger. An unnatural hunger, thinly packaged in a shell of pride. And somewhere in those hazel eyes the expectations hovered like sparrowhawks waiting for a twitch of movement. Waiting to pounce.

In a dream-like state, Tessa heard herself saying, 'I do' and 'I will'. She saw herself floating down the aisle with Paul like a captive fairy, picking her way through a sea of smiles and flowers. A thought echoed from the abandoned caverns of her mind. *It's wrong. Paul is the wrong man. What have you done, Tessa? What have you done? And why?*

The wedding was over. The bells of Monterose Church pealed joyfully. A slate-grey sky hung low over the town, the light bruised with storm clouds, and the West wind drove barbs of rain into the stone porch. It lifted Tessa's veil as if wanting to snatch her back to the distant shores of Cornwall. She smelled salt and heather. She saw Art wading out of the sea, his intense grey eyes burning into her soul. *I love you, Art*, she thought fiercely. *I will carry you in my heart, always and forever.*

PART ONE

CHAPTER 1

Hippies 1964

A bus painted in psychedelic colours rumbled through the streets of Monterose. A few heads turned to watch it disapprovingly. Were the hippies invading the quiet market town?

'That girl in the front – that's Tessa Barcussy! What's SHE doing with the hippies?'

'Disgusting. I mean – it's disGUSTing. A nice girl from a nice family – and she went to Hilbegut School. Now look at her!'

'But then – she always was a bit odd – wasn't she? Moody and rebellious.'

'Keep an eye on them. If they try and set up camp in Monterose, there'll be trouble.'

'Pity. Freddie and Kate are such good people. Sad they've got a daughter like that – and the other girl, Lucy – she went wrong too.'

The bus rattled on, over the railway bridge, and up the

lane, the tyres running softly on carpets of golden leaves that were drifting and zigzagging along the lane.

'Are we nearly there?' Art asked. 'She's running out of petrol.'

'Half a mile,' Tessa said. Her pale blue eyes were luminous and bright as she looked at Art adoringly. His tanned arms with a fuzz of sun-bleached hairs, his mane of hair that always looked as if he was flying over the Atlantic on a surfboard. His frayed denim jacket, the patchwork pockets bulging with a conglomeration of things he used, and things he loved, like the photo of Tessa walking out of the sea in her sea-green bikini. Art had two other photos, one of his gran, the other of a dog he'd loved as a child. He'd got cards with friends' contact numbers on them, a card with a recipe for a Cornish pastie, and cards with poems in tiny writing. All crammed into an Embassy cigarette packet with a flip lid. His diary was stuffed with pressed flowers from the Cornish cliffs where he and Tessa had first made love on a magical day in summer.

Leaving Cornwall had been a wrench for both of them. It had taken three days to drive Art's converted bus to Somerset; the roads were narrow, meandering through towns and villages, over Bodmin Moor and Dartmoor, crossing narrow stone bridges over bubbling streams, and when it rained the autumn leaves stuck to the windscreen like splashes of paint. Art couldn't get the windscreen wipers to work, and Tessa had to lean out and clear raindrops and leaves from the glass. They'd camped on Dartmoor, surrounded by wild ponies, granite and heather.

Somerset felt civilised and flat after the grandeur of Devon and Cornwall. The fields were square, and the Levels stretched into the distance to the gentle blue hills of the Mendips. But to Tessa it was home. The air smelled of cows and apples. The hedges were laden to the ground with bright berries, and covered in a creeping plant known as old man's beard, which shone like foam in the sun. It was a long time, six months since she had been home, and there were issues to be settled with her parents. Number one was Art, and his lifestyle. Number two was her decision to quit college and set up home in the bus with Art.

'How do you know which field it is?' Art asked. 'We don't want to park up in the wrong one.'

'Of course I know, Art, I grew up here,' Tessa said. 'My sister and I ran wild in these fields. It's this next one – where the stream rises. Stop and let me get out. I'll open the gate.'

'Okay.'

Tessa climbed down from the bus. The hedges leaned over her in a tangle of blackberries and coloured leaves of field maples with their bunches of winged brown seeds. Strands of vivid orange bryony meandered through the branches. The gate looked as if it hadn't been opened for years. The bleached seed heads of grasses had woven themselves through the bars; columbine and ivy curled around the posts and along the top bar.

Tessa paused, gazing at the field. It was hers, and she found that hard to believe. A precious square of Mother Earth. She could do whatever she liked with it, or in it. And no one could tell her what to do!

The field was an unexpected inheritance, left to her by Ivor Stape, an eccentric pervert who had abused Tessa when she was only seven. She had run away from school to explore the Mill Stream, the words of Tennyson's poem, *The Brook*, singing in her mind. It had filled her with a yearning to find *the brimming river* and to follow it to *forever* on that long ago May morning. Remembering the story her mother often told, of how Aunt Ethie had drowned in the Severn River, Tessa had been overwhelmed with sadness. In memory of an aunt she had never met she gathered cowslips and floated them on the stream. Finally the Mill Stream led her under a tunnel and into Ivor Stape's gloomy garden where he found her shivering and soaking wet. Feigning kindness, he lured her into his secluded home, and there, in a shadowy room cluttered with old books and geological specimens, Ivor Stape had raped her. It had made her feel bad and dirty, and angry too. Angry at men. Tessa was given no understanding, no therapy or help to deal with it. Instead, the family forbade her ever to talk about it, classifying it as a shameful secret.

Years later Art had finally healed her with his sensitive, romantic love-making. Ivor Stape, whose presence in the village had haunted Tessa's childhood, died and left the field to her as compensation for his behaviour.

Now she stared at the stretch of rough grass leading up to the woods, and the source of the Mill Stream was exactly as it had always been – a secret place under a clump of trees. Even above the throbbing engine of the bus, she could hear the water burbling in its chasm beside the hedge, pouring into the pipe under the lane. From there it flowed down to the water meadows, and on, towards the Mill. Tessa shivered. She wasn't going to think about the Mill and the man who had abused her. She was going to be positive now. That's what Art expected of her. Positive thinking. It didn't come naturally to Tessa.

She tugged at the gate, tearing the wiry tendrils of bindweed with her slim fingers. A silver charm bracelet dangled from her wrist and sparkled in the sun, and spots of colour shone from the beads and ribbons braided into her chestnut hair.

Art jumped out to help her, leaving the engine running and the door of the bus open. Together they lifted the latch end away from its rusty iron hook, and the gate toppled inwards. A robin watched them from the field maple, and as soon as the grass was disturbed a buzzard came circling out from the wood.

It was the cry of the buzzard that disturbed Tessa. She couldn't at first identify the feeling that lodged in her mind like a cold pebble. She froze.

'What's the matter?' Art asked. His eyes were gentle and attentive as always. Yet Tessa felt she couldn't share the illogical feeling with him. Putting it into words would make it ridiculous. So she resorted to one of her mother's tactics. Laughter.

'This gate just doesn't want to open,' she joked.

'You're dead right. This grass has got serious muscles.'

'We need to cut it. What can we use?'

They looked at each other.

'The bread knife!'

Tessa grinned. The bread knife got used for everything from turf-cutting to sawing the legs of jeans to make shorts. Art bounded into the bus and emerged brandishing it gleefully. He squatted down and attacked the tough stalks of grass along the base of the gate. 'No wonder they used to make rope out of this stuff.'

'The Romany Gypsies still do,' Tessa said, 'and they make baskets from grass and reeds, if they can't get willow.'

'You tug and I'll saw,' said Art. 'We ARE going to get this damn thing open. I don't want to leave that engine running too long. She'll get too hot and we won't be able to start her up again.'

As he spoke, the engine of the bus died and the sudden silence pooled around them in widening rings. It spooked Tessa. This was not the way she wanted to be introduced to her precious piece of land. She would have liked to quietly walk there, by herself, get over the gate, stroll up to the source of the spring, and sit there alone, listening, watching, talking to the spirits of the land who might be there, tell them she was a friend, reassure them of her love. Breaking in felt like an invasion.

A chill crept over her skin. Goosebumps appeared on her arms. The feeling hadn't gone away. She looked towards the source of the stream, and stopped breathing as a shadowy figure stepped out from the trees. His cold, dark stare was warning her. 'Something bad will happen here – something bad.' He threaded the words into her mind, and she felt them go in. She tried to ignore them, tried to be brave and bright like her mother. *What could possibly go wrong in such a lovely place?* she asked herself. *Especially with Art by my side.*

'You are not welcome here.'

'Ah – here's the culprit,' said Art at the same moment, pulling at a tenacious ivy root that had grown over the lower bar of the gate. It was too much for the bread knife. 'Can you find the pruners, Tessa? They're in the box under the bed.'

Tessa battled with herself. She wanted to turn and run away like a child, run back home to the safety of The Pines and her mother's kitchen. She wanted her mother to hold her and tell her everything was all right, tell her she hadn't inherited a haunted field and a demon. She wanted her father to come striding up there with her, and sit by the stream and make peace. But what she wanted more than anything was to please Art. Not run away and leave him with a gate that wouldn't open and a bus that wouldn't start.

'So where have they gone in that painted-up bus?' Freddie asked, sitting himself down at the kitchen table. The old wooden top was now covered in a red and white gingham plastic tablecloth, Kate's pride and joy. She hadn't got to scrub it! And in the sink was a brand new red plastic washing-up bowl, another wonder of the age. Freddie wasn't so keen on the plastic cloth. He missed running his fingers over the uneven wood that generations of his family had cared for with beeswax and elbow grease. He wanted to sneak his fingers under the plastic and smooth the knots and ridges of the pine wood.

Kate put a mug of strong, sweet, steaming tea in front of him and opened the biscuit tin. 'They were a bit vague about where they were going,' she said. 'I told them they could park here for a few nights, but Tessa seemed so jumpy about it. I was a bit hurt, to tell you the truth. She wanted to come home, but it felt as if she couldn't get away fast enough.'

'Ah – 'tis him,' Freddie said. 'That hippy she's with. She's got stars in her eyes over him.'

'I made Tessa's bed up so nicely with clean sheets, and she hasn't seen her bedroom since we decorated it,' Kate said, 'but she wouldn't even go up there.'

'She will, when she's ready.'

'I do like Art.' Kate took two bourbon biscuits out of the tin and gave them to Freddie. 'It's a pity he's a hippie. I mean, if he cut his DREADFUL hair and wore a suit, he'd be lovely. But Tessa clearly adores him.'

'She does – but what kind of life is he offering her?' Freddie said passionately. 'He doesn't work, does he? To me they're like two kids playing at life – doing something we could never have done. There's no future in it.'

'But we mustn't intervene,' Kate said. 'If only I could get Tessa on her own I could talk some sense into her, but Art is there all the time, almost as if he's guarding her.'

'Talking sense into Tessa doesn't work, Kate, does it? We've tried to do that all her life, and it makes her worse. Just keep quiet. That's my attitude.'

Kate sighed. She looked into Freddie's steady blue eyes and remembered how his policy of keeping quiet had so often proved to be the healing silence that calmed everyone down. When the girls were small it had been Freddie they ran to for comfort, and he would hold them silently and let them cry. His innate understanding of Tessa's turbulent moods had formed an unbreakable bond with her. The memories circled in Kate's mind as she munched her bourbon biscuit. 'Now who's that?' she said as someone tapped on the back door.

Before she could get up to answer it, the door flew open and Susan Tillerman burst in. 'Thank goodness you're here,' she gasped, and leaned on the table, looking from one to the other with wild, tormented eyes.

'What's up, Sue?' Kate asked.

Susan could hardly speak. 'It's the hippie convoy,' she stuttered. 'They're in our field and Ian's new horses are arriving tomorrow. Those lawless vagrants took the gate off its hinges in the night and just went in and parked their FRIGHTFUL old vans with flowers painted all over them. They've got goodness knows how many dogs – and kids running round – turning the field into a quagmire. They're lighting fires and banging drums. Oh, what am I going to DO?'

Freddie and Kate looked at each other in alarm. They'd heard about 'the convoy', a group of hippies travelling together, setting up camp wherever they could. It had been on the news every night, and in the papers.

'What am I going to DO?' Susan wailed.

'Number one is to calm down.' Kate put her arm round Susan's shoulders. 'We'll do whatever we can to help.'

'But Ian and Michael have gone down there to confront them,' Susan wept. 'You KNOW what Ian's like – and he's taken his gun. He'll end up killing someone, I know it. Oh, what am I going to do?'

'Have you called the police?'

'Yes – but these hippies just laugh at them, Kate – they can't make them move. They have to get a seven-day injunction or something, and by the time they've got it the camp is well established, and it's no good even asking them to move. They just laugh and say the land belongs to everyone, and it DOESN'T.'

'Surely someone can talk to them?'

'I tried – I did try, Kate. I told them we've got some new horses arriving and we need the field. I told them it was ours, by law. And these long-haired arrogant freaks just sneered at me – and the women were awful. They blatantly went on drumming and letting their kids roll in the mud and and—' Susan paused to allow her fury to settle. She wasn't good at anger. Freddie looked at her eyes and remembered her as a child and how he had patiently coaxed those terrified eyes over the station bridge. It had cemented a bond of trust that Susan now seemed to need in her stormy marriage to Ian Tillerman.

'And what?' Kate asked. 'What were the kids doing?'

'Peeing in the hedge,' said Susan, and tears of rage glistened on her powdered cheeks. She looked at Freddie.

'Would you PLEASE come down there with me – you and Kate – PLEASE?'

'What – now?'

'Yes – now.'

Kate and Freddie exchanged glances, both with the same alarming thought. What if Tessa was involved? Were she and Art part of that notorious convoy? It was unthinkable.

Freddie battled with his silent thoughts. Live and let live, he believed. He wasn't going to engage in a confrontation. And anyway, he didn't like Ian Tillerman. Ian Tillerman was an arrogant toff in Freddie's opinion, a man with more money than sense, and it was time he was taught a lesson. 'Sorry,' he said, looking directly at Susan, 'I'm not going to get involved. And that's the end of it.' He got up, pushed his chair in, and walked quietly away.

'I'll come down with you, Sue,' Kate said kindly. 'Maybe we can pour oil on troubled water.'

'Thanks.' Susan glared at Freddie's back as he disappeared into his workshop. 'I just need some moral support.'

'I'll support you, dear.' Kate had the sparks of battle in her eyes. 'I'm not afraid of a few hippies. I'll tell them to go to Putney on a pig.'

Tessa hung her muddy jeans out of the window on the sunny side of the bus and went into the bedroom. She was glad she'd made the bed that morning, covering it with the ethnic blanket Lou had given her, and some cushions she'd made herself in the colours of the Cornish sea – turquoise and purple, with creamy white fringes and touches of gold. She picked one up and buried her face in it, breathing the fragrance of gorse and bracken from the fabric. The familiar old bed welcomed her as she lay down and pulled the blanket over her bare legs. A time to sleep. A golden hour of solitude and rest.

Tessa hadn't intended to sleep. She'd wanted to explore the field on her own while Art had gone to 'catch up with some old mates'. He'd promised to come back with a meal. Fish and chips bundled in newspaper and kept warm under his denim jacket on the walk home. But the exhaustion of the long trip from Cornwall, and the emotional turmoil of seeing her parents again had drained Tessa.

She stretched out, with the noontime sun streaming through the back window of the bus onto her bare toes. A tin lid full of white shell sand from Porthmeor Beach was on the shelf by her side of the bed, along with a black elvan pebble. Tessa picked it up and was comforted by its smooth, cool surface and the way it evoked the eternal symphony of the surf.

Seeing her father again had rekindled a part of her that she'd put on hold. A need to immerse herself in the deep sparkle of his eyes, always more blue than she remembered, brimming with secrets untold, with knowing that didn't come from books. Those eyes were a coming home for Tessa, a coming home to her true self. The astonishment on Freddie's face as she showed him the inside of the bus had been refreshing. His look of wonder at seeing the beautifully fitted cupboards Art had made, the Queenie stove and its chimney which he'd bought from a Romany Gypsy, the extraordinary and comical tap which had to be pumped up and down to produce water from the tank. Freddie was genuinely impressed, and Tessa sensed that he secretly envied their apparently carefree lifestyle.

The feeling emanating from her mother had been quite different. Kate made obvious efforts to be positive, admiring the tie-dyed curtains and the cork-topped glass jar full of seashells. 'I could give you some decent saucepans, dear,' she said, eyeing the battered black objects stacked in the tiny kitchen, 'and – excuse me asking, but how do you MANAGE without a bathroom – I mean – a toilet?' Tessa sensed her mother's disgust when she opened a locker and showed her their toilet bag which consisted of a trowel and an ageing roll of Izal with the words *Medicated with Izal Germicide* printed in green across every sheet.

It had been a relief to escape in the bus with Art, and find her own field on the edge of Monterose, a safe place to camp. Home for the winter, Tessa hoped, home to the woods and fields she loved. She dreamed of finding Selwyn again. Selwyn was a horse, a dappled grey part-Arabian mare Tessa loved, a problem horse who responded only to Tessa and shunned everyone else. Tessa felt Selwyn had been her first-time friend and teacher. Selwyn was not far away. She'd be in one of Lexi's fields further up the lane.

Tessa drifted into a deep sleep, a refuge from the cornucopia of feelings and the creeping shadow of anxiety which had somehow arrived in Somerset with her. In her sleep she vaguely heard the unusual sound of police sirens howling through the quiet lanes. She awoke feeling warm and dreamy, wanting just to lie there and stare out of the window at the sprays of scarlet rosehips bobbing against the sky, listening to a robin singing his poignant little solo, a sound of winter.

The sea was our bathroom, she thought, feeling suddenly grubby and hot. Every day in Cornwall her time in the foaming surf had left her squeaky clean and energised. During their brief camp on Dartmoor she and Art had stripped off and bathed in a fast flowing river, a deliciously sensual time of love-making and playing under a waterfall with magical pips of sunlight darting through the trees. The chill of the water on her skin had intensified the throbbing heat of Art inside her and Tessa had felt like a scarlet flower opening up to a bee in the hot sun.

Moments later it had been spoilt by the ringing voice of a woman walking her dog. 'Don't you hippies have ANY sense of decency? I'll report you to the town council.' The passion had cooled, but Tessa and Art had stumbled into the bus, laughing helplessly, and the laughing had been as wild and energising as the love-making. Pure happiness. Pure unadulterated joy. That was Tessa's life with Art. He was her first and only lover, the love of her life. Nothing else mattered. Until now.

Mum would let me have a bath, she thought, and indulged in remembering how it felt to sink into steaming scented water and lie there until your toes went wrinkly.

Her dreamy thoughts were interrupted by the squelch of heavy boots on the grass. A fist the size of a sledgehammer thundered on the door of the bus. Tessa was terrified. She rolled off the bed, crawled underneath it, and lay there with her heart beating hard and fast against the floor.

The furious knocking came again. A voice shouted. 'Get the hell out of this field you evil, feckless hippies. Monterose doesn't want you here.'

And it was a voice she knew only too well.

She wriggled along the floor to the 'pencil hole'. It was a small round hole in the metal bodywork of the bus, and on stormy nights the wind whistled through it. If it was cold, Art stuck a pencil in it, and on the outside Tessa had cleverly camouflaged the hole as the centre of a marigold.

She slid the pencil out, and put her eye to the hole. She could see Ian Tillerman's leather riding boots standing in the grass, and the gleaming twin barrels of his rifle pointing at the ground. From his belt hung three dead rabbits. The sight of them sickened Tessa. Her fear turned quickly to rage.

Brushing the dust from her bare thighs she stood up and flung the door of the bus open. She was wearing an embroidered smock with tiny round mirrors that winked in the sunlight. Her chestnut hair, full of beads and ribbons, flared back from her face. Her eyes glittered with fury. 'I'll have you know this field is MY LAND, Ian Tillerman,' she yelled. 'And how dare you come here banging on my door with – with those dead rabbits. Shame on you. You're disgusting. Get off my land. NOW.'

Ian Tillerman frowned. His confident eyes swept up and down Tessa's long suntanned legs and then back to her face. 'I don't believe it,' he said. 'Surely it's not – Tessa – is it? Kate's daughter?' The outer edge of his eyebrows flipped upwards like the wings of a buzzard as he scrutinised her appearance. 'What on earth are you doing with the hippies, girl?'

Tessa stepped down from the bus, feeling herself quaking deep inside her solar plexus. 'I'm being ME.' She turned on the full power of her eyes, knowing they were turquoise and gold and charged with the kind of radiance that a being like Ian Tillerman couldn't face. The love that Art had given her burned in her mind like a healing flame. It empowered her to draw back from the jagged edge of yelling, and into the ice fields of being polite to someone you hated.

'This is my land, this field. I have a right to be here, and I would like you to leave.' Tessa walked up to Ian Tillerman. She could smell the salty fur of the dead rabbits. 'And NO SHOOTING is allowed on my land. So go please, and take your silly gun with you.'

Ian Tillerman smirked. It was the retreating smirk of darkness hesitating in front of light. 'You, young lady, are asking for trouble, turning up in Monterose with the hippies. I'm surprised your parents allow it. They're hardworking, honest folk.'

'It's none of your business.'

'Oh, but it is. I live here too – Tessa – and there's a right of way across this field, and shooting rights. You can't keep people out – and – good heavens, girl – look at you! – I wouldn't let my children behave like that.'

Tessa snorted. 'Fiona and – Michael. I'm sure they are paragons of virtue.'

'They're good kids,' Ian Tillerman said, 'which is more than you were, I seem to remember. And don't you dare come near my family looking – like – like THAT.'

Tessa could hardly breathe with the effort of containing her rage. She sensed something similar going on in Ian Tillerman's mind, the embers of his anger blocked with steel bars. Beyond them lurked the secret shame of a man who actually wanted to grab her and throw her down in the wet grass. 'Will you please go,' she said imperiously. 'You're trespassing.'

'And you're asking for trouble, girl. My field has just been invaded by the hippie convoy, and the police have been called to evict them. If you leave the gate open like that, they'll be in here – all of them, and you'll never get them out. Have some sense – Tessa.' He wagged a leathery finger, let his eyes rake over her again, turned on his heel and stalked out of the gate.

Tessa felt the quaking rippling down her legs and through the bones of her arms. She stood, hugging herself, listening to his boots parading down the lane, and the wind in the elm trees whispering after him. Their leaves hadn't yet turned. The elms were always last to go gold, not turning until her November birthday when they shed glorious blizzards of saffron yellow. But now there were dead branches, with dead leaves, a dead, silvery brown that changed the whispering voice of each tree to a song that was hoarse and sad.

Something's wrong, she thought, and with the thought came pulses of grief and longing. Grief for Jonti, her little dog, now buried at home in the garden, grief for her Granny Annie who had died that summer, a longing for her carefree life camping on the Atlantic coast of Cornwall, a heaviness of coming home to her family and her village, a need to have it all in harmony, when it wasn't.

CHAPTER 2

Sensing the Shadows

Kate marched across the Tillermans' field towards the collection of battered camper vans. The lower half of her looked ridiculous in a bottle green pleated skirt, a flowery pinny, and a pair of Ian Tillerman's wellies several sizes too big. The top half looked majestic, her bust lifted high under the red cardigan, her black hair rippling in the sun, her eyes on fire, her jaw set so that her profile resembled a figurehead on a ship. Unstoppable. Strong through wind and weather.

A few dogs trotted beside her, their tails apologetic, their eyes dubious. Susan stumbled a few yards behind, protesting in undertones. 'Kate, don't! Don't get involved. KATE!'

Kate sailed on, undeterred, heading for a group of hippies who were sitting around throwing sticks into a fire. The wind flared and crackled in the flames, tearing smoke towards the woods, with crimson sparks spiralling through the dry leaves of the hedgerow elms. *Thank goodness*, she was thinking, *thank goodness Art and Tessa's bus isn't in here.* She'd said nothing to Susan about Tessa being a hippie. They'd find out soon enough, she figured, if the bus was parked locally.

She felt drawn to a woman who was sitting on the steps of an old horsebox bouncing a baby on her lap. The baby was squeaking with delight and the mother laughing. Kate felt a twinge of envy. She had adored her babies, Lucy and Tessa, and would have had another one if the doctor hadn't told her it would kill her.

The mother looked up with challenging eyes. 'Who are you?' she asked. 'Chairman of the Parish Council?'

'No, dear – I don't sit on committees,' Kate said pleasantly. 'What a lovely baby! A boy is it?'

'Yes – a boy. His name's Willow.' A ghost of a smile twitched on the woman's lips, and the baby turned startling blue eyes on Kate and chuckled.

'Can I hold him?' Kate asked.

'No way! I don't know who you are, do I? Let me guess – a social worker?'

'No, dear, I'm just an ordinary mum, Kate. I live in Monterose, and it's a lovely town – everyone is so kind.'

'Good for you.' The tone was sarcastic, but Kate detected a loneliness in the woman's eyes.

'Willow's granny must be so proud,' Kate said.

'She hasn't seen him. Doesn't know he exists. Anyway – what's it matter to you?'

Kate felt the hostility building. She was aware of a silent

group of hippies gathering around her, watching, waiting to protect the woman and her baby. She sensed Susan hovering behind her with those frightened eyes, and wished she would go away. Her presence wasn't helping Kate's carefully constructed plan. 'Well, dear, I just like to keep everyone happy,' she said. 'I don't do much. I make butter and cheese, and lots of delicious jam and chutney. I could bring you down some if you like – what did you say your name was?'

'Rowan.'

Susan was tweaking Kate's sleeve in a 'don't get involved' sort of energy. She was radiating negativity.

'And who's your friend?' Rowan asked suspiciously. 'Parish Council? It's written all over her!'

Susan tensed with anger. 'I HAPPEN to be the owner of this land,' she announced in a ringing voice.

Rowan smirked, and there was laughter from the group of hippies who had gathered around them. Kate saw her delicate plan collapsing like a snagged cobweb. 'Let me handle this, Sue,' she pleaded, but it was too late. Rowan clicked her fingers, her eyes alight now as she looked across at her friends. A man with a plaited beard, and a pair of drums hanging around his neck on a beaded belt, began to beat a rhythm with the palms of his hands, and the chanting started:

> *This land is your land, this land is my land*
> *From California to the New York Highway,*
> *From the Redwood Forest to the Gulf Stream waters*
> *This land was made for you and me.*

'See what I mean?' Susan whispered in Kate's ear.

Kate looked searchingly into Susan's frightened eyes. 'I think you should go and wait in the car, Sue,' she said kindly. 'Go on – I won't be long. I want a little chat with Rowan.' She turned Susan round and pointed her at the car, and Susan went, hugging herself round the middle and looking at the ground.

Her departure raised a cheer from the group of hippies. Kate stood her ground, her hand fondling the ears of a tatty lurcher dog who was leaning against her legs.

Rowan studied her with a quizzical expression.

'Well, fancy you being named after a tree,' Kate said. 'I'm named after a bird! A golden bird, if you please – shall I tell you the story?'

'Yeah! Go on, lady – we like stories.' The man with the plaited beard stopped beating his drums. He sat down with his back against the wheel of Rowan's converted horsebox, and the rest of the group followed him. Suddenly Kate had an audience. She sat on a wooden box and swept her bright brown eyes over the motley group. *They're just lost children*, she thought, *with nice parents out there somewhere, breaking their hearts – please God, tell me what to say to them.*

'When I was born,' she began, 'here in Somerset, at Hilbegut, my dad carried me over to the window. And there, in the tree outside, was a bright yellow bird, singing its head off. He got the bird book and discovered it was a Golden Oriole, a rare visitor to this country.'

'That's awesome!' The man with the plaited beard was

studying her with intense eyes. 'A Shamanic totem. Did he know that's what it was?'

'No, dear, we don't do that kind of thing,' Kate said, 'but he named me after it – Oriole Kate.'

'Wow – Oriole Kate – Golden Bird Woman. Has the Golden Oriole appeared in your life?'

'Well yes, dear, it has,' Kate said. 'It appeared to my wonderful husband, Freddie, before we were married – and when he saw it he thought it was a messenger, and so he leapt over the church wall and ran down to meet the train I was on – and that was the first time we'd seen each other for months – and we've never been parted since that day.'

'Awesome.'

'And she makes butter and cheese,' said Rowan. 'Golden stuff!'

'And marmalade,' Kate added. She looked around at each pair of eyes fixed on her. The plan was working. She had them in the palm of her hand. Soon she would persuade them to leave Ian Tillerman's field.

It would have worked, she was sure. But something broke the spell. A man in denims appeared at the door of Rowan's horsebox, and the baby squealed and held out his little arms. 'Dada! Dada!'

Art came down the steps and took the baby in his arms. 'Hello, Kate,' he said. 'I'm surprised to see you here.'

Kate went cold. The magic died in her eyes.

'Is Tessa there with you?' she asked.

'No, not right now.'

'I see.' Kate's eyes burned into his. He looked down. *Guilty*, she thought. She lifted her chin and fired the words at him like arrows of deadly ice. 'Then you stay away from my daughter. You – you cheat. You're beneath contempt.'

She got up and marched off across the field, the east wind lifting her hair, leaving the shattered silence twinkling across the ground.

Tessa felt vulnerable after the confrontation with Ian Tillerman. She wanted the comfort of familiar things. Her old bedroom, her books, her dog, Jonti. Even her Granny Annie who had always criticised her so much. She wanted to spend time with her father. She wanted to visit her friend, Lexi, and see Selwyn again.

But Art had asked her to stay with the bus until he came back. Why was he so long? In Cornwall he'd often gone 'to catch up with some mates' on his own, or to visit his parents who lived in Truro. Tessa had never been sure exactly where he went, but she hadn't worried about it. Being 'free' was part of the hippie culture.

She found her watch and looked at it. Ten past twelve. Or had it stopped? She put it to her ear and listened for the tick. It had stopped. She wound it up, guessing by the hunger in her stomach that it was nearer two o'clock. *Mum would give me lunch*, she thought, remembering the taste of Kate's homemade butter, and the apple pies she made from the mellow Egremont Russet apples in the garden. The cinnamon-scented steam. The way the juice soaked into the pastry. *I'll go*, she thought. *Why shouldn't I?*

Tessa locked the bus and put the key under a stone behind the wheel. She glanced up at the source of the spring, tempted to go up there, and decided to wait until she had a Peace Rose in her hand, and Art by her side. Together they would float the petals and make wishes for peace. She walked on up the lane, past the apple orchards, over the railway bridge and into the small town of Monterose where she had grown up. She and her sister Lucy had run wild in the woods and water meadows. They knew every tree, every corner, every old stone farm and hay barn. They knew where the wild orchids bloomed in spring, and where the hedges were heavy with hazelnuts and blackberries in autumn, and where the white button mushrooms appeared in the grass on dewy mornings.

In Cornwall Tessa hadn't missed Jonti. But now she yearned to see the little white terrier trotting ahead of her, always so alert and responsive. Without him she felt unprotected and isolated. Her intense relationship with Art was emotionally engulfing and healing for Tessa. After being sexually abused by Ivor Stape, she had vowed never to allow a man near her – until she met Art. His understanding and his gentle love-making had healed her in body and soul. She no longer felt like a misunderstood loner. She felt LOVED. She felt like someone who mattered, and she wanted to explain that to her parents.

The Pines looked welcoming, its windows open, its

33

red brick walls clothed with Virginia creeper, the leaves in autumn fluttering gloriously in shades of crimson and magenta. Tessa opened the wicket gate and walked up the path through Freddie's vegetable garden where a mini-forest of purple sprouting glistened alongside feathery carrot tops, runner beans and marrows. Her footsteps got slower and slower. She sensed something. A mood.

She listened in surprise.

Kate was banging pots around in the kitchen. Saucepan lids crashing and plates being scrubbed and thudded onto the drainer. It wasn't like Kate. Usually she'd be singing or listening to the radio. Or chatting and laughing with a friend.

Tessa walked in to the kitchen. 'Mum?'

Kate jumped. She spun round and for one terrible moment her eyes were darkly angry. Tessa looked at her in alarm. Her mother's aura, usually so bright, was full of storm clouds and sparks.

'Tessa!' Sunlight spread into Kate's eyes as she saw her daughter. 'What a lovely surprise, dear!' She held out her arms. In the reassuring closeness of their hug, Tessa could feel the tension across Kate's shoulders.

'What's the matter, Mum?'

Kate carefully rinsed the pan she'd been scrubbing with a Brillo Pad and put it to drain. 'Nothing, dear – I'm just being silly.'

'Silly?' In Tessa's memory, 'silly' meant a number of powerful emotions, most of them socially unacceptable. Fear. Anger. Anxiety. Jealousy. 'You don't fool me, Mum.

34

What's wrong?' She steered Kate to the cottage sofa in the kitchen window and sat down with her. Kate's face was flushed as if a maelstrom of worries were whirling in the heat of her mind.

Tessa stared at her wordlessly, and at last Kate met her eyes. 'You're so like your dad, Tessa,' she said, and her voice was low and subdued, not at all like her usual ringing cheeriness. 'Nothing's wrong, dear – I'm quite all right.'

Tessa shrugged. 'I don't believe you.'

But Kate continued to build a shining wall around her obvious distress. Talking brightly of other things. 'You just missed your dad. He had his lunch and he's gone out delivering bird boxes. Have you had lunch?'

'No,' Tessa said, glancing at the clock. It was two thirty. She adjusted her watch.

Kate got up immediately. 'My dear girl. No lunch! What would you like? Shall I boil you an egg?'

'No, Mum, thanks. Toast will be fine – and I'd kill for some apple pie. I can smell it.'

'We ate half of it – but the custard's still warm.' Kate gave her a dish of golden pastry and apple, glazed with brown sugar. She poured custard over it, and watched, satisfied as Tessa enjoyed it. 'Where's Art?' she asked rather sharply.

'He's gone to catch up with some old friends,' Tessa said.

'So where are you parked?'

'In my field.'

'Oh no!' Kate said, and the anxiety clouded her eyes again.

'Why? Why not? It's my field.'

35

'I know that, but—' Kate put two slices of bread under the grill.

'But what?'

'Well, dear – I'm sure you've heard about The Convoy.' Kate lowered her voice. 'It's been on the news every day.'

'We don't listen to the news.'

'Don't you? Well – it's a convoy of – well, they call them travellers – but they're hippies. And yesterday, they turned up in Monterose. The whole town is up in arms. They rolled into Ian and Sue's field in the night, about ten vans and old horseboxes, and they won't move!'

Tessa stiffened. 'So why should that stop me camping in my own field?'

'For a start, dear, it's not legally yours until you're twenty-one,' Kate said carefully. 'We are the trustees – your dad and I.'

'Well, you don't mind – surely?'

'No, dear – I'm delighted to have you home – but the point is, Tessa, if those hippies are evicted from Ian's field, which they will be, they could see your bus and think they can go in there too – then you'd have kids running round, dogs, fires and they'd soon turn it into a dump. And I don't want—' Kate shut her mouth. She'd intended to say she didn't want her daughter associating with them.

'Mum – I AM a hippie.' Tessa looked at her shrewdly. 'I spent the summer with the commune on the cliffs in St Ives. And they're great people. The best I've ever met.'

Kate looked at her silently.

36

'You don't approve, do you?' Tessa asked. She didn't know why it mattered, but it did. She'd been free from those oppressive shadows all summer. Coming home ought to be happy. Didn't it? Her mother looked flushed with anger. A mysterious, judgemental anger that Tessa recognised and no longer understood. Her mother was a warm, beautiful person. Why, why did she choose social prejudice over love? 'You like Art, don't you, Mum? I thought you did.'

'Oh Tessa!' Kate reached across the table and took her daughter's hand. She squeezed it tightly.

Tessa studied her mother's hand. The old familiar fingers were dry and ingrained with the stains of blackberry juice, the nails cut short, the plain gold wedding ring embedded. 'Look what Art has done for me, Mum. You've no idea. He's totally, totally changed my life. I'm so happy now. We're soul mates. Mum, I never thought I'd find a man who loves me the way he does.' She spoke passionately. 'He's a fantastic person – I love him, Mum – I never EVER want anyone else. Our love is transformational, and healing.'

'I've never heard you use those words,' Kate said from between tight lips.

'That's because they were packed away in my mind, waiting for an awesome being like Art to coax them out.'

'But—' Kate was searching for sunbeams. Bright words to rescue them from an ugly confrontation. 'Well – yes – I'm sure there's good in him. But – do you think he'll ever cut his hair and wear a suit?'

'Mum – we're not like that. We're New Age people –

phantasmagorical, multi-faceted beings bringing in the dawning of the Age of Aquarius.'

Kate's eyes widened. Her aura bushed out like the fur
of a startled cat. And Tessa watched it slowly darken again.
Sinking back into convenient ignorance, she thought. 'Jesus didn't
cut his hair and wear a suit,' she added hopefully.

'No, dear – but, supposing the Prime Minister looked
like that.'

'We'd be a nation of peaceful enlightened beings.'

In that moment Tessa saw the spirit of her grandfather
standing next to Kate. His eyes were twinkling as always,
and he had Jonti in his arms. Tessa's eyes filled with tears at
seeing the little dog looking so shining and so at home. She
was glad of her ability to see him, but she longed to actually
feel the warmth of him, the way he wriggled and made con-
versational noises in his throat, the way his eyes gazed into
her very private soul.

'Will you show me Jonti's grave, Mum?'

'Yes, dear.' Kate seemed glad to escape from the threat of
an argument. 'And you must see your bedroom. We decorated it while you were at college. I found the most beautiful
wallpaper with pink roses.'

Tessa winced. Pink roses? *Mum still thinks I'm a child*, she
thought. *She's never going to accept that I'm a woman. Art's
woman!* She hugged the secret thought to herself as she followed Kate through the house and into the garden.

'Daddy made him such a nice wooden box,' Kate said as
they stood under the lilac bushes in the Anderson Hollow.

As children, Lucy and Tessa had made a tiny cemetery there, a place to bury the dead mice and birds they had cried over. Some of the crosses made from lolly sticks were still there, the writing faded. One stood out. The grave of a song thrush Tessa had found dead in the lane. She'd spent ages scratching the words on a piece of slate. *SILENT SPRING*, she'd written, after the book by Rachel Carson, and to Tessa it marked the beginning of her passion for saving the earth from an environmental disaster.

Freddie had carved Jonti's name in beautiful Roman lettering on a slab of golden hamstone.

'He's not supposed to do stonework now,' Kate said, 'but he insisted on doing this. And he's carving an angel for Granny Annie's grave. It's a pity you weren't here for the funeral.'

Tessa felt she couldn't bear to see Jonti's grave a moment longer. 'Let's go and look at my bedroom,' she said. 'There's some books I want. Then I should go home.'

'Go home? But you are home,' Kate said.

'No, Mum. My home is with Art now – in the bus.'

'But you don't need to be camping now that you're back, Tessa. You can stay here with us – where you belong.'

'We're not camping, Mum. It's how we live.'

Kate took her daughter's hand. 'Wait 'til you see your lovely bedroom – you'll want to stay in it,' she said confidently.

Tessa followed her indoors, struggling with remembered powerlessness and obligation. She clung to the fact that

Art loved and respected her. But with that thought came a twinge of pain deep down in her pelvic area. She frowned. Her period was due in three days. She had three pills left. Then what? She would have to go to her old doctor – Doctor Jarvis – and ask him to give her the contraceptive pill. And he was bound to say no.

The night rain was indigo and silver. It pelted on the roof of the bus, and Tessa snuggled up next to Art, enjoying the song of the rain, imagining the diamond drops secretly sparkling on scarlet rosehips, bramble leaves and twigs. Imagining a morning full of mirror-like puddles and glistening grasses. Listening to the gurgle of the Mill Stream and the patter of a fox's wet paws in the lane, a haze of moisture glazing his ruffled fur.

They slept close, like one being, their hands linked on the pillow, Tessa's head nestled under Art's bearded chin. She stayed awake, savouring the happiness after love-making, loving the closeness, admiring him while he slept. The details of him that she loved. The triangle of sun-bleached hair on his torso. His firm hand with its broad, curly thumb, the way his breathing was so powerful and peaceful. Touching him in the pitch dark was like touching the sun and the sea, as if the long hot salt of summer was stored in his body, for her. Sometimes she twisted a lock of their hair together. Chestnut and gold, like a precious candlestick. She loved him so much that she didn't want to sleep. Staying awake was like floating on a cushion of dreams, woven from strands of the loving words that had spun out of him. Words that healed her mind while the intensity of his gaze and the slow, thoughtful, electrifying touch of his hands healed her body. She felt reborn. Cleansed. Whole. Every time.

Tessa was always awake early. Like her father, she was attuned to the natural world, its birdsong, its life cycles, seasons and tides. Today she woke up contented, happy to fling the bus door open and gaze at the raindrops winking in the sun, hanging from every leaf and blade of grass like tiny prisms. She took a bar of soap and a towel and walked barefoot to the stream to wash, shivering in the chill of an autumn morning. The water was clear and icy cold. Full of energy. She played with it, cupping it in her hands and watching the light flicker through it as it poured back into the stream.

Feeling good, and alive, Tessa returned to the bus, dried her tingling feet and got dressed. She unpacked the willow basket she had brought from home, pleased to put Kate's pots of plum jam along the shelf in the window where they glowed red like stained glass. There was a box of eggs from the chickens, a pat of homemade butter wrapped in greaseproof paper, and a 1953 Coronation tin full of golden brown fruit buns, each with a cherry on top.

She took out the three books from her bedroom. A precious copy of Palgrave's *Golden Treasury* which her father had given her, a navy blue embossed leather copy of *The Water Babies*, her favourite childhood book, and *The Rainbow* by D.H. Lawrence, the first adult book she had loved. Tessa's fingers itched to open them, but she put them safely in a wooden cubbyhole which Art had said was hers. Art liked to read with her, and she planned to share them with him later.

Right now she could hear him yawning and waking up. She knew he liked to lie in bed and hear her pottering around, the kettle whistling, the smell of toast. So she lit the little gas stove and made breakfast.

'Aw – this is fantastic, Tessa,' Art said, sitting opposite her at the small table. 'Is this your mum's homemade butter? And plum jam – wow – your mum is awesome.'

'And the eggs are from our own chickens,' Tessa said, happily shaking salt and pepper over hers. Momentarily she remembered a look in Kate's eyes when she had packed the butter into the basket, and the odd tone in her voice when she'd said, 'This is for YOU, dear.' The unsaid words hovered in the air between them. *Not HIM.* Tessa wondered why, suddenly, her mum didn't like Art.

'Mmm, it's delicious,' he said, licking the melted butter from his beard. His grey eyes shone into her soul. 'And you look SO beautiful, Tessa. Your hair is a little bit damp – and sparkly ' He moved a tendril of chestnut curl from her cheek. 'Have you been outside?'

'I went for a wash in the stream.'

'Aw – man! How did I miss that?' Art joked.

Tessa grinned widely, showing the dimples in her cheeks. 'So what are we doing today?'

Art peered out of the window. 'I fancy sitting in a tree and reading poetry. With you, of course.' He stroked his beard and stared out at the sky, as if trying to make a decision, then his eyes looked into hers with startling intensity. He took her hands, his thumb caressing the sheen of her delicate nails and the sensitive tips of her fingers. 'The thing is, Tessa – I've got to go and help a mate move camp this morning – no need for you to get involved – but later I want to do something really special with you, something unforgettable.'

Tessa smiled, trusting him implicitly. 'I've got somewhere I must go,' she said, thinking about Dr Jarvis. 'But later – yes – we'll do something special.' Her mind flew to Granny Barcussy's ruined cottage. She knew it was somewhere on the other side of the wood, but she wasn't sure exactly where, or how to find it.

Art was looking at her expectantly, his rough, suntanned fingers playing with her silver charm bracelet. He reached up and touched the amber bead in her hair.

'Dad used to take Lucy and me to see his granny's ruined cottage,' Tessa said, and sensed Granny Barcussy's bright, bird-like face watching her from spirit, encouraging her. 'It was in an enchanted woodland glade, and I used to see little orbs of light dancing in the trees. I felt peaceful there, and – alive. Dad would sit us down inside the old stone walls and tell us stories, but—'

'But?' Art was listening intently, his eyes locked into hers.

'But sometimes he used to get sad because the cottage was a ruin, and he couldn't do anything about it. His parents had sold it to the estate who owned these woods. He'd go on and on about how they didn't care about the environment.

43

The whole estate was split up into blocks of woodland and sold, and we weren't supposed to go and visit the cottage any more – but,' Tessa leaned forward and kissed him, 'I've dreamed of going there with you – if we could find it. Shall we?'

Art's eyes shone with love and enthusiasm. 'Yeah – I'd love to.'

Tessa found herself tingling with excitement. She imagined lying in the enchanted ruin with Art. A time of magic. She saw Granny Barcussy's spirit beside them, her old hands clasped with joy, her eyes dancing. 'Sometime soon,' she said, happy that Art was gazing at her with love and passion in his grey eyes.

'Sometime soon,' he promised.

CHAPTER 3

'Sometime Soon'

Freddie loaded the last bird box into the back of the pale blue Morris Traveller and tied the back doors shut with a length of baler twine. He tied a red rag on there to warn other drivers it was not fully closed. 'You be careful,' he said to Kate, handing her the keys. 'Don't go speeding round corners.'

'I'll be fine, dear.' She beamed confidently and gave him a kiss. 'I'll be back about tea time – with a roll of cash!' She wagged a finger at him. 'You be good too. No stone dust!'

Freddie's eyes twinkled. He liked the way Kate bossed him around. Pretend to agree, then do it anyway was his usual plan. He certainly wasn't going to tell her what he intended to do today.

Apprehensively he watched her set off, the bird boxes piled high, even in the passenger seat. She wouldn't be able to use the mirror at all. He hoped the police wouldn't stop her. If they did, Kate would be quite capable of charming them into letting her continue on her journey. Today she was going to Dorset, to all the garden centres and pet shops she could find. Freddie felt lucky that Kate was such a good saleswoman. She always came back smiling with an empty car and a bundle of cash, and hilarious tales of how she had persuaded curmudgeonly shop managers to buy the bird boxes. 'No one else makes them like this!' she'd tell them. 'My Freddie has a unique style. These are so elegant – and Japanese-looking, don't you think?' Then she'd point out some plain ordinary bird table in his shop and say, 'I wouldn't have THAT in my garden when I could have THIS one – would you?' All the time flashing her warm bewitching eyes at them, eyes that would melt a battleship.

Freddie stood at the gate, watched her turn at the end of the road and imagined her driving up the steep hill through the woods and away towards Yeovil. There wasn't much traffic on a Tuesday in October. The occasional lorry, the green country bus, and a few cars. The road was dry, the weather still and sunny. Perfect. But he still prayed she would come back safely.

He took an ancient canvas haversack from its peg in his workshop, shook the dust out of it and took it indoors. Kate had left his lunch on the table between two plates. A thick slice of pork pie, a cold boiled egg and a mound of home-grown lettuce. Freddie threw some salt over it and bundled it into greaseproof paper. He stuffed it into the haversack with a crimson Worcester Pearmain apple and a glass bottle of water.

With the bag slung over his shoulder and his mother's ebony walking stick in his hand, he set off down the leafy lane in eager strides. First he called at the church to visit Annie's grave. He stood looking down at the headstone, thinking about the angel he was carving to put there. The doctor had said he must give up stone carving. The dust was making him ill. But he wasn't going to. Damned doctors didn't know everything, did they?

Freddie walked on, through the town and over the railway bridge, his mind now worrying about Tessa. Kate had been so furious with Art. She'd worked herself into a state about him betraying Tessa.

'You don't know that it's true,' Freddie had argued. He was trying to like Art, for Tessa's sake.

'Oh yes I do. He was GUILTY. He couldn't look at me,' Kate said. 'Freddie – he is cheating. Tessa is absolutely head over heels in love with him. He's led her on while all the time he's got another woman – and a baby. He's cheating on her as well. It's the lowest of the low. Tessa will have to be told – but I can't, Freddie, I can't burst her bubble. She's never been so happy in her life, has she?'

'You should keep quiet,' Freddie said. 'If you interfere, she'll blame you, Kate! I don't want to lose Tessa the way we lost Lucy.'

Their conversation was swirling into dark waters. They both fell silent, remembering the ongoing pain of losing their elder daughter. Lucy had been a golden child, perfect in every way, on the brink of taking her A levels when she'd suddenly rebelled and left home to live in a tiny bedsit in Taunton with Tim, a boy Freddie and Kate hated on sight – a timewaster, a spiv, and a drunk, they thought.

'To be fair – we didn't try to get to know Tim, did we?' Kate said sadly. 'I know he's nothing like the kind of man we wanted for Lucy, but there must be good in him somewhere. I've tried so hard to like Art – and Tessa is so much more precarious than Lucy. I'm so afraid for her, Freddie, afraid she'll try to take her life again.'

'I worry about that too,' admitted Freddie. 'And she shouldn't have dropped out of Art College. That upset me more than anything. I'd have loved a chance like that, and Tessa's throwing it away – throwing her life away.'

Throwing her life away! Freddie stood on the railway bridge looking down at the gleaming rails curving away into the hills, his mind replaying the conversation. Kate had begged him to talk to Tessa, but he wouldn't. Tessa trusted him. Even when she was a baby Freddie had been her rock, the only person who understood her dark moods, her anxieties, and the intense power of her dreams. No, he wouldn't talk to her, but he'd listen. He'd offer a healing silence where she could safely share her true feelings.

Dr Jarvis looked at Tessa over the top of his gold-rimmed glasses. He shook his head thoughtfully. 'No,' he said. 'I'm sorry, Tessa, but I cannot prescribe the pill without your parents' consent. You are under twenty-one.'

Tessa felt a cold gust of fury reach her face, from within.

'But – the doctor in Cornwall gave them to me.' She took the foil pack from the back pocket of her jeans and slammed it on the green leather top of his desk.

'And who was this doctor?' Dr Jarvis asked. 'He's got no right to do that. What was his name?'

'I'm not telling you,' Tessa said. 'He was a friend of a friend.'

'Sounds very unorthodox to me. And irresponsible. Did he ask for your medical history?'

'No.'

Dr Jarvis took the foil pack and turned it over, frowning. 'Knowing you, these particular ones are not what I would give you, Tessa. You shouldn't be taking them.'

'I want those BACK please.' Tessa glared at him.

'All right, all right!' Dr Jarvis handed her the foil pack with its two remaining pills. 'I know you very well, Tessa, and your parents. You weren't an easy little girl to treat, were you?'

'No,' Tessa admitted angrily. 'That's because I'm terrified of medical stuff.'

Dr Jarvis had opened the brown cardboard sleeve containing her medical history. 'Not so long ago we were dealing with your suicide attempt, weren't we?'

Tessa touched the thin scar on her wrist. 'I was fourteen.'

'Silly girl.'

The fury reached her throat. She stood up. 'I am NOT a silly girl. How dare you judge me like that. If I was a doctor I'd try to understand. I was desperate. And I wasn't happy until I moved away from Monterose and its old-fashioned attitudes. I'm eighteen now, nearly nineteen, and the man I'm with is wonderful. He's the best person I've ever met, and we are totally in love. I need the pill. I really need it. WHY won't you give it to me?' Tessa felt her hands clench the edge of Dr Jarvis's leather-topped desk with a furious strength that wanted to overturn it with one flick. Her slim arms were wire-strong after the summer of swimming in the Cornish surf.

'That is precisely why.' Dr Jarvis was playing his words like cards, with the ace of spades hovering. 'Look at you. Relax your hands, girl, and stop murdering my table.'

Despite her anger, Tessa found herself grinning at the wise old doctor who had treated her all her life. He had a way of deflecting extreme emotion with gentle humour. She remembered that she did actually like him.

'Seriously, Tessa – talk to your mother. She's very open-minded. I'm sure she'd rather try to help you than be kept in the dark.'

'But she doesn't believe in sex before marriage. She thinks it's a sin. I can't possibly tell her. Please don't you tell her either, or Dad.'

'I won't. What about Lucy? Can you talk to her?'

'No. She hates me, always has.'

Dr Jarvis looked flummoxed.

'Why should I have to talk to someone? It's my life,' Tessa said.

'And can't you say no to this wonderful young man?'

'No. We LOVE each other.'

'Well – there is an agency you can go to. The Brook Advisory Clinic. I think there's one in Bristol.'

'Bristol?'

Tessa took the leaflet and trailed out. Bristol! It sounded like the other end of the earth. She'd have to hitchhike. And Art wouldn't like it. Contraception, and money, and getting to Bristol were outside the sphere of phantasmagoria where he seemed to live. Even now he'd be sitting in a tree reading poetry, while she trudged the streets of Monterose worrying about contraception. She didn't want it to put a damper on their love.

What should she do?

Tessa meandered down the familiar street, not looking at anyone, and turned in to the small Post Office Stores. She wanted a stamp for the letter she'd written to her friend, Faye, who was at College. She'd told Faye about Art, and about their carefree summer on Porthmeor Beach, and explained why she was dropping out.

As she walked up to the counter a man grabbed her arm. She turned, expecting it to be someone she knew, but it wasn't. A grey little man with angry eyes was looking at her in a challenging way, his face an unhealthy red as it popped out of his immaculate collar and tie. 'No hippies,' he said. 'Can't you read?' He waved a sinewy arm towards a notice in the shop entrance. 'Out you go. OUT. That way!'

Tessa stood her ground, in disbelief.

'I just wanted a stamp,' she said.

'I don't care. We don't serve hippies. OUT.'

'I'm proud to be a hippie. They're beautiful people. You should get to know us instead of being so prejudicial.' She tried to speak quietly and slowly, like her father would have done. Calm words lapping the shores of a great ocean of frustration. 'And Monterose is my home town. I grew up here.'

'I don't care if you grew up in Buckingham Palace. OUT.' His breath ponged of garlic. Tessa backed away. She stepped round him and marched to the Post Office counter. The woman behind it had a face like a boxer dog. She gave Tessa a silent snarl and slammed the hatch down.

'Supposing I came back dressed as a housewife?' Tessa said. 'In a flowery pinny and slippers – and rollers in my hair. Would you serve me then? I need to post this letter.' She slammed the letter to Faye on the counter. 'Will you please sell me a stamp?' The pitch of her voice was rising and the quaking started in the muscles of her stomach. First Ian Tillerman, then Dr Jarvis, now this. Tessa felt like trashing the Post Office. All she wanted was a peaceful day with Art. Why these obstacles?

Her temper was under control, but only just. She knew that her grandfather, Levi, had died from losing his temper. She'd had years of practice and patient teaching from her parents, and threats of what might happen if she lost it. Yet still she walked precariously along a cliff edge, her feet on solid ground, her eyes warning her of the endless crashing, down, down into a life of broken glass and splintered bone, a friendless life where temper was a lonely outcast dictator. *Don't go there, Tessa,* she thought, gathered the shreds of herself into a regal silence, and walked out of the shop into the sunshine.

She headed home to the sanctuary of the bus, half hoping that Art wouldn't be there. Time alone to calm down was what she needed. But when she turned into the field she was surprised to see a horsebox parked in there. It had little windows with rainbow curtains, and a woman in a flowing velvet skirt was sitting on the steps breastfeeding a baby.

Freddie leaned against the green Morris Minor, his fingers smoothing the well-polished roof. 'Why are you selling her?' he asked.

Todd Whitcombe's eyes looked at him candidly from under his tweed cap which was dark with oil. 'She belonged to Lady Fontwell up at the Manor House – she died recently.'

'Ah – I heard she'd gone,' Freddie said. 'Bit of a character, wasn't she?'

'She were a witch, people say!' Todd's eyes twinkled. A bit of scandal added romance to his life as a car dealer. 'She were practising some weird kind of medicine.'

'Herbalism?' asked Freddie.

'No – it were even weirder than that. She had this black box that sent out rays or something. They say she had clients all over the world.'

'I've never heard of that,' Freddie said. He felt the back of his neck prickling. 'Sounds a bit dodgy, don't it?'

'Anyway – she were a Lady. Old money, if you know what I mean. I sold her this car, new, and serviced it for her. She was always charming, always – but her eyes used to look right through you.' Todd hesitated as if unsure whether to trust Freddie with the next morsel of scandal. 'And d'you know what she said to me once?'

'What?'

'Well, one day I had a bad back – awful it were – made my work hell – and she came round for some petrol. She looked at me out the car window and she said, "Todd, you've got a back pain, haven't you?" I said, "yes", and she said, "I'll put you on the box."'

Freddie's eyes rounded. 'Go on.'

'She opened her handbag – scruffy old leather thing – and took out a pair of nail scissors. "Cut me off a snippet of your hair," she said.'

'And did you?'

'Ah – I didn't want to get on the wrong side of her, so I did it. Gave it to her through the car window and she put it in an envelope and wrote me name on it. That's all she did – she went off and I never saw her for a month – but d'you know what?'

'What?'

'That back pain were gone the next day, and I never had it since.'

The two men looked at each other over the roof of Lady Fontwell's car, letting the mystery settle into silence. Like a bird settling into its nest after flight. Freddie felt a stirring in his mind as some long-forgotten energy began to uncoil the tip of its tail.

'How much do you want for it?' he asked.

'Seventy quid.'

'Ah – that's too much. It's not worth that. Shame.' Freddie buttoned his jacket, ready to walk away.

'Make me an offer.'

Freddie frowned. He walked round the car and found some rust along the bottom edge of the doors. 'That's bad, see. Needs a lot of work doing. I could give you fifty quid, I suppose. That's all the cash I've got.'

'Can't you find another fiver? I'd take fifty-five, but only from you.'

Freddie took out his brown leather wallet and counted out fifty pounds. 'Sorry – that's all I've got.'

Todd stared at him. A twinkle of knowing passed between them. 'Oh – all right then. Fifty quid.'

'Done,' said Freddie and they shook hands.

It was nearly lunchtime. Freddie got into the driver's seat and set off towards Langport. The straight half-mile of road leading out of Monterose was a good place to test a car. He put his foot down and drove flat out in the little car, wanting to see if the engine would cope without boiling. It made a lot of noise, but it was fine, and as he topped the crest of the hill he pulled into a gateway with a view across the Levels to the distant Quantocks. Only then, in the sudden stillness, did he realise someone was in the car with him. A woman with a coil of silver hair and burning blue eyes. Her voice was a silvery whisper with long snake-like vowels that pinned him to the seat so that he couldn't move.

'You were driving her much too fast,' she said. 'But, yes, this is the right car for Tessa.'

Freddie was electrified. How did she know he had bought the car for Tessa? He waited, too shocked to speak.

'You have nothing to fear,' whispered the voice. 'This car is full of my energy and my love. I will be Tessa's guardian. It is part of the plan. She has my gift.'

Freddie felt a smile of recognition stretching across his cheeks. He'd bought a haunted car. A car haunted by a spirit who knew what he knew about his beautiful daughter. A benevolent spirit who wanted to help her. He turned to look into those burning blue eyes, and as he did so she vanished like threads of silver silk blown away by the wind from the sea.

It had been so long since this had happened to him. He'd been like a soul asleep on the hard bedrock of survival, marching on like a warrior through shellfire. And now he'd reached a bright horizon, a distant place where clouds parted into a rose gold smile of light.

Tell no one, he thought. *Tell no one. It's too fragile to share. Too precious.*

Hungry for his lunch, Freddie turned towards the Polden Hills, intending to eat his picnic up on the ridgeway and gaze out across the peat moors towards the sea. But the spirit of Lady Fontwell hadn't finished with him. Her voice whispered insistently through his consciousness. 'Tessa needs you.' He tried to ignore it, thinking Art would be there. He wanted his daughter to himself. After lunch he had to get on with some work. The Morris Minor was going slower and slower, as if it had a mind of its own. The voice kept coming. 'Tessa needs you.'

Freddie sighed. He pulled into a gateway, turned the car and headed back through Monterose. He actually felt shy about going into Tessa's field and knocking on the door of the bus. The fear was old family stuff, imparted by his mother. It had dripped through his lifetime like the cold tap over the Belfast sink in the scullery. He'd fought it and mostly overcome it, but in the last few years his confidence had cracked. Losing Lucy. Tessa's suicide attempt. His illness. Dr Jarvis's voice telling him he could no longer do the work he loved.

It turned out that he didn't have to go and knock on the door of the bus. He found Tessa in the lane, leaning over the gate to Lexi's horse field. She was by herself. He gave the horn a little toot and pulled the car onto the grass verge. He wasn't going to tell her he'd bought it for her. He'd tinker with it first, and give it to her on her birthday, or maybe Christmas.

Tessa swung round. 'Dad!'

Freddie knew Tessa very well. He knew the way her face pouted when she was guarding pain, the way her pale blue eyes lost their light. He got out of the car and stood in silence, looking into her soul.

'Oh Dad.' She studied his eyes for a moment of trying to hold herself together.

'Whatever's the matter?' he asked, and Tessa collapsed against him, her body heaving with sobs. Freddie held her silently, his hands smoothing the tresses of chestnut hair that hung down her back, feeling the beads and ribbons she had woven into it, the denim jacket, the heat of her crying. He found it difficult, sometimes impossible, to use the word 'love' but he felt it intensely. He hoped Tessa would sense how much he loved her.

'Have you had lunch?' he asked, eventually. It was the only thing he could think of to say.

Tessa shook her head.

'You get in the car with me – I were gonna eat my lunch up on the ridgeway,' he said. 'There's enough for two. Lardy cake as well.'

She looked up at him, her face covered in tears.

'Come on.' Freddie opened the passenger door and steered her inside. He drove in silence towards Hilbegut, through the village and up the steep wooded lane, sensing Tessa calming down beside him, the sobs ebbing away. She'd tell him, all in good time, he figured, and if she didn't, it wouldn't matter.

'Is this a new car, Dad?' She managed to sound normal, though her voice was low.

'Ah. I only just bought it. Hold tight – I'm not sure if she'll go up this blimin' hill.' Freddie changed gear and put his foot down. The car took off like a bumble bee. Two wings of steam leaked out from under the bonnet as he pulled into the gateway and stopped. 'She's boiling. Hear it?' He got out, lifted the bonnet, and clouds of steam wafted away into the trees. 'We'll go and have our picnic and let her cool down.'

The narrow path to the ridgeway was colourful with pink

and orange spindleberries, clusters of blue-black sloes, and the yellowing leaves of hazels still laden with nuts. The turf was carpeted with layer upon layer of fallen leaves, opening out onto the hillside grassland, nodding with seedheads of grasses and knapweed. Freddie and Tessa walked in silence up to the skyline where the light shone white through the geometric tufts of thistle seed. The view was a breathtaking chessboard of greens and golds, all the way to the silver brown shores of the Bristol Channel, twenty miles away. A misty sheen of water, and the sapphire blue outline of the Welsh coast beyond.

'I missed this place,' Tessa said.

The sun was warm on the turf. Freddie took off his jacket and spread it out for them to sit on. 'Kate and I always came up here,' he said. 'It's a good place to – to think.' He just stopped himself reminding Tessa that she had chosen this wild hillside for her suicide attempt.

'I wanted to die in a beautiful place, Dad, in case you're wondering about it,' she said, as if sensing his thought. 'It was Art who found me. He was good to me.'

'Ah – he were.' Freddie unwrapped the greaseproof paper. He broke the slice of pork pie in half and offered it to her.

Tessa shook her head. 'No thanks, Dad. I'm vegetarian now. And not hungry. You eat it.'

Freddie restrained himself from airing his views on vegetarians. 'I'll do the eating, and you do the talking,' he said.

Tessa sighed and wriggled close to him, as close as she could get with the two of them sitting on his jacket. 'Suddenly my life is crowded with obstacles,' she said.

'Ah – obstacles – but, are they obstacles or are they choices?'

'They are obstacles, and no matter what I say or do they won't go away. They just won't.'

Freddie heard remnants of the sobs buffeting her breath as she talked. He picked up an acorn which had blown down from a nearby oak tree. 'You've gotta be a tree,' he said. 'If a tree root comes to a rock, it doesn't try to go through, it goes round. But what you gotta remember is that the rock will make the tree's root system stronger in the end, so it can hold tight when the wind blows.'

He watched her eyes. They were thoughtful as she fingered the plump golden acorn in its knobbly cup. 'If you close your eyes, you can feel its life force,' she said. 'Art taught me that. You should try it, Dad.'

'I'm eating me lunch,' he said, but stored the idea away in a corner of his mind.

'Art's taught me a lot,' Tessa said, and then she began to talk. Everything, except the contraception issue. Ian Tillerman. The Post Office. The build-up of anger and frustration.

Freddie listened, sensing she was leaving something out, some women's stuff, he figured. But the anger which had been pouring out of Tessa was slowing down, drifting now, allowing her to breathe and look at the world again.

'When you saw me,' she concluded, 'I was looking at Lexi's horses. Selwyn is my special horse and I really wanted to see her and make sure she was okay. I kind of hoped to see Lexi too – she was a good friend to me.'

'Ah – she was,' agreed Freddie. Tessa had spent the previous summer working for Lexi between school and college. She was proud of the way Tessa had managed to calm and understand Selwyn who was suffering from a back injury. The beautiful dappled grey mare had responded to Tessa's love, and shown her that she could heal.

'I was worried because Selwyn wasn't there.' Tessa hesitated. Freddie saw a new pain surfacing in her eyes, a shadow of what was to come. 'But the worse problem was that I – I couldn't go home.'

That was it, Freddie thought. Those four words, 'I couldn't go home' had come out of her as a cry from the heart. Now she was silent again, looking at him, her fingers twiddling an amber bead that glinted in her hair. The amber echoed the flecks of gold in the centre of her light blue eyes. 'Why not?' he asked.

'Because – THIS WOMAN was there.' Suddenly Tessa was angry again. 'She said her name was Rowan – and I hated her, I just hated her on sight. Her eyes are like flint, and she's bitter and challenging, if you know what I mean, Dad. People like her really wind me up. I could kill her! – And she's got a baby which she brandishes at the world. You can't touch me 'cause I've got a baby – that sort of attitude.'

'So – was she in the bus?'

'No – worse. She lives in a converted horsebox and she had the cheek to just drive it in and park – in MY field – and when I confronted her she smiled in a patronising way and said Art had invited her to camp there. Then she said Art had gone to help a mate fix a stove in his camper van. She said he'd asked her to keep an eye on me, for goodness' sake. And I don't want her there, Dad, I just wanted peace and solitude. I asked her to leave and she wouldn't – she sat there flaunting her superiority, trying to make me feel like a silly child. She didn't respect me at all. I HATED her.'

Freddie put his arm around Tessa and gave her a kindly pat on the shoulder. 'Why don't you come home? Stay with us while Art's away – I don't like to think of you alone in that bus. I know it's all nicely fitted out – he's made a good job of it – but you can come home, Tessa.'

'But Dad – I WANT to live with Art. It was working beautifully in Cornwall – we were in the sea every day –and the commune were so friendly. They just accepted me – no questions – no judgements. And you have to understand this, Dad – my life with Art is the most beautiful and precious thing. I have to make a go of it, whatever it takes.'

CHAPTER 4

The Tide in London

The mysterious mist that hung low over the Somerset Levels was reputed to be the ghost of an ocean which had been there centuries ago. It turned the hills into islands. Glastonbury Tor, Burrow Mump, Dundon Beacon and Lollover became the enchanted isles, floating on the expanse of shining mist. There was even a legend of a phantom ship – the Argo Navis, the ship of the sun that sailed into the west and disappeared.

Tessa imagined it now, as she walked home an hour before sunset. A tall ship with translucent sails, its timbers glistening with encrusted salt, gliding soundlessly on the white tide of mist, nearer and nearer to the water meadows of Monterose. She paused to lean on a gate and dream with it. A lucky ship it would be. A love ship for her and Art. Lucky, and private, and eternal.

The evening sun flung stripes of rose pink light across the surface of the mist, turning the windows of Monterose into mirrors of gold. Tessa was feeling better after the time with her father. She'd stayed for tea and Kate had arrived home, jubilant, with an empty car, a roll of cash and a beaming smile. They'd laughed and laughed over the tale of how she'd parked illegally in Lyme Regis and duped a policeman into holding two bird boxes while she delivered an order to a pet shop.

Kate had given Tessa a warm hug, a five-pound note, and yet another basket of goodies to share with Art. They'd talked about the woman with the baby, and Kate had said, 'You hold your head up, dear, and be proud of who you are. We're proud of you, aren't we, dear?' and Freddie had said, 'Ah – we are.'

Tessa felt nurtured and confident. She'd be polite to Rowan, but make it clear that Art was hers. They were lovers. Lovers across time. And no one could come between them.

She watched the tall ship she had imagined. Or was it real? Momentarily there was a blurred edge between fantasy and reality, a shore of crinkling silk and lace, a shore of deception. She heard the creak of timbers, the snap of the mast and she saw the floating black splinters, the billowing sails ripped and torn into rags. The cries of sailors as the charred carcass sank below the waves with terrifying speed.

Disturbed by the dark vision, Tessa walked on quickly, reassured by the friendly weight of the willow basket over her arm, a bit of home comfort – bright apples and home-made ginger cake, a Pyrex dish with one of Kate's pies. The windows of Monterose darkened, the mist shone pearly white, the air chilled as she hurried down the lane, a tingle of excitement in her spine.

Walk tall, she thought, and turned into the gate of the field. She'd be bouncy and radiant. Confident and full of light, the way Art liked her to be.

The basket fell to the floor. She stopped, suddenly death–cold. The field was empty. The horsebox had gone.

And so had the bus.

Tessa couldn't move. She felt herself sinking into cold wet estuary sand, down, down into the dungeons of the bedrock. The sparkle of her bright spirit was leaving. Not flying gloriously into the gold–rimmed cumuli of evening. Not dancing in the glittering waves. But sinking. Going deep into paralysing mud. Leaving. Opting out. Earth to earth. Ashes to ashes. Dust to dust.

Her eyes picked out something white in the hedge. An envelope, in the front pocket of her rucksack. *I can't read it*, she thought. But her feet plodded towards it. Her eyes looked down. The rucksack was open at the top, and all her stuff had been hastily crammed in there. Lou's ethnic blanket. Her spare clothes. Her green bottle of Silvikrin shampoo. Her diary stuffed with monochrome photos of Selwyn and Jonti. The jar of sand from Porthmeor Beach, the black elvan pebble and seashells. In the middle of it the gold–rimmed pages of *The Water Babies* glinted.

Tessa's hand reached out and picked up the white envelope by its corner. The name stung like a nettle under her fingertips.

TESSA – in Art's stylish, curving capitals. *Who am I?* she thought. *I'm not that person and I can't read that letter. Not yet.*

She heaved the heavy rucksack onto her back and walked out into the lane. The lights of Monterose twinkled and cosy squares of firelight glowed from cottage windows. The Pines looked far away, standing apart from the village, with bright yellow lights in the kitchen and living room. *I can't go home*, Tessa thought. *Not after this. Not with this letter like a poisoned wafer in my pocket.*

She turned her back on Monterose and headed up the lane towards the main road, letting her legs take her in punishing strides through the violet dusk.

And she didn't look back.

The willow basket was left where she had dropped it in the grass. A pair of crows flew down to investigate. They pecked the apples, and pushed the lid off the Pyrex dish. Soon there was a circle of crows, magpies and jackdaws, squabbling and tearing Kate's pie to bits, flying up with beaks full of pastry and dropping it all over the field. A fox came and sniffed at everything. He took the whole ginger cake in his jaws and ran off into the wood with it.

Tessa walked up the lane, hearing only the rhythmic thud of her footsteps and the haunting cry of the tawny owls hooting in the wood. A heron passed over on ponderous wings, heading for its roosting place in the tall ash trees.

When she reached the main road it was getting dark. Tessa paused by the black and white signpost on a triangle of grass. She touched the cold lettering. *MONTEROSE. Goodbye*, she thought, and fought back the cyclones of grief that loomed and circled in her innermost mind. She touched *ILCHESTER* and *YEOVIL*, the raised letters gritty and wet under her fingers. London was far away, but the road would lead her onto the A303 at Podimore. Then over the chalk downs of Salisbury Plain, past Stonehenge and on towards London.

Tessa saw London as a rabbit hole. Alice in Wonderland's rabbit hole. A great place to disappear. To enter a labyrinth of anonymity and possibility. A place where no one cared who you were or what you had done.

She knew how to hitchhike. Her friend Faye had taught her at college. Doing it on your own was scary, and 'inadvisable'. But who cared? Who cared about her now? A dropout. A hippie. That had seemed exciting and creative while she was Art's woman. But who was she now? A reject. Reject, REJECT.

She swung her rucksack down and propped it against the signpost. She listened for a car, but heard only the velvet pattering of leaves falling onto the tarmac. The stillness and the quiet were unnerving. To be running away but standing still. *I'm broken-hearted*, she thought suddenly, and saw herself running and running for the rest of her life to avoid facing the paralysing pain that waited in the stillness.

At last the sound of a car struggling up the steep hill, its gears grinding, the headlights sending dazzling shafts of yellow scissoring through the trees. Tessa stepped to the edge of the road and lifted her arm to thumb a lift.

*

Three days later, Freddie and Kate stood looking at the Morris Minor outside The Pines. 'What a dear little car!' Kate said, giving the new car an appreciative pat on the bonnet. She walked round it and peered in the windows. 'It's got nice green seats, and it's so clean. I'm thrilled, Freddie. Fancy you going off and buying Tessa a car. She'll love it.'

'Well – I hope she don't go painting daisies all over it,' Freddie said.

'She probably will!' Kate opened the door and smoothed the driver's seat, imagining her daughter driving it, looking capable and sophisticated like Fiona Tillerman. 'And you didn't tell her? Didn't you even give her a hint it was for her?'

'No.' Freddie's eyes twinkled. ''Tis for her birthday.'

'In three weeks' time. I can't wait to see her face,' Kate said. 'I shall tie a big bow of red ribbon round it, and put her card inside. And will you be teaching her to drive?'

'Ah – I will,' Freddie said, and the twinkle in his eyes misted over. 'And I'd have done the same for Lucy if she hadn't gone off with that blimin' Tim.'

Kate put her arms around him and studied his face with that searching, kindly gaze he loved so much. It was the look that had first drawn him to her, for no one else in his life had looked at him so caringly, before or since. Kate had power. She could make him feel like a millionaire with one glance, and she could heal him with another one. 'Lucy will come round,' she said now. 'I'm so sure she will. Let's not give up on her. Remember how good she was.'

'Ah.' Freddie stared at a heron flying majestically across the sky. He watched it go down, slow and graceful, into the water meadows.

'Can we go for a drive in it?' Kate asked.

'What – now?'

'Well – I'd like to just drop by and see Tessa,' Kate said, 'and take her some eggs. The chickens have laid so many. I know I gave her a basket of stuff a few days ago – Saturday it was – and I've made another fruitcake. They'd love a wedge of that.'

Freddie looked at her shrewdly. 'Is that the only reason?'

'No,' admitted Kate. 'I'm a bit anxious about them being in the field, especially if that other woman is parked in there. It said on the news that the convoy had been evicted from Ian and Sue's place – and they're heading for Glastonbury now.'

'Best place for 'em, too,' Freddie said. 'You know what I think of hippies.'

'Yes, dear, I do know.'

Kate packed the eggs and cake into a cardboard box. She looked in the larder and added a tin of corned beef, a tin of spam and a jar of home bottled Victoria plums. She'd missed spoiling her girls. Tessa had been away for six long months, at college and then in Cornwall. Kate had lain awake night after night worrying about her being alone, sleeping rough in St Ives with no money, and no address or phone number. When Tessa had sent a postcard telling her she'd met Art, Kate had felt better. She didn't like the way Art chose to look, but he was kind. He had rescued Tessa from her suicide attempt, but Kate hadn't foreseen that Tessa would fall in love with him so young and so passionately. When the two of them had turned up in the bus, Kate was overjoyed at the change in her daughter. Tessa had always been hypersensitive and difficult. Now, with Art, she was radiant and confident, sparkling in fact. Kate had tried hard to open her heart to Art, and to help Freddie to accept him. Then she'd seen him with Rowan and it had all collapsed into fury. Maternal fury, which was a magnificent version of normal anger. Kate had kept it to herself for once. She didn't want to make things worse and drive Tessa away. Wait and see what happens was Freddie's attitude. Don't wade in and confront the guy.

She put the box of goodies in the boot of the Morris Minor and got in next to Freddie. Immediately she had a funny feeling as if the person who had owned and driven it was watching them both. *Don't be so silly*, she thought, and sat back to enjoy the ride. The streets of Monterose flew past like the city of leaves, the roads and pavements piled with drifts of them and the speed of the car sent them skittering down the middle of the road. 'I love the autumn,' Kate said. 'I wish I was out picking blackberries.'

Her mood changed when they pulled into the empty field.

Freddie's eyes glistened with disappointment. 'Gone,' he said, and the word hung in the air like a hawk.

Kate felt devastated. After all her effort, Tessa had moved on without a word. 'She could have said goodbye – told us where she was going – couldn't she?' Her voice lost its cheerful resonance.

'I don't like to see you hurt,' Freddie said, and they sat in the car in silence, staring at the place where Art's bus had been parked.

'We should be used to it by now,' Kate said, 'but I never will be – never.'

Another bitter silence swirled around them.

Kate got out of the car. 'I'll just have a look round – in case they left a note. Maybe they've gone to Glastonbury with the convoy.'

It was Freddie who made the grim discovery. Sticking out of the long grass was the handle of a basket. He got out to look at it. Kate's willow basket. Her best one. On its side in the mud. Around it was a mess of half-eaten apples, lovely apples from their garden tree, now rotting and crawling with flies. A Pyrex pie dish lying in the grass with a ring of crumbs left inside. Freddie stooped and picked up a feather. It was black and white with a sheen of blue. *A magpie,* he thought, and a sense of foreboding coloured his mind in the same metallic blue. Why had the birds been allowed to plunder the gift Kate had prepared so lovingly?

Freddie stood still as the air unfolded a veil of chiffon light in front of him. Blue eyes, like his own, shimmered within it, and an old familiar voice boomed in his mind. 'I told you, didn't I? Tessa's gonna get hurt.'

'Mother!' he gasped, and Annie appeared, her silver hair shining like a halo, her cheeks apple-red, her apron snowy-white. In seconds she was gone, snuffed out like a candle flame. A whiff of perfume hung in the air. Rich red cottage roses. The coke oven. The aroma of fresh bread.

Kate had walked along the hedge, searching for clues. She came towards him, her hands empty, her eyes anxious. 'What is it, dear?' she asked, and Freddie suddenly wanted to cry, to cry like Tessa, in big sobs. Not for himself. He'd been used to pain. But for Kate. The distant hours of happiness, her joy at having two little girls, were aeons away. Now it lurched from one disaster to the next. He felt helpless. He didn't want her to see the basket, but she did.

'Birds,' he managed to say. 'Crows and magpies. Had the lot.'

'Why? Why, Freddie?' Kate looked shocked. She picked up the basket, shook the crumbs out of it, retrieved the dish and put it inside. Her hands were shaking. 'Tessa wouldn't have just left it there in the grass. That was such a nice pie.'

'Ah – something's happened,' Freddie said.

'We must find her,' Kate said in a panicky voice. 'Let's get in the car and go to Glastonbury.'

Freddie knew he shouldn't let Kate go on her own. But he felt powerless, as if his feet were rooted into the earth. 'I told you. No. I'm not getting involved with those hippies. You go.' He handed her the car keys. 'Go on, you can go. I'll walk home in a minute. I need time to think.'

He knew from the way Kate's eyes darkened that she was furious with him. Her cheeks were crimson, her lips pursed, maybe she wanted to scream at him, but she never would. She was hardwired to dignity and good behaviour.

'All right, dear. If that's what you want.' She took the keys and Freddie watched her drive off in the unfamiliar car.

Slowly he padded up to the source of the spring. He parted the tendrils of old man's beard and elderberry branches and sat down on the mossy oak log.

It was something he'd always known – that if he sat perfectly still, and listened, and waited, wisdom would come to him. Sometimes it came as a bird or an animal. Sometimes a voice on the wind, or a shift in the light.

The moon and the tides had always fascinated Tessa. Gentle childhood tides on Weymouth beach that left the sand in wavy ridges. The excitement of running to the water's edge on little feet, water-baby feet, hers and Lucy's. Sisters. Always together. Then the amazement of Cornish tides in St Ives, crystalline waters on white shell sand, ebbing for vast distances, crisp with light, revealing pools of myriad colours, underwater gardens, dazzling reflections to explore in the endless sunshine. Clean curly seashells in ivory and gold, pink and ultramarine blue. All disappearing under the majestic roar of the incoming tide creaming across the sands, the flash of green through a towering wave, the dance of lemon sunlight interlaced in the foam.

She was remembering.

And now she was watching a new tide, dark and vigorous, oily and heavy, relentless. The tide from the North Sea. The tide in London, surging up the River Thames, casually reflecting the coloured lights of the city, stitching them in silks of scarlet, emerald and amber. A line from Coleridge, *The water like a witch's oil.*

Tessa was watching. Not thinking. Watching, as if she watched her own hand painting a picture, painting bright shoals of goldfish on the swirling ebony water.

Not thinking. Remembering. Aunt Ethie drowning, streaming up river on the Severn tide, her face to the sky, her face twisted with anger, her mouth shaped by regret, her dying eyes suddenly loving and at peace.

Aunt Ethie's favourite book was in Tessa's rucksack. She could feel the brick shape of it against her back as she leaned on the cold grey metal of Hungerford Bridge. Metal that rang and thundered under the wheels of trains. Passing over. Over her head, her aching tired head. The gold-rimmed pages of Charles Kingsley's story would go down with her, this time, its words splayed out like the wings of a dying swan.

And yet there was something in that book – a story within a story that burned a candle in Tessa's mind. Her mind was not thinking. Just following candles.

A woman was in the book – a spirit woman who appeared in a number of disguises. An old woman in a red shawl. A water fairy. A horrible teacher and a loving teacher. And finally – Mother Carey who sat on the 'Allalonestone' and loved all the creatures of the ocean, especially the wicked and the lost.

Who was she?

Clinging to the bridge, Tessa listened. In case there was a voice for her. A voice that would care. A loving spirit, like Mother Carey, who did not judge.

As dawn came over London, Hungerford Bridge

resounded and vibrated with thousands of footsteps pounding their way into the city. Tessa could feel the surge of their focused energy. She sensed their forgotten dreams trailing like georgette scarves, so thin, so transparent and vulnerable, snatched away by the North Sea tide. Hungerford Bridge. She toyed with the name. A derivative of *hungry* and *ford*, as in crossing the river. Transformation.

In the midst of the rush hour, there was a clock. It had chimes like her mother's clock, but huge and sonorous. *Big Ben*, she thought, and counted seven gong-like chimes. She wound her watch up and set the hands to seven o'clock. *Why am I winding my watch up when I'm going to die?* she thought. *I'll drown, like Aunt Ethie, and then they'll throw rose petals into the river and remember that sometimes, just sometimes, I was good.*

She waited, hoping for just one rose petal on the water, in the pink light of dawn that dimmed the candle flame she'd been following. She listened. In the heart of Aunt Ethie's book was a voice, the seed of a voice, so quiet that it planted a word into her mind. *DIARY.*

Lou's ethnic blanket was wrapped around her. She let go of its homely fuzziness and took her diary from her top pocket. It was dog-eared and stuffed with information. As she turned the pages, a card fell out, into her hand. Taped to the back with yellowing sellotape was a tiny sliver of citrine crystal. She touched it, and remembered. The eyes. The voice. Starlinda, Faye's mother, a clairvoyant medium and healer, had given her the card. 'If you ever feel like killing yourself again – ring me,' Starlinda had said.

Tessa was cold and her clothes were damp. She'd spent the night wedged into a corner of the great bridge over the River Thames. Her rucksack, still strapped to her back, had been her one solid, comforting link. No one had noticed her there – a young girl with chestnut hair, bundled in a blanket, even though her shoes were visible. The tall legs in neatly pressed trousers walked on by, and so did the women's legs in high boots and miniskirts. Not a single face had turned to look at her with searching kindness. And no one looked at her now as she unfolded her stiff limbs. *I stink*, she thought, *but who cares?*

She trudged back towards Waterloo and found a vacant phone box. It stank of urine and tobacco, and it had an alarming small mirror where she confronted her own face. Ugly and tired. Worthless. Her eyes like two cracks of aquamarine light, almost hidden in swollen cheeks after another night of misery and adrenalin.

With a pile of pennies and sixpences ready, she dialled Starlinda's number. No answer. She imagined the cream telephone ringing and ringing in an empty flat. Tessa tried three times but no one answered. Starlinda lived in Belgravia. Could she walk to Belgravia from Waterloo with her heavy rucksack? She was starving and tired. Why bother? Why not go back to the bridge and just do it? Put an end to it. She stared at the inside of the phone kiosk and a small notice caught her eye. *SUICIDAL? Talk to us – we can help you – any hour, day or night. Ring Mansion House 9000, for free.*

A spark danced in her mind. She dialled the number. A voice answered immediately. 'Samaritans. Can I help you?'

Tessa froze.

'My name's Dorothy. Please talk to me.'

Still she froze.

'Is something troubling you? Are you there?'

Her throat felt padlocked, but she hung onto the phone.

'Would you like to tell me your name?'

'Tessa.'

CHAPTER 5

Catharsis

Tessa walked into the crypt of St Stephen's Church, Walbrook, the founder centre of The Samaritans. 'I came to see Dorothy,' she said to the reassuringly ordinary young man who greeted her. He wore a faded black t-shirt, and flared jeans, and there was light in his eyes. 'I'm Tessa,' she said. 'I spoke to Dorothy on the phone earlier.'

'Right – okay, Tessa, come this way.' He led her down a corridor under the stone vaults of the ancient crypt which was cosily lit with soft lamps in each recess. 'Would you like a coffee?'

'Yes please – with sugar.'

'Okay – I'll bring it down straight away, so you won't be disturbed at all,' he said, and showed her into a tiny room. It had two friendly old armchairs with orange cushions, a small table, an ashtray and a box of tissues.

Tessa heaved the rucksack from her back and sat down.

She glanced at Dorothy who was sitting in the other chair, and saw only her eyes. They were serious. Tessa sank into a chair, and looked at the floor, occasionally noticing Dorothy's swollen ankles bulging over a pair of flat black slip-on shoes, and one of them had a squashed sultana stuck to the sole. Then she stared into her coffee mug, wrapping her frozen hands around it. Coffee had never tasted so good and so hot.

'You take your time,' Dorothy said. She didn't push Tessa to talk, but sipped her own coffee thoughtfully. On the phone she had said, 'We don't give advice. We just listen.' And Tessa sensed her doing exactly that – listening, waiting, expecting nothing. At the same time she felt Dorothy wasn't going to give up on her. She was tenaciously patient – like a horse.

'It's complicated,' Tessa began. 'I was okay until three days ago. I was fine. I was happy. Happier than I've ever been in my life – and then ' Suddenly she couldn't breathe. She felt trapped in an earthquake of emotion where sentences were either splintered or boulder-shaped and threatening to crush the life out of her. 'My boyfriend, Art – oh, boyfriend is the wrong word – he was – IS the love of my life. We were soul-mates, and lovers.' She glanced at Dorothy to see if she was shocked, and found the same attentive horse-like concern. 'And then he – he totally abandoned me. I didn't do anything wrong. We didn't have a row. We loved each other – I thought it was forever. I was so happy. Then he – he betrayed me. I don't understand – why? Why me? WHY?' Tessa sobbed uncontrollably, on and on, hearing her heartache echoing through the stone crypt under St Stephen's Church. The rest of the story tumbled out in jagged fragments.

Dorothy hardly moved, but she listened, her head tilted in a kindly way. She murmured innocuous little phrases like, 'Oh dear,' and 'You poor girl,' and 'It's so unfair.'

'I've always been a bad girl,' Tessa wept, 'always in trouble and I never intended it to be that way. No one understood me – except Dad, and he was out working most of the time. Mum couldn't cope with me, and my granny hated me. She kept saying I was evil and a curse on the family – even if I was nice to her she pushed me away. And my sister, Lucy, was angelically good. People kept on at me to be like Lucy, smile like Lucy, think like Lucy.' Tessa's voice rang with pain. 'And I COULDN'T.'

'Of course you couldn't,' murmured Dorothy.

'It went on all my life and I was sick, sick, SICK of it. Lucy and I played together, but we're so different – we're like strangers now. I couldn't talk to anyone like I'm talking to you,' Tessa wept, 'not even Dad. He's a sculptor and a creative person and I'm so proud of him. But no one wanted ME to be creative. It just got me into trouble and––' She paused, reaching a barbed-wire fence, stretched tightly across her life so long ago.

Dorothy waited, totally engrossed in her task of sacred listening.

'You're awesome,' Tessa said, suddenly noticing her. 'Aren't you tired of me moaning?'

'No, dear. I'm fine. You were saying? About being creative?'

'Well—' Tessa hesitated. 'There's something I'm not supposed to talk about.'

'You can talk about it here. You need to, don't you?'

Tessa nodded. Her skull felt like an eggshell being cracked open.

'A woman I know told me once that I was clairvoyant. She said it was a wonderful gift and I should use it. And when I was little, I did. I used it all the time. I saw spirit people, like my grandfather, and I had spirit friends, real friends, who I talked to, and in school when we were studying poetry, I saw the poet. Once I got expelled when I told the teacher I could see Alfred Lord Tennyson in the classroom. She hated me, hated everything I did – and mostly she hated my eyes! "Don't look at me with THOSE EYES," she'd say. I used to think she looked like a badly weathered clothes peg – all grey and full of splinters. I mean – what's wrong with my eyes, for goodness' sake?'

'Nothing, Tessa, they're beautiful,' Dorothy said warmly.

'Art loved my eyes. He said they were like the eyes of an angel.'

'I agree with that.'

Tessa managed to raise her eyes from staring at the floor to look at Dorothy and it was the first time the two women had eye contact. Dorothy's eyes were compassionate and sustaining. Tessa touched the skin around her own eyes and it felt hot and sore. 'I must look a proper wreck,' she said, 'after all that crying.'

'You look fine, especially after what you've been through.'

'I should go,' Tessa said, and looked at her watch. 'Oh no! I can't believe I've been here for two hours!'

'It's okay – I've got plenty of time. You talk as much as you need to, Tessa.'

'No, really, I should go.'

'Okay – but will you come back? Tomorrow? There's a lot more, isn't there?'

Tessa looked at Dorothy in silence. She felt hollowed out like a Halloween pumpkin, and two hours of crying had left a burning ache in her throat and shoulders. She hadn't eaten since she'd read Art's letter, sitting under a tree by the River Thames.

'I'd like to ask you two questions, Tessa,' Dorothy said, 'if that's okay. But you don't have to answer them.'

'Okay.'

'First – have you got somewhere to go? Somewhere to sleep tonight?'

Tessa looked at the floor again. She looked at the endearing sultana stuck to Dorothy's shoe, and imagined her as a slim teenager, like herself. She wondered what kind of journey had brought Dorothy to this quiet, life-saving listening. Life-saving! *People are always saving my life*, she thought. *Why can't I save my own life?*

'I've got a lovely home, in Somerset,' she said, 'and nice parents. But they want me to CONFORM – and if anything

82

bad happens, they won't talk about it. They shove it under the carpet. It's like they don't want to know the real me. They seem – afraid of me – and I'm afraid. All my life I've been terrified of doing or saying something wrong. And the fear comes out as anger. Whichever way I turn, it's there, like a guard dog – a dog with red eyes.'

Dorothy nodded, still patient, still listening with her velvet-grey serious eyes fixed on Tessa.

It was like a door opening. A door that had been slammed shut all those years ago. 'We don't TALK about it, dear,' her mother had insisted, and Tessa had grown up like a time-bomb. 'I can't possibly go home,' she told Dorothy. 'I have to be strong to go home and maintain the image of the successful daughter. Even now, I can't – daren't – talk about it, even to you. But maybe I will, if I can come back and see you again.'

'I hope you will, Tessa. Come tomorrow, if you like.'

'What was your other question?' Tessa asked, fidgeting. She needed to move now.

'When you thought about killing yourself – was it because you really wanted to take your life, or was it because you didn't know where to find the kind of help you needed?'

Tessa was silent. Art had saved her life. Cornish lifeguards had fished her out of the sea. Jonti and Selwyn had saved her. That thought persisted. *Why can't I save my own life? Maybe I just did,* she thought.

'I didn't really, truly want to die,' she said, 'but I don't know which way to turn. I'm so useless. I don't know what I'm supposed to do with my life!'

Kate knocked on the door of Art's bus. Her heart had almost stopped when she saw it parked in a layby high up on the Polden Hills. She'd been searching all the morning, driving through the lanes around Glastonbury, and was on her way home, tired and worried sick about Tessa.

When no one answered the door, she tried the handle. It was locked. Kate walked round it and peered in the windows, looking for Tessa's little corner where she kept her books and seashells, and she was alarmed to see they were gone. Instead, a pile of grey-looking towels and a grubby white pot of zinc and castor oil cream were there. Kate frowned. She couldn't see a single item that belonged to Tessa. She looked at the washing line strung between the back of the bus and the hedge. Two pairs of jeans, a threadbare towel that had once been yellow, a frayed black bra in a small size. It would never have fitted over Tessa's beautiful size 38 bust, and anyway Tessa didn't like black underwear.

Kate sat down on the steps, and allowed the chill of knowing to dawn in her mind like a November morning. She waited for an hour, hungry and very thirsty. *Both my girls have gone*, she thought sadly. She'd been so happy to see Tessa come home. Now she had vanished again in typical Tessa fashion. Kate was afraid Tessa had found out about Rowan. She tried to imagine how she herself would have felt if Freddie had betrayed her, but he never had, and never would.

In the afternoon light, she saw Art and Rowan coming across the hillside, walking together, talking. Holding hands, Kate observed. As they came closer she noticed Rowan had the baby in a sling against her chest.

'Hi, Kate!' Art looked surprised to see her standing there.

'Don't you "Hi, Kate" me, young man. I'm Mrs Barcussy to you.'

'Golden bird woman,' said Rowan, and grinned in a way Kate interpreted as insolent.

Kate ignored her. 'Where's Tessa?'

'Didn't she come home?' Art asked.

'No, she did not.'

'Aw – shit!' Art said. He looked genuinely concerned.

'Don't you swear at me, Art. Where is my daughter?'

'I don't know.'

'And don't care by the sound of it.'

'That's not true. I've been good to Tessa. I tried to build her confidence – she didn't have much – and I brought her home to what I thought was a safe haven, to people who love her. She's a great girl. She became emotionally dependent on me, Kate. I had to cut loose. I'm a daddy now, and I want to support Rowan and little Willow.'

'But what did you tell Tessa?'

'Exactly that. I wrote her a beautiful letter, and a poem.'

'It was beautiful,' agreed Rowan.

'We packed all her stuff and left her rucksack in the hedge for her, with the letter.'

'So – Tessa came back to you, with a nice basket of apples and a pie. She was so happy. She must have been DEVASTATED.'

Kate thrust her furious face closer to Art's surprised one. 'What a dreadful thing to do, Art. So cruel! I thought you were better than that. It's despicable. The lowest of the low.'

Art stood there looking bewildered. He put down the basket of blackberries and hazelnuts he'd been carrying, and spread his stained hands in the air in a gesture of innocence.

'Don't pretend you didn't know it was wrong,' Kate said. 'You've led Tessa to believe you loved her, and she trusted you. She ADORED you, Art. How could you do that to her? You've ruined her life, after all she's been through. She's been missing for three days now – and we didn't even know about it 'til we saw the bus had gone – and my basket of food was just dumped in the field. The birds had eaten it, and Tessa was nowhere to be seen.'

Rowan looked at her scornfully. Her eyes narrowed. 'You should ask yourself why, not blame Art,' she said. 'I knew you were trouble the minute I saw you. Judgemental, moralistic do-gooders like you are the reason why we choose to be hippies. We want to live in peace. Art and I both came from affluent homes with pushy parents like you.'

'I don't care what you think, dear,' Kate said contemptuously. 'I'm proud of my home and family. I shan't waste my time trying to talk to you.'

'Hey – hey, let's not have a cat fight,' Art said amiably, and turned back to Kate. 'I thought you liked me.'

'I did,' Kate admitted.

'I'm still the same guy. So what happened?'

'You have hurt my daughter – in a disgustingly under-handed way. You may even have killed her,' Kate said. 'She—'

'Aw – hang on a minute. That's a serious accusation. I loved and admired Tessa.'

'You used her.'

'That's not the point.'

'We don't believe in monogamy,' said Rowan smugly.

Kate was trembling with anger. And Art noticed. He tried to touch her but she shook him off. 'Don't you dare touch me. You – you – scum. That's what you are. Scum of the earth. Get out of my way.' She swept past him and marched back to the car.

'You shouldn't drive when you're that mad,' Art called after her. 'And if I see Tessa, I'll tell her you're looking for her.'

Kate was terribly upset and shaking. She managed to start the car and drive away, resisting the urge to speed recklessly through the lanes. She had to be calm. Freddie needed her. She must arrive home smiling and positive, no matter what.

She wished Lucy was there for her to talk to, but she wasn't. Kate thought of her own mum, Sally, who lived in Gloucestershire. Sally hadn't got a telephone and couldn't afford one so Kate's only contact with her was by letter. Sally hadn't spent much time with her granddaughters, but she'd been there when Tessa was born, and she'd immediately declared the tiny baby to be exactly like Ethie. It had seemed like a bad omen. The thought haunted Kate as she drove home. *My daughter is in the river*, she kept thinking, *I know it*.

The woman in the frugal navy cardigan reminded Tessa of the teacher she had hated at primary school. But the eyes were different. Thoughtful and medium-bright. The hands were different too – they were small and pale, and there was a wedding ring, as if someone actually loved her.

'You must have an address,' she said. 'No one is likely to employ you if you're of no fixed address.'

'Can't I give my parents' address?'

'Not unless it's in London.'

'But how can I get an address when I haven't got any money?'

'That's for you to sort out, not me. I can give you a leaflet on how to apply.'

Tessa pushed the leaflet back across the table. 'Thanks, but I have two of these already.'

'Good. Then, there's nothing else I can do for you.' The pale hands patted the scattered papers together in an irritatingly pernickety way. She looked over Tessa's head at the man standing behind her. 'Next please.'

Tessa felt his hand tug at the back of the chair she was sitting on. She smelled alcohol and damp dog. She turned angrily. 'Excuse me. I haven't finished.'

His lip curled and the yellowy stubble on his chin bristled.

The frugal woman held up her hand. 'Wait please, Mr Parsons. Let her get up from the chair please.'

Tessa sat mutinously. She straightened her back and gave the woman an assertive stare from her pale blue eyes. 'I thought you were going to give me some advice about jobs.'

'I will do that when you give me a London address.'

'But I can't just pluck an address out of thin air.'

'No, but come back and see me when you do have one.'

'I can't just come back. I walked miles across London to get here. I need to sort it out now. Will you please at least give me a list of jobs? It's urgent.'

'Everyone's need is urgent.'

Tessa felt her temper rising. She wanted to get up and hurl the miserable chair across the room, break its legs and jump on it. She'd trudged through endless noisy streets, the rucksack too heavy and too hot on her back, a disintegrating paper map of London in her hand. She'd had nothing to eat or drink that day and was beginning to feel lightheaded and close to yet another emotional precipice.

'WHAT is the matter with you people?' she stormed. 'Why can't you treat me like a human being?'

'I'm just doing my job, madam – and we don't tolerate rudeness.'

'You are not doing your job,' Tessa insisted. 'You were supposed to give me some advice about jobs.'

'I'll give you some advice, darlin',' said the man. 'You

won't get nowhere if you come in 'ere looking like an 'ippie, and arguing like an 'ippie. If I were you I'd go 'ome, take that junk outta yer 'air and grow up.'

Tessa jumped to her feet and slapped his face so hard that his stubble burned her fingers. 'How dare you criticise me. Look at the state of you. You stink to high heaven.'

The man laughed at her with a set of mustard-coloured teeth. 'Go 'ome, Princess.'

His mocking tone magnified her frustration, and the fear that had burst into her mind from the slap, and the need to conceal it. Tessa stood there, trembling, looking at a room full of shocked, judgemental eyes. Those old demons! 'I hate you,' she yelled. 'I hate the lot of you. I wasn't born to be tormented by a bunch of morons in a bureaucratic, dysfunctional, malodorous dump like this.'

She grabbed her rucksack and swung it onto her back with such force that she felt something snap inside her shoulder. She flicked her mane of chestnut hair, its bright beads and ribbons flying, and walked out, through the double doors and down the steps into the heavy air of London. *Sod them*, she thought, *sod the lot of them. I'll do it by myself.*

The two rhythms began again. The furious heartbeat and the thud-thud of her footsteps embedded in the roar of London traffic. And the new thought pounding in her mind. *Sod them, I'll do it by myself.* The thought was wholesome and sustaining, like a Somerset apple, rosy-skinned and ripe, and somewhere deep inside it was a seed, a perfect dark pip that could grow into a tree.

She walked blindly through endless streets, and came to a halt on a corner where there was a small park. Across the road was a little paper shop. A woman in a beautiful turquoise sari was outside arranging fruit and vegetables in wooden boxes. The pain in Tessa's shoulder was suddenly sharp and alarming, sending echoes down her back and arm. She felt weak and unaccountably shaky. Dizziness loitered ever closer, like a rain cloud.

Tessa crossed the road and looked at the prices on the fruit. She picked up a really lush Jaffa orange. She looked at the bunches of bananas. 'Can I buy just one banana?' she asked.

The woman studied her with eyes the colour of black coffee. 'You are all alone?' she asked. 'And you have pain. Bad pain?'

Tessa was too choked to answer. She nodded.

'This box has cheap bananas – too ripe – I choose a good one for you,' said the woman, and rummaged in the box. She took out the biggest banana. 'That is one penny.'

'Thanks,' Tessa whispered. She followed the woman into the shop, entranced by the jewel-like colours and patterns in the flowing sari. The colours of the Cornish sea – jade, purple, white and gold. 'Have you got any drinks that aren't fizzy?' she asked, looking at the glass bottles of Tizer and Dandelion & Burdock. 'I wish there were bottles of water.'

'Wait there. I give you a glass of water.' Moments later she was back with a tall glass of water, and a screw top bottle also full of water. She tucked that inside Tessa's rucksack.

'Aw thanks. That's kind of you.' Tessa drank it down without stopping. She looked around the shop and chose a bread roll and a Crunchie bar. She picked up a local newspaper.

Again the woman in the turquoise sari seemed to be reading her mind. 'You have no home?' she asked.

'No.'

'Plenty adverts in there,' said the woman. 'What is your name?'

'Tessa.'

'I'm Nita.' She put the fruit, bread and newspaper into a brown paper carrier bag and gave her the change from half a crown. 'Good luck, Tessa,' she added warmly.

Overwhelmed by the kindness from a total stranger, Tessa crossed the road and went into the park. She sat under a majestic plane tree and shared her picnic with a squirrel and a crowd of sparrows. The tree was rustling and full of afternoon sunlight. It felt like a benediction, sheltering her while it gently dropped spectacular orange-gold leaves, each one of them an art form. Seeing them stirred a momentary longing to take out her sketchbook and pastels, and a sudden wave of regret at having dropped out of Art College.

She ate everything except the orange. It was too beautiful to eat. Holding it, smelling it, contemplating its journey from the blossom gave her spirits a small oasis of joy. Discovering that something as simple as an orange could shine a mysterious lantern in the desolation of her broken heart. She decided to keep it for a while. She'd write a poem about it. Maybe her creativity was invincible, like her father's. Freddie had often told her about the stone angel on their bedroom window sill. It was his first ever stone carving. Herbie, the stonemason, had bet him a pound that he couldn't carve an angel out of a stone gatepost, and he'd done it. At the time he had been broken-hearted, like Tessa was now, thinking he'd lost Kate forever. His story had a happy ending when Kate had come back to him.

Would Art change his mind? Would he one day come back and declare his undying love for her? Admit he'd made a mistake. Beg her to take him back.

Tessa took Art's letter out of the secret pocket in her denim jacket. She'd only read it once and it had made her suicidal. But since talking to Dorothy, it had begun to settle into a kind of grieving. She made herself read his words again. They weren't unkind. He'd velvet-gloved it. Dumped her, rejected her, but done it poignantly, romantically. But that was Art. A poet. A dreamer. A Romeo. She loved him, and hated him. It was a stark choice between the pain of loving and the destructive power of hating.

She'd come a long way in three days, from the first terrible night wedged into the iron bridge above the river, to sitting under a plane tree with an orange. To holding a newspaper and hyping herself up to open it, to scan the adverts for accommodation and 'Job Vacancies'.

She knew she ought to ring home and tell her parents where she was. Telling them Art had dumped her was beyond her pain threshold. Then explaining why she was in London. Her mother would fly off the handle and beg her to come home. Tessa felt too emotionally fragile to face that kind of confrontation. She wanted to talk to her father, but Freddie seldom answered the phone, and when he did he was tongue-tied and awkward.

The late afternoon light was a soft, butter-yellow under the plane tree. Only an hour of daylight was left. Tessa opened the newspaper to the *JOB VACANCIES* pages. She only knew what she didn't want to do. Cleaning, being a waitress or a shop assistant didn't appeal. Typing and secretarial work was out of the question. A job in an art gallery? A job as a groom with the Queen's horses? She dreamed a little, and searched a lot. Nothing! She sighed and turned to the last page. An advert in a box jumped out at her. *I couldn't do THAT,* she thought. But her eyes kept going back to it. *Why me? But maybe it's ME they need.*

A sliver of light filtered into the shadows. She counted her money. There was enough for a few phone calls, a bus ride, and a meal. But how would she look the morning after another night of sleeping rough in London? Another night of being cold and scared and grubby.

I have to try, she thought.

In the noisy, orange-grey twilight of a London park, she took out a comb, and began to remove the beads and ribbons from her hair. Each bead had a meaning. A link with a time, or a colour, or a person who had given it to her. It was painful to be parting with them and she tried not to think too much about the nostalgia. Hardest of all was the amber bead that Art had given her. She left it until last, ending up with a little pile of beads and ribbons, a handful of forgotten rainbows. She put them into the white paper bag Nita had given her, and stuffed it deep down into her rucksack.

Then she headed across the park to the line of red telephone boxes.

CHAPTER 6

Wild Child

'Can you come for an interview on Friday morning? Will ten thirty suit you?' The voice on the end of the phone sounded warm but cautious. Tessa visualised a square-faced woman with permed hair, shoulder pads, and goatie ankles.

'Yes, I'd love to,' she replied eagerly. An interview! She had an interview.

'Make sure you have the names and addresses of two referees. Have you got a map of London?'

'Yes.'

'Good – the nearest tube station is Kilburn High Road.'

Tessa listened carefully to the directions, writing it down along the white space at the edge of the newspaper.

'I look forward to meeting you. See you on Friday.'

'Yes – and thanks.'

Tessa replaced the phone and did a silly little dance inside the phone box. She looked at her shocked eyes in the mirror.

Her face was pale with shadows under her eyes. Without the beads and ribbons, her hair hung limp and greasy. Her denim jacket looked grubby. *What am I going to do?* she thought, panicking. *I look AWFUL.*

On an impulse she rang Starlinda again, hoping to get invited to stay the night, have a bath, and wash her hair. But as before the phone rang and rang and there was no reply. The problem seemed to be growing out of its space. She couldn't possibly go to an interview looking and smelling like a vagrant. She couldn't go dragging a dirty old rucksack bulging with an ethnic blanket and survival stuff.

She thumbed through her diary. The only other London contact she had was Paul. He'd been part of the hippie commune in St Ives, and at the end of summer he'd opted out and gone home to London to study music. He'd told Tessa he fancied her. She thought about it for a moment and decided, no, she didn't want to get involved with him. She remembered how his hazel eyes had looked when she'd rejected his attempt to kiss her. There was an edge to Paul's affable image, an edge that was too close, like the cliff edge on a starry night. A 'don't go there' edge.

Tessa folded the page with the information on it and tucked it into her purse. She picked up the rest of the newspaper, and a headline caught her eye. *HIPPIES IN TRAFALGAR SQUARE.* There were photos of the flower children handing out chrysanthemums to tourists, and of long-haired hippies draped over one of the lions. Freedom people! The only people Tessa trusted. It was like finding her tribe. *I'll go there*, she thought, *and wash my hair in the fountain!*

The sky over London was slate-coloured, the air motionless and thick with the smell of chip shops and traffic fumes. Tessa bought a bag of hot chips, wrapped in newspaper, and returned to the plane tree in the park. She intended to sleep there. The sound and scent of the leaves were comforting, the solidity of the tree trunk and the sense of its roots spreading a cradle under her was reassuring. She rolled herself in Lou's ethnic blanket, put her head on her rucksack and tried to settle down. Her mind, and her shoulder, were hurting. Grief, rejection, and fear dipped in and out of her exhausted sleep. She clung to the one bright star, her interview. She hoped the sun and the wind would help her to dry her hair in time.

As if in response to her wish, the morning dawned bright and a cleansing wind blew from the west, clearing flocks of crisp leaves from the plane trees. Tessa's limbs felt stiff with cold. She debated whether to eat the beautiful orange or save it. She glanced at the shop and was surprised to see Nita emerge, wearing a black coat with the collar turned up, and carrying a tray. Nita crossed the road and came into the park, right up to the plane tree. 'I keep an eye on you, Tessa,' she said, and her dark eyes shone. 'I bring you hot breakfast.'

'That's UNBELIEVABLE!' Tessa said. 'Thank you!'

Nita took the lid off the bowl on the tray. Sweet-smelling honeyed steam spiralled into the air. 'I bring you hot porridge with golden syrup. It do you good.' She handed Tessa a spoon.

Tessa started to cry. 'You don't know how much I needed this.'

Nita smiled. She sat down and waited while Tessa warmed her hands on the hot china and began to eat.

The smooth oat porridge felt like swallowing fire. 'This tastes absolutely divine,' she said, between mouthfuls.

'I like – help people,' Nita said. 'Today is a lucky day for you – something good happen.'

'Do you think so?'

'I know,' Nita said. 'I know things you can't see.'

Tessa felt as if Nita had lit a candle in her mind. 'I know things like that too,' she said.

Nita nodded. 'One day you help someone like I help you – many, many people, Tessa. And it begins – today.'

Tessa could hardly speak. 'Thank you,' she whispered. Nita said no more, but gave her a loving patchouli-scented hug, took the tray and walked quickly away with it. Tessa felt dumbfounded. *She's like the old woman in* The Water Babies, she thought, *a spiritual godmother who appears when you most need her and says the words you most need to hear.*

Big Ben was chiming ten o'clock when she reached Trafalgar Square, tired and sore from the long walk. There were pigeons everywhere, and a few tourists with expensive cameras. A group of Hari Krishna people with tambourines were chanting in one corner, and the hippies and flower children were sitting around Nelson's Column, tucked in a sheltered spot between two of the lions. A man who looked like Art was already up on the lion's head, greeting the sun with his arms akimbo and hair flying in the wind. Tessa gulped. Every hippie was going to remind her of Art. There was no escape from the inner grief. She'd have to live with it and deal with it.

The fountains were peppermint white and magnificent, the wind whipping the spray eastwards in the morning light. The water would be freezing cold. But Tessa had been used to plunging into the Atlantic surf every morning in Cornwall. She was ready for this. She was wearing her sea-green bikini under a sweater and jeans. It would raise a few eyebrows in London, but she didn't care. This had to be done quickly, before some interfering London policeman noticed what she was up to.

Tingling with excitement she marched across to the group of hippies. Who should she trust? She felt drawn to a group of women who were watching her. They had flowers in their hair, long skirts, big boots and voluminous ethnic cardigans. 'Hi, sister,' said one of them with an open friendly smile. Two of them stood up, their eyes wide with astonishment. 'Tessa!'

'Lou and Clare!' she cried, excited. 'What are you doing in London?'

'We're just passing through – well, no, actually we're in a squat,' Lou said. 'For the winter, or 'til we get chucked out.'

Tessa gave them each a hug. Lou and Clare had been part of the commune in St Ives, and Lou had given her the ethnic blanket and taught her sacred drumming. Lou still had her drum, hanging over her shoulder on a wide strap woven from vividly coloured threads. She wore a beaded headband around her black hair, and her brown eyes were warm and shrewd. Clare hovered beside her like a butterfly, her eyes vacant. 'She's stoned,' Lou said, and Tessa nodded. Nothing much had changed.

'So what about you?' Lou asked.

Tessa didn't want to tell her about Art. Lou and Clare had tried to warn her, and she hadn't listened. So she said, 'I need your help – again! I'm going to wash my hair in the fountain – I've GOT to – before any policemen notice me, and I need someone to mind my rucksack.'

'Oh, you're not going in there, Tessa. You're mad,' Lou said. 'It's freezing cold – and never mind the police, the press are skulking around just waiting for us to do something outrageous.'

'I have to do it quickly, like now,' Tessa said, dumping her rucksack at Lou's feet.

'Okay – we'll look after it.'

'It's got all my essential stuff in it. I can't live without it,' Tessa said, pulling out her towel and draping it over the rucksack. She took off her shoes, socks and jeans, bundling them into a heap.

'Yeah – we know – don't worry, we'll mind it for you, Tessa. I don't believe you're going in there!'

'I am.' She held up her green bottle of Silvikrin shampoo. Then she peeled off her sweater and stood there in her sea-green bikini. A cheer went up from the hippies, and there were wolf-whistles. 'I've got to do it quickly,' Tessa said, suddenly nervous, and annoyed with the men. Her pulse roared in her ears as she turned and ran barefooted to the fountain and got in, gasping at the icy cold water, her feet slipping and sliding.

She didn't notice the cameras clicking and the men hurrying over to see the girl in the sea-green bikini who had dared to strip off in Trafalgar Square on an October morning. She just felt the power of the falling white water blasting through her hair, cleansing her, making her fresh and alive again. She didn't hear the clapping and cheering as she lathered the shampoo through her chestnut hair and let the fountain swoosh it away. Even the wind was gleefully blowing clods of foam away across the square. The water was magic therapy to Tessa. She loved it. Loved rinsing the suds from her wavy tresses of hair until they were squeaky clean, splashing and scrubbing her body until she felt pink and glowing. It was like a daydream. A time when she was blissfully lost in a different dimension, in a world of dizzy-white, rainbow-spattered energy.

She emerged, radiant, to find a circle of cheering faces, mostly men, an odd mixture of hippies and tourists. Embarrassment and anger quickly eclipsed the joy she'd felt. A man who looked like an immature wolf with spectacles pushed a microphone in her face. 'What's your name? What made you do this? Are you a hippie? Are you homeless?' He fired bewildering questions at her without waiting for an answer, and took photos of her with the complicated camera dangling around his neck.

'Have you considered nude modelling?' asked another

eager reporter with a camera and flash-gun. 'I could get you work!'

'Where are you from, darlin'?'

'How old are you?'

'Do your parents know what you're up to?'

Lou and Clare pushed their way to Tessa, who was now shivering and bewildered. 'Don't speak to them!' Lou said urgently. 'Don't tell them your name.'

Tessa's eyes widened. 'Why not? I already did!'

'They'll crucify you. It's the press,' Lou said, thrusting a towel at her. She shoved the reporters aside. 'Piss off, you vultures. She's freezing cold. Haven't you got anything better to do?'

Lou and Clare stood either side of Tessa. 'Come with us,' Lou hissed. 'Come on – don't be a naïve idiot. You'll be all over the papers in the morning. Come on. MOVE!'

'Down the loo,' said Clare, and Tessa gave in and allowed them to bundle her across Trafalgar Square, her bare feet leaving neat wet footprints. The three girls started to giggle, dashing down the steps to the *LADIES* with Tessa in her bikini, meeting disapproving coat-clad, leather-booted women coming up. Once down there on the blue and white tiled floor, they were laughing so hysterically that more coat-clad, leather-booted women were peering down from the top of the steps, too frightened to go down there.

'We thought you'd gone to Somerset,' Lou said, when she could speak again. 'Where's Art?'

Tessa looked at her wordlessly.

'He hasn't dumped you, has he? I'll kill him,' said Lou fiercely.

Tessa nodded. She couldn't speak. The grief rose up like a monster from the deep, devouring everything, her courage, her hope, her moments of joy. She leaned against the cold ceramic tiles and sobbed bitterly. 'I've been sleeping rough in London. I was suicidal. I've got an interview for a job tomorrow morning and I'm in such a state. What am I going to do?'

Freddie was daydreaming as he ate his breakfast. He hardly tasted the egg, bacon and fried bread that Kate had put in front of him. He was thinking about the two wild swans he'd seen on the river, and planning a carving of them. It would have to be wood, not stone, because of the long necks. A pair of swans with their elegant necks entwined. Beautiful birds who mated for life. Like him and Kate. He looked at her across the table, sad to see the shadows of tiredness under her eyes. Kate caught his gaze and smiled. Then she craned her head to look out of the window. 'Uh oh! Here's Susan. Now what?'

Susan Tillerman came hurrying up the path, a newspaper under her arm. She burst into the kitchen without knocking. 'You HAVE to see this, Kate,' she said breathlessly. 'I know you don't take a newspaper so I brought ours. Ian's already read it.' She thrust the newspaper in front of Kate.

Freddie glanced at the headline: *WASHING HER HAIR IN THE FOUNTAIN*.

'Hippies again!' Kate said resignedly.

'But Kate – look at the photo,' Susan said. 'There's more inside.'

Kate looked at the bikini-clad girl with wet hair, climbing out of the fountain in Trafalgar Square. She went pale.

'It's TESSA,' Susan said, gloating. 'I'd know that pout anywhere.'

'Freddie – you'd better see this,' Kate said in a precarious voice. He moved his chair around and sat beside her, hardly believing the shocking images of his daughter on the front of a national newspaper. Together they read the report which was lavish and untrue, describing Tessa as a sex-bomb and a brazen flower-child. Surly and abusive, they said she'd been. Refused to talk to reporters. Went off giggling with her friends. Should have been arrested. What kind of parents let their daughter behave in this publicly disgraceful way?

'Tessa always was a wild-child,' said Susan.

Freddie got to his feet, furious with her. He picked up the newspaper and handed it to her. His voice shook with emotion. 'I think you'd better go, Susan.' He steered her towards the door. 'And take your newspaper with you.'

'No, you keep it.' Susan threw it back onto the table. 'You're going to need it, believe me.'

'Will you please GO HOME,' Freddie thundered and Susan backed away, her eyes startled. 'Kate's not well and she doesn't need this first thing in the morning.'

'But I thought you should know,' protested Susan. 'I felt it was my duty to tell you.'

'Right, well, you've told us. Now will you go, please?' Freddie opened the door and stood by it firmly.

'And – don't spread it all over Monterose, Sue – please,' Kate said.

'Of course I won't. I'm not a gossip! But it's already the talk of the town, you'll find.'

When she had gone, Freddie and Kate sat looking at each other, with the offending newspaper still on the table.

'It's typical Tessa,' Kate said. 'And I'm sure she didn't intend it to get in the papers. But they're so cruel, these reporters. So cruel. How can they say such nasty things about a girl they don't even know?'

Freddie saw the stress on Kate's face. She didn't deserve this. 'Mother would turn in her grave,' he said, grim-faced.

'Tessa's brought shame on our family,' Kate said. 'We'll never live it down. Never. We'll have to move house. Go and live in Gloucestershire with my mum.'

'What? Leave The Pines?' Freddie was horrified. 'No. No, Kate – 'tis our home. We were born and bred here. Why should we let this drive us out?' The phone rang as he was speaking. 'If that's Tessa, you let me talk to her. I shall have some harsh words to say. She's made her bed – she can lie on it.'

Kate answered the phone in an unusually subdued voice. 'Mrs Barcussy?'

'Yes.'

'I'm Robin Tell, the reporter for the local *Gazette*. I'd like to talk to you about your daughter, Tessa. Could I come and see you?'

Kate covered the mouthpiece with her hand and whispered to Freddie. 'It's Robin Tell from the *Gazette* – about Tessa!'

Freddie shook his head. He took the phone from Kate. 'Hello, this is Mr Barcussy. We are not gonna talk to you, or any other newspaper.'

He was going to put the phone down but Robin Tell's voice came through urgently. 'You must agree to talk to me, for your daughter's sake. If you don't, then we can only take our information from what is in the national press, and you wouldn't want that, would you?'

'Well – no.'

'Especially as your daughter, I understand, went to Hilbegut School.'

'"Tis nothing to do with Hilbegut School.'

'And there are other incidents in her past, aren't there?'

Freddie felt suddenly threatened, as if the whole of Tessa's turbulent childhood was about to erupt into a scandal. He struggled to be polite. 'You come here at ten o'clock,' he said curtly, 'and we'll talk. Goodbye now.' He put the phone down, and looked at Kate. 'They've got us over a barrel,' he said bitterly. 'If we don't talk, they'll print what's in that – that blimin' rag.'

'I don't know how our own daughter can do this to us,' Kate said.

'Ah – she didn't do it to us,' Freddie said wisely. 'She didn't do it to hurt us. 'Tis those reporters. They're savages. Hell bent on ruining someone's life. I hate 'em.' He felt the colour rising up his neck and over his cheeks. He desperately wanted a cigarette. He'd given up smoking on doctor's orders last winter, and it had been hard.

'I'll make us a cup of coffee,' Kate said, 'with a dash of rum in it and some cream. Don't you go reaching for the fags again. You're so much better without them.' There was love in her bright brown eyes, love for him. He felt its warmth, and the moment passed. He sat down again at the table and watched Kate whisking the hot coffee. She had just put the rum into it when there was a tap at the door. 'Now what?' she said, and went to answer it.

A girl with blonde hair stood there. She wore very high heels, neat stockings with straight seams, and a royal blue winter coat with the collar turned up. In her hand was a newspaper, and her eyes were full of indignation.

Kate gasped.

'LUCY!'

Tessa walked briskly along a leafy avenue in North London. Her hair was rolled into a bun on top of her head, and she wore a navy blue pleated skirt belonging to Lou's mother, a white nylon blouse with ruffles that Clare had lent her, and Lou's black sling-backed patent-leather shoes. She hoped she looked neat and sensible, even though Lou and Clare had screamed with laughter at her new image. It had been good-humoured banter, and they'd let her stay the night in the empty house where they were squatting. There was no electricity or water, so it was candlelight, orange boxes, and mattresses on bare floorboards. But the mattress and pillow felt heavenly to Tessa after her nights of sleeping rough, and she'd slept deeply. Lou had given her a bowl of Cornflakes with milk and sugar, then coffee, and lots of advice. Tessa hadn't listened to most of it, but one nugget had lodged in her mind. 'Stop punishing yourself, Tessa,' Lou had said.

She felt like an alien. But different. The ruffles on the nylon blouse made her feel womanly and feminine. She'd unearthed her make-up bag from the bottom of the rucksack and done her face with the dwindling supply of Max Factor Crème Puff and Dusky Pink lipstick. The rucksack was left with Lou and Clare, and she carried only a small beaded handbag.

Twenty-five past ten. Perfect timing. She paused outside the gates, admiring the lovely old white painted town house, now a school for children with special needs. Its walls echoed with the sound of their playtime – screams, laughter, running feet. Tessa felt unreasonably apprehensive. *What am I doing here? I'm not even going to like these children,* she thought.

The playground had high wire fencing, and in one corner was a mature horse chestnut tree. Children were running everywhere, playing with the fallen leaves, and with skipping ropes and balls. Tessa opened the gate and went in, her eyes on the entrance door opposite, which was painted in bright reds and yellows.

'Hello, Miss.' A little girl ran to her. She had grey skin, and a grey vest under a cardigan that looked like a dishrag. Her blonde hair was pathetically thin and wispy, but her eyes shone up at Tessa like the eyes of a precious doll. 'I'm Della, Miss.'

'Hello, Della.' Tessa squatted down and looked into the child's eyes.

'I love you, Miss.' Della put her arms around Tessa and hugged her tightly. Tessa was astonished. She sensed Della's desperate need to love and be loved. She felt her sadness, and her happiness, like pepper and salt next to each other on a table. But the ultimate surprise was the shimmering light around this unkempt little urchin.

'What a lovely welcome,' Tessa said softly, and Della just went on hugging her and beaming into her eyes.

'You're an angel, Miss,' Della said. 'I love you. Are you going to stay here, Miss?'

'I hope so,' Tessa said, and found herself using the kind of voice she used to heal animals. A low, musical, crooning voice. She didn't know where it came from, but it was calming, for her and the recipient.

Another child, a boy with lonely huge eyes, came close and touched her shyly. 'Hello, Miss. You very pretty, Miss.'

Tessa was mesmerised by the inner beauty of these children. She straightened up, with Della still hugging her, and suddenly the playground went quiet and more and more children came to her as if drawn to her light. She felt like a big magnet. Wordless and strong.

The spell was broken by a voice of authority. A woman with cropped silver hair and vibrant blue eyes. 'You must be Tessa.'

'Yes.'

'I'm Megan – Mrs Burns. I'm the headmistress – or trying to be!' She laughed heartily and held out her hand to Tessa. 'Let go of the lady, Della,' she said, looking down at the clinging child. 'You can hug her again later. And the rest of you – go and enjoy the playtime. Go on – shoo! Shoo, shoo, shoo.' She clapped her hands humorously and pretended to be chasing them off. 'This is a happy school,' she said brightly to Tessa. 'And I can see that the children clearly like you already. Shall we have a chat over coffee?'

Tessa followed the dumpy figure into the spacious building, which was painted in vivid primary colours. The children's artwork was splashed over the pin boards, each piece lovingly mounted and labelled.

'I love children's art,' Tessa said. 'These are fantastic.'

'We're very proud of them.' Megan turned to smile at Tessa. She led her upstairs to the staff room. 'This is our haven of peace,' she said, switching on the kettle. 'And it's got an all too tempting biscuit tin.' She prised the lid off. 'Would you like one?'

'I would – if this wasn't an interview,' Tessa said, eyeing the custard creams and bourbons.

Megan laughed. 'Well, at least you're honest,' she said, spooning Nescafé into two mugs.

Something was happening in Tessa's mind while she sat watching Megan make the coffee. *I can be honest with this woman,* she thought, and suddenly felt as if her dad was there with her, right inside her mind.

Megan sat down next to her. She looked at Tessa's sleek brown legs. 'My goodness – is that a suntan? Or have you got stockings on?'

'It's a suntan. I spent the summer in Cornwall.'

'In Cornwall. Lucky girl. What were you doing there?'

Tessa took a deep breath and turned her pale blue eyes on Megan. 'Being a hippie,' she said. 'I dropped out of Art College after my first year.'

Megan's eyes cooled a little. She looked thoughtful. 'Tell me about yourself, Tessa, and why you want this job.'

Tessa tried to draw on the collection of responses she'd mentally rehearsed. Instead, she found herself following a signpost her dad had put there. It said *HONESTY*.

'I'm hypersensitive,' she said, 'and creative. I grew up in rural Somerset. I know quite a lot about the country-side – animals, birds, trees and wild flowers. I'm also quite practical – I can make bread, and willow baskets, grow seeds, look after animals. But—'

'Go on,' Megan said warmly, 'the best bit usually comes last, I find.'

'I feel – I can understand people,' Tessa said. 'I'm intu-itive – and, because I've suffered a lot myself, I can relate to other people's difficulties and needs. It's something I want to develop. That's why I was drawn to this job. I feel I can really give something to these children – something they're searching for and not getting at home. I understand, deeply, how children get hurt and emotionally damaged. And,' she added, quoting directly from her dad's wisdom, 'that knowledge hasn't come from books – it's come from LIFE.'

Megan stared at her. She nodded her head slowly. 'Hmmm – an old soul,' she said, and studied the handwritten CV Tessa had given her on a single sheet of lined file paper. 'You've had a good education. What made you drop out of Art College?'

'It was irrelevant to the kind of life I wanted,' Tessa said. 'I do enjoy art – but I wanted to be out there interacting with people, at the grass roots – and when I saw this job it just seemed perfect.'

'Have you had any experience with children?'

'Not much.'

'This job is for a full-time classroom assistant,' Megan said. 'You would work mostly with one teacher. The children here have a variety of special needs. We have children with autism, aphasia, dyspraxia, epilepsy and some with undiagnosed, deep emotional problems – children from difficult backgrounds, some of them heart-breaking. They can be VERY challenging, and very surprising. We need someone with a big heart and lots of love to give. Do you think you're that person, Tessa?'

'I'd like to give it a try. It isn't just because I need a job. I need THIS job – and I believe you need ME,' Tessa said firmly. She was secretly amazed at how the right words were coming out of her mouth with such quiet strength. 'I'm lucky that I've got a wonderful dad,' she added. 'He was incredibly kind and patient with me, and tolerant. I want to do that for children who haven't had a kind person in their life.'

Megan put the lid on the biscuit tin. 'I'll take you down to see the class you'd be working with – see how you feel. Finished your coffee? Bring it with you if you like.'

Tessa followed her down the stairs and through the building to a spacious annexe full of light and colour. There were just eight young children, and they were not sitting at desks as Tessa had imagined, but happily occupied with brightly coloured toys. A wooden railway set was laid out in one corner, with two boys totally engrossed in it. There was a Wendy House and a dressing-up box, a cosily carpeted book corner with beanbag cushions, and an art corner where a boy was carefully painting a curious labyrinth on blue sugar paper.

A boy with crossed eyes and a beguiling smile came up to Tessa and claimed her straight away. She squatted down to talk to him.

'This is Billie Ku,' Megan said. 'He'll look after you – won't you, Billie? Can you show Tessa around the classroom?'

Billie beamed. He took Tessa's hand. 'I like you, Miss,' he said. Tessa smiled back. His eyes were astonishing. *Old,* she thought, *like a little old man. Yet here he is in the body of a handicapped child.* 'Where shall we go first?' she asked, and Billie led her to the book corner. He picked a book called *Mike Mulligan and his Steam Shovel* and gave it to her. 'Read me a story, Miss? Please.'

Tessa glanced at Megan.

'Please, Miss!'

'I'll leave you here for half an hour,' Megan said. 'Is that okay, Tessa? This is the teacher – Diane. Okay, Diane, if I leave Tessa with you? She needs to know what she's letting herself in for!'

Diane grinned at Tessa and said, 'Hi – make yourself at home,' and Tessa was surprised to see she wore jeans and a flowery smock. She could have passed as a hippie! She was sitting at a desk with a silent, solemn little girl cuddled on her lap. 'We'll chat in a minute,' Diane said. 'I'm kind of occupied.'

'That little girl is Zoe,' Megan said, 'and she doesn't talk at all. She chats at home, but in school she's silent. So far. We live in hope!'

The half hour flew by. Tessa felt completely at home and interested in the children. One by one they sidled up to her as she read stories, her eyes looking up, pausing to make contact with the eyes looking at her. Before long there was a child on her lap, and another two with their arms around her neck. She could read the emotions in their eyes. There was anxiety, loneliness, disappointment, confusion, all of it overlaid with hope and waiting to erupt into fury. Tessa felt as if her father was there with her, inside her mind. Now, at last, she was using the rich storehouse of patient, silent love he had given her. *I really want to do this,* she thought, *and I can, I know I can.*

When Megan came to fetch her, Billie Ku had a monster tantrum. He flung *Mike Mulligan and his Steam Shovel* on the floor, planted his legs a yard apart and jumped up and down, his face contorted with rage. Diane waded in and tried to restrain him, but he pushed her away angrily. 'I wanted Tessa to stay,' he roared. 'It's not fair! I hate you. I hate all of you.' He collapsed against the wall, rocking and banging his head.

'I'll come back and see you, Billie,' Tessa said gently, trying to get him to look at her. He pushed her away.

'Leave him, Tessa. I'll deal with him. It's pretty standard behaviour,' Diane said.

'I could calm him down,' Tessa said. 'I know how he feels.' She wanted to tell them that not so long ago she herself had been like that, a child full of frustration, a child forever trapped in the wreckage of her crushed dreams, a child confronted with the dark holes where hope and light had died.

Instead, she followed Megan out into the corridor, the sound of Billy Ku's rage and Diane's very loud voice echoing after her.

Megan turned and looked into her soul. 'The job is yours, Tessa, if you'd like it. We'd love to have you.'

CHAPTER 7

A Soul in Exile

Kate watched Lucy walking away down the path, a lump in her throat. She'd been moved by the way Lucy had defended her sister. 'Tessa isn't THAT bad, Mum,' she'd said, 'you should ring the paper and complain. Or I will.'

Her words had fired Kate up, but it had hurt when Lucy declined her offer of tea and biscuits. 'Some other time, Mum, I'm really busy.'

Kate picked up the phone and dialled the *Gazette*.

'I am beside myself with fury,' she told the startled girl who answered. 'I want a word with Robin Tell – now, please.'

'I'm afraid he's out of the office.'

'Then who can I speak to?'

'Our senior manager is here, but he's in a meeting.'

'I don't care,' Kate said icily. 'You bring him to the phone, right now, or I will be on your doorstep in fifteen minutes with a tin of red paint, and I shall paint *LIARS* across your door.'

The girl sighed. 'I'll see if Mr Swithins will talk to you.'

Kate waited, feeling her temples bursting with a hammering pulse, her hands ice cold, her stomach in a tight knot. She wasn't well. Desperate for news of Tessa, she'd spent the last few nights in a chair by the phone, terrified it would ring in the night and she'd miss a vital call. Freddie had been exasperated with her, and he'd gone to bed grumpy and alone. But Kate couldn't help it. She feared that Art's betrayal would destroy Tessa. And whatever Tessa had done, Kate wanted her home safe in her pink bedroom.

She could hardly stop herself from screaming at Mr Swithins when he came to the phone. His voice was cultured, cold and intimidating.

'I'm disgusted with Robin Tell's ridiculous and grossly unfair report on my daughter, Tessa,' she began. 'He came here to see us, and I don't know why he bothered. He didn't listen to a thing we said. He just reprinted the lies from the tabloids – the gutter press.'

'And can you substantiate that allegation, Mrs Barcussy?'

'My daughter is not a sex-bomb for a start. She is innocent and wary of men, and she doesn't deliberately flaunt herself. She is not a narcotic – how DARE you label her like that when you don't know her. You are damaging a young girl's life with your LIES.'

'But I assure you Robin Tell is—'

'Don't even think about defending that WORM,' Kate

ranted. 'My daughter is trying to recover from a broken heart. She's a caring, sensitive girl, and to have this – this hideous scandal perpetuated by your guttersnipe newspaper in her own home town is appalling. To accuse her of being a narcotic! She's never taken drugs in her life. This is libel, Mr Swithins, libel, and I want to know what you intend to do to put it right.'

'But, Mrs Barcussy—'

'Don't you dare Mrs Barcussy me!' Kate felt like a huge cat with a mouse twitching at the end of the phone. One wrong move and she'd have him. She pictured a grey little man, bald and bewildered.

She was hyping herself up for the kill when his calm voice oozed down the phone. 'Excuse me but I have a meeting to attend to. I suggest you ring back when you have calmed down.' It was followed by a click, and the big black telephone in Kate's hand felt empty and useless. She put it down with deliberate care.

Freddie was hovering in the doorway.

'Are you here or not here?' Kate asked.

Freddie just looked at her, and steered her to the cottage sofa which stood in the sunny window. He sat down with her.

'I don't really want to sit down,' she said. 'I'm seething.'

''Tis no good upsetting yourself, Kate,' Freddie said. 'Let 'em get on with it. It'll all blow over, you'll see.'

But Kate shook her head. 'I can't stand by and let them destroy our daughter.'

'They won't destroy her. Tessa's stronger than that. She probably doesn't even know she's in the papers.'

'If only I could talk to her,' Kate leaned on his comforting shoulder, 'but I'd probably say the wrong thing right now.'

'Ah – you're not yourself at all, I can see that.' Freddie's steady blue eyes still had that secret sparkle. Kate let herself gaze into the rejuvenating sanctuary where Freddie seemed to keep his soul, intact in a mystic land beyond the sparkle.

They both jumped when the phone rang.

'Leave it,' Freddie said. 'Let it ring for once.'

Kate couldn't. She darted into the hall and picked it up, shaking with a lethal blend of anger and anxiety.

'Will you accept a reverse charge call from a London telephone box?' asked the exchange.

Her heart leapt. It had to be Tessa. 'Yes,' she croaked, and beckoned Freddie to the phone.

'Go ahead, you're through,' said the voice, and after a few clicks and bleeps, Kate heard what she had longed to hear for the last few terrible days. Tessa's voice.

'Hello, Mum.'

'Hello, dear – oh, I'm so glad to hear your voice.'

'Sorry I left like that,' Tessa said. 'I'm really sorry, Mum, I was utterly desolate – because Art just finished with me.'

'I know, dear, he's behaved very badly – a rotten thing to do,' Kate's voice was breaking. She was afraid of saying the wrong thing. Freddie was close to her, listening.

'I'm in London, Mum,' Tessa said, and her voice brightened. 'And – I've got a job! I thought you'd be proud of me.'

She's never going to come home, Kate thought. She wanted to shout and scream at her daughter. Instead, she retreated into a simmering silence. Her cheeks flared red. She handed the phone to Freddie, shaking her head.

'Mum?'

'Your mum's not well,' Freddie said to Tessa.

'What's wrong?'

'Nothing a good night's sleep wouldn't cure,' Freddie said. 'She's been sitting all night by the phone in case you rang. We've been worried sick, Tessa. Are you all right? That's what I want to know. You're precious to me – you know that, don't you?'

He could hear Tessa breathing at the end of the phone, and he visualised himself there with her, his arms around her, his mind still picturing the beautiful, troubled child with chestnut plaits and big eyes that changed as quickly as the skies on an April morning.

'Shall I come up and fetch you home?' he offered.

'Oh Dad – no, thanks. I'll be all right.'

'Do you need some money?'

'I do – but I'm staying with friends, Lou and Clare, and I've got a job, Dad, a job I really want to do. I start on Monday.'

Freddie glanced at the newspaper on the table. He figured Tessa had no idea that she was the centre of an unfolding scandal, and he wasn't going to tell her. Maybe she was better off in London, away from it all. Away from memories of Art, and away from the vitriol of the family grapevine. It would blow over, he was sure. He hoped her employer, whoever it was, didn't know about it either.

'I'd like to tell you about my job,' Tessa said, 'but I need to start it, find my feet, if you know what I mean. Then I'll write and tell you all about it – and send you an address.'

'Ah – all right, love. You keep in touch – always – you promise me that, Tessa.'

'Okay, yes, Dad, and don't worry.'

'And – you look after yourself in London.'

Tessa's silences were getting longer, and he could hear her sniffing. *She's crying,* he thought. He wanted to ask her why she wouldn't come home – why live in London when she could live in Monterose? Why make it so hard for herself? But then, she'd always chosen hard options, he remembered. The words wouldn't come, so he said, 'I wish you lots of luck.'

'Thanks, Dad.'

He put the phone down and went to comfort Kate. She wept and ranted in his arms. 'I should have said God Bless and told her I loved her.'

'Ah – she knows that,' Freddie said. 'I don't think she knows about the newspapers, and I'm not gonna tell her. She's got enough to cope with.'

'It's good that she's coping at all, after what Art did,' Kate said, drying her eyes on an embroidered hanky. She put her arms round Freddie and gave him a kiss. 'I don't know what I'd do without you, Freddie. You're so wise.'

Freddie smoothed her brow with his gentle-giant hands. 'I told her you weren't well – and you aren't – are you?'

'No.'

Kate didn't usually admit to feeling ill, so Freddie's concern deepened. 'Why don't I take you away for a few days?' he suggested. 'How about Weymouth?'

Before she could answer there was a shuffle of heavy footsteps outside. The door was pushed open, cautiously, and Freddie's two sisters, Alice and Betty, came in. They had identical permed hairstyles, gloomy green overcoats steeped in the scent of mothballs, and identical expressions. They both fixed accusing eyes on Kate, and Alice slammed a newspaper on the table. 'Look what your wicked daughter has done NOW. She's brought shame on our family. I hope you're going to punish her.'

Grieving for Art cast pools of darkness over Tessa's life. Her job with the children shone, isolated and bright as the moon while her sorrow swirled into ever-shifting shadows that moved through her life in London. The landscapes of Somerset blazed in her memory, like stained glass, set into the stories that built walls in her mind: the starry skies, the nightingales, the water meadows of Monterose.

'I was looking forward to going home,' she said, in one of her regular sessions at The Samaritans with Dorothy. 'I wanted to spend the beautiful autumn there, with Art. I wanted to spend time with Mum and Dad, and see Lexi and Selwyn. I thought we'd be there for the winter, and see the great silver skies, and the floods, and the frosty mornings. Art had a little Queenie stove in the bus, and we were going to be so cosy – our own fire – toast in bed on a frosty morning. We talked of all those things, Dorothy. Our dreams were the same – we loved the same kind of things – we were so happy. Why? Why did it happen? To me!'

Always she would talk herself to that point, like the edge of a cliff where you had to stop. The edge was always the tears that no longer came in sobbing but in a hot bolt of pain from ear to ear. And still Dorothy listened devotedly, patiently riding the wordless chasms. Her responses changed subtly from the blind sympathy of their first talk. Now she often said, 'You'll cope. You will.' And she said it so often and with such kind, motherly conviction that it rang like a comforting mantra in Tessa's mind.

'Maybe – I am coping,' she said.

'You are, Tessa. You've got a job – and a place to live.'

'I've got to stay in London.' Tessa felt the moment of recognising that she was coping begin to spiral downwards again. 'I still feel I can't go home. I can't LIVE in the places I love – because – because of who I am.' She looked at Dorothy's velvet eyes. 'Who am I anyway?'

'You're a lovely girl, a gifted girl too.'

'So why – why did the man I adored just dump me? For some flinty-eyed slut who was clever enough to have his child! Why couldn't I do that?'

'Did you want a child?' Dorothy asked gently.

'Well – no – I didn't. I went to great trouble to get myself on the pill,' Tessa said. 'But Art wanted kids. He tried to persuade me a few times, but – this is hard to admit, but I'm terrified, you see. I'm terrified of childbirth.'

'Why is that, dear? What scares you?'

'I'm not brave and stoical like other women. I can't even watch a woman having a baby on television. I have to leave the room. They're always screaming. It's always, always horrific – and in the novels I've read. I can't stand hearing about it. My aunties, and my granny used to glory in talking about it in lurid technicolour, and I was so terrified, I used to faint! Or I'd run out of the room and they'd laugh at me, which was awful – and it made me so ANGRY with them. It was like they absolutely relished frightening me like that. I hated them for it. And it made me feel even more oddball.' She paused to sip the sustaining mug of hot coffee, which somehow tasted like the warmly lit stone arches of St Stephen's, Walbrook. It was Saturday morning, and she'd just finished her second week at Parkwell School.

'So how do you feel with the children at work?' Dorothy asked.

'I love them,' Tessa said, and a few sparkles drifted through the sadness in her pale blue eyes. 'It's strange because I didn't expect to feel like that. I thought it would just be a job where I could make a difference. I expected the kids to be difficult – like I was – and they are, but they're beautiful, and so LOVING – and their horizons are so different. They are so happy with a tiny, tiny bit of success, like tying a shoelace, or catching a ball, or copying their name. They've all got huge issues to deal with, and in a way being with them is helping me to cope with my life.'

'That's good to hear,' Dorothy said. 'So is your life getting any better, Tessa? Better than when you first came in here?'

'Yes – definitely,' Tessa said. 'It's just the weekends, and evenings. I don't mind being on my own. But Art haunts me. Everywhere I go I think I see him. Every day I long for a letter from him. I still can't believe he could cut me off so abruptly, after the love we had. I feel like a soul in exile, banished to a distant island to wait for a ship to bring my love home to me, like Tristan and Isolde. And I feel cheated and rejected. That never changes.'

'It will, dear. It will change,' Dorothy said in her comforting voice.

Tessa looked at her. 'You've helped me so much,' she said, 'and, one day, when I'm better – if I ever am – I'd like to do what you're doing.'

'Then you probably will,' Dorothy said, and a constructive silence followed, a time when castles of possibility manifested between them, a time when Tessa found archways in the long wall of her grief. The glimpses through those archways were mystical and enticing. Gardens in the sun. Glittering sea shores. Cocoons where kindness was turning itself into butterflies.

Tessa unlocked the heavy front door of the house in Nottingham Place. The thick cold air of London seemed to follow her inside, chilling the walls, adding mildew to the damp, dark red carpets. On the third step of the stairs was a dead mouse. She stood looking at its cute, pink, shell-like ears, its pale, sleek belly, its exquisite little paws, and remembered how tenderly she and Lucy would have buried such a creature under the lilacs at home. She picked it up in her gloved hands. It weighed nothing. *I've got nowhere to bury it,* she thought, *and mice don't matter in London.* She took it outside, and placed it tenderly under the leaves of a dandelion plant that had fought its way out of the bricks.

She trudged up the stairs, past the first landing where plastic bags of rubbish were stashed outside closed doors, and on up to the second floor to her bedsit. At least it was hers. It was home. A narrow, high-ceilinged slot of a room, with the bed against the wall, a cream enamel sink unit along the opposite wall, next to a square of Fablon-covered worktop with a single gas ring under a slot meter that ate shillings. There was just room to walk between the sink and the bed. The saving grace was the tall sash window, facing south, where the sun streamed in on good days, lighting the dust motes. Tessa had replaced the heavy, brown damask curtains with a brightly coloured pair she'd found at a jumble sale. Lou's ethnic blanket covered her bed, and two orange and white Habitat cushions Lucy had given her for Christmas were propped against the wall.

In her bag was a slim bundle of green daffodil buds which she took out and arranged in a glass milk bottle on the window sill. London in December was depressing, and she'd found that spending a shilling on a bunch of buds from a street barrow was worth it, for the contemplative joy of watching them slowly come open into optimistic golden blooms. It helped her stay alive.

Under the window sill were three wooden orange boxes which she'd painted in psychedelic colours. They held her books, a Roberts radio, her jar of sand from Porthmeor Beach, her black elvan pebble, and photos of Jonti and Selwyn, and of her parents outside the front door of The Pines. The photos were monochrome and tiny, with white borders and curling edges, done with her Brownie Box camera. Tessa had glued them into a wooden frame she'd bought for sixpence in a junk shop. She'd painted it apple green, filling the woodworm holes with thick paint.

Her photo of Art was in her diary, inside a cream envelope which she'd decorated with hearts. She couldn't bear to look at the photo, but kept it hidden. She'd drawn the hearts as symbols of eternal romance, a thin trail of hope that he would come back to her. She'd wanted to add a broken heart, jagged and tragic, and coloured black, but her pencil had stopped in the air. *Don't spoil it,* she'd thought, *even if he never comes back, the memory is still a love story.* Sometimes she couldn't even open the diary in case she saw that cream envelope covered in hearts.

Saturday mornings had settled into a predictable routine. She paid her rent, two pounds and ten shillings, to the greasy-haired landlord who lived in the basement. It was done by remote control. She handed it to him through a hatch, and he took it, grunted, signed the rent book and handed it back through a haze of nicotine, his eyebrows fiercely shielding a pair of cloudy, expressionless eyes. He never looked at Tessa, and she wondered if anyone was actually in there, a soul, a spirit, even a person dwelling within the tweed-jacketed lump.

Today she returned home after seeing Dorothy, and found her mum's little blue letter stuck in the post rack in the hall. Nothing from Art. The usual jolt of pain. There had been times when Tessa had sat in the window, perched on the end of her bed and craning her neck to watch the postman going from door to door along Nottingham Place, waiting for him to arrive at the front door. Hope and dread were woven together in her mind, and when he did arrive she tore down the two flights of stairs to find – nothing. On weekdays after work she emerged from Baker Street tube station and ran down the wide pavements of Marylebone Road, past the dome of the Planetarium, and into Nottingham Place with every beat of her heart yearning for a letter from Art, only to find – nothing. Each day of nothing took her further and further into a desert of sorrow where the crystal sands scorched her feet, blew dust through her hair and into her eyes, a nothing place where no trees grew, a place where the only option was to lie, exhausted, on the fiery sand and pray for rain.

Today she was pleased to find the predictable letter from her mum, full of homely news, threaded with subtle euphemisms and always a cry at the end. A 'when are you coming home?' cry, and still the silent, unspeakable answer loitered in Tessa's mind. *NEVER*.

She sat on her bed with her back against the wall, and opened the envelope. Her mother's letter was brief this time. She wasn't well. Lucy had been to visit, and Tim refused to come into the house, and Freddie had stubbornly stayed in his workshop. Kate felt she was the only one still flying the flag of unconditional love. Inside Kate's letter was a bit of treasure – a letter from her dad in his copperplate script. It was folded neatly into four, and when Tessa opened it, a pound note fell out.

Freddie wanted her to think about the field, and what to do with it. He'd been up there with Herbie and fenced off a strip of it close to the woods, and planted the lime trees he'd grown from seed. He'd gathered acorns, walnuts and beechnuts and planted them in pots. He hoped she'd come home one day and help him in his lone mission to plant trees for the future.

Tessa closed her eyes, holding his letter between her hands. She could feel his energy in the paper. The noon-time sun streamed through the tall window, warming her hands and face. A memory hummed in her mind. A glaze of light over an oasis in the desert of grief. Gaia. The Rainbow Warriors. The hippie dream of saving the earth from destructive chemicals and pollution. Saving the wild creatures. *What am I doing here?* she thought. *How far away have I come from my true self?*

At the same moment she heard footsteps on the stairs, heavy male footsteps. In soft shoes. She tensed, listening, expecting it to be one of the other tenants on his way home. She listened for the sound of a key turning in a lock, a rustle of shopping bags being carried in. Instead, the man stopped outside her door. She could hear him breathing.

Tessa got to her feet, her eyes big with fear, watching the door like a startled animal. She felt cornered.

There was a minute crackling sound, like cellophane. Then a polite tap on the door.

The warrior surfaced, and she opened the door wide and positive, ready for battle, a shoe in one hand.

A pair of hazel eyes confronted her. A tall young man, clean-shaven and rangy, his jeans too clean, his cheeks too eager, a bunch of carnations in his hand.

'Hi, Tessa!'

'Paul!'

He looked suddenly bashful. 'I got you some flowers. Are you angry?'

'Well – thanks, they're lovely,' Tessa said, sniffing the heavy clove-like scent of the carnations. 'And, no, I'm just surprised. You look so different.'

'Yeah.' Paul ran his fingers through his new boyish crew cut. 'The sun-bleached locks had to go. Didn't fit my old man's image of a son.'

'I know what you mean,' Tessa said. 'My beads had to go.'

'Are you going to ask me in?'

She studied his hazel eyes, remembering how they had looked when he was rescuing her from the sea. Steady. Boring. But safe. *Well – safe-ISH,* she thought, remembering the wounded-wolf look he'd given her one day when she'd rejected his attempt to kiss her.

'You can come in for a quick coffee,' she said. 'Then I'm going out.'

'Right.' He followed her inside and shut the door. Immediately Tessa felt uneasy. Trapped. His fidgety shadow between her and the door. His needy soul already drawing energy from her light, or what was left of it. She'd never lost the habit of using her ability to see the human aura, and Paul's was an acid yellow with chinks of flinty darkness. He had the aura of a loner, a misfit who had survived by swinging wildly between being a bully and being a fairy-tale prince.

She didn't trust him.

'How did you know my address?' she asked.

'Your mum gave it to me.'

Tessa's eyes rounded. 'She did?'

'I saw you in the paper, in the fountain. It blew my mind! I thought, yeah, that's Tessa. And Barcussy isn't a common name. I asked directory enquiries for it, in Monterose, and they gave it to me. Your mum answered, and I put on my best upper class accent and told her I was an old friend, that I'd rescued you from the sea. I told her I lived in London, and that Dad was a lawyer, said I was concerned about you being alone in the big smoke, and she gave in like a little lamb and told me your address.'

Tessa nodded. Kate had sent her the cutting from the *Gazette* and Tessa had screwed it into a ball and binned it.

Obviously Kate had fallen for Paul's charm, and his accent, and his credibility. *Damn,* she thought, *Mum has got to learn not to do this to me.*

132

'Your mum sounded nice.'

'She is.'

'She kind of – chatted to me in a confidential sort of way. She told me about Art and what he'd done to you. That dreadful hippie, she called him. I mean – are you all right, Tessa? After what that bastard did?'

'Art's not a bastard. He's a beautiful person, and he changed my life, Paul. Yes, I'm broken-hearted, and angry with that woman – Rowan. But I'm okay. I'm coping. And I've got a job, and this little place – it's not much, but it's home.' Tessa smiled to herself as she heard those words emerging. *Thank you, Dorothy,* she thought.

'I always admired you, Tessa. You're so brave.' Paul sat down on the bed, his long legs hunched against the sink unit. 'Mind if I sit down?'

'I'm not brave. It's just an act.' Tessa sat down too, in the one chair by the window. She didn't want to get too close to Paul. His eyes roved over her legs, and up to her face.

'You've still got the sun-bleach in your hair,' he remarked. 'The sun is just catching it now – golden – a golden girl.'

'No way,' Tessa said. 'My sister, Lucy, is the golden girl. I'm the black sheep of the family.'

'Your mum didn't give me that impression. She really loves you, Tessa. I could tell.'

There was a pregnant silence between them. *I wish he'd go away,* Tessa thought.

'I'm envious,' Paul said. 'My parents don't love me like that. I'm just an extension of their ego trip. They hated me being a hippie. Dad was all set to disown me 'til I came home and cut my hair. But he still doesn't like what I'm doing.'

'What are you doing?'

'Studying music. Violin and clarinet – I'm hoping to get into an orchestra, a big one like the LSO, and travel the world doing concerts.'

'I like classical music,' Tessa said.

Paul's eyes sparkled mysteriously. He reached inside his jacket and pulled out two tickets. 'Well – what a coincidence. I just happen to have two tickets for the Royal Albert Hall – tonight! – It's Beethoven's *Violin Concerto* – you'd love it. Will you come with me?'

Tessa hesitated, remembering how much she had enjoyed a concert with Faye. They'd hitched up to London from college, and it had been Tessa's first ever experience of a symphony concert. The music had been Brahms's *Symphony No 1*. Its eight note theme had haunted Tessa forever, especially as Faye had described it so passionately as 'a light in the forest'. It had been a huge, and welcome, emotional rollercoaster. She had the LP which Faye had given her for Christmas, but it was sitting on top of her record player at home, along with the other LP she had – *The Planets* by Holst. After that difficult Christmas, she'd spent hours in another world, lying on her bed listening to those two LPs. *Neptune* from *The Planets* was magical and contemplative, truly the music of dreams.

But all that had happened before Art. Before their Summer of Love on the wild shores of St Ives in Cornwall.

'You're taking a long time to answer,' Paul said, and the tiniest crease of a frown appeared.

'Thanks, but no thanks,' Tessa said.

Paul looked miffed. His eyes changed shape as the frown deepened, and the pupils went pinhead small. His top lip tightened. 'So what's the excuse?'

'Do I need one?'

'It would help me to understand why, Tessa.' He managed to make her name sound like an accusation. 'Are you going out somewhere already?'

'No.'

'Surely you're not going to sit here on your own on a Saturday night – in this cupboard – are you?'

Tessa stared at the wall. 'I'm fine on my own. I'm not going to manufacture an excuse. And it's not a cupboard. It's a nest.'

Paul's back went rigid. 'Is it the concert you don't like? Or is it me?'

'It's neither. You have to understand – I'm like a wounded animal right now. I need to stay in my cave.'

'Your mother seemed to think it would do you good to go out.'

'Yes – well, she WOULD,' Tessa said angrily. 'She's a going-out kind of person, and I'm not. And anyway I do go out. ON MY OWN.'

'Okay, okay – don't bite my head off.'

Tessa glared at the wall. She felt like a trapped lioness. *I'm being horrible,* she thought, looking at the carnations in their

135

cellophane cone. 'I'm not rejecting you, Paul,' she said gently. 'And – are you sure you want me to have these flowers?'

His face softened a little. 'Yeah, of course, I bought them for you. Maybe we could do something else – a walk in the park? Or the Planetarium?'

'Not today, but some other time, when I feel better – if I ever do.'

'Fine. That just leaves me with another lonely Saturday night. There's plenty of girls around, but I don't fancy any of them. I've never met a girl like you, Tessa. You're special, and very beautiful.' He leaned closer. 'I'm not going to give up on you, and – I really hope you don't give up on me.'

Tessa suddenly felt sorry for Paul. He looked crestfallen, as if the pendulum had swung out of its anger zone and into genuine disappointment. He tucked the offending tickets away in his pocket. 'So what will you do tonight?' Tessa asked.

He shrugged. 'Go on my own.'

Tessa was tempted to give him a kiss on the cheek, but a warning neon light flashed in her mind. *DON'T*, it said in scarlet letters.

Another part of her mind knew it would not be long before she and Paul were going out together. She felt caught in a tide of expectations. Girls were expected to get married, and if they didn't they would be labelled as 'odd' or 'frigid', incapable of love.

CHAPTER 8

Working With a Broken Heart

'I could calm her down,' Tessa said in a quiet voice.

The walls rang with raucous screams coming from the child who lay on the floor. Chandra was a heavily built dumpling of a girl, six years old, known for her mega-tantrums and endless whining. Three teachers and two therapists had given up on her, and so had her mother, who delivered her screaming daughter through the door in the mornings with a sigh of relief.

Tessa was pinning the children's artwork on the corridor walls when it started. The teacher in the classroom next door to hers was Helga, a mountain of a woman with a bust like an army tank. She had a booming voice and the children and most of the staff were petrified of her.

So Helga looked taken aback when Tessa, a mere classroom assistant, quietly offered to do her job for her. 'I doubt that, Tessa. But you have a go.' She gave a battle-weary laugh and let go of Chandra's arm which she'd been using to drag her across the floor. 'Little madam. She's playing up because she's got to go to the nurse for an injection. Anyone would think the nurse was going to cut her head off. It's only a little needle, Chandra. Silly girl.'

Her words fired new energy into Chandra's screams. She pounded the floor with her small feet.

'Go on – you have a go,' said Helga, and her eyes bulged at Tessa. 'See if you can drag her to the nurse. I'll be in my classroom if you want me.' She strode off, in a pair of red platform heels.

Tessa sat down on the floor. Chandra was eyeing her through two slits of swollen cheek, like a growling dog, ready to attack. But in there somewhere was hunger for love, love that was forever unreachable for a child like Chandra.

The power of silence was something Freddie had given Tessa all her life. It had rescued her countless times from the furthest edges of frustration and fury, edges that glittered like broken windows. Tessa was sure in her heart that Freddie was a secret healer.

So she sat still, and looked at Chandra kindly, praying that Helga wouldn't intervene and break the spell with her loud voice. Chandra's aura had the angry colours of an open wound. Tessa waited, imagining the soothing blues of the ocean, the diamond cold of its waters, swirling around the distressed child.

One of the problems in managing Chandra was the child's

strategy of lying on the floor when things weren't going her way. Sometimes she would crawl under the desks and tables and stay there for hours. She was so heavy that most of the adults in her life had given up trying to get her to stand. They left her there under a cloud of recriminations and the occasional kick from one of the other children. Chandra's life was a thunderstorm of negativity.

Tessa was interested in finding the real Chandra hidden inside the layers of resistance. The soul who had been born as a magical, shining being. Where was she now? How had it come to this?

Those two words, 'silly girl', were used relentlessly on Chandra. Hearing them again was salt in the wound. The rage was a furious sense of injustice. An unanswered question. Why? Why did no one actually try to understand and respect her feelings? To Chandra the world was a cruel and hostile place.

So when Tessa sat quietly beside her, not criticising, not pressurising, it was a new experience for Chandra. After a few minutes, she quietened down and her eyes began to open and focus. Tessa caught a glimpse of a wild creature inside Chandra, a beautiful phantasma like a turquoise damselfly on a reed. Something so bright that you weren't sure whether you had really seen it, or whether it belonged to the solid, physical world at all. Tessa encouraged it with a spontaneous, magical smile, feeling the dimples twitch in her cheeks. It was the rare smile that Art had loved. The smile of a soul recognising another soul.

A magic moment, coaxed out by the silence. A time to use her special voice. The voice she had used to heal Selwyn.

'What's the matter, darling?'

No one ever called Chandra 'darling'. No one ever spoke to her in such a hypnotic, caring tone of voice. No one else looked into her soul with the bewitching eyes of a healer.

But there was so much the matter in Chandra's life that the child didn't know how to begin, how to choose from the chaotic jumble of words and emotions. Her eyes scanned the space for danger, like a songbird checking to see if it was safe to fly into a garden.

'Chandra?' Tessa spoke her name in a special way.

The child breathed in, and forgot to breathe out in the first enchanted moment of eye contact. Helga loomed in the open doorway of her classroom. *She's waiting to pounce,* Tessa thought.

Chandra managed to select a word. 'Nurse,' she whispered.

'Nurse? Does she frighten you, darling?'

Chandra nodded miserably, and the colour rushed over her cheeks again. Beads of sweat crept along her hairline. Anxiety burned in her eyes, and Tessa saw its endless shadow, years and years of it.

'Don't be too soft with her, Tessa,' Helga called from the doorway. 'She has to be held down kicking and screaming if the nurse just touches her.'

Tessa bit back a furious retort. Crossing swords with Helga could ruin everything. She continued gazing at Chandra. 'Shall we go for a walk outside?' she suggested. 'Sit under the magic tree?'

Chandra looked surprised, but she nodded, and stood up.

'I'll take her for a walk,' Tessa said to Helga, and without waiting for a response she took Chandra's hot little hand in hers and walked out into the sunshine.

'Don't take her off the premises,' Helga called after her.

Chandra walked trustingly with Tessa, looking up at her in awe. Once outside under the cool coppery skies of London, she grew calmer. Against the predictable roar of traffic and aeroplanes, a dove was cooing to another dove, who was answering, their plump soft bodies hidden in the trees.

Tessa led her to the big horse chestnut that hung over the playground. Under its dappled light was a bench. 'Shall we sit down?' Tessa said. 'If we're quiet we might see the squirrel.'

Chandra sat looking at her. She stretched out a chubby hand and touched the braid in Tessa's hair. 'You hair's lovely, Miss. I wish I had those pretty ribbons in my hair.'

'I'll do a braid in your hair if you like,' Tessa said, 'and you can choose the colours. I'll bring my ribbons to school.'

Chandra's eyes lit up with delight. Then they went black again with anxiety. 'But do I have to be good first?'

'No,' Tessa said. Obviously Chandra had anticipated the bribe she'd been thinking of making. So that wasn't going to work. 'I'll do it out of kindness.'

'Why?'

''Cause I like being kind,' Tessa said.

'Can I come home with you, Miss?'

'No.'

141

'Why?'

''Cause you're not my little girl.'

Chandra leaned against her. She pointed across the playground at the main building. 'She's in there, Miss, the nurse.'

'So what will you do if she comes to fetch you?'

'Kick her.'

'And then what will happen?'

'She'll tell my mum, and then all of them will hold me down and make me have an injection. And they always say it doesn't hurt when it does.'

'Maybe we can find a better way,' Tessa said. She stroked Chandra's hot face, moving strands of hair away from her brow. She began to talk in her special voice, telling the avidly listening child about the buds on the horse chestnut. It was late February, and the sticky buds had opened like candles burning a pale green light against the gloomy brickwork and smoking chimneys of London. 'When I was a little girl,' Tessa said, 'I had a magic trick that helped me cope with pain.' She noted that Chandra was listening with wide, rapt eyes. 'Because once I was like you. I was terrified of nurses – and the dentist – I used to kick and scream just like you.'

'Did you?'

Tessa nodded. Then she whispered, 'But I learned a magic trick. Shall I teach it to you?'

'Yes please.'

'Well, first you have to remember what the four winds look like – when you see them in story books. Like this.'

Tessa blew out her cheeks and made a face she hoped was like the North wind.

Chandra copied her, and they both began to giggle.

'When I have an injection,' Tessa said, 'I don't look at the needle. I look the other way and take a big breath in. Then when I feel the pain, I blow it out – like the North wind, and it's gone, like magic.'

A thought hit her, almost knocking her down. *If only I could blow away the pain of Art like that, but it's too big. It's like an immovable boulder.*

She looked up, aware of loud footsteps. She watched the light die in Chandra's eyes as Helga came barrelling across the yard, her grey hair looming like a thundercloud. 'Tessa, it's nearly home time and Diane needs you. Go quickly. I'll take Chandra to the nurse.'

Freddie was in the Post Office when the feeling started. It began as mild uneasiness, a vague sense of being unwell. He was in a queue, boxed in between the shelves of writing paper, carbon paper, bottles of Quink and fountain pens. In his hand was the telephone bill which he had to pay at the counter. He didn't know any of the people in the queue, except Herbie's wife who was at the front. Freddie focused on her reassuringly portly back. At the same time he didn't want her to turn around and notice the sweat on his cheeks and the tremor in his hands.

As the queue shuffled forward he had a memory of being a small boy clutching an earthenware jar. His mother, Annie, had sent him out after school to queue for a ration of treacle. Exhausted and malnourished he'd arrived home with it, and crashed to the floor in a dead faint. He remembered how everything had swayed crazily, the kitchen dresser, the walls with their copper pans, the coke oven, all gyrating like a carousel.

It was happening now, in the Post Office, in that very public place. The shelves of fountain pens and paper were moving, like barleycorn in the wind. The sound of his own pulse hissed in his ears, louder and faster with every passing second. Sweat prickled under the rim of his cap. *I'm gonna die,* he thought, *here in the Post Office. Drop dead, like me father did.*

He wanted something to hold. Something that wasn't moving. He touched the shelf. Sturdy, thick wood. Well polished oak. His fingers clamped over its edge and he told himself it wasn't moving. He remembered Kate saying, 'Take a deep breath, dear,' and he tried. But his breathing was rapid and shallow, beyond his control.

The yellow lights of the Post Office dimmed, and shone out again, and darkened like a garden under stormy skies. The bottles of Quink and the fountain pens tilted and spun. *I'll bring shame on the family,* Freddie thought, *I mustn't collapse in the Post Office. I gotta get out.*

He turned and fought his way to the door, the phone bill crumpling in his hand. The eyes of the queue bobbed accusingly at him, and he heard a woman's voice tutting and saying he was drunk. He felt ashamed, and terrified.

Outside the Post Office was a wooden bench against the

sunny south wall. Freddie sat down on it, glad to feel the breeze cooling his skin. His hands gripped the bench, his feet pressed hard on the ground, his back safe against the blue-lias stones of the wall. *Nothing is moving,* he told himself, and the giddy feeling settled into stillness. The solidity of wood and stone had somehow anchored him to the earth.

He looked at the ball of paper in his hand. He'd have to smooth it out and present it, creased and cracked, to the critical eyes of the postmistress. But he couldn't go back inside. Maybe he could never go in there again. And he had to get home. With his heartbeat still hissing furiously in his ears, his breathing shallow, his legs unsteady. No matter what, he had to get home.

It had taken him five minutes to stride down to the Post Office in the morning sun. Now, suddenly, the distance between him and The Pines felt like a hundred miles of shingle.

Kate stood on the slipway at Aust Ferry, the wind streaming through her hair. It was always an emotional journey for her, the memory of her sister Ethie drowning in that speeding, merciless tide of the Severn Estuary. She watched the Severn King, the oldest of the ferry boats, struggling against the current, the chugging of its engine ringing painfully on the wind. Kate thought nostalgically of trips across the ferry with Lucy and Tessa. Lucy had always been seasick, but Tessa had loved to stand in the front of the boat with her chestnut plaits flying. Then she would run to the back to watch the wake of churning brown water. It had been hard to keep her safe. All that effort, Kate reflected, and now she had no way of knowing whether Tessa was safe. Her letters from London were mostly about the children she worked with. There was nothing about her social life, nothing about how she was coping with a broken heart. And still nothing about that nice young man, Paul, with the cultured voice Kate had liked on the phone. She'd pictured him striding through the city in a pin-striped suit.

On this cold gusty day in February, Kate was going over on the ferry by herself to fetch her mother, Sally. She hoped Sally would decide to live with them at The Pines, now that she was getting old and needing care. Freddie hadn't wanted Kate to go on her own. He worried about her driving the car on and off the ferry boat, a scary task when the weather was rough, the boat rocking wildly and water slopping over the ramp. Kate didn't care. She felt confident she could do it, in Tessa's little car, the green Morris Minor.

The Severn King edged up to the jetty and the big fat ropes were flung across the gap and secured around the plinths. The ramp was lowered and cars disembarked, their engines roaring up the slippery jetty. Kate got back into the Morris Minor and started her up.

'Steady, steady, Mrs!' the boatman called as she shot up the ramp onto the deck. 'No need to go like a bull at a gate, dear.'

Kate grinned and gave him a cheery wave. She parked neatly and got out again to enjoy the wind in her hair. Loaded with cars, the Severn King laboured out into the sweeping brown tide, its engine grunting and spluttering. Kate leaned on the prow as it steamed towards Beachley on the opposite bank, at midstream passing the Severn Queen on her way over. Crossing the water always gave Kate a sense of separation, and this time it was strong. Inexplicably there was a sudden sense that something was wrong with Freddie. He hadn't wanted her to go. A little voice inside Kate's mind told her she shouldn't have left him on his own. *Of course, he would be fine*, said the voice of reason. But Freddie had never been alone. His mother had always been there, and now she had gone. Annie had been a sweet but sometimes difficult old lady, and she had particularly hated Tessa.

As the boat drew close to Beachley jetty, Kate debated whether to stay on board and simply go back home again. What could possibly go wrong? She'd left a pie in the fridge, and a trifle for Freddie's lunch. He only had to feed the chickens, and pay the phone bill. She thought of her mum, Sally, waiting excitedly at Asan Farm, her suitcase packed and ready. They'd agreed to visit the graves of Ethie and Bertie that afternoon, Kate would stay the night and they'd head back to Monterose the following morning. *I can't let Mum down,* Kate thought.

Tessa glared at Helga in disbelief, her heart aching for Chandra who had again flung herself on the floor. 'I was just getting through to her,' she said. 'Couldn't you leave me with her a bit longer – as long as she needs?'

'Oh, Madam Chandra needs all day,' Helga thundered.

'She's had you all to herself for half an hour – and now look at her!'

'I was teaching her a magic trick to help her cope with the injection,' Tessa said.

'Magic trick? Oh, I don't think so, dear. We don't want that kind of mumbo-jumbo. You get back to the job you SHOULD be doing, Tessa, and don't interfere in future. Leave MADAM to me.'

Tessa held back the fiery response and maintained a steady, indignant glare straight into Helga's eyes. It was as much use as glaring at a thunderstorm. The edges of Helga's lips went white with spittle, her eyes rolled like marbles. 'Don't cross me, Tessa. You are a classroom assistant, not a Clinical Psychiatrist,' she hissed, and what she did next was unbeliev-able. She reached down and yanked Chandra up by her arm. 'And YOU,' she bellowed, 'get up off that ground. NOW. Before I give you something to cry about.'

Chandra's howl of pain went right through Tessa. Fire ripped through her belly, and she lost her temper totally.

'Stop it, you bully,' she yelled at Helga. 'You're hurting her. Can't you see Chandra is really frightened? She's a sensi-tive, anxious little girl and you're not just hurting her, you're wounding her, deeply and forever, wounding her, body and soul. Body and soul, Helga.'

'Don't be so ridiculous. I've taught more children than you've had hot dinners. Go back to your job – or you'll regret this, my girl.'

Tessa stood her ground. 'No, I will not, Helga. I don't

148

care who you are. I'm not going to stand here and watch
you bully a six-year-old anxious little girl. I know what I'm
talking about. I was bullied by a teacher. You are misusing
your power, Helga. It's wrong – and you know it's wrong.'

There was an obstinate silence. Chandra's howling paused
and she looked from one to the other in bewilderment.

Helga looked shaken. Her marble-hard eyes momentarily
softened, allowing a rare glimpse of who she might once have
been. While she reassembled her defences, Tessa had another
go. 'You agreed to let me take Chandra for a walk,' she said
more calmly. 'Now let me finish the job. I will take her to the
nurse, and you can go back and explain to Diane.' Tessa felt
power gathering inside her, power she'd always had, power
to use her anger, to fill her turquoise eyes with altruistic fire.
'I mean it, Helga. Let go of her, please.'

Helga wilted under the glare of light coming from those
eyes. Her shoulders twitched, and she huffed righteously. She
let go of Chandra's arm as if she was chucking litter into a
bin. 'You'll regret this, my girl. It'll cost you your job.'

'I don't care,' Tessa said proudly. 'Get me sacked if you
like. At least I will have rescued a child. Chandra's a lovely
little girl, and she MATTERS.'

Helga lifted her bust and walked away, her shoes clanking
over the tarmac.

Tessa felt the anger still fluttering inside her like a bird
trapped in a window. But she felt calm as well. She cuddled
Chandra, and rubbed her hurt arm, and used her special
voice while new amazing concepts flooded her mind. *I am*

in control, she thought. *I've got my mother's fire and my father's calm, and together they are powerful.*

The healing moments settled around them like rose petals, like the peace rose.

And five minutes later, Tessa and Chandra walked hand in hand across the yard to the nurse's room.

Freddie sat outside the Post Office until his breathing slowly returned to normal. Warmth and colour crept back into his cheeks and hands, and the shaking gradually stopped. He fished a Fox's Glacier Mint out of his pocket. It was so old that the paper was welded to the sweet and he spent some time picking it off with his fingernails. He sucked its glassy mintiness thoughtfully. What had happened to him? Had he had some kind of heart attack? Or was it the low blood sugar Herbie had warned him about? Or something more sinister? He wished Kate was at home to reassure him and make him smile again. He wished Lucy wasn't in Taunton, and Tessa even further away. He wanted his family round him, caring about him, needing him. The joy of feeling his children's soft little arms around his neck, and the wonder of that light in their eyes was something he sorely missed. The work he was doing was lonely now. Chipping at stone. Smoothing wood. Coaxing engines into life. He missed the camaraderie of his haulage business, the banter, the happy bustle of the station.

Something had gone wrong in his life. It had lost its essence. He wanted it back.

But right now he must try to go home.

Outside the Post Office on a triangle of grass between two streets stood a huge elm tree, hundreds of years old. Freddie got up and walked gingerly over to it. He felt okay. The panic had just been inside the Post Office. He couldn't go back in there, but he could begin to walk home.

He put his hands on the bark of the elm, and he could feel that it was springtime. Winter was coming to an end, and the elm tree knew, deep in the heartwood, that its bead-like buds were slowly turning red with life, the calyx getting brittle and thin, ready to split like the skin of a snake and release the soft baby leaves.

Freddie glanced up the hill at the Old Coach House where Dr Jarvis had his surgery. He knew he should go to the doctor. But he just wanted to get home.

He picked up a stick which had fallen from the elm tree. It would help to anchor him. *The journey of a thousand miles begins with the first steps,* he thought, and as he began to walk he noticed a bright little face in the grass. Something running alongside. Not following but leading. A dog. A little white dog like Jonti, leading him home through the long afternoon.

'Will you come to the office please, Tessa? Now.'

Tessa's heart sank when she saw Megan waiting for her at the gate on Monday morning. Had she lost her job? She'd told Helga she didn't care. But she did. The job with the children was a sustaining factor in her life, financially, emotionally, and spiritually. She'd done everything as well as she could, cutting up paper, mixing powder paint in jars, tying shoe laces, zipping tiny anoraks, reading stories, and sitting on a tiny wooden chair helping a child read, or build bricks, or count buttons. She'd grown to love those children, and she believed they loved her.

For once Megan sat behind her desk, her eyes serious. Tessa sat in the chair opposite, the nerves already twanging inside her.

'Tessa, I've just spent twenty minutes with Helga,' Megan began. 'She's very angry, to put it mildly.'

Tessa wanted to say that Helga was a bully, but she deemed it wiser to keep quiet. She liked and respected Megan. Surely Megan would be fair – wouldn't she?

'This is your first job, isn't it?' Megan asked, shuffling through some papers on her desk.

'It's my first real job,' Tessa said. 'But I worked part-time with horses when I was still at school.'

'How important is this job to you?' Megan studied Tessa's eyes, her hands clasped on the desk, her expression grave.

'Very important.' Tessa's heart began to thump nervously. 'I really love the children – and I get on fine with Diane. It's not just a job for paying my rent, it's a job that matters to me.'

'Hmmm.' Megan looked thoughtful. 'I'm afraid Helga was adamant that you should be dismissed.'

Tessa felt her skin flushing. The embers of the fire burned inside her, burning down, burning to ashes. Megan was watching, waiting for a reaction. And Freddie's calm eyes were in her heart, telling her to hold on, stay quiet. What did Megan want? Flames? Tears? Tessa waited.

'I can see it means a lot to you,' Megan said kindly. 'We all make mistakes, me included. Would you like to explain how this happened, Tessa, from your point of view?'

A lifeline, Tessa thought, *she's throwing me a lifeline.*

'I was deeply concerned for Chandra's wellbeing,' she began. 'I know only too well how fear can manifest as anger. That little girl is sensitive and extremely anxious. She lies on the floor because it's her only way of defending herself from the relentless, destructive attacks on her personality from most of the adults who purport to care for her. Love and kindness are a rare oasis in the harsh desert of her life. She's lost, you see. Lost in a merciless world where everyone hates her, everyone calls her a silly girl – for being frightened. I tried to offer her something different, something healing and magical, and I believe it did help her.'

Megan's mouth fell open in astonishment.

But Tessa hadn't finished. She couldn't stop the river of brilliant words that flowed through her. 'It helped because I tuned into who Chandra really is – a beautiful little soul who finds herself in a hostile, bullying world – a flower who can never bloom because it is crushed under thoughtless feet. She's like the epitome of Yeats' poem, *Tread softly, for you tread on my dreams.* That's why I'm here, in this job. Okay, I'm cutting up paper and mixing paint and tying shoelaces – but I'm being gentle and kind to these damaged children, and I think that should be the beating heart of this school – don't you?'

'My God, Tessa!' Megan looked stunned. 'Shakespeare would be proud of that speech!'

Tessa kept her face and her body very still, maintaining the solemn stare. Minute tingles of excitement crawled up her spine.

'And how about being kind and gentle to Helga?' Megan raised her eyebrows enquiringly.

'She's a bully.'

Megan nodded ever so slightly. 'Honesty is all very well. But tact is needed too. The fact is, Tessa, you were openly argumentative and rude to a senior member of staff. You undermined the work Helga was doing with Chandra, challenged her authority, and took a vulnerable child outside for half an hour, without reference to Diane.'

Tessa stared at her with passion, trying to stay on the chair. She imagined herself getting up and swanning out. Telling Megan to stuff her job.

But Megan held up her hand, as if she'd sensed the shift in Tessa's mood. 'No – don't walk out on me, Tessa. It's not all bad news,' she said. 'But I had to tell you how Helga felt. I know Helga is a bit of a dragon, but she's goodhearted and very experienced. If you have any issues with her again, Tessa, will you please come to me? Don't get into an argy-bargy with her. Okay?'

'Okay.' It came out as a whisper. Tessa's throat felt like a tight painful knot. *If only you knew,* she thought, *I'm working with a broken heart.*

Megan's face brightened. 'However – there is some good news,' she announced. 'Chandra's mum came in this morning and asked me to say thank you to you. She was thrilled that Chandra managed to have her injection without fuss, the first time ever – and she said she came home a different child, smiling from ear to ear.'

'That's great!' Tessa said.

Megan pushed the box of Kleenex over to her. 'I can see you're very stressed. I should go and get a coffee and calm yourself down – and keep on the right side of Helga!'

'Thanks.'

CHAPTER 9

Violetta

'What if they don't like me?' Tessa asked as Paul led her down a leafy avenue in Richmond.

'They can stuff it,' Paul said. 'It's not an exam, Tessa — come on — I love you and that's all that matters.'

Through the months of early summer in London, Paul and Tessa had been dating regularly. Walks by the river, concerts at the Royal Festival Hall, picnics in Regent's Park.

Tessa felt apprehensive about meeting Paul's parents. It hadn't been an issue with Art, but Paul seemed intimidated by his parents, and his sister. Despite his bravado, she sensed he was seeking to impress them — with her. 'What should I wear?' she'd asked.

'Be who you are,' Paul said, then frowned. 'Maybe not too hippyish.'

An eternal conflict was bugging Tessa, between wanting to be the 'people-pleasing Tessa', and wanting to be rebellious. In the end she chose a cream cheesecloth blouse with an embroidered yoke, flared stone-washed jeans and her flowery boots.

The house looked imposing, with brick and stone balustrades and tiled steps leading up to a white front door with two pristine urns planted with geraniums.

'Hello, Mum — this is Tessa.'

Paul's mother looked like an expensive Fortnum and Mason chocolate. Tessa eyed her flawless beige skirt, cashmere twin set and triple row of pearls. The coffee-cream image ended with a bitter chocolate bob of hair, a pair of pencilled eyebrows, and a leonine stare.

'Pleased to meet you, Tessa.' She held out a manicured claw and Tessa felt repelled by its touch. She looked at the eyes. Hostile and suspicious.

'What should I call you?' Tessa asked. 'Penny?'

'Penelope will be fine.'

Penelope led them inside with a swirl of expensive skirt. The house smelled of scrubbed marble and scorched linen as if Penelope spent her time ironing table napkins. 'Tea is in the drawing room.' She ushered them into a room with voluminous chintzy sofas and highly polished sideboards laden with porcelain figurines and silverware. Family photos in silver frames were grouped on a table, mostly formal portraits, and none of them smiling.

Tessa paused to look at them. 'Is that you, Paul?' she asked, pointing to a photo of a wistful-looking boy with neatly combed hair.

'Yeah – that's me.'

'Aged eight,' said Penelope. 'In his first term at prep school.'

'I hated it,' Paul said.

'No, you didn't. It was good for you.' Penelope picked up another photo of a curly-haired girl holding a trophy. 'And this is Amelia, Paul's sister, when she won the cup for best all-rounder of the year at her prep school.'

Tessa glanced at Paul and saw a look come into his eyes, a look she understood only too well. 'I had a clever sister – Lucy,' she said. 'It was hard to follow in her golden footsteps.'

'But you're quite clever, Paul tells me,' Penelope said.

'No.' Tessa looked candidly into the leonine eyes. 'It's not one of my priorities.'

'Oh.' Penelope looked taken aback. 'But – you went to a good school, Paul said. Didn't you?'

'Does it matter?' Tessa asked, a touch too loudly.

'She went to Hilbegut,' Paul boasted.

'Hilbegut!' Penelope didn't look impressed. 'Rather a controversial reputation, I seem to recall. What made your parents send you there?'

Tessa was beginning to feel cornered. She wanted to ask 'Does it matter?' again, but Paul had his arm round her shoulders and his fingers were sending cautionary mini-prods into her arm. It wouldn't do to fall out with his mother at this early stage of their enforced relationship. Further down the line Tessa clearly foresaw a big bust-up. She sensed how Paul longed to trash the top of the sideboard with one sweep of an angry arm.

'I was there on scholarship,' she said.

'Oh dear, you poor girl. Were you bullied?' Penelope asked. 'I've heard that scholarship girls are, usually.'

'No. I had a fantastic art teacher – Mrs Appleby. She changed my life. I was—'

Paul gave her an extra hard dig. 'Mother dear, don't interrogate Tessa when you've only just met her!'

The pale amber eyes cooled. 'I know how to conduct a conversation, thank you, Paul.'

Tessa sensed Paul's light getting dimmer by the minute in the presence of his mother. *Distract her*, she thought, and looked out of the window. 'You've got a beautiful garden.'

Penelope softened, just one degree. 'Do you like gardens?'

'I love gardens.'

Paul gave her an approving squeeze. 'Shall we go for a quick look? Dad's out there messing with the roses.'

He led her through a hall and down some steps. Penelope followed, her shoes tapping importantly.

Tessa breathed in the scent of roses. It was the first time she'd smelled roses in London. The heady fragrance took her back to her home garden at The Pines. Her dad's blue eyes. The carrot bed. The lilacs over Jonti's grave. 'It makes me homesick,' she said, and Penelope softened another degree.

The roses were planted in lines, on straight little standards, and around them was bare earth. The lawn was a sterile green sward, like a bowling green. Tessa felt drawn into the garden by the ambience of the roses with their coils of plush petals that seemed to reach towards her like cats, inviting

159

her to touch, to smell, to begin to sense their flower power. She made a beeline for a rose she knew well. A peace rose. She remembered Freddie bringing her one in hospital. She'd been fourteen and had tried to take her life. She'd lain in bed staring into the heart of the flower, its cream petals flushed with pink. Its vibrant gentleness had spoken to her soul, spoken of healing love, and it gave itself to her, totally, until it dropped apart in her hand. So many petals on the sheet, like leaves, like the autumn of the flower. It had allowed her to use it until it no longer existed, and its corpse was a geometric star on a wine-coloured stem.

The rose she was looking at now was remote. Not involved. But beautiful with droplets of morning still gracing its petals.

'Tessa!' Paul's voice cracked into her dream and it fell away like an eggshell. She hated it when he did that. She felt her eyes glaring at him, and the cold of Penelope standing behind him. She longed to be alone in this garden.

'Come and meet Dad.' Paul towed her down the path to a shed where a wispy wizard of a man was sharpening a pair of clippers with a whetstone. He looked up at her with tired green eyes that came suddenly to life when he saw her.

'This is Tessa, Dad.'

'Tessa?' The voice was like that of a spider, had it chosen to speak. 'Tessa who?'

'Tessa Barcussy.' She offered her hand and he took it in both his blue-veined, suntanned hands, and held on as if trying to find her bones.

'Your hands are very dirty, Marcus,' Penelope complained. 'And we are about to take tea, in the drawing room.'

A glimmer of humour passed through Marcus's green eyes, but he held on to the bones inside Tessa's hand.

'It doesn't matter,' Tessa said. 'I'm a country girl – used to dirty hands. I can see you're a working man – and I love the roses. They are awesome.'

'Awesome!' Penelope tutted disapprovingly.

Tessa beamed at Marcus, showing the dimples in her cheeks, and he was instantly hooked. He gazed at her raptly. 'We've been waiting for you,' he said. 'Tessa Barcussy indeed.' He let go of her hand and opened the door of the shed. 'I keep everything,' he said, waving a wand-like arm at towers of yellowing newspaper stacked in the dim interior. 'And it's all in order.'

'Oh for goodness' sake, Marcus. Tessa doesn't want to see your ludicrous hoard of tabloid vitriol,' Penelope said.

'I do actually,' Tessa said. 'It looks fascinating.'

'Yeah, Dad – but maybe later,' Paul said. 'Why don't we show Tessa the end of the garden? Before it rains.'

'Evasive as ever,' said Penelope acidly. She followed them through the roses to an archway cut into a tall box hedge. 'Yes, this end of the garden is rather special, we think.'

Through the archway was a circular patio surrounded by a neat mosaic of flowerbeds. A white wrought-iron table and chairs stood there, and in one of the chairs sat a regal old lady, looking at Tessa with azure-blue, expectant eyes. She wore a full-skirted dress of royal blue velvet, sweeping to the floor, a high lace collar and lace cuffs. On the table in front of her was an oak box, wide open, showing an array of embroidery silks in colours as bright as the roses. She smiled right into Tessa's questioning eyes. The noise of London faded as if heavy folk-weave curtains had been drawn around the secluded garden. Tessa forgot about Paul and his parents. She wanted to talk to this intriguing old lady.

'Hello,' Tessa said, and smiled warmly. She held out her hand. 'I'm Tessa.'

A bewildered silence hovered behind her.

'Who are you saying hello to?' Penelope asked.

'The lady in the royal blue dress. Is she your grandmother?' Tessa asked. 'Is this her special garden?'

Penelope's high cheekbones went white. 'There's nobody there,' she said firmly.

But Marcus clasped his hands together like a child who'd been given a present. 'Can you describe this lady?' he asked.

'She's beautiful, and so tranquil, like a lily,' Tessa said eagerly. 'And I'd really like to talk to her, and look at the box of silks she's got – but I don't think she's hearing me – it's like she's – she's somehow in a place beyond – beyond this world.' She felt her voice wavering like a reflection on water. Something similar was happening to the lady in the royal blue dress. The image of her trembled, shimmered, and vanished. Only her eyes lingered momentarily, and some words drifted in, 'We must talk. Here in the garden – in the garden.'

Tessa found herself looking at an empty chair and table.

Marcus bombarded her with questions. 'What kind of blue dress?' 'What hairstyle?' 'Who was she?' Anger and confusion closed in on her, from Paul, and Penelope.

She'd made a terrible mistake. It was irreversible. In front of Paul's difficult mother and his dad who looked like a wizard. Tessa felt it was a catastrophe. But why should it be? She hadn't done anything wrong. Why, suddenly, was she under attack? A lethal mix of conflicting emotions overwhelmed her. She pushed Paul away. 'Leave me alone. All of you. I need to be alone.'

She slumped into the empty chair, her head in her hands.

'Come on – pull yourself together, Tessa.'

Tessa looked up at Paul with tormented eyes – hoping to see some empathy. There was none, his stance judgemental and annoyed. He put his head close to hers and hissed, 'Did you HAVE to start that mumbo jumbo stuff here? In front of Mum and Dad? It was humiliating for me. What about me? What about my feelings?'

Tessa jumped to her feet and fled through the rose garden, up the steps and back into the drawing room. She grabbed her bag and ran out of the front door and away, down the leafy street. She wasn't running away from Penelope. She was running away from her own anger, leaving it circling through the rose garden.

'Ah – you can't afford pride.' Herbie put a chipped blue and white mug on the table in front of Freddie. 'That's a good brew. Stand the spoon up in it, you could. Cure anything, my tea. The missus don't make it like that. "Don't be so extravagant, Herb," she'd say.'

Freddie eyed the steaming, orange-coloured tea. 'Did you put sugar in it?'

'Ah – six spoonfuls – that'll sort you out.'

''Tis tooth-rot,' Freddie said, but he wrapped his hands around the familiar old mug and sipped gratefully, feeling the hot, sweet liquid warming his shaking body. He'd dragged himself as far as the stonemason's yard and found Herbie, covered in dust, chipping away at a slab of Portland stone. Herbie's shrewd eyes had noted Freddie's flushed cheeks and trembling hands.

'What's up with you?' he'd asked, steering Freddie into his office.

'I dunno.' Freddie sat down, gingerly, on a chair which was tied together with baler twine. 'I had a funny turn – in the Post Office. Couldn't get out of there fast enough. Didn't even get me stamps or pay the phone bill.'

'Why didn't you tell someone you was ill?'

Freddie shook his head miserably. 'I felt silly. Getting in this state over nothing. To tell you the truth, it frightened the hell out of me, Herb. I thought I were gonna drop dead like me father did.'

Herbie had made him the cup of strong tea in silence, then handed it to him with the advice about pride. 'Fag?' he asked, offering a packet of Embassy. 'Go on, it'll calm you down.'

Freddie had given up smoking after being ill with bronchitis. 'Ah – I wish I could,' he said, 'but if I had one fag I'd be back on twenty a day in no time. I miss it. A good smoke used to calm me down.'

Herbie's dog, Jilly, crept out of her basket and leaned against Freddie's legs, looking up at him adoringly. As soon as he touched her silky head, Freddie felt better. But there was still the distance between him and home. How could he possibly tell Herbie, or anyone, that he was frightened to walk home? He wished Kate was there, and he wished they still had Jonti. Jonti would have escorted him home briskly and cheerfully, like a nurse.

'Kate's away, isn't she?' Herbie asked.

Freddie nodded. 'Gone to fetch her mother from Gloucestershire.'

'And Tessa – where's she?'

'Gone to London.'

'London!' Herbie bit back the questions he wanted to ask. The two men sat in silence, as they'd often done over mugs of tea, this time contemplating the evils of London.

'I'm gonna take you home,' Herbie announced, taking the keys to his pick-up truck from a nail on the wall.

Relief flooded into Freddie's mind. He finished his tea and climbed thankfully into the front seat of the truck, his feet wedged between boxes of tools and oily rags. Jilly jumped into the back, barking and wagging her tail.

'I'll just tell the missus where I'm going.' Herbie went into the house at the end of the yard, and emerged five minutes later, looking furtive and determined. *He's up to something*, Freddie thought.

He soon found out what Herbie had stealthily done. A few minutes after he'd settled down in his chair by the window, Freddie was alarmed and irritated to see Dr Jarvis walking up the path with that ominous doctor's bag in his hand.

'Herbie rang me, Freddie,' he said, coming in uninvited and assessing Freddie with those all-seeing eyes. 'He said you'd had a funny turn.'

'I wouldn't have called you, doctor,' Freddie said.

'I know you wouldn't. Good job you've got a friend like Herbie.' Dr Jarvis unpacked his stethoscope. 'Let's have a listen.'

Freddie rolled his shirt up, reluctantly. He was frightened of what the doctor might find. He'd rather not know. Rather just get on with life and forget about the funny turn.

'Your lungs are all right – and your heart is steady, if a bit too rapid,' Dr Jarvis said. He shook his thermometer and took Freddie's temperature, then his blood pressure. 'Everything is all right – normal,' he said, and sat down at the table. 'So what exactly happened?'

Freddie was silent. Pictures of his mother, Annie, loomed in his mind. 'Don't tell the doctor,' she'd insisted after one of her panic attacks. 'He'll say I'm mental and then they can shut me up in an asylum.' Annie had drummed that into him. An asylum was the 'mad house'. The final punishment. Like Hell and Damnation, only worse.

Dr Jarvis was looking at him enquiringly.

'Well – I'm all right now,' Freddie said. 'Since Herbie gave me a cup of sugary tea. I didn't have no lunch, see. That can make you shaky – can't it?'

'Indeed it can. Low blood sugar. Why no lunch?'

'Kate's away – and I couldn't be bothered.'

Dr Jarvis tutted and started packing up his medical bag. 'Are you sure it's not anxiety? Like your mother had?'

'Oh no – definitely not.' Freddie looked at him steadily, hoping the shrewd old doctor couldn't see the denial in his eyes. He was relieved to see him go, leaving Freddie with a hastily scribbled prescription in his hand. A tonic. The same kind of square shouldered glass bottle of a foul-tasting iron tonic that Dr Jarvis gave everyone.

'I'm afraid she's gone home.' Breathing hard, Paul looked down at the laden tea trolley in the drawing room. The best bone china tea set. The moist slices of ginger parkin, the dainty triangles of egg mayonnaise sandwiches, the expensive tin of Fortnum and Mason biscuits. He reached out and took a chocolate one.

'Wait until you've got a plate,' snapped Penelope. 'We don't want crumbs on the carpet.'

'I haven't dropped a single crumb. Promise.'

'You're the only person I know who can infuse the simple act of eating a biscuit with such appalling arrogance,' complained Penelope. 'And what's the matter with Tessa? Such disappointing behaviour after you said she was so wonderful.'

'She was just overwhelmed, Mother dear, plus being nervous about meeting you.'

'Nervous? Well, she'll have to get over that.'

'She will,' Paul said, more confidently than he felt. He'd chased Tessa down the street and around the corner, but when he'd seen her disappear into the tube station, he'd given up and gone home to face his parents.

'We'll have to have tea without her. How tiresome.' Penelope handed him a plate and a napkin. 'Your father's in the kitchen scrubbing the skin off his hands. He was about to rummage through those dreadful newspapers and unearth something (controversial I don't doubt) to show Tessa. As for the lady in the chair – Paul, that really spooked me. There was nobody there – nobody. But—'

'But what?'

'We all know the person Tessa described – my grandmother, Violetta. She lived, and died, in this house, Paul. That velvet dress is in a trunk in the loft. Have you shown Tessa a picture of her?'

'No. Never. Haven't even got one.'

'Then – how did she know?' Penelope's eyes narrowed, demanding an answer.

'Tessa's got a vivid imagination.'

Penelope looked sceptical. 'No. It's more than that. She's WEIRD. She's not normal, Paul, and I don't want her here. That kind of thing belongs in a gypsy caravan at a fair. Not here.'

'Don't be judgemental, Mother dear. If you take the trouble to get to know Tessa, you'll find she's actually very caring and capable. She cares enough to work with special needs children.'

'Hmm – she'll soon lose her job if she goes around seeing ghosts.'

'She won't, and she doesn't.'

'Have you met her family?'

'No. Not yet.'

'For all you know, they could be gypsies – living out in the country like that. Bucolic, and weird.'

'Her dad is a lorry driver and a sculptor, and her mum was a nurse, an SRN.'

'Well, they haven't made a good job of raising Tessa, have they? If she behaves like that and then runs off. It's the height of bad manners.'

Marcus appeared in the doorway, in his socks, a newspaper in his now pink, scrubbed hand. 'Wait 'til you read this!' he gloated. 'Haven't I told you how important it is to keep information? I knew exactly where to find this newspaper.' Marcus sidled up to Paul and pushed the paper under his nose. 'There you are! That's your wonderful Tessa.'

Paul blinked at the photo of Tessa washing her hair in the fountain at Trafalgar Square back in October. *Hippie Goddess Bares All.* 'I know about this, Dad. It's history. Why rake it up?'

Penelope sat down, the newspaper in her hand. 'It's even worse than I thought,' she said tersely. 'Scandalous. And you say you knew about it? How can you even THINK about associating with that girl? She's a dirty, rebellious hippie and I won't have her in OUR family.'

'That's a shame,' Paul glared at his mother, hating her, 'because, like it or not, Mother dear, I intend to marry Tessa.'

There was a fractured silence, and the three of them turned to see Tessa standing in the doorway, her eyes blazing with defiance.

'Sorry,' she said, 'I just freaked.'

'Freaked?' Penelope's eyebrows disappeared into her fringe. 'Freaked!' she repeated, picking the word up in disgust as if it were a dead mouse being dropped into the dustbin, by its tail.

Tessa remembered her mother's unique gift of blending grace with courage, using those bright brown eyes to bewitch people. She thought of her father and his silences, the way he would quietly say, 'Now you listen to me,' and everyone did listen, hypnotised by his simple power. *I can be both of them*, she thought, *if I tell the truth with eloquence and joy*.

She picked up the newspaper Marcus had put on the black glass coffee table. 'Yes – this is me,' she said, deliberately putting sparkle into her eyes as she looked around at the three of them. 'And I'm proud of what I did. I was homeless, and broken-hearted at the time, and I simply needed to wash my hair so that I could go to a job interview. I'm proud of my hippie friends for helping me. I got the job, and it's a super job, with children who need my depth of understanding.' She paused, seeing the three faces as if they were painted on a window looking in at her. Penelope was open-mouthed, Marcus gazing adoringly, Paul frowning in alarm. 'I'm proud of who I am,' Tessa continued, 'and, yes, I do see spirit people. It's a gift, not a curse, a God-given gift, and I intend to use it. I'm a warrior, you see, a warrior of the rainbow.

This earth, and its people are in trouble. The trees are dying, the birds are dying. The delicate, exquisite web of life is collapsing. It's your planet. Don't you care?'

Silence.

Tessa's cheeks burned. Paul's frown was transforming into an awestruck grin. She sailed on like a ship with golden sails, set free by the winds of truth.

'Why don't you see the good in me?' she demanded, 'instead of condemning me for something you don't understand. Accept me for who I am – because if you don't, I want nothing more to do with this family. And as for gypsies – I've met Romany Gypsies, and hippies, and I'd rather live like they do, lovingly and with respect for our planet than live – like – like this!' She waved her long creative fingers at the porcelain-laden sideboard. 'Life is not about STUFF. It's about being and doing and caring.'

The silence was now in a thousand twinkling pieces.

Then Marcus gave an appreciative little cheer and clapped his hands. 'Magnificent!'

'No one asked your opinion, Marcus.' Penelope looked shell-shocked.

'And – just for the record ' Tessa added, 'I have not agreed to marry Paul.'

CHAPTER 10

The Ring

Tessa lay awake in her narrow bed in Nottingham Place. It was three o'clock in the morning. Her window was open, with a sooty wind wafting the curtains. She could hear the gurgle of rain falling on the street and the scrabbling of mice picking holes in the trash bags stacked on the landing outside her door. There were mice in her cupboard under the sink, squeaking fiercely as they scurried along the pipes and out into the stairwell.

She'd learned to disentangle meaningful sounds from the constant roar of the London traffic; the lone quacking of a duck in the park; the wind in the plane trees; the rain. Always it was the rain that loosened the confines of the city, allowing her to dream, to go home to Monterose, to the garden of The Pines where the rain would be pure and silver, scattering rhinestones over the hedges, turning the Mill Stream to a foaming torrent twisting around the roots of willow and poplar. Rain falling on her abandoned field, seeping through the grass and into the lane where the puddles pulsed with rings from the raindrops. At home she would hear the unearthly yelping of foxes, the hooting of owls, and the voices of trees. As a child she had learned that the four winds had different personalities. The South wind tasted of orange groves; the North wind smelled of snow and the ruffled fur of wolves; the East wind was bitter and smoky. Tessa's favourite was the West wind, tasting of sea-salt and heather, its voice a symphony of psalms from distant islands. Together, the wind and the rain brought to her the world beyond London, its rolling blues and greens, its cottages with coral lights in windows. The West wind made her homesick.

Tessa got up and sat in the open window, a candlewick dressing gown wrapped around her shoulders. She tried to taste the sea on the West wind as it freckled her cheeks with rain. It tasted sour. Tasted of London.

The ache of homesickness filled her body and soul, as if there was no room for any other kind of feeling. She badly needed to talk to Dorothy. The Samaritans were open day and night. She didn't want to use the tenants' payphone in the hall. It was too public. Everyone in the building would eavesdrop on her distress. Going out would involve getting dressed and braving the night streets to find a phone box. Not worth the risk of getting mugged.

She switched the light on, stuck a shilling in the meter, and lit the gas ring. There was no kettle in her bedsit, so she boiled water in a chipped enamel saucepan and made hot chocolate, adding some Carnation milk from a tin. With her hands wrapped around the mug she sat in the window again, watching the street light making orange cobwebs in the filigree branches of a birch tree. She could see its tiny catkins and the swelling buds on the ends of twigs. It was nearly Easter. Summer was coming. And how could she bear to be in London?

Everything. Every single thought was a sharp pain of longing.

One more week of the school term. Then holiday. A black hole.

No Easter eggs. No picnics in the bluebell wood. No going out in the morning sun and finding a hen proudly parading a clutch of newly hatched chicks. The joy of picking one up and feeling it tremble in her cupped hands, seeing the black spark of its eye, hearing its plaintive cheeping.

Everything hurt. Everything.

I have to escape, Tessa thought. *From London, and from myself. Find the spring. And the light on the water.*

She spent an hour writing a poem, trying to sculpt with words a picture of her longing. She felt the dawn long before it came, and it was the dawning of an idea. A rescue. She had to rescue herself. Again!

Excited, she took a map down from the bookshelf and unfolded it on the bed. The way out of London. The way to a beach where the West wind made sparkles on the waves. Her eyes were drawn to the south. Brighton! She'd go to

Brighton. It was Saturday. But Paul wanted her to walk in Regent's Park with him. After lunch, he'd said. Tessa frowned. It didn't feel right. She'd leave him a note, pinned to the door.

At five in the morning Tessa finally went back to bed and slept heavily until she was woken at eight o'clock by a pigeon tapping on the window with his beak. She smiled and got out of bed to give him some biscuit crumbs. The pigeon had become a friend. Sometimes he would even walk in through the sash window on his little pink feet. He listened attentively to everything Tessa told him, making mysterious crooning sounds in his throat and watching her with one bright eye. She called him Toby.

'I'm going to Brighton!' she told him as he walked about on the crumbling window sill, his plumage iridescent with pinks and greens in the morning sun.

She lit the gas ring and made herself a fried egg sandwich and a coffee. Then she fished out the sea-green bikini, rolled it in a towel and put it into her rucksack with half a packet of chocolate digestives and a banana. She scribbled a note for Paul, folded it and pinned it to the outside of her door with a brass drawing pin.

With an old forgotten feeling of freedom and adventure, she swung her rucksack onto her back and headed for Victoria Station.

'Where the hell have you been?' Paul was standing, white-faced, in the street as Tessa returned from Brighton. Her eyes were bright and her complexion rosy and fresh from a day in the sun on Brighton beach. Her pockets were full of interesting chalk pebbles and sun-bleached bits of driftwood. She felt happy, until she saw the look on Paul's face.

'Brighton!'

'Brighton.' Paul digested the word as if it was a jail sentence.

'What's wrong with Brighton?' Tessa felt her smile disappearing under a stone. But she was unprepared for what happened next.

'THIS is what's wrong with Brighton!' Without warning, Paul slapped her across the side of her face, so hard that she fell sideways against the railings. Stunned and bewildered, she slid to the floor, clutching her face. She stared wildly at the man who was supposed to love her.

Blood was running from a cut above her eye where she had hit the railings. 'Look what you made me do,' she yelled, getting to her feet. 'How dare you hit me in the street like that, Paul. I haven't done anything wrong! I had a lovely day in Brighton. What's got into you?'

'How dare YOU go swanning off to bloody Brighton?' Paul shouted. 'I thought we agreed to walk in Regent's Park. I came all the way here and waited around for nothing.'

'I left you a note.'

'I don't want your bloody note.' Paul fished it from his pocket, screwed it into a ball and flung it into the gutter. The sight of Tessa cowering away from him seemed to ignite another volley of rage. Aware that people in the street were watching him, he lowered his voice to a rasping whisper and moved his face close to hers. 'YOU are going to let me in, make me a coffee, and bloody well explain yourself, woman.'

'Don't call me woman.'

'Bitch then! BITCH.'

Tessa felt scorched by the closeness of his anger. What had she done? She didn't understand. And why didn't he care that her eye was bleeding and she was now shaking violently? Terrified, she backed against the railings and began to sidle up the steps. Get to the door, then shut him out was her plan. She didn't want to be alone in her room with Paul in that mood.

The communal front door was usually left open and off the latch during the daytime, then locked at night. Tessa paused on the top step, pressing a screwed-up tissue to her wounded eyebrow. Then she moved quickly, in through the door, whipping around to shut Paul out, her hand on the Yale lock, her heart pounding with fear. But she hadn't moved fast enough.

'Oh no you don't.' Paul heaved at the door. 'You are NOT going to shut me out, you bitch.'

They scuffled, one each side of the heavy old door, and Tessa fell backwards, screaming. 'No, Paul. No. Get away from me. Leave me alone.'

'What's going on here?' The landlord came up the steps from his basement flat in a cloud of sour-smelling pipe smoke. For once, Tessa was glad to see him, even though he was glaring fiercely at both of them. She pulled herself up and clung to the hall table. 'Is this man hassling you?' he asked, looking up at Paul with bulldog eyes. Paul was visibly crumpling in the presence of this solid little man who stood there calmly in a pair of leather slippers, baggy trousers held up with braces, and a nicotine-impregnated tweed jacket with very square shoulder pads.

Paul's eyes were silently threatening Tessa, daring her to speak.

'Will you please tell me what's going on?' repeated the landlord. 'This is my house, and I will not have this kind of rumpus.'

Tessa's voice trembled. 'I just came back from Brighton – I've done nothing wrong.'

'Alcohol,' said the landlord. 'It's a curse on society.'

'I haven't been drinking,' Tessa said, and burst into tears. 'Why should I have to stand here like a cornered animal? I've done nothing wrong.'

'That's right, turn on the tears,' said Paul nastily.

The landlord looked at him contemptuously. 'Right – you – out. Out of my house and don't come back. Go on. Go. There's the door.'

Paul backed away from the bulldog eyes. Throwing Tessa a look of seething resentment, he left in two long strides and the Yale lock snapped shut behind him.

'And you . . .' The landlord turned to Tessa, his voice gentler. '. . . I suggest you go upstairs and get that eye seen to. Have you got some first aid?'

'Yes.'

'Well, go on then. And make sure this never happens again.'

'I'm sorry,' Tessa said. 'I couldn't help it – and I have to work on Monday!'

The landlord looked at her hard, as if he wanted to say a lot more. He relit his pipe and blew clouds of smoke into the hall. 'I'm not going to get involved. As long as you're all right. Are you?'

'Yes – thanks – I'll be fine,' Tessa said, but she didn't feel fine. She felt abused. She climbed the stairs on trembling legs, glad to reach the sanctuary of her small bedsit. Still with the tissue pressed to her eyebrow, she curled up on the bed and stared out at the grey London sky. She'd come home from Brighton feeling good, her mind full of pictures of the sparkling water and the steeply shelving pebble beach. Paul had taken it all from her. He had sucked the joy from her spirit.

Tessa spent Sunday in a state of tension. Paul had a habit of lying in bed until mid-morning so she felt safe for the first few hours of the day. She arranged her Brighton beach treasures on the window sill where the early sunshine lit the strangely shaped chalk pebbles. *Dad would love them*, she thought. *I could get him a big lump of chalk to carve.* And again – the homesickness. What would her dad say about the cut over her eye? What if he knew about the way Paul had treated her? *He'll never know*, she vowed.

She went for an early walk in Regent's Park and gazed at crocuses opening their saffron-hearted blooms to the sun.

Was it over with Paul? Would she have to admit to failure? Failure to sustain a relationship? Failure to be a normal person, a normal girl who wanted marriage and babies. Kate had only spoken to Paul on the phone and thought he was wonderful, and as for the wedding bells, it was Kate and not Tessa who had stars in her eyes. *I can't let her down*, Tessa kept thinking. Her walk around the park was like a drawing she had studied by her favourite artist, Paul Klee. An ink drawing entitled *Flight from Oneself*. It was how her walking felt now. Harder and faster, more and more desperate, but never, ever fast enough or strong enough to escape from herself. The old, creative Tessa was trapped inside a new chrysalis built from endless skeins of people-pleasing and duty and responsibility. It hung by a thread in a hard dark corner.

Mid-morning, she returned to Nottingham Place, dreading to find Paul angrily waiting. But he wasn't there. Perhaps he'd given up on her, she thought, with mixed feelings. She paid her rent and the bulldog eyes looked at her through the hatch in an unfriendly way. 'Make sure that young man comes and goes quietly in future,' he said. 'Otherwise I'll be giving you a week's notice.'

Tessa blanched. Dumped by Paul. Chucked out of her flat. It spelled failure. She'd made the tiny room into a cosy nest. The sun streamed through the window, and there was Toby, her little pigeon friend. 'Please don't do that,' she said. 'I really like it here and I need to stay.'

The bulldog eyes misted over as he searched the light in her pale blue gaze. Light was something he'd given up on long ago. The moment of eye contact was fragile, but Tessa sensed the shadow of unhealed pain in him. She felt he liked her, but no longer knew how to express the concept of liking someone. It was a soul thing, a hopeless longing for an angel. *All his angels are cardboard*, she thought, watching his fat fingers signing the rent book. He handed it back with a dismissive grunt.

She spent the rest of Sunday reading and sleeping, snacking on biscuits and coffee. There was no sign of Paul.

But in the morning, in the Monday rush hour, Paul was waiting for her outside Baker Street tube station, shamefaced, a gift-packed red rose in his hand. 'Forgive me, darling. I don't know what came over me. I shouldn't have hurt you like that.' He reached out and tenderly ran a finger over the cut above her eye which she'd tried to disguise with makeup. 'Friends?' he asked as she stared at him.

'Friends,' she affirmed reluctantly, and watched the light flood back into his eyes. She imagined him as a lonely, embittered old man, like the landlord, with shadows steeped in nicotine.

'Thank God,' Paul said. 'I had such a miserable day yesterday. Couldn't even play music. All I could think of was losing you. I'd be gutted, Tessa. I need you in my life. You're the best thing that ever happened to me. Please don't dump me for one flash of bad temper. I'd never, ever hurt you again. Please believe me.'

'It's okay, Paul – but I'm on my way to work.'

'Yeah – I know. Give us a kiss then.'

He kissed her with unusual tenderness, and Tessa felt an odd mix of relief and confusion. The brilliance of her day in Brighton sped past her like a lost window of freedom, closing now, as if she'd been a canary let out of its cage, just for one day, to taste the salt wind, to discover the wings within her soul, wings that could fly, only to creep home at the end of the day to the safe cage.

I don't hate Paul, she thought as she sat on the tube train, jammed in with remote-eyed commuters. *I just don't love him the way I loved Art. And now I don't trust him either.*

Tessa had always wanted jewellery. Wood and plastic wouldn't do. It had to sparkle. As a child she'd played for hours with her mother's necklace of clear faceted crystal, especially if she could have it out in the sunshine, letting it slip through her fingers and make rainbows on her skin and on Jonti's white fur. 'It's only glass,' Kate told her. 'You don't want glass – diamonds are better,' and she'd shown Tessa her diamond engagement ring and explained how Freddie had given it to her on the edge of the sea when he'd proposed. Tessa loved to gaze into the window of the pawnbroker's shop in Monterose, and study the rings. She wanted one so much. 'Certainly not,' Kate had said firmly. 'Children don't have rings.'

'Why not?'

'Because rings are valuable and expensive.'

'Why?'

'Because the stones have to be dug out of the rocks.'

'But, Mummy, there's a green one, and a red one. How can stones be bright colours?'

'Oh, I don't know, dear, but they are. That green one is an emerald, and the red one is a ruby.'

Tessa had frowned, imagining far below her feet the rocks of Planet Earth full of bright, winking coloured stones. 'Does the Queen have them in her crown?'

'Yes, she does.'

'Why?'

'Because she's rich, and important.'

'But why, Mummy? Why can the Queen have rubies and emeralds when she's got arms and legs and a face like me? Why can't I have a ring, a real one?'

Kate would get exasperated and drag Tessa away from the pawnbroker's window. 'Don't be so tiresome.'

In the Coronation year of 1953, Tessa had spent hours making a St Edward's Crown out of a Primula Cheese box. Annie had given her scraps of velvet and silk, and sequins. Freddie contributed pipe cleaners for the structure of the crown, and Tessa had glued and stitched, pricked her finger and cried, but worked obsessively until she'd finished the glittering model. Kate still had the lopsided crown on the dresser at home.

But no one had ever given Tessa a ring. Lucy had one, out of a cracker, with an impressive sparkly 'stone', and Tessa had begged and begged to be allowed to have it. Finally Lucy had swapped it for a windmill on Weymouth beach. Tessa had spent an ecstatic hour with the dazzling ring on her small finger, then lost it in the sea, and cried bitterly for the rest of the day.

Now she had a few sets of ethnic beads, her silver charm bracelet, and the precious amber bead that Art had given her. She still couldn't pass a jeweller's window without gazing and dreaming, and one day, in Portobello Road market, a stall appeared with fascinating displays of tumbled gemstones. The dark-eyed man who was selling them had a stone-tumbler running, polishing pebbles. Glad to be on her own, Tessa spent a long time browsing, picking up stone after shiny stone, liking the colours, the mysterious patterns within the translucent gems. They had labels with words she'd never heard, like agate, obsidian, tourmaline and lapis-lazuli. There was a pink one she particularly liked. She didn't understand how a rock could be pink.

'That's rose quartz,' the man said, 'it's the kindness crystal.'

Tessa looked at him in surprise. He was hippyish, she thought, with dreadlocks, silver bangles and a silver necklet with an enormous turquoise stone.

'The kindness crystal? What do you mean?'

His eyes lit up at her interest. 'You can use gemstones for healing,' he said. 'They have different frequencies and energies. Here – feel this one.' He put a smooth purple stone into the palm of Tessa's hand. 'Close your eyes,' he advised, 'it helps your awareness to kick in.'

Tessa stood there, mesmerised, holding the purple stone. The moment she closed her eyes she felt a cool, calm vibration from deep within the stone. She didn't want to put it down. 'What is this?' she asked, remembering that Portobello Market was not the sort of place to stand around with your eyes closed.

'Amethyst,' he said, and added, 'from Cornwall.'

'Cornwall?'

'Oh yes. Cornwall is full of crystals – deep in the rocks.'

Tessa opened her eyes in astonishment. She'd spent the whole summer there, without knowing about gems like this amethyst hidden in the rocks beneath her feet.

'Are you drawn to that one?' he asked, watching her reluctantly replacing it on its tray.

'Yes.'

'Then you should have it. Amethyst is brilliant for fear and anxiety. It's the calming crystal.'

She had to have it. 'How much is it?'

'A shilling.'

'I've got to pay my rent.' Tessa searched in her purse, found two sixpences, and handed them over. She watched the man lovingly wrap her precious amethyst in white tissue paper.

'Don't let anyone else handle it,' he warned. 'Keep it only for yourself, a secret amulet. I keep mine in a little bag – always with me.' He pulled a faded velvet pouch from his top pocket. 'I've got carnelian, for my solar plexus, rose quartz for kindness, and a fluorite for happiness.'

'And what's that blue stone round your neck?' Tessa asked, intrigued.

'Aw – that's turquoise – real turquoise – as used by the

Native Americans. It's a sacred stone. It holds the knowledge of the ancient world. You should have one,' he added seductively, 'to match your very lovely turquoise eyes.'

'I'd love one – but not today,' Tessa said, carefully putting the tissue-wrapped amethyst in the inner pocket of her bag. She lingered, wanting more of this man's unique knowledge. 'How do you know so much about crystals?'

'It's my passion,' he said. 'I've travelled the world collecting them. My name's Nick, by the way – and yours?'

'Tessa.'

'Well, Tessa – I hope to see you again sometime. I run workshops on crystal healing. You'd be good at it, I can tell.' Nick's eyes were magnetic as he studied her face, then he rummaged in a tin with a dented cream lid, and produced a leaflet. 'What I'm teaching is ground-breaking. You're welcome to come on one.'

'I might do that, thanks – Nick.' Tessa took the leaflet and tucked it away to study later.

She debated whether to tell Paul about her exciting discovery. *He won't like it*, she thought sadly, *and he'll think Nick was chatting me up.*

Keep it secret, she decided.

The first of many secrets she needed to hide from Paul.

'I hate my mother.' Paul picked up his violin with an angry flick of his arm. He settled it under his chin, and Tessa watched his expression change from hating Penelope to loving music. She didn't ask him why. By now she was used

you, Tessa, the day we fished you out of the sea in Cornwall. I – loved you – yes – loved you, fell in love with you the minute I saw you. I made myself learn to play the Bruch concerto, for you, so that one day I could play it to you, perfectly, and – and give you – this.' He uncurled his long musical fingers to reveal a small, dark blue velvet box in the palm of his hand.

'Paul!' Tessa gasped in surprise. At last! She was to be given a ring! And in that moment she again saw Violetta, the azure-blue eyes looking over Paul's shoulder, looking down at the ring box like a mother watching a child unwrap a most treasured gift. *It's her ring!* Tessa thought instantly. She didn't dare tell Paul. Keeping it to herself was so hard, almost impossible, for it was stunning to encounter a loving spirit, a spirit who loved Paul, who had always loved him since he was tiny. She thought Violetta was an angel and a grandmother, and a gift of joy. Violetta had helped Paul to play the music. She was helping him now, eagerly, to give the ring, wanting to see it sparkle as if it had stayed locked away for years. A ring in waiting. For her.

'Open it, Tessa.' Paul was shaking with excitement.

Tessa picked up the tiny box, with reverence, her eyes glancing into his. She opened the hinged lid, and the ring inside came instantly to life.

'This is – unbelievable,' she whispered, looking down at the twinkling, deep purple stone. An amethyst. Set in rose-gold, with minute diamonds on each side. 'It's beautiful, and perfect.'

'It's not new,' Paul said. 'It belonged to my grandmother. She left it to me, and I hid it away for years, hoping I'd one day find you, Tessa.' He looked at her soulfully. 'Will you wear my ring? On THIS finger?' He took the ring finger of her left hand and kissed it tenderly. 'Will you? Will you marry me, Tessa?'

CHAPTER 11

Starlinda

'There's somebody up there, in Tessa's field.' Freddie stood at the landing window in The Pines. It had a view over the roof tops of Monterose towards the wooded hills beyond, and in the winter when the trees were bare it was possible to see the top edge of Tessa's field where it adjoined the wood. 'I can see smoke rising.'

'Not the first time, is it?' Kate said, joining him. 'Here, use Dad's field glasses.' She handed him Bertie's binoculars in their brown leather case.

Freddie put them to his eyes. 'Whoever it is has got no business up there, lighting a fire.'

'How long since you've been up there?' Kate asked.

'Not for a long time,' Freddie said guiltily. He hadn't been to the field since his panic attack. In fact, he hadn't walked anywhere. 'We should go and take a look,' he said, 'before dark.'

'I've got a cake in the oven,' Kate said. 'You go.'

'I don't intend to confront anyone, not on me own,' Freddie said. 'It could be Romanies, or it could be hippies.'

Kate took the binoculars back. 'Let me have a look. Are you sure the smoke's in Tessa's field? Or is it in the edge of the wood? It could be the forestry people.'

'No,' Freddie said. 'That wood's been sold. Herbie told me. The woods along the hill were part of Mileswood estate, and they've been split up into small plots and sold to private buyers, and some of them have ruined the wood. Cut it all down. Breaks my heart to see it.'

'And the nightingales don't come any more,' Kate said. 'We didn't hear them once last summer, did we?'

'No one seems to care,' Freddie said. 'If they go on like that, the day will come when those hills will be barren, and our ancient woods gone forever. Our bluebell wood. Granny Barcussy's cottage is up there somewhere on the other side of the wood. I used to go up to it through the sheep fields, but it's hard to work out which section of the wood it's in now, and who owns it. If I'd had the money, I'd have bought it and done it up. Last time I saw it, the roof had fallen in. It's nothing but an overgrown ruin now – breaks my heart.'

'You took the girls up there a few times, didn't you?' Kate asked.

'I did – and they loved it. I used to sit on a log and think about Granny Barcussy. She was wonderful to me. Lucy and Tessa used to play inside the ruined cottage – they thought it was magic. Especially Tessa. You know what she was like. She even told me she could see Granny Barcussy in there.'

'We should tell Tessa what's happening to the woods. She might get her hippie friends to come with *SAVE THE TREES* banners.'

'That doesn't work,' Freddie said. 'It didn't save the station, did it?'

'No.' Kate looked sad. She and Susan and half the population of Monterose had campaigned with banners to stop the station being closed under the Beeching cuts. It had changed the town, and changed the community.

'I'll pop up to the field in the lorry,' Freddie said.

Kate looked surprised. 'Have you given up walking?' she asked. 'You always enjoyed a good walk.'

Freddie mumbled an excuse and went out. He hoped he'd never have to tell Kate about his panic attack. He wanted to be strong and reliable for her, not someone who couldn't even walk home on his own.

He started the lorry, noting that the fuel gauge was low, and drove it down through Monterose and up the lane to Tessa's field. The thin column of smoke expired as he pulled into the gateway. Someone had seen him arrive and put the fire out. Taking his mother's ebony walking stick from the cab, he climbed the locked gate and padded upwards close to the hedge. Goldfinches bobbed ahead of him, pausing to feed on teazels and thistle heads. Pathetically few, Freddie thought, remembering the vast flocks he'd seen in his youth.

He counted them. Seven. *Seven goldfinches left in the world*, he thought, *and where are the yellowhammers and linnets?*

Halfway up he paused, looked back at the comforting sight of his lorry, then at the edge of the wood, and between the trees a shadow moved swiftly, and in silence. The shadow of a man in black, with a black hat pulled down over his brow. Instantly Freddie had goosebumps along his arms and up the back of his neck. The winter afternoon was still, each blade of grass crisp like a carefully pencilled drawing. Down on the Levels, mist crept across the fields, tinged by the last pink hour of sun.

Someone was watching him, he was sure. *Pretend you haven't noticed*, he thought, and walked on, pleased to see the young trees he had planted sticking up out of the rough grass. Lime, oak and beech, now about six foot high. Their fallen leaves lay round each sapling and filled the wire rabbit guards. Freddie touched the tightly closed ruby red bud of a lime tree. It felt good to have grown them from seed.

He walked on, determined to go right to the top, watching the copse with a sidelong glance. Whoever it was didn't want to be discovered. There was no further movement, only the uncomfortable sensation of being watched. Freddie thought about the times when he had seen spirit people. Was this a spirit? He didn't think so.

The wood had always been fenced off by a simple barrier of posts and wire, low enough to step over. Freddie was shocked to see a brand new fence glinting in the sunlight, higher than his head, the dense wire netting ferociously topped with two taut strands of barbed wire. A notice painted in red on an old door said *PRIVATE LAND. NO SHOOTING*. He could hear the blackbirds in the wood making a fuss, sending warning cries zipping through the wintry silence.

Freddie had always felt at home in the woods and fields. It was his homeland. Why this hostile fence? He walked along it, touching the unfriendly wire, and right at the end, in the corner of the field, was a metal gate set into the fence. It was padlocked, and a well-trodden footpath led down towards the copse. Someone was fetching water from the spring. Someone living behind that new high fence.

It's HIM, Freddie thought. *It has to be him.*

'I'm not wearing that,' Tessa scowled at Penelope. She put the camel coloured suit firmly back on the rail.

'Why not?'

'I wouldn't be seen dead in it.'

'Open your eyes, dear,' said Penelope smoothly. 'This is a classic. I'm surprised you haven't already got one in your wardrobe. It's such good taste.'

'This one has our own exclusive label,' said the sales assistant who had been standing patiently. She turned the corner of the jacket and revealed the sleek satin label. 'It would make you look elegant and classy.'

'Won't you at least try it on?'

Tessa looked at Paul who sat in one of the green velvet chairs, his long legs crossed and his foot tapping the air in annoyance. 'Don't pressurise her, Mother dear,' he said. 'We only came in here for coffee!'

'I am not pressuring anyone. I know how to choose clothes. Now try this on, Tessa, please. You'll be surprised at how good you'll look.'

Tessa took the suit into a changing cubicle, resentment smouldering in her eyes. 'I can manage, thank you,' she hissed at the sales assistant who came teetering after her on her stilettos. She took off her skirt and coat, and slipped into the camel suit. The fabric felt smooth and expensive, and the satin lining slid easily over her bare arms. She looked at herself in the mirror, and a stranger stared back, a lost child in a camel jacket with huge shoulder pads, her embroidered white cheesecloth blouse looking crumpled and ridiculous inside the lapels of the jacket. It was the colour she hated.

'Stand up straight,' Penelope said as she appeared from behind the curtain, but Tessa stood limply, her mouth pursed, her arms hanging.

'Don't bully her, Mother dear.'

'It's a beautiful fit on you,' said the sales assistant. 'With a different blouse and some smart shoes, it will look perfect. It is a classic. I have two in my wardrobe. I wouldn't be without them.'

'I hate it,' Tessa said. 'And when would I wear it?'

'You're just being awkward,' Penelope said.

'No. I'm being honest. I hate the colour. And I wouldn't wear it at work. I work with special needs children and we all go to work in jeans.'

'Yes, but you'll be giving up that job when you marry into our family,' Penelope said.

'No, I will not.'

'Oh, you'll soon change your mind when you've got Paul to look after, and a house to run,' Penelope smiled patronisingly.

'We don't want that kind of life, Mother dear. This is the 1960s,' Paul said.

'We've got suits in other colours,' said the sales assistant. 'How about navy? Or bottle green?'

'No thanks. I need a colour with resonance and energy. Like aquamarine or apricot.'

'Apricot?' Penelope lowered her voice a whole octave, as if apricot was some kind of disease. 'But – how vulgar.'

'There's no demand for those kind of cheap colours in our store,' agreed the sales assistant. Ignoring the glare in Tessa's light blue eyes, she smoothed the camel jacket, tweaking and adjusting it to flatter Tessa's 38-24-38 figure. 'It really is nice on you. It's what everyone is wearing this season.'

'Excuse me – but I'm a person, not a ceramic mannequin,' said Tessa, twisting herself out of reach. 'And I'm taking this off.' She caught Paul's eyes gazing raptly at her and realised he was enjoying her standing up to his mother. She retreated to the cubicle and changed back into her denim skirt and her extravagant Afghan coat.

'Please don't waste your money on this, Penelope,' she said, handing the camel suit back to the sales assistant. 'I'll never wear it – I wouldn't be seen dead in it.'

An Arctic chill glazed Penelope's eyes. She tapped her fat cheque book on the counter. 'What do you think, Paul?'

'Me?' Paul looked uncomfortable and annoyed. 'I think you should put the cheque book away, Mother dear. Tessa likes to choose her own gear.'

'Gear? Paul, I'm merely trying to offer her some guidance on the kind of life she will have as a member of our family. I didn't expect rudeness and ingratitude.'

'She's just being honest, Mother dear.'

'Don't you speak to me in that patronising tone.'

The sales assistant stood awkwardly, arranging the camel suit back onto its hanger while Paul and Penelope argued in undertones. But Tessa was staring across the rails of clothing at a pair of bewitchingly powerful blue eyes. A Goddess in a white trouser suit was walking towards her, her golden hair tumbling softly around her shoulders, a bright turquoise, beaded bag sparkling, a pair of turquoise ankle boots peeping from under the flared white hem. Her aura was huge and magnetic, a drift of gold and aqua in the air around her, and she was looking directly at Tessa with those extraordinary eyes.

'Starlinda!'

Tessa felt so drawn to her that she almost ran across the store, weaving her way through the rails of clothes. As soon as she was close to Starlinda she felt different. Calm, and excited, and at home.

'Wonderful to see you, darling!' Starlinda gave her a jasmine-scented hug, then looked deeply into her eyes. It was like being unwrapped. The layers of anxiety and resentment flaked away, and the real Tessa began to emerge like a creature awakening from hibernation.

'Is Faye with you?' Tessa asked.

'No – she's at college, and I wouldn't get her in here. Portobello Road is her shopping place.'

Tessa smiled. 'Me too. It's been so long. I tried to ring you.'

'I've been in India.'

'India?'

Starlinda wasn't going to waste time on normal chitchat. She looked searchingly at Tessa. 'Who was it? Who hurt you so deeply?'

The eyes went on looking at her. They were full of light. Tessa felt stunned. 'Art,' she whispered.

Starlinda closed her eyes for a moment, then opened them again. 'Yes,' she said, as if in agreement. 'I see it. I see him. It's his karma. But you—' She put a warm hand on Tessa's arm, and the touch seemed to go right through her until it reached a place where she was still curled up in a ball of pain. 'You need to spend time with me, sweetheart. I can show you how to clear that pain forever, and use your gifts. You're so special. It's not by chance we met today.'

'It's an awkward time for me,' Tessa said, glancing round at Penelope and Paul.

'Ring me. Have you still got my number?'

'Yes.'

'Come and have a vegetarian supper with me – and we'll talk.'

'Okay.'

Penelope was bearing down on them. She looked disapprovingly at Starlinda's white trouser suit. But Paul's eyes lit up and he gazed at Starlinda as if he thought she was a film star. Tessa wanted to introduce her, but Starlinda threw them a contemptuous glance. 'I'm not going to engage with those two. I must dash. I've got an appointment.'

'But Paul is my fiancé,' Tessa said, flashing her engagement ring.

Starlinda didn't react like most people did, with warm wishes and congratulations. She stared at Tessa in silence for a moment. Then she opened the turquoise bag and took out a white diary with a golden pencil attached. 'How about Thursday evening? About six. Can you manage that?'

'Yes, I can.'

'See you then. Got to dash.' Starlinda turned and floated towards the lift, and when she had gone the store felt gloomy without her light, as if thick rain clouds had rolled over the sun.

'Who is SHE?' Paul asked, his eyes savouring the last glimpse of Starlinda disappearing into the lift. 'And where are we going on Thursday night?'

'That's Faye's mother. Starlinda.'

'Starlinda, eh? She looks like a film star. Why didn't you introduce her, Tessa?'

'Thank goodness you didn't,' said Penelope. 'I can't stand flamboyant women like her.'

'She's lovely,' Tessa said defensively. 'She's been very kind to me. And she's a clairvoyant medium.'

'WHAT?'

200

The rails of coats trembled with the shockwave from Penelope's disapproval. 'I hope you are not associating with such a person, Tessa. Wicked charlatans, that's what they are. Don't you dare ever bring HER near my family.'

'Sounds like we're going to dinner with her, Thursday night!' said Paul and his eyes danced mischievously. 'Isn't that right, Tessa?'

Penelope turned on him like a sand dune in a dust storm. 'You stay away from that woman, Paul. I won't have some witch in a white trouser suit getting her jasmine-scented claws into MY son.'

'Calm down, Mother dear. You're making a scene.'

'Paul wasn't invited anyway. I'm going on my own,' Tessa lifted her chin defiantly at Penelope, 'whether you like it or not.'

Tessa felt nervous as she rang Starlinda's doorbell. She didn't know why. Something major was going to happen, and she didn't feel ready. The feeling floated in and out of her mind as if it didn't belong there.

She heard voices, and Starlinda came to the door with a wealthy-looking woman with sculpted silver hair and a bright pink coat swathed in a pink silk scarf with pink elephants and little golden tassels around the edges. She gave Starlinda a hug. 'Thank you, my sweet angel. You've changed my life. I feel all joyful and exuberant!'

'Do come back if you need to,' Starlinda said confidentially. 'Enjoy the journey!'

'And who is this ANGEL?' asked the pink lady, looking at Tessa. Her gaze felt like an illuminating searchlight.

'I'm just an ordinary lump,' Tessa said, embarrassed.

The two women looked at each other. 'Watch this space,' Starlinda said confidently. 'This is Tessa.'

'Good luck, darling. Good luck on your journey,' crooned the pink lady and her eyes sparkled at Tessa.

'I'm not going anywhere,' Tessa said.

'Oh, but you are, darling angel – today's the day.' The pink lady swept her pink scarf around her square little shoulders and floated off down the street, turning once to wave a manicured hand.

'That's Stella Luna,' Starlinda said. 'She's a healer. Come on in, Tessa.'

Starlinda's daughter, Faye, had once said to Tessa, 'No one, but no one just goes to have coffee with Mum. She's always got some devious agenda.' Her scathing comment rang in Tessa's mind, and so did Penelope's slitty-eyed judgement about 'wicked charlatans!' – Starlinda didn't seem like that to Tessa.

'Coffee? Or a cold drink?' Starlinda asked, leading her into the kitchen. 'I've made us a vegetarian lasagne for later.' She turned the heat down on the electric oven.

'It smells wonderful,' Tessa said, sniffing the wholesome aroma. 'And I'd like something cold to drink, please.'

Starlinda gave her a tall glass of water with ice cubes and a slice of pink grapefruit. 'We'll go into the sanctuary,' she said. 'Take your shoes off, please.'

Tessa followed, her bare toes sinking into the pale apricot carpet. 'I've never been in here!'

'You've never been here without Faye. I'm afraid Faye's energy is too dense to cope with the sacred flame.'

As soon as she stepped inside the sanctuary, Tessa had goosebumps. It was like a cocoon. The walls and ceiling were draped in a soft white fabric, like butter muslin, the floor covered in lush white rugs and huge cream silk cushions with discreet motifs of Chinese lettering. A golden Buddha sat in a softly lit alcove, emanating stillness and peace. A tall candle stood in the arched window which overlooked the river, and two tall statues of Egyptian temple cats sat regally, one each side of it. In the centre of the room, on the floor, was another candle, burning inside a lantern, and an enormous clear quartz crystal. Next to it was a bell, and a turquoise bowl of water. There was no furniture at all.

Tessa felt oddly at home, sitting on a cushion in the silent, soothing space. She felt like curling up there for a blissful snooze. She didn't want to talk. It was indeed a sacred space, a pearl of silence in the turmoil of London, a place to listen.

She was glad Starlinda didn't seem to expect conversation but just let her sit and absorb the shared ambience of peace.

Before she arrived, Tessa had made up her mind to say a firm no if Starlinda offered to do anything 'spooky', as Faye called it. 'Shall I teach you to meditate? NO. Shall I contact your dead granny? NO. Shall I give you some healing? NO. The answers were all lined up like tennis balls ready to bat.

But it wasn't necessary. Starlinda simply sat there with her and said in a quiet voice, 'Let's close our eyes and be very still.' And Tessa found her eyes closing and her body becoming light and motionless, like the Buddha. The feeling was a blessed relief from the constant pressure and watchfulness of living in London, a rare sense of being loved, invisibly, unconditionally.

When Starlinda did begin to speak, her voice was velvety and confident. 'Do you trust me to take you on a beautiful journey, Tessa?' she asked. 'Just say yes or no.'

'Yes,' Tessa heard herself whisper. The contents of her mind sailed past her like pieces of litter on a stream. Penelope's comments about 'charlatans' were there, and Paul's admonitions about 'mumbo jumbo'. Then older stuff, from her childhood. The Reverend Reminsy's face close to hers, barking: 'This nonsense has got to STOP'. Her mother saying, 'Even if you do see ghosts you are not to talk about it'. And her dad's heavy silence, the look of knowing in the blue of his eyes as if an undiscovered world glistened distantly, a forbidden world. She let it all drift by as she listened to Starlinda's velvet voice.

'Imagine your heart as a golden flower,' Starlinda said, 'a shining flower with twelve golden petals open to the sun. It wants every petal open, so that you can receive all the light, all the love that is there for you.' She paused, and then gently asked, 'How many petals of your heart-flower are open, Tessa? Give me the first number that comes.'

'Two,' Tessa said immediately.

'Then take your time, and allow all twelve beautiful petals to open. It's very easy to do – it's so soft and gentle.'

Tessa held the vision of the golden flower. It felt so right, like something she had always known from the moment of her birth. She knew how slowly petals opened for she had observed them many times, sitting in the wild flower meadows of Monterose, or by the river staring at the yellow bottle lilies, or in the garden watching a tulip open in the morning sun. It was something so magical that even breathing seemed too loud, too fast, too human to belong to such enchantment. She felt it now, as if time was suspended while she allowed the twelve petals of her heart-flower to open fully.

'Welcome.' Starlinda's voice changed and became even softer, more whispery, and the quality of listening became intense. It sparkled with magic. 'Welcome,' she repeated, 'for you have come home, Tessa, you have come home to the heart. In this space you will find the tranquillity you have longed for.'

Tessa's eyes were closed, yet she was seeing colours brighter and more vibrant than any in the real world.

'Go into the centre of your beautiful heart-flower,' continued Starlinda, 'and you will find a sacred, eternal flame. Within the flame is a precious pearl. This pearl is your true self. It has always been there, in the heart of the heart, across time. It is the essence of who you are, and it will never leave you. Go into the centre of this precious pearl as if it were a room, a sacred space where you may rest, a sanctuary where the angels and guides who have always loved you can come and talk with you, or sing with you, or just give you divine love and joy.'

Afloat in the shining silence, Tessa sensed the space inside her 'pearl'. It was changing, image melting into image, until it became an alcove inside a temple garden. The earth was alive and vibrant under her feet, the air infused with an exotic fragrance.

'Where are you?' Starlinda asked quietly.

'In the temple garden.'

'What are you sitting on?'

'A curved stone seat, set into a wall, and the wall is full of twinkling crystal.'

'Can you describe it more fully?' Starlinda asked. 'What sounds can you hear? What plants are growing nearby? What time of day is it?'

'It's very still,' Tessa said. 'It's early morning, and there are song thrushes singing all around me.' She paused, feeling the sudden lurch of tears in her voice.

Starlinda led her on, with confident skill. 'You can do this, Tessa. The sadness will pass, like a gentle breeze, and you will emerge, joyful and refreshed. Just breathe.'

'I can hear the sea,' Tessa whispered, and her serenity vanished into turbulent waters, rapids and foam, tearing her away into darkness, into heartbreak. 'I need to go home,' she wept, and curled up in a ball on the floor. 'I need to go home SO much.'

CHAPTER 12

The Kundalini

The sound of drums echoed across the frozen earth. Not war drums, but peace drums. The hippies were gathering at Stonehenge, wending their way through the freezing fog, along the switchback roads of Salisbury Plain. The roadside verges were a wonderland of seed heads, ferns and grasses encrusted in a ghostly frost that glistened with a light of its own. Beech and hawthorn trees hung over the lanes, traceries of twigs glazed with ice crystals, rustling and tinkling if anything moved below their canopies.

The hippies were arriving in small groups, in their Afghan coats and ethnic shawls, some in camper vans, others on foot, having hitchhiked or trudged for miles.

'You're not really going to MARRY him, are you, Tessa?' Lou asked as the three of them plodded towards the stones, Lou with her drums strapped to her back, Clare trailing behind, vacant-eyed and silent. Around them the icy fog seemed infused with the mystic lustre of pearls.

'I am, yes,' Tessa said heavily. She flashed her engagement ring at Lou.

Predictably, Lou was not impressed. 'Why don't you just shack up with Paul?'

'It's hard to explain.'

'Try.'

'Okay – Lou – it's family stuff.'

'Expectations?'

'Yeah.'

'Who from? His folks or yours?'

'Both. But mostly my mum. She broke her heart – seriously – over Lucy, and she's dreamed for years of a white wedding – a fairy-tale wedding like she and Dad apparently had.'

'But you can't wreck your life, Tessa, for your mum's fantasy.'

'I'm not wrecking my life. Paul really loves me, and he needs the security of marriage – he's actually insecure.'

'He's moody.'

'So am I,' Tessa said. 'We're two moodies together.'

'Oh God, Tessa!' Lou's eyes smouldered from under the wide-brimmed brown felt hat she was wearing. It was coated in frost. 'That's a recipe for disaster.'

'No, it's not. I'm strong. Stronger than him. I can give him the support he's never had from his folks. He's a brilliant musician, and they don't appreciate him. They want him to study law like his dad. They belittle him all the time. No one's ever believed in him like I do.'

'But, Tessa – come on – you still love Art. I know you do.'

Tessa sighed. 'It's over, Lou, long ago.'

'But what if he came back to you? You two were SO fantastic together – but – well, you wouldn't trust him ever again, I suppose.'

'Probably not,' Tessa said. 'I'm hoping Art won't be there at Stonehenge. I couldn't bear it, if I saw him – I really couldn't.'

'We'll be there with you.' Lou tucked her arm into Tessa's in a friendly way. 'You can sit with me and do some drumming.'

'Thanks.'

Tessa was quiet as they drew close to Stonehenge and saw the monolithic slabs of stone towering over them in the mist. There were hippies everywhere, leaning against the stones, or sitting in circles around the glow of a fire. The air smelled of incense and sage leaf. Tessa found herself wishing she hadn't come – she felt lost and deeply cold, and all she wanted to do was wander about, searching hopelessly for the familiar psychedelic colours of Art's bus. Was Lou right? Was she still totally, hopelessly in love with him? Could she bear to see him with Rowan and their precious child?

Paul had refused to go with her. A music exam, he'd claimed. He'd offered to borrow his dad's white Mercedes and drive her down to Monterose. He didn't want to be part of the hippie scene any more, especially, he said pompously, if it involved festivals like the winter solstice. But Tessa was passionate about celebrating the solstice. All through her childhood Freddie had taken her and Lucy into the woods and hills on what he called 'the shortest day'. It was like the turn of the tide, he'd said. You could touch the earth and feel the change in your bones. You could touch a tree and feel it waking up. They'd sit in the red–gold beech wood and listen for song thrushes, and there always was one singing at noon on the day of the solstice. The song had been a symbol, a confirmation that everything was all right, spring would arrive and the earth would once again be warm and fragrant with bluebells. And when the thrush had begun its song, Freddie would take them into the orchard and lift them high on his shoulders to pick mistletoe. The white berry, he said, represented the returning sun. Then he'd remind them it was Granny Barcussy who had given him all that knowledge.

'I need to be on my own,' Tessa said.

'No, you don't.' Lou put her favourite drum into Tessa's cold hands. 'You can't go wandering off in the mist. There's nowhere to go around here.'

They joined a circle of drummers around a crackling fire. Drumming and chanting and dancing. Despite herself, Tessa couldn't resist the invigorating rhythms of the five elements which Lou had taught her. It was powerful. She began to feel warm and alive, part of something special. She sensed the earth below her listening, responding in some mysterious way. Earth, air, fire, water and the human heartbeat. She danced with Clare and a group of other women, generating heat in the frosted night. In the last hour before dawn, the Druids appeared, and everyone fell silent. The mist cleared, the fires softened into embers, and the silence hummed with anticipation.

Tessa sat cross-legged, facing East in perfect stillness. And as the first rose-gold ray of the rising sun touched her chestnut hair, she felt an intensity beyond anything she had ever experienced. It shot up her spine, like a golden flower growing through her, opening its petals at the crown of her head. In that moment she saw the cold winter sky criss-crossed with geometric flower patterns like a celestial kaleidoscope. She saw the earth become bright with limitless lines of gold, ancient paths, perfect and straight, connecting the sacred sites of churches, holy wells and stones, Celtic crosses and beacons. Spellbound, she found her mind flying along one particular line. A line right through Monterose, through the garden of The Pines where she had played, and on towards Glastonbury.

She sensed that every single person gathered at Stonehenge in the dawn was infused with the same sparkling energy. They were more than people. They were geometric fountains of light, complex mandalas, diverse and perfect as snow crystals.

She felt herself being lifted by an incoming tide of sound, as if sound had declared itself as a power, a presence, a part of the shining web of energy. It was music. It was resonance. The essence of spirit. The unseen.

Nothing had ever moved her so profoundly as the sound

211

of the Druid's horn greeting the sun, the way people were humming and singing a single note, making an incredible sound, their hands lifted to the sky, like a field of ripening corn.

And when it had finished and the sun was an icy disc in the winter sky, everyone slept, huddled against the great stones. No one talked. Drums and guitars lay silent. Everyone slept in clumps like kittens, keeping each other warm.

Only the policemen stayed awake, watching from a respectful distance, their minds safe and sensible under frost-glazed helmets.

Freddie came home at noon on the day of the winter solstice. He parked his lorry and listened in surprise to the sound of music coming from The Pines. Kate was playing an LP of Christmas songs: *Little Donkey*, and *Jingle Bells*, and *I'm Dreaming of a White Christmas*.

Something's happened, he thought, walking up the garden path. He paused to inspect the vegetable plot, pleased to see the twinkle of frost on the chunky-stemmed Brussels sprout plants, their pale green stalks covered in knobbly sprouts. They always tasted better for having the frost on them.

He was bemused to find Kate dancing round the kitchen in her favourite red dress and pinny. 'What's going on?' he asked.

'Oh Freddie!' She came to him, bright eyed and radiant. *Like she used to be*, he thought. 'Guess what? Go on – guess.'

'I dunno,' Freddie said. 'You won the pools?'

'No.'

'You backed a winner?'

'No.'

'What then?'

'It's TESSA!' Kate was crying tears of joy as she looked up at Freddie. 'She's coming home for Christmas!'

Freddie's blue eyes sparkled with hope. 'Oh, that's good, good news. It's been a long time!'

'Fifteen months,' Kate said. 'AND – she's bringing Paul! Look, here's her letter – and she says they've got something exciting to tell us. Ooh – I can't WAIT. Dance with me, Freddie, come on, crack your face, dear.'

Freddie had misgivings about Paul. But he soon got caught up in Kate's excitement and found himself laughing and smiling as they whirled around the kitchen.

''Tis good to see some colour in your cheeks again,' he said as they collapsed on the cottage sofa. Lucy's Dansette record player was making clicking noises. 'Dust on the needle,' he said and got up to lift the arm away from the LP before harm was done. He blew the dust off, set the arm back away from the LP, and turned it off. Kate was talking non-stop as she made his coffee, adding a dash of rum and a blob of cream, the way he liked it. 'You spoil me,' he said when he managed to get a word in edgeways.

'We must get a Christmas tree. Can you get one from Tarbuts Timber?' Kate asked, and babbled on without waiting for an answer. 'And I must make mincemeat. I haven't made any yet. A good job I made all those Christmas puddings – there they are – look ' She waved at the dresser where a line of twelve white earthenware basins stood, each covered by a cloth tightly tied on with string. 'I put sixpences in them this year, and lots of brandy. You wait 'til you taste one, Freddie, with some of my rum butter. And – oh my goodness, I must get some wrapping paper – and we'd better give Paul a present. Whatever can we get him? A tie? Socks? We don't know what he likes. And what if it snows, Freddie? Where's the old sledge? They might want to go tobogganing down The Skiddins.

''Tis in the shed,' Freddie said, inspired by her enthusiasm. 'It's got woodworm. I'll get it out later and give it a brush over – and I'll get a tree after lunch.'

He could drive up to Tarbuts Timber. That would be okay. He hoped Kate wouldn't ask him to walk anywhere, or go to the Post Office. She gave him one of her searching, caring gazes. 'Are you all right, Freddie?' He looked down at her clear eyes and was tempted to tell her about the panic attack and how deeply it had shaken his confidence. Telling her now would spoil her happiness. So he kept quiet.

'Tessa will want to show Paul her field,' Kate said, skilfully changing the subject. 'We ought to get our wellies on and go up there.'

'It's very overgrown,' Freddie told her, 'and Herbie said he'd seen a hippie up there. I walked up there, as you know. I was shocked to see that fence. Someone is camping in the wood, and fetching water from the spring, I reckon. I wouldn't mention it to Tessa – she might not even want to go there, after that blimin' layabout broke her heart. I'm surprised she's got over it so well, to be honest.'

'Well, it looks like Paul is her knight in shining armour,' Kate said, smiling. 'I can't wait to meet him. Do you think he's a townie? I wonder what he'll think of our country ways?'

Freddie let Kate go on fantasising about Paul while he thought about Tessa's field. Over the year he'd worried a lot about what would happen to the lovely little field. Would Tessa ever want to go there again after what had happened? Freddie wanted her to keep the field, and plant trees with him, create a wood of their own. He wanted to care for it and use it, not let it go wild and become an impenetrable thicket that could never be reclaimed. Worse, he feared she might be tempted to sell it for a few hundred pounds. Money that would soon be gone. He had an uneasy feeling about Paul. He actually felt that Paul was stealing his beloved daughter away, just when he most needed her.

Tessa woke up at Stonehenge with an odd feeling that nothing would ever be the same again. She'd slept wedged between Lou and Clare, in Lou's faded one-person tent. It had been hard for her to switch back from creature comforts to the frugal reality of being a hippy. Paul wasn't wild about her decision to go to Stonehenge. She looked at the ring on her finger and sighed. She felt like two people. The Tessa who paid her rent, went to work, and mothered Paul, and the

Tessa who longed to go on crystal workshops, paint angels, and heal animals. The two Tessas seemed to be drifting apart.

She told Lou about her experience at the solstice. 'It came right up my spine,' she said, 'this incredible buzz of energy – and it opened up at the top of my head like a golden flower made of light.'

'Wow!' Lou's knowing eyes warmed with enthusiasm. 'It's the Kundalini, Tessa. You had a Kundalini awakening!'

'The Kundalini? What's that?'

'It's a release of power from the base of your spine,' Lou told her. 'It's a life-changing gift, Tessa. Go easy on yourself. You're in a state of transition.'

'A lot of other people had it too,' Tessa said. 'I saw it. And together we filled the universe with golden, geometric mandalas. It was connected with the sunrise, the earth energy, and the music – like a mysterious blend of mathematics, music, and spirit.'

'Wow,' breathed Lou, studying Tessa's eyes. 'Not much impresses me now – but THAT is mind-blowing.'

Tessa nodded slowly. Lou was looking at her with such intensity, it was almost frightening.

'But, Tessa ' Lou said, urgently, 'don't go back. Don't go back to being a human.'

'I HAVE to,' Tessa said, looking at Paul's ring on her finger. 'But I know what you mean, Lou.'

'Don't waste your life – like I did,' Lou said. 'I'm nearly forty now, Tessa, and I wasted most of my youth on a binge of people-pleasing. It was a total waste, a mad, stupid delusion, and nobody got anything out of it except a sense of failure. I didn't wake up spiritually until I was thirty five, and by then it was so hard to disengage from the family scene, stuff I'd spent my whole life building, blindly believing it was right. I'm warning you, Tessa, don't do the same thing. Don't build yourself a cage and sit in it. You're a tiger, girl.'

'Yeah – *Tyger, tyger, burning bright / In the forests of the night,*' Tessa quoted. 'That's me – a misunderstood tiger.'

'Why am I not surprised?' Lou's eyes smouldered at Tessa from under her wide-brimmed hat. 'You remember what I said.'

'I will.'

'So where are you going now, kiddo?'

'For a mooch around. I want to see if Art's bus is here.'

'It's not,' Lou said. 'And I asked a few guys who know him. No one knows where he is. No one's seen him.'

Tessa still needed to look for herself, and see the stones in the morning light. 'Then I'm going back to London to make myself look civilised, and tomorrow Paul's taking me down to Mum and Dad's place for Christmas.'

Lou groaned. 'Family Christmas, eh? I used to like that once. Now I shall go up Glastonbury Tor with a sandwich, and sit there drumming out a message to the world.'

Tessa crawled out of the tent and looked at the encroaching line of policemen. The mist was rolling away into the distance, unveiling lemon sunlight on the bare white fields. A flock of redwings were working their way along a hawthorn hedge, some of them sitting around on the frozen ground, their feathers fluffed out in the cold, and a robin was pecking around the tents, searching for crumbs.

It didn't take her long to see that Lou was right. Art's bus wasn't there. It hurt, but she was glad. A meeting with him now would set her right back into emotional turmoil. Starlinda had brought her out of that with a few chosen words. 'You have to rise above the emotional body,' she'd said, 'into the shining light of your spiritual self.' It had been a revelation to Tessa. Starlinda and Lou could not have been more different, yet she felt both women were guiding her. She leaned against one of the massive stones, thinking about what Lou had said. *I have to be that tiger,* she thought. *I have to burn brightly, not get negative. I have to keep that Kundalini energy.*

Freddie planted the Christmas tree into a metal bucket of soil and carried it indoors.

'Don't drop mud everywhere,' cried Kate. 'What a lovely bushy little tree.'

'Ah – I made sure I got one with roots,' Freddie said, and his eyes sparkled. 'They wanted to sell me a dead one! I told 'em I didn't want one chopped off – I want one I can plant afterwards. They let me dig this one up myself.'

'It's wonderful – well done.' Kate's smile made him feel wonderful too. Pleased, Freddie stood holding the vibrant Norwegian Spruce while Kate wrapped the bucket in scarlet crepe paper. A plywood tea-chest full of decorations was stashed under the table. He pulled it out, feeling the old excitement starting as he glimpsed familiar baubles and tarnished tinsel, dilapidated angels and Santas the girls had made when they were children. Relics of happy Christmases. Complete Christmases.

''Tis still like half a Christmas without Lucy here,' Freddie said. 'I wonder if she misses it. If she thinks about us.'

'Of course she does,' Kate said brightly. 'We've got the parcel she sent – and the letter. Maybe one year we'll go over there and have Christmas on the beach. Now – shall we leave the decorating for Tessa and Paul to do? I hope he likes our cardboard angels.'

Freddie glanced out of the window. 'That's not them surely?' he said, seeing a car turning into the drive. 'That's a posh car – a Mercedes Benz.'

Kate was beside herself with excitement when she saw Tessa stepping out of the white Mercedes, looking fabulous in her Afghan coat, a mini skirt and high boots. Paul towered over her, in an expensive looking black overcoat with the collar turned up. Exactly the type of man Kate had dreamed of for her daughter. She beamed at Freddie. 'He looks NICE, doesn't he?'

'We'll see,' Freddie said.

'Let's not make the same mistake we made with Tim,' Kate said anxiously. 'We've got to try and like him, even if we don't.'

Freddie hardly heard her. He was already heading out in eager strides to meet Tessa. He waited on the doorstep, and Tessa ran across the frosty lawn and flung herself at him. 'Dad! Oh Dad – I've missed you SO much.'

Freddie couldn't speak. He smoothed her chestnut hair with his large hand, anticipating the moment when she looked up at him. Those pale blue eyes with a core of gold. Now they were full of stars, and the long curved lashes shiny with happy tears.

'And Mum!' Tessa opened an arm to include Kate in the hug, overwhelmed to see her radiant smile and feel her mum's sturdy little body, always so solid and rooted firmly in the earth. *Invincible*, Tessa thought. 'I'm so lucky to have you, Mum,' she whispered.

Kate started to cry. 'You've never said that before.' She looked at Paul who was standing back respectfully. 'Now who's this handsome young man? I can't wait to meet him.'

'This is Paul.'

'Paul,' Kate repeated as if Paul was a pure gold ingot. She held out both hands, her bright brown eyes shining into his. Paul glowed. He put down his bag and let Kate hold both his hands and gaze at him with her irresistible warmth. Tessa smiled to herself, proud of her mum's way of making a stranger feel like a long-lost friend.

Freddie held out his hand and the two men eyed each other. 'Come in then,' Freddie said. ''Tis cold out here, and we've got a roaring fire going.' He picked up Tessa's bag which was bulging with parcels. 'And Kate's got mince pies in the oven!'

Kate gave the white Mercedes a little pat. 'What a fabulous car.'

'It's not mine,' Paul said. 'It's my parents' car.'

'Better keep it clean, then,' Kate said in a conspiratorial whisper. 'It's too nice for the kind of mud we have around here.'

Paul grinned. 'I've already been threatened.'

Freddie followed them indoors, thinking about what he had seen in Paul's hazel eyes. So different from Art's steady confidence. Paul had the eyes of a damaged soul. His eyes didn't match what his lips were saying. *Not another one,* Freddie thought privately, *not another blimin' conman who's going to hurt my daughter.*

On Boxing Day, Freddie suggested he took Tessa for a driving lesson. Tessa's first thoughts on seeing the Morris Minor had been *I could live in it* and *I can escape in it.* She was already sketching her plan for painting it up in psychedelic colours. 'Don't go painting daisies on it. You'll ruin the bodywork,' Freddie warned, but Kate said brightly, 'Well, it's her car now. She can do what she likes with it.'

Paul seemed a wee bit jealous. 'Lucky girl. My parents never gave me a car, even when I passed my test. But Amelia got a brand new Mini for her 21st. You can count me out,' he added, 'if this is a driving lesson. I don't want to sit in the back with Tessa at the wheel!'

'Very wise,' said Kate. 'You go, Tessa. Paul and I will sit by the fire and have a lovely chat.'

Tessa looked at Freddie, sensing his need to spend quality time with her, just the two of them, and she wanted that too. She wanted to tell him about Violetta, and about the solstice at Stonehenge.

'We'll go out on the old airfield, as you haven't got your provisional licence yet,' Freddie said, and he drove them to Westonzoyland, and let her get used to the feel of driving a car.

He was a patient teacher, encouraging and reassuring her. 'You're taking to it like a duck to water.'

But Tessa was shaking with nerves as she brought the car to a halt. 'I'm not really a machine-friendly person, Dad, but I'll get there.'

'Can you get lessons in London?' Freddie asked. 'I'll give you the money for them – but you shouldn't take the car up there 'til you've passed your test.'

'Thanks, Dad, you're so kind to me.' Tessa turned to look into his eyes. 'Was this what you wanted to do today? Or is there something else?'

Freddie hesitated. She read the expression in his eyes. Concern, for her. Need. What did he need so badly when he had a good life with Kate? It came to her in a flash. Her dad needed her the way the children did; he needed inspiration and reassurance. He needed her light.

She told him about the solstice at Stonehenge and the Kundalini awakening. She held nothing back, and was rewarded by seeing him come alive, his eyes rounded with interest. Then she told him about Violetta, and he listened intently.

'I know you banned me from talking about spirits,' she said, 'but the world is changing, Dad. People are waking up to spiritual truth and light like never before.'

222

'Kate banned you from talking about it,' Freddie said, 'but I hope I never did.'

'Living in London has changed me so much, Dad. I have to be careful what I say at work, and with Paul. But working with the children has been fantastic. They've taught me a lot.'

Freddie studied his daughter in surprise. 'How could – what do you call 'em special needs? – how could children like that teach YOU?' Privately he thought Tessa was wasting her life in such a job, but he wasn't going to tell her that.

'They need me, Dad. They suffer constantly, from failure and frustration, and relentless pressure from the adults in their life. What I can give them is simple, caring love. I accept them as they are, because I can see the shining light in their eyes, and all around them. They're like angels in disguise, Dad.'

'But what about your art?' Freddie asked. 'Don't you ever paint a picture now?'

'I don't need to right now. But it's always with me. I AM my art, Dad. Art can be invisible. I paint angels in children's minds.' She paused. The answer seemed to both satisfy and startle Freddie. She watched his aura grow brighter. 'And I encourage them to study the natural world – yes, even in London. We watch buds opening, and plant seeds, and feed the birds. One day I caught a Red Admiral butterfly in a jar and the children were so excited and interested; they said the most amazing things, and when we set it free they cheered and clapped – why? – because they know in their little hearts that freedom matters, and caring for wild creatures matters.'

Freddie nodded silently. Her impassioned speech had moved him beyond words.

'Dad.' Tessa spoke quietly now, intensely, her hand on his sleeve. 'I'm doing for them what you did for me, all my life.'

'What was that?'

'You inspired me, Dad. Like the times you took Lucy and me into the woods at the winter solstice – to touch the trees and feel them coming alive, listen for the song thrush, and find mistletoe. The times when you took us to the river to watch water voles and dragonflies, and the stories you told us about Granny Barcussy, and the times we played in her ruined cottage in the woods. It was precious, Dad, and it will stay with me, always.'

Freddie nodded, his eyes glistening softly.

'But the BEST thing you did for me,' Tessa concluded, 'was that you loved me when I was horrible.'

They sat in silence for a few minutes, letting the words settle into manageable calm.

'Well – I hope Paul appreciates you,' Freddie said, looking at Violetta's amethyst ring on his daughter's slim finger.

'He needs me.'

'Well – I hope he doesn't need you too much.'

'What do you mean, Dad?'

Freddie hesitated. 'I can see it in his eyes – an emptiness.'

'You're right. Paul had a terrible childhood, nothing like mine. No one believed in him, and he's a brilliant musician. He comes alive when he plays music.'

'So why do you want to marry him?'

'He loves me, and I believe a good marriage will change him. I want to give him the love and support he never had.'

'Ah, he's not gonna change. People don't. You be careful, dear, please. You can't spend your life helping lame dogs over stiles.'

Tessa felt defensive now. She didn't agree with Freddie's warning, but she didn't want to spoil the special time with him.

'Shall we go and see the field?' Freddie asked, rescuing her.

'I'd rather go up to the ridgeway,' Tessa said, meeting her Dad's eyes. 'I don't want to go to the field – not yet – maybe not ever. It hurts too much.'

PART TWO

1970

CHAPTER 13

Honeymoon

The first cracks in Tessa's relationship with Paul appeared just hours after the wedding.

An enthusiastic group of friends and family followed their car with its tin cans, balloons and streamers flying, to Castle Cary Station, armed with bags of confetti and rice. They gave chase as Paul and Tessa ran, giggling, over the footbridge. Tessa felt strange in her 'going away' outfit, a heavily textured Crimplene jacket and skirt in 'duck egg'. The colour suited her, but the fabric felt scratchy and toxic. 'But you MUST have a hat,' Kate had insisted, and Tessa had reluctantly chosen the smallest possible hat, a crescent of blue feathers curled uncomfortably over the top of her head. It felt like a dragon's claw. The hairdresser in Monterose had dragged her hair back and created an extravagant bun held together with sharp hairpins. It felt like a teazel.

Paul had nodded approvingly. 'Very ladylike!'

Tessa didn't want to look ladylike. She felt hot and itchy and longed to get on the train and hang her head out of the window, let the claw and the teazel unravel and blow away, let the wind stream through her hair. She was fed up with acting the radiant bride, smiling at aunties, sipping champagne when she wanted water, and striving to light a spark of approval in Penelope's leonine eyes.

The hardest bit had been saying goodbye to her dad. Face to face on the platform as the train from Paddington came in, Freddie's steady blue gaze was full of anxiety. She knew that he knew. 'You remember your old dad,' he said, 'and remember you can always come home.'

I'd like to go home with you right now, Tessa thought, but her lips said, 'Thanks, Dad. Don't worry about me.'

They boarded the train under a hail of rice and confetti. Cameras with big flash guns flickered too close to their faces.

Kate blew a kiss, her eyes brimming with emotion. 'Goodbye, darling,' and she wagged a finger at Paul. 'You look after my little girl.' The train was moving now, and they hung out of the window waving, watching the loving faces getting smaller and smaller. *It's like dying*, Tessa thought, *watching your entire life vanish into a multi-coloured dot*.

With her soul disappearing into infinity, she had a burning need to know where Paul was taking her. He'd relished keeping it a secret, his eyes twinkling stubbornly whenever she asked. She hoped the train was going to Southampton to catch the boat to France. But as the sleek diesel engine hummed past her on the platform she'd noticed the proud lettering on the side. It was the Cornishman. Surely, surely Paul wouldn't be taking her there?

'Now will you tell me where we're going?' she asked as they settled into two window seats.

Paul twinkled. 'This train stops at about twenty stations so you'll have to keep guessing! Or we might change trains. Now – come here, Mrs Selby, it's time I kissed the bride properly.' He pulled her towards him and kissed her long and hard, his hands grinding the rice and confetti into her back. Tessa felt like screaming. 'What's the matter with you?' he asked. 'You're my wife now. I can kiss you whenever I like!'

'No, you can't.' Tessa pulled away, glaring at him.

'Hey – hey, don't go all huffy,' he said. 'We're on honeymoon.'

'Honey and moon means sweetness and light,' Tessa said, 'not grope and grab.'

'I wasn't groping.'

'Yes, you WERE.'

Paul looked affronted, and patronisingly amused. 'You'd better calm down, Mrs Selby,' he said. 'You're a married woman now.'

Tessa fumed silently. Her new name sounded mildly insulting and alien. She clawed at the neck of her blouse and fished out a handful of confetti and rice. 'This is what's

231

bugging me.' She tried to smile brightly like her mother would have done. 'It's down inside my clothes. I need to go into the loo, strip off and shake it out.'

Paul's eyes lit up. 'Oh boy! Can I come?'

'No.'

Tessa escaped down the corridor and into the loo, slamming the bolt shut with a sense of relief. She confronted herself in the mirror. A young woman she didn't recognise stared back with angry eyes. *I look frumpy*, she thought. While the train careered across the Levels towards Taunton, she stripped off and shook the confetti and rice grains all over the floor and into the toilet. She put on just the skirt and blouse. She liked the blouse for its motif of tiny white horses with their manes and tails flowing, and the satin felt good against her skin.

Her mind was racing like the train as she unpinned the complicated bun and let her hair roll down her back. Paul knew how passionately Tessa loved Cornwall. They'd met in St Ives, as hippies, that long-ago summer. But Tessa felt she could never go there again. To her it was sacred space, not to be revisited because it belonged to her intense love affair with Art. Her memory had sealed it in a golden bubble, forever floating over the wild and rocky cliffs out at Clodgy where she and Art had first made love in the hot grass. Kindred spirits. Lovers across time as if they'd lived many lifetimes together. She could never imagine St Ives without seeing Art's serious grey eyes and feeling the sensual beauty of his warm, tanned body close to hers, feeling his love transforming her into an ethereal creature like Botticelli's painting, *Birth of Venus*.

When they'd discussed the honeymoon, Tessa had tried to explain to Paul, without hurting him, that she never, ever wanted to go back to St Ives. He had listened, with a kind of darkness flowing through his eyes. It wasn't there all the time. Only when he talked about his childhood. How his parents had favoured his sister, Amelia. How they'd pushed him mercilessly, and criticised the choices he made. How Amelia had ballet and piano lessons while Paul, who was musically gifted, was never even allowed to touch the piano. Instead he had to do macho stuff like rugby and rowing.

Tessa felt sorry for him. She could relate to those kinds of problems. She wanted to do for him what Art had done for her. Bring out the best in him. Show him he was worth loving. Nurture his music.

She went back to their compartment and sat down, running her fingers through her hair. 'There, I feel like me again.'

Paul didn't look too pleased. 'Aw, I liked your new look,' he said. 'I like you looking ladylike and mature.'

'Too bad,' said Tessa. 'I'm happy like this.'

The train rattled on through the March countryside, past flocks of sheep with baby lambs, and stretches of newly sown wheat and barley just showing their green blades. After Taunton they entered the rich red clay beds of Devon, then Exeter, and along the coast of the red rocks. Dawlish and

Teignmouth flew by and they moved inland again. Tessa got increasingly anxious. She didn't tell Paul, but sat beside him, her hand in his, her head on his shoulder as they talked and laughed about the wedding and the aunties.

'Ah – the Tamar Bridge,' Paul said as the train slowed down after Plymouth. 'Isambard Kingdom Brunel. What a name – and what an engineer. Your dad would love this.'

'He would,' agreed Tessa. She leaned out of the window to taste the cool air rising from the silvery water.

'Look at those battleships!' Paul said.

'I thought we might get off at Plymouth?' Tessa said, 'and get the ferry to Roscoff?'

'No luck.'

'But we must be in Cornwall now.' Tessa felt her face begin to burn with frustration. 'Paul – come on – I really need to know where we're going.'

He sighed. 'Don't keep on about it. Enjoy the mystery.'

'I'm not enjoying it. I'm worrying.'

'Worrying? What – about a honeymoon with your handsome new husband? Don't you trust me, Tessa?'

Tessa was silent.

'For God's sake, smile,' Paul snapped suddenly. 'You're not going to a funeral.'

'I'll smile if I want to smile.'

'Be like that then.' Paul took a bottle of brandy from his pocket and swigged it. He put his feet up on the opposite seat and went to sleep.

It was getting dark. The train belted onwards. Liskeard.

Bodmin. Parr. St Austell. Names Tessa remembered. She stared at Paul's shiny black shoes propped on the seat. She eyed their precious luggage stored overhead in the string luggage racks. It crossed her mind that she could grab her nice new blue suitcase and get off at the next stop while Paul was asleep. She could make a run for freedom, and be a homeless hippie all over again. Except that Art would not be there.

When they got to Truro she was still on the train. She gave Paul a prod. 'Wake up. There's not many stations left and I don't know where we're getting off, do I?'

Paul yawned and stretched. He pressed his nose against the window. 'Truro Cathedral. All lit up. You'll soon find out, and you're going to love it, Tessa.'

'I need to know now, not soon.'

'Don't you think you're making an unreasonable amount of fuss?'

'No, Paul. That's not fair. I carefully explained to you why I didn't want to go to Cornwall, and in particular St Ives.'

'St Ives is a beautiful place,' Paul drew a piece of cream paper from his wallet and unfolded it, 'and we're staying in the lap of luxury.' He thrust the paper in front of her with a flourish. 'Ta-da!'

Tessa stopped breathing. A hotel in St Ives! For a week. And Paul's eyes eagerly awaiting her reaction.

'I can't believe you've done this,' she whispered. 'You know how I feel about St Ives. Being there will be emotional torture for me.'

'Don't be silly, Tessa. You'll get over it. You've got me now.'

Silly? The word danced in front of Tessa's eyes like a wasp. One wasp for every time she had ever been called silly. Another half of her mind floated alongside, and it was the people-pleasing half. The wedding. The gifts of towels and saucepans. The aunties. But mostly it was about her mother's dream of a white wedding for her daughter. The way Kate had opened her heart and her home to Paul. The way she kept saying, 'You'll be so happy, dear, when you get your own little home together.' Kate had even helped her write the thank-you cards. 'Thank you for the lovely Crown Derby tea set. It will look so nice in our new kitchen.' 'Thank you for the lovely embroidered napkins. They will come in very useful for entertaining.' 'Thank you for the Mrs Beeton's cookery book. It's just what every girl needs.' The list went on and on.

And somewhere among the sets of saucepans, Tessa's soul had gone missing. She felt like a troubled child again. She'd forgotten how Starlinda had taught her to rise above the emotional body. She was no longer in charge of her life.

'Don't look so stricken,' Paul said. 'I chose this place because I knew you'd love it. We've got a balcony with a view out towards Clodgy.'

It got worse.

'You should have asked me,' Tessa said.

'I knew you'd say no,' Paul explained. 'I've done it for your own good, Tessa. It will help you get over that bastard Art. Once and for all.'

'It's not like that.'

Paul stared at her. Too late she saw a flow of darkness eclipsing the light in his eyes. 'You still love him, don't you?' he hissed, and his cheeks turned white with anger. In one quick, robotic movement, he clamped her arm with an iron fist as the train belted on through the starless night. He pushed his face close to hers. 'Don't you? Go on – admit it.'

'You're hurting me. Let go.' Tessa was terrified. Everything rose up from the depths of her life. Everything that was black and merciless. Demons that had followed her. The colours of the day faded, and she became once more a dark shell of a creature who wanted to die.

'Redruth. This is Redruth.'

The train's brakes squealed on the metal as it pulled into the small Cornish station where the doors and the railings were painted red, and tubs of daffodils shone yellow in the light from the train windows.

'I'm getting off. Let go of me.' Tessa twisted her arm out of the iron grasp and with all the strength of her anger she pushed Paul away, grabbed her suitcase from the rack and turned the door handle.

He charged back at her, breathing hard, his high cheek-bones white and skull-like, his eyes glinting like broken china.

The train door flew open, and Tessa fell out. Her head hit the concrete with a sickening crack, and she lay still, her chestnut hair spread across the platform, her eyes closed, her face suddenly shell-like and peaceful.

Her new blue suitcase had burst open and lay beside her on the platform, her carefully packed honeymoon negligee tumbling out like the foam from a wave.

Paul leapt out and knelt beside her, aghast. 'Tessa! Oh God – what have I done? Open your lovely eyes, darling, please.' He howled and shook as people came running. 'Oh God – help us please.'

'Well, what a wonderful day we've had.' Kate kicked her shoes off and sank into a chair. 'My feet are killing me. But it was worth it. Worth every penny.'

'Ah. It went well.' Freddie had taken his tie off and loosened the stiff collar which had been chafing his neck all day. He was kneeling on the hearth rug, lighting the fire.

'Tessa looked so pretty,' said Sally.

'She can look pretty – when she's happy,' Kate said. 'What did you think of Paul?'

'He seems a nice lad. I can't wait to see the photographs. How long will they take?'

'About a week,' Kate said. 'And they're going to be in colour!'

'You can get colour TV now,' Sally said.

'Susan's got one,' said Kate.

'Ah – the Tillermans would, wouldn't they.' Freddie held a sheet of newspaper against the fire to make it draw. Flames roared up behind it, a spark jumped, and he quickly screwed up the burning paper with his bare hands and crammed it into the fire.

'I wish you wouldn't do that,' Kate said.

''Tis all right. I've done it all me life.'

'I wonder where Tessa and Paul are now?' Sally said. 'He was so mysterious about the honeymoon.'

'The Channel Islands – or even France, Tessa was hoping,' Kate said. 'We won't know 'til we get a postcard.'

'I'd worry,' Sally said, 'if I didn't know where my loved ones were.'

'We do, Mum,' Kate said. 'But, with Tessa, we've got used to it. We're seasoned worriers now.'

'She always was a bit of a problem, wasn't she?'

'But she's much more tenacious now – isn't she, Freddie?' Kate said. 'We were so worried when she went through that hippie phase, and that dreadful man let her down – she was broken-hearted – but it was a blessing in disguise. Now she's got Paul and he comes from a decent family. His father is a lawyer. You like Paul, don't you, Freddie?'

'I'm not sure about him,' Freddie said.

'Why? What's wrong with him?'

'There's just – something in his eyes,' Freddie said. 'He seems all right. But time will tell. I hope he treats her right.'

'Pity he lives in London, though,' Sally said. 'Tessa won't be happy there, will she? Not for long.'

Kate was looking at Freddie. He had a way of going tense and moving his eyes when he was listening to something outside. 'What are you listening to, dear?' she asked.

239

The three of them went quiet, and the sound of the rain sighed in the darkness. The wind howled through the telegraph wires and rattled the shutters.

Freddie looked from one to the other. 'Can't you hear it? A dog howling.'

'No,' said Kate.

'I can't hear it.' Sally shook her head.

They listened again as the fire crackled in the grate and water gurgled in the storm drains.

Freddie went to the door and stood gazing out at the night, his whole body tense and alert.

'He spooks me when he does that,' Kate whispered, 'but I don't disturb him.'

Freddie stepped outside and shut the door behind him.

'He's gone out in that rain!' said Sally.

'He's just standing on the doorstep, under the porch,' Kate said, and they could see Freddie's shape against the glass.

Freddie stood so still that he almost forgot he had a body. It was a full moon and between showers the white-gold moon appeared and disappeared from the night palaces of cloud. He was hearing Jonti. He remembered the moment at the altar when he and Tessa had both heard an eerie howling, as if the spirit of Jonti was still around, still warning them – of what? Freddie waited. And he saw a pair of eyes, pale blue with a core of gold, Tessa's eyes, coming out of the night, calling to him from a place of stone. He saw her chestnut hair spread out over cold stones, her hands curled like the feet of a dying bird. She needed him. And he couldn't reach her. He couldn't pick her up and hold her close. Or could he? Freddie knew he had only to remember how to use his own power. Something had happened to Tessa. He imagined holding her against the beat of his heart, giving her the silence of his love as he'd always done.

He was terrified that the link was broken. He visualised his hand, turned to gold, and reaching through silent miles of night, to hold on to her, to anchor her, to call upon the silver cord that binds the generations.

Paul felt hollowed out with grief as he sat in the waiting room of the Royal Cornwall Hospital. Guilt and failure were not new to him. Those two imposters had shadowed him for most of his life. Sometimes they loitered on the brim of his consciousness, and other times they charged in like Viking warriors, with stormy skies mirrored in the blades of weapons, the sun sparking triumphantly from helmets. And Paul was never armed, never prepared. They got him, every time. Guilt and failure.

He blamed his father's machoistic approach to parenting. He blamed his sister for being born, and his mother for choosing status over love. Tears threatened, but he fought them back as he stared at the floor, at his reflection in the floor, at the ache of accusation that seemed etched on every wall, window and door handle in the hospital.

Paul's mind was not his friend. Instead of helping him cope, it kept taking him back to that confetti-spattered moment when he had emerged from Monterose Church

241

and Tessa had given him a heart-stopping smile, her dimples velvet in the sun, her huge turquoise eyes glowing with love — for him. Paul had felt a rare sense of achievement, with Tessa as the glittering prize. In those unique moments, Paul had felt the tingle of magic, he had worn a star-spangled cloak that defined him as a rich, successful, conquering prince.

But now he was a frog again, guilty and crawling into cracks between stones, hiding from the sun's penetrating stare. *Nobody must know*, he kept thinking, and hoping Tessa would feel the same. The honeymoon must be salvaged, reconstructed in time for them both to return to their London jobs a week on Monday. Eight days.

He hadn't meant to hurt Tessa. Had he pushed her out of the train? Paul couldn't remember. Already the memory was hardening, baked like brick in the kilns of his need to survive.

The hospital clock ticked on, through the night, capping the bubble of their wedding day with bead-black minutes. Paul was glad no one expected a phone call from him. They thought he was blissfully on honeymoon with Tessa. At the same time, he wished someone kind would sit beside him. Someone who wouldn't judge or lecture him. There never had been a person like that in his life. Paul had dealt with emotional traumas on his own from a very young age, and the only strategy that worked for him now was the shell of cold steel, the shrug, the bolshie retort, the menacing stare.

At ten minutes to midnight a doctor in a white coat came towards him down a corridor, and Paul felt utterly vulnerable, at the mercy of this confident young doctor who was everything he wasn't.

'Mr Selby?'

'Yes.'

'I'm Doctor Parker.' The starched white coat brushed against Paul's knee as he sat down. 'About your wife.'

'She's not dead, is she?'

'Goodness – no. But she did suffer a severe blow to her head. We were concerned that she may have a fractured skull.'

'Oh God – no!'

'No – she hasn't. We have x-rayed her. That's why it's taken so long. There's no fracture. What we are concerned about is that she may have a blood clot on the brain from the injury. The next twenty-four hours will be crucial. She's still not conscious, and until she is, we can't tell whether there's any brain damage.'

'Brain damage?' Paul blanched. A horrible image of his beautiful Tessa helpless in a wheelchair came into his mind. He wouldn't be able to cope. He'd run away, disappear and live in a distant town. *My life is ruined*, he thought, *because of her silly attitude!*

'We will monitor her constantly in case there is a need for surgery.'

'Surgery?'

'If there's a blood clot, Tessa will need an operation to

remove it from her brain. We are doing everything we can, rest assured, to prevent it.'

Shock settled like ice crystals clustering around his bones. Paul felt rigid as if he was the only strong unmoving object in a spinning world. He put his hand over his eyes to shut out the giddiness. He didn't want the doctor to notice.

'I suggest you go home now, and come back tomorrow. There's nothing you can do here. Try to get some sleep, eh?'

'I want to see her, please.'

'She's not conscious. And she needs to be kept still and quiet.'

'But – look, I've heard that people in comas can hear if you talk to them. Can't I do that?'

The doctor frowned. 'If you believe it will help her, then you can – but only for a few minutes. Can you respect that?'

'Sure.'

'And talk to her kindly and quietly. No dramas! Okay? Can you do that?'

'Okay.' Paul got up and followed the doctor down the corridor, his hand on the brandy bottle still in his pocket.

He stood by the bed staring desolately at Tessa's dark eye-lashes curled over the ivory-pale skin. It was like looking at a closed book. A book whose pages shivered with evocative stories and enchanted places. But closed.

He sat down on a chair the nurse pushed towards him. He took Tessa's hand, his finger stroking the new gold wedding ring that meant she was his. 'Darling,' he whispered, 'it's Paul. I'm here with you.'

There was a scarlet silence. Then the bleep of the heart monitor raced alarmingly. Without opening her eyes, Tessa snatched her hand away. She tore the ring from her finger and threw it spinning across the room. 'Go away,' she cried. 'I never want to see you again.'

CHAPTER 14

Tresco

Tessa turned her head away when she saw Paul come into the ward, his arms full of gifts, his eyes anxiously seeking hers. She didn't want him there. Her head ached and the bruise under her hair was tender and swollen. The doctors had said she would be okay after a few days' rest, but she didn't feel glad. She almost wished she was worse so that she wouldn't have to leave hospital and go with Paul.

He stooped over the bed. 'I brought you a bottle of Lucozade,' he said, 'and some grapes – and a Crunchie bar. I know you like them.'

'Thanks,' she mumbled ungraciously.

'And – I brought you this.' Paul slid a cone of rustling tissue paper in front of her face. The paper had little hearts on it, and inside the cone was a single red rose, and a card. 'Please don't throw it at me,' Paul said. 'It's a peace-making rose, just for you, Tessa. I wanted you to have a flower to gaze at – a love flower. Remember Flower Power?'

She grunted.

'Shall I pour you some Lucozade?' She heard the squeak of yellow cellophane as Paul unwrapped it from the glass bottle. Then the glug and fizz of the golden liquid being poured into a glass. The sound of Lucozade reminded her of childhood illness times when Kate would bring her that tall sparkling bottle and she'd spend the rest of the day looking at the world through the yellow cellophane.

Tessa contemplated the red rose's spiral of velvet, and sighed. Hating took so much energy.

'Come on, Tessa – or I won't be able to resist drinking this,' Paul said.

She read the words on the card. *Please forgive me, darling. All my love, Paul xxx*. The discreet sizzling of the Lucozade was too much. She turned over and propped herself up, trying not to look at him as she savoured the burn of the fizzy drink on her tongue.

The same words came from his lips. 'Please forgive me, darling. I truly never wanted to hurt you. I – I just snapped.'

Tessa managed to look at him then. *He's my husband*, she thought, *and he's only a boy. A haunted, lost boy.* She fingered the soothing petals of the rose and studied Paul's face. He had deep shadows under his eyes. 'Where did you sleep?'

'On a bench in the waiting room.' He fished in his top pocket. 'I've got your rings,' he said. 'They're precious to me – you are precious – darling – and I hope you'll reconsider – take them back and give me another chance. Our love means everything to me. I don't want to live without you, Tessa.'

She looked at the rings in his hand. There was something disarming about seeing the palm of someone's hand. Vulnerability. Truth. Like seeing a badger's feet.

'Have you told anyone what happened?' she asked.

'No,' Paul said passionately. 'I didn't think you'd want your mum and dad to know, after all they did for the wedding. And I didn't want my folks to know either.'

'Thanks. I appreciate that.' Tessa swallowed some more Lucozade.

'I'll do anything to make it right,' Paul said, 'anything you want, Tessa. We're still on honeymoon, and when you're well enough we can go wherever you want. I'm sorry I got it wrong.' His voice broke and he looked at the floor. She heard him taking big breaths.

Compassion unfurled in Tessa's mind, wrapping the unwelcome anger in a swathe of silk. She reached out and touched his hand. 'It's okay, Paul.'

He clasped her hand and looked up at her searchingly. She didn't pull away but let him hold her, both of them breathing in the sweet colours of peace.

'Forgive?' he asked.

'All forgiven,' Tessa said. She'd forgive, but not forget. The trust was damaged and she would forever tread cautiously, learn to recognise that flashpoint in Paul, those old remembered hurts that exploded into anger.

'Thanks,' he said. 'I won't let you down.'

Tessa accepted the pledge in silence. It was like walking down the church path all over again. Seeing the freedom stretched out around her, but choosing the shadowed door.

She let him put the rings back on her finger.

'It's only Tuesday,' he said eagerly. 'If they let you out today, we can go anywhere you want. I cancelled the booking I made in that place we don't mention. But we're here in Truro. We could go up country and stay in Devon – Torquay or Paignton – OR—' his eyes brightened like a magician pulling rabbits out of a hat, 'we could go to the Isles of Scilly – on the boat. It's a ship really, and it sails daily from Penzance which is an easy hop on the train. It's a two-hour sea trip, and apparently you sometimes see dolphins. Then you can explore lots of beautiful islands, some of them uninhabited.'

'I'd like that,' Tessa said immediately. 'I hope I'll be well enough. Let's see what the doctor has to say – here he is now.'

The doctor shone a torch in her eyes and asked her questions. Then he said, 'You can go home tomorrow morning, Tessa. But don't expect to be back to normal for a while. You may get headaches and feel irritable, perhaps need to sleep more than usual.' He looked at Paul. 'Can you remember that, too?'

'Sure. I'll keep an eye on her.'

'If there's any nausea, or dizziness, or unusual drowsiness, see your doctor immediately, or bring her back here if you're on holiday.'

Tessa smiled. 'We're going to the Isles of Scilly!'

'Lucky you.' The doctor momentarily dropped his professional expression. He looked at them with dreamy eyes. 'I recommend Tresco. It's a paradise island – white sand, a tropical garden, and it's full of magic and legend.'

'Tresco!' repeated Tessa, and a shiver of excitement passed through her mind like a wave. White sand. Magic and legend. Something ancient already touching the forgotten recesses of her soul. Had she been there before in some distant dream?

'I'm tired now,' she said to Paul. 'I need to go to sleep.'

'Sensible girl,' said the doctor. 'I'll leave you to it.'

'Okay, darling – I'll go and find a phone box, see if I can book us in somewhere, and book the boat – *The Scillonian*, it's called.'

Paul kissed her tenderly, and left, his eyes excited, his walk full of new life and enthusiasm.

Tessa settled back onto the starched pillows and closed her eyes. Tresco! It was like being given a cloud. A new, silver and white, untainted cloud, catching the sunlight from the last hours of an ancient land. A transformational cloud. She let it enfold her in softness, and as she floated into sleep, she heard a song on the wind.

Tresco had answers. Silent answers to silent questions, stitched in filaments of lights into the minds of those who could still access the magic.

'I can't get up. Can't see straight. Sorry, love, I'll just have to lie in bed.' Paul was stretched out on the bed in the Island

Hotel, Tresco. 'And draw the curtains please. I can't stand the light.'

Tessa stood looking down at him in bewilderment. She felt fine, happy in her jeans and sneakers, a rucksack on her back with a packed lunch for two inside, provided by the hotel. A perfect spring day with cerulean skies and hardly a breath of wind. Her sea-green bikini under her clothes, a towel in the rucksack.

On their first day on Tresco, it had been Paul, not her, who was irritable. She thought the stress of the wedding and the accident had affected him badly. Despite her blow on the head and the concussion, Tessa had benefited from the long peaceful hours of sleep. And she loved the boat trip across the dazzling ocean, loved the salt wind in her hair and the swoosh of the waves. Dolphins raced alongside the great white ship, leaping out of the water in arcs of spray. She felt they were looking right at her – at no one else, just her – and smiling, communicating pure joy.

Sailing into the quay at Hugh Town, St Mary's, Tessa noticed some small blue-black diving birds on the water, agile and fascinating in the way they flipped into a dive, like a hybrid between a bird and a fish. 'Manx shearwaters,' someone told her, and a man handed her his powerful binoculars and let her look at the tiny bright-faced birds. Paul wasn't interested, and as they waited on the quay for the boat to Tresco, he'd been oddly silent, his eyes hidden behind sunglasses.

The ultimate surprise, for Tessa, was landing on Tresco,

walking up the stone jetty and hearing a song she recognised. It haunted her dreams. A song thrush. And not just one, but many, shouting melodiously to each other across the island.

'I love song thrushes,' she said. 'They remind me of the woods back home in Monterose. It's my Dad's favourite bird. And it's now an endangered species.'

Paul grunted. He frowned over the map in his hand.

'Once when I was in London, in the middle of the traffic, I heard a song thrush,' Tessa said, 'and it was high up on top of Selfridges, singing its heart out – and nobody listening. It made me feel amazing. They're inspirational, don't you think?'

'What are?'

'Song thrushes.'

'You're potty about birds.'

'So?'

'So it's annoying.'

'So is your obsession with maps.'

'I am TRYING to see where our hotel is. Or don't you think that matters?' Paul's sunglasses flashed angrily. 'I hope it's a decent place. It cost a fortune. I'm surprised at this scruffy-looking place.'

'It's not scruffy! It's an island – a wild island with no traffic. And look at these flowers, Paul – sea pink and white campion – and those massive tufts of leaves with giant seedheads. I wonder what they are?'

'Agapanthus,' growled Paul. 'Mum's got some in our garden – remember?'

Tessa bounded forward to look at something else, a prostrate, creeping plant with a pink flower. 'These are like sweet peas! Oh, I wish I'd brought my wildflower book.'

Paul was not impressed. 'I've brought us here to look at Tresco, not study weeds. Come ON, Tessa. We need to get into our hotel. I need a cup of strong coffee.'

'Low blood sugar?' she asked.

'Something like that.'

She stumbled after him, carrying her suitcase, and they climbed onto the trailer with seats pulled by a small tractor which took them to the hotel.

'It's fantastic!' Tessa said happily as they were shown into the honeymoon suite. A luxurious, soft lit bed, a bathroom to themselves, and two windows full of the shining skies and the blue sea. She longed to go out, but Paul didn't seem interested. He didn't want to make love either. He just wanted to sleep.

Heavy clouds rolled in and rain spattered the windows, and outside in the hotel garden the fat palm trees fluttered and flickered in the wind.

'What's wrong?' Tessa asked. She sat beside Paul on the bed and studied his face. It was pale as a wax candle, the skin clammy and taut across his brow.

'I've got a migraine.'

'Aw, you poor thing. What can I do?'

'Get me some black coffee, and an aspirin. I can't eat anything. I'll be sick.'

'What brought it on?'

'The bright sunlight – and probably the stress we've been through.' Paul looked up at her and his eyes looked weak and reluctant. His aura was full of oscillating tendrils of sharp lemon light.

'I can feel your pain,' Tessa said, stroking his brow. She slid cool fingers into his hair and gently massaged his throbbing scalp.

'That's awesome,' he murmured. 'I'm sorry, love, but I'm pretty useless right now. I get terrible migraines. Sometimes they last for days, and no one seems to know what causes them. I hang together when I'm under pressure – I keep going and make the right noises, if you know what I mean – then, as soon as the pressure stops, the migraine arrives. Like it's stopping me having fun.'

Tessa put her arms around Paul and cradled his head against her breast. He gave a deep sigh, and she felt him relaxing, letting go of whatever he was guarding so tightly. She wanted to give him healing, to talk quietly in her special voice, to send him colours and music through her fingertips. But it changed, in a flash of energy. Paul reached up and tweaked her nipple through the satin of her blouse. He sat up and looked at her with starved black eyes. 'God – I need you, Tessa. I need you so much.'

He didn't ask if she was okay. He just pushed her into the deeply sprung, quilted bed and rolled on top of her. Tessa felt a sudden throbbing power from him, from his eyes first, then from the wire strength of his muscles. 'I'm not ready,' she tried to say, but he smothered her in a kiss that took her breath away. She felt him tearing her skirt, unwrapping her savagely like a forbidden parcel. *He's my husband. I've got to let him*, she thought. And she was afraid. Afraid, as if the migraine had an unstoppable alien power to turn love into violence.

'Go on – scream,' he said. 'I like that. I like you to scream.' He got hold of her hair and yanked her head sideways, then his arms held her bare shoulders down. As he thrust himself inside her, all she could feel was his desperation and his need.

It was over very quickly, leaving her crying silently, feeling the heat of what might have been. Frustration. Betrayal. Self-hate. Darkness. And a name, crying in her heart. Art. Always Art. Always and forever.

Paul groaned, turned his back on her and went instantly to sleep, the migraine still a taut, white mask across his cheeks. Tessa ran a bath for herself and found her bottle of expensive bubble bath. Tiara, by Lenthéric, Lucy's wedding gift to her. 'You only need a capful,' she'd said. But Tessa was feeling abandoned, disappointed and dirty. She tipped the entire bottle into the bath and immersed herself in the foam.

In the morning the migraine still had Paul in its grip. 'You go and explore the island,' he said. 'I'll be better tomorrow.'

'Are you sure you don't need a doctor?'

'No, I don't need a quack. I'm used to it. It's like a storm, Tessa. There's nothing I can do but hunker down and let it blow over.'

Tessa walked out into the pristine morning. *I'm free*, she thought, and a burst of euphoria lifted her spirits. A day to herself, on an enchanted island. Alone with the song thrushes and the seabirds. Exactly what she needed.

Kate was lying in wait for the postman, hoping every day for a card or a word from Tessa and Paul. They'd gone off so happily, but she needed to know where they were. The end of the wedding had left a gaping hole in her life. While Freddie got on with making bird boxes, she and Sally set about cleaning up the post reception chaos, slowly restoring their home to normal. Kate worked at the sink in the window so that she could see the postman arrive.

'He's got a card!' she cried, and ran out. She exchanged the usual banter with the postman, and stood on the garden path in the morning sun, tingling with joy as she saw the colourful postcard. A white ship on a dark blue, foam-flecked ocean. *The Scillonian*! Kate burst into Freddie's workshop. 'They've gone to the Isles of Scilly! Isn't that wonderful? How clever of Paul. Oh, Tessa will love it.'

'Ah, she will.' Freddie wiped his hands on an oily rag, and they put their heads together to read the treasured words on the back of the card. Dolphins. Manx shearwaters. Tresco. A world away from Monterose.

'I'm so happy for them,' Kate said, 'and I can see you are too.'

'We shall see,' Freddie said non-committally.

'How I'd love to go out there on that white ship,' Kate said.

'Well – we can – what's stopping us?'

'Money?'

'Ah – money.'

Freddie picked up his hammer again and continued nailing slats of larch on the roof of a bird box. 'We can't go on like this, Kate. I gotta get the lorry going again. No matter what the doctor says.'

'If you think so, dear.' Kate knew the wedding had cost them a lot of money. It would take time to build their savings again. She took Tessa's card into the house to show Sally.

'Lucy rang,' Sally said. 'She's coming over this afternoon, with Tim. She said they'd got something to tell you.'

Kate gasped. *Grandchildren*, she thought immediately. *Lucy might be expecting.* She saw herself knitting matinée coats and booties.

'Don't get your hopes up, Kate,' Sally said.

'Why not? What did she tell you?'

'Nothing, dear – it was just her tone of voice.'

'Well – it's either grandchildren, or trouble,' Kate said, deflated.

Sally was looking at her with serious eyes. 'I know you'd love a grandchild, Kate – but maybe you and Freddie might have another baby – I know you wanted a boy.'

'Mum, I'm too old,' Kate said. 'I'm in the change of life now. Hot flushes and all that.'

She was glad to see Lucy and Tim arriving.

Tim didn't usually come in. He still felt awkward, despite Kate's efforts to accept him. She'd worked at it and felt they were progressing. Tim would even look at her and give a curt sort of smile, but he never really cracked his face.

They were both in jeans and baggy sweaters. Lucy had her hair cleverly twisted into a deliberately untidy bun, with tendrils escaping like graceful springs around her face. She wore a pair of diamond-shaped enamelled earrings.

'Tessa and Paul are on the Isles of Scilly!' Kate said proudly, pushing the postcard across the table.

'Good for them,' Lucy said with carefully guarded sarcasm. She hardly glanced at Tessa's card. She seemed edgy.

'I'll go and make some tea,' Sally said tactfully, 'and leave you to talk.'

'Where's Dad?' Lucy asked.

'In his workshop.'

'I'll go and get him,' Lucy said. 'We've got something to tell you – both of you. It's okay, Mum. Don't look so anxious – and no, I'm not pregnant.'

Kate hoped Freddie wasn't going to go wooden and refuse to come in. But he did, in long strides, his face wary and vulnerable under his cap. He sat down as far away from Tim as possible, and the two men eyed each other uneasily.

Kate tried to break the ice with chat about the unseasonably warm weather. She sat close to Freddie, feeling protective towards him. His little Lucy, the child with the bouncing curls and laughing eyes, was all grown up and hard-faced. It hurt Freddie to see her with Tim, and he'd dealt with the pain by shutting it off, losing himself in his work.

'Mum, you don't have to talk about the weather!' Lucy said. She and Tim looked at each other, and Tim lit a fag. He offered one to Freddie.

'He's given up smoking,' Kate reminded him, and Tim shrugged and blew smoke towards the ceiling. She wished he wouldn't smoke. It was hard for Freddie to see someone else enjoying a fag. She took a box of New Berry Fruits from the sideboard and offered them round.

'Mm – I like the raspberry one,' Lucy said, taking it.

They sat munching the fruit jellies which had a hard capsule of sugar at the centre, with a sharp tang of juice inside.

'So what have you come to tell us?' Kate asked, licking the taste of lemon from her lips.

Lucy swallowed the rest of her raspberry sweet. She took Tim's hand and looked at him. He nodded, and Kate saw him squeeze Lucy's delicate hand. The silence felt prickly.

'Well – Mum, and Dad.' Lucy hesitated and Kate saw her eyes grow ominously bright. 'This might be a shock – but, the fact is – Tim and I are going to Australia.'

'Australia!' The word splashed down into the silence like a huge pebble being dropped from a great height into a lily pool.

'To live,' Lucy added.

Time alone on Tresco had a profound effect on Tessa.

At first she stood, mesmerised, outside the hotel, gazing at opaline views of rock ridges and tantalising islands, scattered cottages and boats. Dazzling light on turquoise seas. Hot yellow squares of bulb fields nestled between stone walls. Primroses bursting from granite walls, impossibly abundant as if painted there in the palest cream. The scent of them on the salt air was soporific.

On hushed feet she wandered, listening in awe to the song thrushes, her eyes seeking out each individual bird, always alone, high up, trembling with energy as they sang. Though the song was different, it called up her memory of nightingales in the woods of Monterose. Tears hovered, and she let them roll down her cheeks and dry in the crisp sunshine. Tears of joy this time. Welcome, healing tears. She didn't long for Art, or Paul, or her dad, or even Jonti. She loved, loved, loved being alone.

Enormous Monterey pine trees grew in clumps all over the island, and especially around the Abbey Gardens. Tessa felt drawn to explore, but first she wanted the beach. Appletree Bay was a perfect crescent of moon-white sand. Tessa took her shoes off and paddled along the shoreline of glass-clear water, lattices of sunlight spangling her toes. It was deliciously cold. With her jeans rolled up she stood knee deep, listening. The song thrushes were distant now and there were seagulls and the high-pitched cries of oyster catchers. Beyond the singing was an unfathomable ringing sound from the sea, something she remembered from St Ives. Here on the Isles of Scilly it was stronger, from the bell buoys far out at sea.

Tessa sat down on soft sand, her hand full of shells she had gathered. Limpets in myriad colours, sea snails in bright yellow and russet, pink cowries and fragments of pearl. She planned to take them home to London and make something with them, a trinket box or a lamp, something to touch and dream of Tresco.

It was annoying to feel tired and headachy. She'd wanted to swim, but the echo of her concussion made her more cautious than usual. A feeling of being fragile. Needing to sit still and just be.

Appletree Bay was deserted. It was all hers. Tessa lay back in the sand, the March sun warm on her face and legs. She allowed herself to daydream, something she hadn't done for a long time, not since Art. It had been too painful.

Her mind responded instantly, as she gave it permission to dream, and it focused on the shining sea stretched out before her, with the islands of Bryher and Samson floating in the jade green waters. They were hill tops, Tessa thought, the mountains of a drowned land. And she had lived there! She had climbed those rocks, she had dreamed on those summits and gazed at emerald valleys far below.

The ringing sound from the sea became intense, drawing her into a tunnel of resonance, down, down into a place of chiming bell towers and pale stone palaces. Her city. The city under the sea.

I'm home, she thought, *it's where I lived, centuries ago, before I became Tessa.*

She saw herself strolling between pillars of polished stone, where ancient sunlight glistened in the crystals of white granite. She saw her robe of silk and sea-pearls swirling as she walked, her hair tumbling from a jewelled tiara. Then came the alarm bells, and the screams. Hundreds of people fleeing for their lives, dying like ants in the tsunami, their hair flung like seaweed into the mountain slopes. While she still lived, high on the mountain, in a safe palace of white granite. Forever haunted by an overwhelming thought: *My work is not finished.*

She sat with her back against a rock, her fingers caressing the white sand, watching points of light from grains of sand and the winking colours of seashells. Then she did something Starlinda had taught her. With her eyes closed and the palms of her hands upwards, she sat still and sent the question into the light. *What work? What is the unfinished work? Who am I, and what is my destiny?*

She waited.

And waited.

The lapping of the waves and the piping cries of seabirds faded. She found herself in her field, under the elder tree at the source of the Mill Stream. The water was burbling, and Art was there, playing his guitar, looking at her with immense love in his grey eyes. He got up and walked away, up the field and into the wood. He went through a gate, and locked it behind him. Tessa frowned as her reasoning mind kicked in and reminded her there was no gate, and no fence such as the one she was seeing. And why couldn't she follow? Why lock the gate? She saw the glint of a chain and a heavy padlock, and it hurt. It was like a symbol. The way to his heart was locked.

Starlinda had trained her well. At one time, Tessa would have wallowed in the pain. Now she was able to lift her consciousness, rise above the pain and into the world of light. *What is my work?* she asked again, and felt an ache of intensity woven into the question. The answer came, swiftly, like a shimmer of wings against the sun. Just four words. *You are a healer.*

She longed to ask *How?* and *When?* and *Where?* but she remained still and let the words flow into her heart, and as she did so, a garden sprang up around the source of the Mill Stream, with lilies and roses, and a path winding through trees. The field had become an enchanted garden where bees and dragonflies flew with the sun on their wings. The winding path led down to a building at the bottom of the field; strangely, it was a barn that looked like a temple. Even stranger was the queue of people waiting at the door, some with cats and dogs in their arms. *They're waiting for me,* Tessa thought, coming suddenly awake from the meditation, holding the dream in both hands like a precious jewel.

Driven in from a distant time, the dream alighted in a corner of her mind like a windblown seed arriving in the place where it intended to grow. At the top of the beach there were dandelions in the grass, in full bloom. Tessa studied one of the yellow flowers, so total in the way it opened its thousand petals to the sun, so mystically perfect in the way it made the seed head into a geometric globe. Another memory surfaced, of Freddie carrying her round the garden as a baby. She'd been crying, and he'd picked a dandelion clock and shown it to her. He'd made his face look like the North wind in a story book as he'd blown it, counting 'one o'clock, two o'clock ', each time looking at her with his blue eyes sparkling, until she'd felt a smile ripple her cheeks and heard the startling sound of her own laughter.

Thanks, Dad, she thought now, *you were the only person who knew how to reach me. The only person who believed there was a bright soul inside that screaming bundle of a child. And now I'm doing the same, for Chandra and all the children I work with.*

Another, less welcome thought arrived like the tolling of the deepest bell. The death bell.

I have to do the same for Paul – and he's supposed to be my husband.

CHAPTER 15

Silent Spring

''Tis the saddest day of my life.' Freddie held Kate's hand tightly as they waited at the garden gate of The Pines.

'We should go indoors,' Kate said, 'and get on with something.'

Freddie shook his head. He put his arm around Kate's shoulders, his fingers finding comfort in twiddling strands of her hair. 'I gotta stand here. 'Tis like – a funeral,' he muttered, and the words hurt his throat. *Men don't cry*, he thought, annoyed to feel a tear trickling through the stubble on his cheek. He wanted to rage at God, and shout at the sky, tell the world he cared and why didn't they care?

'Don't upset yourself, dear.' Kate slipped her arm around his waist, her work-worn hand loving on the edge of his old tweed jacket. Then she tensed, listening. 'They're coming!'

They clung together, shocked by the finality of it as three huge lorries roared past, making everything tremble. They pulled in and parked on the grass verge outside The Pines. 'Look at that,' Freddie said in disgust. 'Three of them – blimin' great things. What do they need THREE for?'

'Well, one's got a crane on it – and the tools, I suppose,' Kate reasoned. 'What a lot of men in tin hats. Do you think I should make them some tea?'

Freddie looked down at her bright brown eyes. 'You stay here with me, Kate. I – I need you by my side. No need to make tea for that lot.'

'I'm going to make you a ham sandwich and bring it out here,' Kate said firmly. 'You've had no lunch. I won't be long.' She put a wooden garden chair next to him, and disappeared into the house.

Freddie sat down, numbly. It seemed easier to think while he was sitting. He watched the nine helmeted men unpacking chainsaws and coils of rope. *Butchers*, he thought, and his mind trawled back through the years, creating a requiem for the land he had loved since boyhood.

The elm trees had always been there. He had trudged to school under their guardianship. Trees that stood, invincible, through wind and weather, and wartime. He'd spent happy hours playing in the drifts of golden leaves that filled the lanes in autumn. He'd watched flocks of linnets, yellowhammers and fieldfares moving through the branches, and caterpillars of the tortoiseshell butterfly making their cocoons in a crevice. He'd seen woodpeckers high up drilling for insects, and the red of hibernating ladybirds hidden in the texture of the bark. The elm trees supported a vast range of wildlife which he had studied as a boy. Elms grew profusely along the hedgerows all over Somerset. Thousands had died, leaving their bare trunks like white bones, leafless and dead, killed by Dutch Elm Disease. Without them, the countryside would be desolate.

Freddie's ham sandwich lay untouched on the willow-patterned plate, and Kate sat on a rug at his feet, her arm over his knees. He knew she felt powerless, as he did, against the whine of the chainsaws. 'It's like they're cutting me friends down,' he said. 'And no one seems to know or care about the wildlife. Where's it gonna go? All that life? Even the dead wood had dozens of insects, and birds, and fungi. There'll be nothing left but a sterile world.'

'It's like *Silent Spring*,' Kate said, referring to the book by Rachel Carson they'd both read in the fifties. A grim prediction of what would happen if the widespread use of herbicides and pesticides continued. 'We've lost so many birds and butterflies already – and those lovely meadows full of clover and cowslips – and moon daisies. It's very sad. But there's nothing we can do.'

'Tessa was passionate about it. Wasn't she?' Freddie said. '"Til she ended up in London.'

'She still is, I'm sure,' Kate told him, 'and she'll come home one day, I know she will.'

'Good job she's not here today. She'd break her heart.' He jumped when the first giant carcass of an elm tree cracked and hit the ground with a thump, scattering splinters across the lane. It left a new kind of silence, a vacancy in the sky.

267

Freddie felt it in his heart and through his veins. They watched the blue-painted crane lift the tree trunk and dump it on the back of one of the lorries.

Kate looked up at him, and he realised suddenly how pale her cheeks were. Her skin was the colour of the dead wood. Why had he never noticed it until now? 'You don't look too good,' he said, expecting the usual response – laughter and a bright, dismissive smile, a reassuring affirmation that all was well. He was alarmed when Kate's head went down and she stared at the ground. 'There's nothing wrong – is there?' he asked.

Kate shook her head, but wouldn't meet his eyes. 'I'm tired. I don't know why I'm so tired, but I am.'

Freddie chilled. He felt as if the splinters of the fallen elm were like poison arrows. Kate's illness had come slowly, like the death of the elm trees. Suddenly the loss of thousands of elm trees was nothing compared to Kate's life. His Kate. She'd been rosy-cheeked and vibrant. Her plump figure had been homely, the way he liked it. Freddie pulled at the soft fabric of her dress. It was loose.

'You're losing weight,' he said, and added tactlessly, 'your clothes are hanging on you.'

'Oh, I'll be all right. It's just old age, dear,' Kate joked. 'I must get the sewing machine out and take some tucks in my dresses.'

'You should see the doctor.'

'I don't want to make a fuss. I'll be fine.'

'But will you see him? Please, I think you should.'

'I might – or I might not.'

A second tree crashed to the ground. A smell of rotting timber and crushed grass drifted through the garden of The Pines. Kate looked at the line of washing strung across the lawn. 'Our sheets will smell of sawdust,' she said brightly. 'I must go and get them in.'

By the end of the afternoon, fifteen trees bordering the garden and the lane had been felled and stacked onto lorries. When they had gone, a few crows and jackdaws flew down to pick over the bruised ground, and a breeze whisked saw-dust along the tarmac in drifts. The sky looked silver-white and shocked, and the earth trembled. Freddie could feel it in his bones, even inside the house. *We live on a dying planet*, he thought, imagining the earth blanched and barren like the moon. Even in bed he still felt the shock rippling up walls and through floorboards.

Next morning when he was shaving in the bathroom, he heard a new sound, a tearing, crunching sound, and the throb of a tractor's engine. He opened the window and looked out. A new red Massey Ferguson tractor was power-ing slowly up the lane towards The Pines, with the long arm of a flail-cutter viciously chopping the hedge. It was cutting the new tender shoots of ash, maple and bramble, sending shreds of twig flying. Freddie could smell the sap. Horrified, he watched it shearing the blossom from a hawthorn tree, the petals scattering like snow. A pair of blackbirds flew up with shrill cries of distress.

Freddie had vowed, long ago, never to lose his temper.

But now, something snapped in his mind. With his face half covered in shaving foam, he dropped his razor into the basin, and ran downstairs two steps at a time. He thundered through the kitchen where Kate was frying bacon, out of the back door and down the garden path with his pulse roaring in his ears.

Crying with fury, he ran towards the tractor, waving his arms. 'Stop. STOP!'

Tessa and Paul had set up home in a rented attic flat near the river. Paul had chosen it as a place where he could practise his violin without disturbing anyone. The lounge window looked out into the branches of a plane tree, which Tessa liked, and there was a bathroom and two bedrooms, one just big enough for the double divan bed, a wedding gift from Marcus and Penelope. The other bedroom was small and Paul had quickly claimed it for his music study. They'd agreed on Tessa being the breadwinner until he had finished his three years at music school. 'Then I'll be able to get a decent, highly paid job,' Paul promised, 'and we can think about buying a house with a garden, and then having a family. I fancy two boys and a little girl.'

'I don't want children,' Tessa said.

Paul looked horrified. 'Why not?'

'I'm terrified of childbirth,' she admitted. 'I could never get through it.'

'Is that all?' Paul said coldly. 'Well, Tessa, you'll have to grin and bear it, the way other women do.'

Tessa reacted furiously. 'No, I will not. It's MY body, and you can't dictate how many children we shall have.'

'I'm not dictating. It's every man's right. I married you, and I expect you to have my children.'

'Then you'd better change your expectations,' Tessa said. 'How can you be so insensitive, Paul?'

'It's not ME being insensitive, it's YOU being stupid. Women have children. Full stop. Get used to it, girl.'

'I don't HAVE to have children. Especially not yours if you're going to be dictatorial.' The words were out of her mouth before she could stop. Paul went white. He'd promised never to hit her again after the incident on the train, but Tessa knew it was only a matter of time before it happened again.

'I didn't start this war,' he said.

'Neither did I, Paul. Why can't you be kind instead of bullying me?'

'I am not bullying. I'm asserting my rights as a husband.'

'What about my rights as a wife?'

'I haven't got TIME to argue.' Paul slammed out and disappeared into his music study with an arrogant twist of his shoulders. Tessa sighed. *Keep off the subject of children*, she thought, adding it to a list of things she and Paul couldn't talk about. Being married was more difficult than she'd thought. It wasn't all bad. Mostly they enjoyed weekends in London, walking by the river, or rowing on the Serpentine in Hyde Park. Paul seemed happy with his life, except on the days when he clashed with his rather volatile music teacher.

271

But Tessa longed for the green hills and woods where she had grown up. She sometimes thought sadly about her field and how happy she had felt to have her own plot of land. She'd had a vision of what it could become. The source of the stream would be landscaped into an idyllic water garden with a curved stone seat, a place where she would meditate, plant cowslips and cuckooflower, a place for nightingale picnics and creative dreaming. She felt guilty about the way she had abandoned it. Because of Art. Their time together in the precious field had been brief, three wonderful days, and in three days they had planned its future as a sanctuary for wildlife, a bluebell wood, a glade for butterflies, a pond. The dream was part of her grief.

'You should sell it,' Paul said, one day when they were short of money.

'Certainly not.' Tessa was horrified. 'You can't make me sell it.'

'I can,' Paul said, 'if we get into debt. It will be counted as a joint asset. Ask Dad.'

'I don't believe you,' Tessa said furiously. She added the field to the list of things they didn't talk about for the sake of peace. She tried to live more frugally, but it wasn't easy in London. There was little money left over at the end of a month, and Tessa felt she was struggling to pay the bills while Paul blithely spent his student grant on what he called 'music related expenses', travel expenses, and fags. Sometimes he even bought cigars, which Tessa hated for the way they filled the flat with smoke.

She'd passed her driving test back in the summer and had bravely driven the Morris Minor up to London. At first she and Paul enjoyed having a car, using it for weekend outings to Box Hill, or the Sussex coast, always at Tessa's expense. If she asked Paul for a contribution, he would adopt a cold, judgemental expression and say, 'You chose to have a car. You maintain it.' And if she complained that money was tight, he would wave his musical fingers at the car and say, 'Sell that heap of tin you keep parked there at huge expense. It's a vanity thing. Get real.'

'You're doing brilliantly, Tessa,' Starlinda said in her calm voice. 'You've come a long way since that first meditation.'

Tessa beamed. 'I feel happy, and on fire,' she said. 'It's a luxury to be my true self, after a lifetime of pretence.' She leaned back against one of the sumptuous cushions in Starlinda's sanctuary. 'It's kind of you to teach me.'

'It's my joy, darling,' Starlinda said quietly. 'Someone did it for me, taught me meditation, and it was the greatest gift I have ever been given. So I'm just passing it on, and you will do the same one day, when you've got your own healing centre.'

'It doesn't look possible at the moment,' Tessa said.

'Hold the dream,' Starlinda said, and her eyes shone like blue fire. 'Hold the dream, no matter what. Let no one take it from you.'

Tessa went home with a smile on her face and in her heart, as she always did after an evening of spiritual enlightenment

273

in the ambience of Starlinda's sanctuary. Usually she felt so good that she'd go home and be much nicer to Paul. She even changed her attitude to housework. 'Nurturing my living space,' Starlinda called it. 'Places respond to care as well as people.' Tessa began to find joy in keeping their modest flat sparkling and harmonious. She made cushions from remnants of velvet and silk. She put plants and crystals on the window sills, and burned incense cones of sandalwood and pine. Paul didn't say much, but she felt he appreciated her homemaking skills, especially when Penelope was impressed.

For the first time in her life, Tessa felt successful at being 'normal'. There was a degree of contentment at having made a lovely home out of a boring box of a flat.

On that particular Thursday, she chose to walk home along the river and through the busy streets. A fresh wind was blowing through London, upriver from the North Sea. Tessa loved to feel the wind on her face, even if it had spatters of rain in it. She felt it was cleansing London, making the leaves ripple and the gulls scream as they flew over the swirling river. It brought a touch of the wild into town.

She was enjoying the walk home when something happened, in a moment, that was to change everything.

Two streets away from home, Tessa noticed a cat crouched in the doorway of a derelict chapel. A cat with soft, dark tortoiseshell fur and a sweet little face.

'Hello!' Tessa stopped to stroke her, concerned for the cat's wellbeing in the busy street. 'I've never seen you before. Are you okay?' she asked, and the cat looked up at her, wildly, with eyes that didn't sparkle. In answer to Tessa's question, she meowed piteously, clearly asking for help. 'Can I pick you up?' Tessa slid both hands around the cat's tummy and lifted her up gingerly, shocked to find she weighed almost nothing. She was a bag of bones and fur. She clung to Tessa as if she'd found an angel.

'You're starving, and lost. Does no one want you?' Tessa asked, and felt the cat's whiskers tickle her face. The cat sniffed her cheek and rubbed her head against her, purring, her claws fastened into the collar of Tessa's coat. 'I'm taking you home.'

It was obvious the cat didn't want to let go of her. Tessa carried her down the road and into a newsagent's shop. 'Do you know who this cat belongs to?'

'No.' The shopkeeper didn't seem interested. 'It's a stray.'

'Have you seen her before?'

'Never.'

'Then – will you sell me a tin of cat food – and a bag of cat litter? – and a tin of tuna in case she doesn't like Kitekat.'

Tessa took the cat home, awkwardly with her bag of shopping over one arm. She unlocked the front entrance door, and the cat clung to her tightly, looking everywhere with big eyes as they negotiated the stairs.

Paul was out. He'd left her a scribbled note about an audition at Covent Garden, and he'd underlined Covent Garden three times and put a row of exclamation marks. He'd signed it, 'cross-fingers for me – Paul'.

'I'm not going to abandon you.' Tessa carried the cat into

the kitchen and stood holding her. It was so long since she had cuddled an animal, and the feel of her soft fur was touching a deep need in Tessa. The cat's delicate, needle-like claws clinging to her coat, the way her ears were pink inside, and her tiny nose pink and inquisitive. The rapid heartbeat and the purring. The love that emanated from this weightless bundle of life. 'I must give you a name,' Tessa said, in her special, crooning, animal voice, and the cat listened attentively. 'I'll call you Benita. It means gift. Because that's what you are – a gift to this earth.'

She put Benita down on the kitchen floor, noticing her legs were wobbly and weak, probably from hunger. Hungry, scary hours of being lost and homeless in London. Being unwanted. Tessa felt an instant, emotional bond with Benita.

She got the tin opener and opened the can of tuna while Benita meowed and wove herself around Tessa's ankles. She gave her a dollop of tuna and a dollop of Kitekat on a saucer, and watched, satisfied to see the pathetically thin creature eating. When she'd finished, Benita made a beeline for the sofa and sat there washing. Being in a strange place didn't seem to bother her.

Tessa made herself toast and coffee, kicked off her shoes, and sat down next to Benita. It wasn't long before the little cat crept onto her lap, and when Paul came home late he found the two of them asleep in the lamplight. 'A cat!' he exclaimed, and Tessa woke up immediately. Benita opened her eyes just a slit, checked out Paul, and shut them again, purring softly in her sleep.

'This is Benita,' Tessa said. 'I found her in the doorway of that derelict chapel. She's terribly thin and can hardly walk.'

Paul sat down beside her. He stroked Benita gingerly. 'She doesn't smell very nice.'

'Neither would you if you were homeless and starving.'

'And she's probably got fleas, Tessa.'

'I can deal with those.'

'She's really sweet,' Paul said. 'But we can't keep her, Tessa. You do know that, surely?'

'Why not? She won't do any harm.'

'It's in our rent agreement. No pets. You signed it!'

'But she needs a home, Paul. And she needs to go to the vet. I'll take care of her. You won't have to do anything.'

Paul was getting increasingly tense. That taut, judgemental pallor was creeping over his cheeks. 'What part of this do you not understand, Tessa? We can't keep a cat here, no matter how sweet. She will have to go.'

'I love her, and I'm keeping her.'

'Don't be so pig-awkward. You can take her to the RSPCA, can't you? Do the humane thing.'

'No, Paul. Benita is a gift. I believe she was sent – to me. I've committed to her, and she's staying.'

'She is not. If she's not gone when I come home tomorrow, I'll take her to the RSPCA myself.'

'No, you will not. How would you like to be taken to the RSPCA? Have a heart, Paul. Benita has only just found me. She needs to stay with me. With ME, not be put in some soulless wire cage.'

'We signed an agreement.'

'I don't care.'

'No, you wouldn't, would you. Awkward bitch.'

'It's no good attacking me, Paul. Why should I be called names for LOVING a little lost cat?'

Paul rolled his eyes. 'Spare me the emotional blackmail,' he groaned. 'And by the way, IF you're interested, I won't be playing in the Covent Garden Opera orchestra – I made a mess of the audition. They didn't even say, "Come back next year". They were totally po-faced and off-putting. I feel like giving up. I worked SO HARD on that Paganini. Are you even listening, Tessa? Oh, sorry, I forgot, it's the cat who matters, not me.'

'You're right,' Tessa said quietly, with power in her eyes. 'This little cat is homeless, hungry and unloved, and you are none of those things, Paul.'

'Do you have to be so sanctimonious?'

Tessa looked down at Benita who was still purring and enjoying being stroked and loved. Paul had a way of winding her up. She remembered what Starlinda had said. 'Hold the dream. Let no one take it from you.' Had she said that because she knew that Paul was becoming more and more controlling?

He leaned close to her so that she saw the glint of menace in his eyes. 'YOU.' He jabbed a finger close to her face. 'Make sure that cat is gone by the time I get home tomorrow.'

Tessa felt tears gathering in her throat. She didn't want to give Paul the satisfaction of seeing her cry, so she fought them back, concentrating on the love and light she was sending into Benita's painfully thin back. *What am I going to do?* she thought, remembering tomorrow was Friday and she had to go to work. At the same time, she knew in her heart exactly what she was going to do.

Kate listened in alarm to the shouting going on in the lane outside. She quickly turned the cooker off and put a lid over the pan of sizzling bacon. She'd wanted to giggle when Freddie had shot through the kitchen with blobs of shaving soap flying from his face. But now she could hear the pain in his voice, against the sound of a tractor idling in the lane. *I must go out*, she thought, *and pour oil on troubled waters*. Or was it best to leave the men to have their argy-bargy? She chose to go out to stand staunchly beside Freddie.

She hurried down the path, and was alarmed to see Freddie in such a state. She'd never seen him so angry. He was standing in front of the tractor, banging his big fist on the bonnet and shouting up at the driver who was rolling his eyes and pushing an unruly mop of black hair away from his brow.

'You are NOT gonna cut our hedge like that,' Freddie shouted. 'This is our hedge, between the garden and the lane. There are nesting birds in there and I won't have 'em disturbed.'

'I work for Somerset County Council Highways Department, and I've got to do my job,' the driver yelled back. 'I keep telling you that and you won't listen.'

'Over my dead body,' Freddie bellowed. 'I'm not moving

and you'll have to drive over me if you dare – and I reckon you would too, since you don't care tuppence about the wild birds who live in that hedge. You've already destroyed their source of winter food. That hawthorn will have no berries now, 'cause of you and your posh tractor. 'Tis bad enough with the elm trees being cut down, without an idiot like you destroying the hedges as well.'

'Don't you call me an idiot. Look at you – a demented old man with shaving soap on yer face. Why should I listen to you?'

Kate squared her shoulders and walked into the road.

'Stay out of it, Kate,' Freddie pleaded.

Kate marched up to the tractor and flashed her bright brown eyes at the driver. She wagged a finger. 'Now you turn that engine off and get down here,' she said, 'and we'll talk this over nicely.'

He stared at her.

'I'm waiting.'

He rolled his eyes, and turned off the engine.

'That's better, thank you,' Kate said pleasantly. 'My goodness, you look so intimidating up there in that huge tractor. It's like a tower. I was a farmer's daughter, and my dad never had a tractor like that. He had a little grey Ferguson. We used to play on it as children. Now, are you going to get down, or shall I come up and get you?' she added, mischievously.

The man actually smiled. 'All right, missus. Keep yer hair on!'

He opened the cab door and climbed down, and the

atmosphere changed immediately as a human being emerged from the mechanical monster.

'Well, you're only a lad,' Kate said appraisingly. 'Fancy you being in charge of that intimidating machine.'

Her kind voice coaxed another smile out of him. Kate looked at Freddie. His face was purple, but his eyes glistened with regret. She sensed him calming down. She reached up and gently brushed the last of the shaving soap from his neck. 'I thought the house was on fire, dear, the way you thundered through the kitchen.'

The ghost of a twinkle appeared in Freddie's eyes. He looked at her with awe, and gratitude.

Kate took his arm. 'Now you – and you,' she looked at the young lad, 'come and sit down on the lawn and I'll bring you both a cup of tea. Then you can talk about this nicely.' She towed the two men to the seat under the cherry tree. 'Now isn't this lovely? Look at the blossom. And the bees on it!'

She left them sitting there meekly while she made tea. Later, she planned to turn it into a funny story she would relish relating to friends even though it was a serious matter. Kate believed tea and good humour would calm the troubled waters. She opened the biscuit tin and popped a few custard creams and Cadbury's Chocolate Fingers on a plate, put it on a tray with three mugs of tea and took it outside, pleased to see Freddie was himself again, quietly explaining something about nesting birds to the young man who was listening, mesmerised, by the emotive power of Freddie's storytelling, a gift inherited from his father.

What would Freddie do without me? Kate thought, sipping her tea. *He'd be lost.* With a heavy heart, she made a decision she ought to have made months ago. *I should go to the doctor,* she told herself. *I can't run away from this forever.*

CHAPTER 16

I've Lost Everything

The morning after Tessa had found her, Benita sat on the sofa, washing her face elegantly with a carefully curled paw. Her eyes were watching Tessa darting around the flat, stuffing clothes, shoes and books into a bag. Tessa was singing along to her favourite song, The Beatles' hit, *Let It Be*. It suited her mood right now.

> *There will be an answer*
> *Let it be*

The song was exactly what Art would like. Tessa allowed herself to imagine him playing it on his guitar, and singing the words in his husky voice. It sent a shiver down her spine. The years had passed, the wound had healed over, but the scar was deep. Deeper still was the longing in her soul. Tessa had never stopped searching for Art. Every day, every place, every hippy in the distance. In truth Art had never left her. He was in her heart every day, and in her dreams at night. No one knew where he was. Lou and Clare told her Art had gone missing. No one had seen him. *All my life, I'll search for him*, Tessa thought, stuffing her flared jeans into the rucksack. She knew that if she did find Art, her marriage to Paul would be over.

'Do you like The Beatles, Benita?' Tessa asked, and the little cat blinked her eyes in reply. She already looked a bit better, her legs less wobbly, her eyes happier. 'Now you stay here and be contented. I've got to go out, but I won't be long. I'm not abandoning you, darling.' She felt terrible when Benita followed her to the door and meowed, looking up at her pleadingly. 'I'll be back soon.' Tessa locked the flat door, took the packed bag downstairs and stuffed it into the boot of the Morris Minor.

She hurried down the street and into the bank. It was the end of the month and she'd just been paid. She drew out her entire month's salary, leaving nothing to pay the rent, and not caring for once. With the cash safely zipped into her multi-coloured Indian bag, Tessa ran on, dodging the early morning shoppers, and arrived at a pet shop. She bought Benita a luxury travelling basket with a cosy tartan cushion inside. After a browse around the shop, she bought her a brush, a tin of flea powder, worming pills, a catnip mouse and a red velvet collar. She bought vitamin pills, and tins of Felix.

It was May, and heat was already rising from the

pavements of London, the sun blazing from the windows of tower blocks. Tessa was boiling hot, and anxious, her heart racing, worrying in case Paul might decide to come home early and find Benita alone in the flat. What would he do? What would he say when he saw the travelling basket and the bag of goodies from the pet shop? He'd cross-examine her about why, and how much money she had spent. Tessa didn't think she could stand yet another row. Lately it had been bad. Paul was stressed over his final exams, his auditions, and his migraines which seemed relentless.

She hurried back to the flat, feeling rebelliously jubilant at the thought of the money tucked in her bag. She'd earned it. Why shouldn't she spend it for once? She loved carrying the cat basket home, and the stuff she'd bought for Benita. She was looking forward to helping the little cat recover from her ordeal, seeing her coat glossy and her eyes alive and happy.

But when she looked up at the flat window, it was open, and she'd left it closed in case Benita tried to escape. Paul must be there! Tessa paused at the front door and debated whether to put the cat basket straight into the car. *Why should I have to hide it?* she thought. *I'm proud of what I've done. But the money! He'll take it off me.*

Tessa put the bag under the driver's seat of the Morris Minor and locked the car, hoping Paul wasn't watching her. She hid the car key in a crack between two bricks next to the front door.

Paul was at the kitchen table, sipping black coffee and frowning over a pile of sheet music. 'Hi,' he said, without looking up. Benita was nowhere to be seen.

'Where's Benita?'

'How should I know?'

'I left her in the flat while I went shopping. Where is she, Paul?'

He went on studying the sheet music, teasing her.

Tessa's heart raced with anxiety. She searched the flat, looking under chairs and the sofa, under the bed, behind the fridge, in the broom cupboard. Anger came, burning along the threads of her anxiety, igniting a bomb inside Tessa. 'WHERE IS SHE?'

Paul went cold. 'Don't shout at me.'

'What have you done with my cat?' Tessa yelled.

'Don't get hysterical. I haven't damaged your precious cat. I let her out.'

'You did WHAT?'

'She meowed at the door. So I let her out and she ran downstairs and out into the street – where she belongs.'

'How could you, Paul? How COULD you? You – you're not human. Benita doesn't belong in the street. No one belongs in the street. She needs a home, and I rescued her.' Tessa was distraught. 'She could die on the street – and – and she'll think I abandoned her.'

'Stop screaming at me. How can I work with a bloody head-case like you around?'

'I am not a head-case. I'm a caring, compassionate person,

286

Paul. And, in case you hadn't noticed, you can work, thanks to me paying for everything.'

Paul's shoulders stiffened. He pretended to be looking at the sheet music, but his eyes fired bullets of contempt in her direction. 'And don't you just LOVE reminding me,' he quipped.

'I don't love it. I hate having to and I wish you appreciated what I do.'

'Like blowing our housekeeping money on a luxury cat basket for that flea-ridden bag of bones off the street.'

'I'm being kind. Or hadn't you heard of kindness?' Tessa turned her back, intending to go out and search for Benita. She forgot how much Paul hated her to walk away.

In seconds he was on his feet, sending his chair crashing to the floor. He grabbed Tessa's wrists and held her in a vicelike grip, as if he hoped her bones would snap like chair legs. Her silver charm bracelet dug into her skin. His breath drowned her in an acrid cloud. 'You've been drinking,' she said, wincing, 'and you're hurting me.'

'GOOD,' he growled. 'You asked for it.'

It was what he always said.

'Let go of me,' Tessa screamed. 'I need to find the cat.'

'Oh – it's the cat now, is it? I'm just your husband. What do I matter? Eh? Eh? – Go on, answer me.' He shoved her against the wall with such force that a picture hook tore out from the plaster and sent the picture crashing to the floor. It was one of Freddie's watercolours. The river bridge in summer, with its yellow bottle lilies and reeds. It glowed up at them through the shattered glass.

'Dad's picture.' Tessa bent to pick it up, a rush of tears in her throat.

Paul kicked it aside. 'Leave it,' he raged, his knuckles white as he pushed her shoulders back against the wall. 'Stop bloody whingeing about a stupid picture. Stop bloody looking at it.' He gripped her chin and turned her head to look at him, his fingers digging into her cheeks.

Tessa froze. Images streamed through her mind. Freddie sitting by the river with his box of Reeves Watercolours and a jam jar of water. Benita, lost again, cowering out in the echoing streets. The smile in her mum's bright brown eyes when she'd given her the picture. 'I had it framed especially for you – for your first little home with Paul.'

The images closed together like curtains, shutting out the black window that was Paul. Long ago, in her childhood, Tessa had learned how to freeze, to go still and silent, diving under the anger and fear, diving deep to survive.

She waited, while Paul glared, his eyes demanding a reaction. She sensed him moving along the edges of his anger, crawling, clinging like a man trying not to fall over a precipice into the destructive maelstrom of his own fury. She remembered the times when Freddie had rescued her from that same dark shoreline. He'd never rescued her with words. He'd rescued her with silence. His big hands patting her shoulders. His blue eyes believing in her.

It took all of her strength to stand there and keep quiet, keep the lid on her own feelings. She hated Paul. She was terrified. But she had compassion for him. 'I won't let you do this, Paul,' she said quietly, and slipped her arms around his shoulders.

Predictably he crumpled, letting go of her and sinking to the floor. He took his head between both hands and banged it against the wall. Then he looked up at Tessa and held a fold of her skirt against his face. 'Don't leave me,' he pleaded. 'You're my LIFE, my whole world. Please – please – don't leave me.'

Kate was unusually silent as she lay on the narrow couch in Dr Jarvis's surgery. She'd been a nurse. She knew how to read a doctor's face. So she studied Dr Jarvis's expression as he examined her swollen tummy. He was frowning as his clean, confident hands pressed and prodded. He did a lot of tapping and listening, his eyes occasionally meeting hers over the top of his glasses.

When he had finished, there was an uncomfortable silence. While Kate readjusted her clothes and slipped her shoes on, he sat at his desk writing notes with a black fountain pen. Kate felt very frightened. She knew, from her nurse's training, what it could be, and Dr Jarvis knew that she knew.

'Take a seat, Kate.' She sat down on the brown leather chair while he shuffled papers, as if putting off the moment when he must tell her. Finally he met her eyes. 'I'm afraid you might need surgery, Kate. There's definitely something there that shouldn't be there. But – unless we open you up and have a look, we don't know what's going on. Let's hope it's just a cyst which can be easily removed.'

'And what else could it be? Please be honest with me, Doctor. I need to know.

'I will be – but let's not speculate. Wait and see what the surgeon finds, Kate.'

'So – when have I got to go to hospital?'

'Now.'

'Now?' Kate was shocked. She'd expected him to say in six weeks' time. She gripped the arms of the chair tightly. She saw summer disappearing like a picnic rug snatched from the lawn. 'But I can't just drop everything. Freddie depends on me. We have a business to run.'

'Freddie's a big boy,' said Dr Jarvis, 'and he would want you to have the best treatment we can get for you – wouldn't he?'

'He's got a deep fear of hospitals,' Kate said. 'It's in the family. His mother was the same, only worse – and it's in Tessa too. I'm the one who holds the family together.'

'I appreciate that, Kate. But the sooner we get you into hospital, the sooner you can get well. I'll try to get you in on Monday.'

'And Lucy's in Australia,' Kate added.

Dr Jarvis nodded. 'It will be all right, Kate,' he said firmly. 'Your family will rally round, and friends.'

'I don't want to be a nuisance,' Kate said in a small voice.

'You won't be. You couldn't be a nuisance if you tried, Kate. You've looked after everyone else over the years. Now it's your turn for some TLC.'

'TLC? What's that?'

'Tender loving care.'

Going under the surgeon's knife didn't sound like tender loving care to Kate. She considered refusing treatment. Reasons to say no loomed in front of her like a flight of stairs. Number one was that Freddie would panic. Who would look after him? Kate wanted to cry. The deepest pain was Lucy being in Australia. So far away. So unavailable. And the resentment still stubbornly brooding between Lucy and her father. *In the old days*, Kate thought bitterly, *Lucy was our pride and joy, our golden girl. She would have managed everything so beautifully. What if I die and never see Lucy again?*

Kate got up in a daze. 'I need to think this over, Doctor. I'll go home now.'

'Yes, of course,' Dr Jarvis looked at her shrewdly, 'but, Kate – don't leave it too long.'

Kate was glad Freddie was out when she got home. The lorry was gone and he'd left a note on the kitchen table. *Gone to help Herbie load some stone.*

Everything hurt. Even seeing her lovely home and garden. Kate took her bike out of the shed. She needed to be out in the sunlit countryside, sailing along the lanes with the wind in her hair. *I'll go to Hilbegut*, she thought, *and look at the old family farm.*

She hadn't ridden her bike for a while, and at first she felt fine, sailing down through Monterose and out across the Levels. But her swollen tummy felt awkward and uncomfortable, and soon she was overwhelmingly tired. Again she wanted to cry. She stopped on the river bridge, propped her bike against it and sat on the warm stone parapet, gazing down at the pea-green waterweed waving in the current, the marsh-marigold and sedge grass along the bank. She smiled as a water vole emerged, swimming downstream with his fat cheeks and bright black eyes.

The rhythmic hum of swans' wings made her look up, and a pair of swans flew over, perfectly together, perfectly snowy white. Kate knew that swans mated for life. Like her and Freddie. *I can't die*, she thought. *I can't die and leave Freddie all alone.*

Heat shimmered on the tarmac as Tessa drove down the A303, her bruised wrists on the steering wheel a stark reminder of the state of her marriage. *It's over*, she thought, not for the first time. *I can't go back.* Then the voice of reason told her she had to. Paul's desperate, pleading eyes begging her not to leave. His hand clutching her skirt. His words calling out to her compassionate nature. She'd supported Paul and built his self-esteem, tried to heal the wounds he carried from a lifetime of rejection. It wasn't working. Instead of gratitude, there was anger. Sometimes she thought he hated her. He'd blamed his parents for everything, and when they'd refused to support him through music college, a new surge of bitterness took hold of Paul. Hell-bent on proving them wrong, he'd invested his hopes and emotions in Tessa. It had become increasingly scary for her, coping with his moods, and being the sole breadwinner. 'Don't walk out on me NOW!' Paul had yelled. 'I'm almost there, Tessa. Another few months and I'll have a great job and a salary – money in the bank! Don't pull the rug out now.'

'It's not like that,' she argued.

'Oh, isn't it? So how are we going to pay the rent now you've blown it on cat stuff? You silly bitch.'

Tessa was deeply hurt, and frightened, as her mind recycled the argument while she was driving. It wasn't the situation. It was his attitude. The way he spoke to her. It wasn't fair. She'd done her best to survive in London. She'd longed for a dog or a cat to love. She'd longed to spend some of the money she earned. Working with the children was emotionally rewarding, but exhausting, especially with the journey she now had to make across London. There were times when it hurt to go out on a beautiful morning, and taste the traffic fumes, and spend the summer days cooped up in a building or a tube train. She longed for the silver-blue skies and the water meadows of Monterose, the silence, the deeply scented lanes and the starry nights. She missed her father's mystic peacefulness, and her mum's bright cheerfulness.

Benita was surprisingly quiet, but awake, her lamp like eyes watching Tessa constantly from her basket on the front seat. Most cats would have panicked on a journey. It was odd. Tessa began to sense another presence with her in the car, a guiding spirit, someone who was keeping the little cat calm. A blue-eyed lady, closely resembling Violetta – but the eyes – those eyes – angel eyes that had shone into Tessa's consciousness all through her life.

Tessa hadn't planned to stop, but she pulled into a layby just outside Wincanton, turned the engine off and let the sweet perfume of hawthorn blossom and hayfields drift in through the open windows. There was little traffic, and between the swish of the occasional passing car, the songs of skylarks rippled through the blue air.

What have I done? she thought suddenly. It was Friday. She hadn't phoned Megan to say she wouldn't be there. Her job would be at risk if Megan thought she just hadn't turned up. And what would happen when the standing order for a month's rent was presented to her bank and there was no money to pay it? Worse was the thought of Paul's reaction when he found she had run away.

She'd done it all for Benita. A simple act of love that was sweeping her frail canoe towards the rapids.

Nothing had worked out as she'd planned. Paul's callous reaction to a needy little cat had shocked her into impulsive action. She felt like a child again, running away for some passionate reason. 'I'm going to find Benita,' she'd said firmly to Paul. 'You go and make yourself a coffee.' And she'd picked up the cat basket and hurried downstairs, her own pain and fear secondary to frantic concern for Benita.

She'd paused in the street, looking up and down the road, and was overjoyed to see the little cat come running to her from under a parked car, with her skimpy tail up and her sweet face bright and trusting. 'Darling! Thanks goodness.'

Tessa had scooped her up, feeling the cat's bone-thin body vibrating with her purr. 'I can't risk taking you upstairs again.' Benita touched noses with her, and pushed her head against Tessa's neck. How could such a poor, neglected creature be giving her so much love? Uncomplicated, unconditional love. It seemed sacred.

Fearing for her safety, Tessa had put Benita straight into the basket, grabbed the car key from the slot in the wall and driven out of London, shaking deep inside, wanting to cry but feeling herself going into lockdown. She'd intended to take Benita to Starlinda's place, but the car seemed to have a mind of its own. Someone else was driving. Steely blue eyes. A voice echoing in her mind. Home. Go home. Home.

Sitting in the layby, Tessa heard the voice again, whispering words to her. Surprising words. 'Benita is not your cat. She is a messenger. She has come to lead you home. Nothing happens by chance.'

'Who are you?' Tessa asked, aloud, trying to see the spirit who was talking to her.

'I am who I am,' was the haughty reply, and suddenly the voice changed to a shout. 'Get out of the car. Out. Now. Quickly. And the cat – take the cat. Quickly.'

Tessa grabbed the cat basket and got out. She smelled hot rubber and petrol fumes. Alarmed, she touched the bonnet of the car and found it burning hot. Too late, she realised she had forgotten to top up the water tank and smoke was drifting from under the car. *I should open the bonnet*, Tessa thought. She hesitated, unsure what to do. The blue eyes frowned at her, a vivid urgent blue, and the voice shouted, 'Get back – back – away from the car.'

Benita was yowling inside the basket. Clutching it, Tessa stumbled along the rough tarmac of the layby. An invisible force seemed to be pushing her. 'My bag,' she protested, 'I need my bag! – my money.'

She put the cat basket down in the grass at the roadside, and turned to run back.

The explosion lifted her off her feet and flung her face down onto the tarmac. A white-hot flash, then a curdle of blood-red fire engulfed the Morris Minor and everything inside. It burned like dragon fire, crackling horribly, the fractured metal glinting, and triangles of glass skittering across the road. A mushroom of blue-brown smoke, laden with sparks, billowed into the sky.

Tessa lay in the road, feeling as if all her bones were broken. She heard Benita's terrified meows. 'It's okay, little cat, I'm coming,' she cried out. A spark landed on her hair and she smelled it burning. 'Oh God – no!' She beat it out with her bare hands. A scorching pain from her fingers made her giddy, and just before she passed out, she heard the sound of running feet pounding towards her.

Kate's way of cheering herself up was to make Freddie an especially nice lunch. His favourite cottage pie with a sliced apple under the rich beef mince, topped with creamy mashed potatoes, smothered in butter and browned to a crispy gold.

She'd pulled, scrubbed and cooked baby carrots from the garden with fresh spring greens. Followed by their own sweet, lush strawberries and clotted cream.

She wasn't hungry after her consultation with Dr Jarvis, but Freddie didn't seem to notice the small portion on her plate. He ate with relish, his eyes gazing out at the garden. 'Bloomin' pigeons,' he said intermittently, watching the portly grey woodpigeons raiding his vegetable garden, despite the squares of foil he'd strung over it, and the scarecrow with its bottle top eyes glaring from under a broken panama hat. ''Tis a lovely meal,' he said, eyeing the strawberries, 'and all of it free – except the meat. You're such a good cook.'

Kate swelled with pride. *I can't tell him*, she thought again. Freddie looked well, suntanned and contented, the way it should be. With just the two of them at home they had developed a habit of sunbathing after lunch in two deckchairs, snoozing to the sound of bees and chirruping sparrows. The upset over the elm trees wasn't going to go away, but in May there was still so much to enjoy. The haze of buttercups over the meadows. The young lambs playing like kittens with over-the-top leaps and chases in the field opposite The Pines.

While Freddie set out the two deckchairs, Kate made coffee and took it outside on a tray, the *Daily Express* under her arm. He was watching a blue Bedford van which had pulled up at the gate. 'Now who on earth is that?' she asked, setting the tray down on the lawn between the two deckchairs. Kate usually welcomed company, but today she didn't feel like seeing anyone. 'People just descend on us,' she said, and they watched to see who was going to emerge from the van.

The driver got out and walked around to the passenger door to help someone out. 'It's no one we know,' Kate said, and then her eyes changed. Her hand flew to her mouth. 'Oh my goodness, Freddie. It's Tessa! And she's hurt.' Kate bustled down the path with Freddie padding behind, his eyes full of concern.

The man brought Tessa to the gate. She was obviously in pain and her face looked bruised and swollen. In her hand was a cat basket and Kate could see a sweet little face peeping out with big golden green eyes.

'Mum!' Tessa could hardly speak. Sobs lurched through her body and made her crumple forward like an old woman.

'What is it, dear? What happened?' Kate hugged her daughter close, horrified to see a strand of her beautiful chestnut hair singed, and appalled to feel the power of those deep sobs which seemed to go right back to childhood. She'd thought Tessa was okay, settled at last, enjoying London and her job, building a home and a marriage.

'I've – lost – everything. Everything, Mum!'

The man beside her looked awkward. He met Kate's enquiring eyes. 'I'm Jim,' he said. 'I brought her home. She wouldn't go to hospital. Her car caught fire on the 303 outside Wincanton.'

'Oh no!'

'It's a burnt out shell. Nothing could be done. But at least she's safe.'

Kate's mind raced. What was Tessa doing, on a Friday, driving down? Where was Paul? So many questions. They would have to wait until Tessa was calm enough to talk.

'I'm sorry, Mum,' she gasped. 'It's my fault. I've ruined everything.'

A wail from the cat basket distracted them, and spawned another bout of crying from Tessa. 'Mum – this is Benita,' she wept. 'She's a darling cat. I rescued her from the street and Paul went crazy. I brought her here – and – I've let her down, Mum – I've let everyone down – my whole life is collapsing. I can't go on – I really can't.'

'Oh, it will all blow over, dear,' Kate said, reassuringly she hoped.

'No, it won't, Mum.' Tessa's face hardened. She took some deep breaths, trying to fight the inner fury, remembering how Kate had never understood or accepted anger. She managed to calm herself, in a resigned sort of way, as if her mother's attitude was old territory, not to be revisited. 'We have to get Benita inside, Mum. She's been cooped up and she was fine until the car caught fire. Now she's upset again and it's all my fault.'

Leaving Freddie talking to Jim about the car, Kate and Tessa took Benita into the kitchen and shut the door.

'This little cat is my only reason for staying alive,' Tessa said, unfastening the door of the cat basket. Kate expected the frightened cat to run under the furniture, but Benita didn't. She took her time emerging, her sensitive face assessing the new space. 'She's terribly thin,' said Tessa. But Benita fluffed her fur and strolled out with her tail up. She made a beeline for Kate.

Kate melted. She picked Benita up and the cat immediately started to purr, gazing into Kate's eyes as if she understood everything. *She knows*, Kate thought, *she knows I'm ill*. A tear rolled down her pale cheek.

'You've brought me an angel.'

Tessa smiled. 'Will you have her, Mum? Please?'

'Have her? I'd LOVE to. I – need a kitty angel right now.'

'Thanks.' Tessa looked full of tears again. 'I wanted to keep her so much, but I can't. It seems – I'm not meant to have anything that loves me.'

'Doesn't Paul love you?' Kate asked sharply.

Tessa shrugged, her eyes bleak and silent.

Something's very wrong, Kate thought in alarm. But in that moment Tessa was watching, with a touch of envy, as Benita delicately licked the tear from Kate's pale cheek.

'You don't look well, Mum,' Tessa said, suddenly becoming the compassionate adult again.

I can't tell her, Kate thought. 'Oh, I'm all right, dear,' she said brightly. 'Just a bit off colour. I expect it's only a virus going round. But never mind me, I want to hear your news. Whatever happened to the car? And this poor kitty – she's so thin.' Kate put Benita on the floor and scraped the remaining mince from the pie dish into a saucer. They watched her tucking in.

'I bought stuff for her,' Tessa said sadly, 'food, and flea powder, and a brush and a red velvet collar. It's all gone up in flames, Mum, and my case of clothes – my Afghan coat, my best jeans – everything. And my bag. It had cash in it, my salary. I drew it out – and it's gone.'

'What bad luck,' said Kate kindly.

Tessa shook her head. 'No, Mum – it's my fault. I don't know what Dad will say. I forgot to put water in the car. I left in a hurry because . . .'

'Because?'

Tessa stared at her in silence.

'Paul?'

'Yep.'

Kate's cheeks flamed and she looked at Tessa with fierce eyes. 'What did he do?'

'I don't want to talk about it, Mum. I need to lie down.'

'You must be in shock.' Kate steered Tessa to the sofa in the kitchen window. 'You really ought to go to hospital.'

'NO.' Tessa sank into the familiar sofa. It still creaked in the same places, and smelled of marmalade and tweed. Kate pulled out her father's old milking stool and sat close, watching her daughter's slim body still racked by deep sobs that persisted long after the tears had dried. Kate wondered why, after all these years, Tessa still suffered so much, and why it was so hard to understand. Tessa was never satisfied with the things Kate treasured – a good marriage, a home and family, a simple, wholesome life. What Tessa wanted was somewhere out there beyond love, beyond the reasoning mind. There had always been a cut-off point in their mother/daughter relationship. Usually a straight 'no' or 'I don't want to talk about it', or a certain look in Tessa's pale blue eyes, a closed door Kate could never open.

'My whole life is collapsing,' Tessa wept, again. 'What am I going to do, Mum? What am I going to DO?'

CHAPTER 17

Let the Heart Remember

'There's always a reason why things happen,' Starlinda said in her calm, confident voice.

Tessa had slept for most of Saturday, relieved to be back in her own bed at The Pines with the fragrance of new mown hay drifting through the open window. She'd woken in the afternoon light, feeling rested in a deeply satisfying way, a special blend of contentment that permeated her entire being, a feeling of coming home. Her first thought was to phone Starlinda and try to make sense of what had happened. Then she wanted a long talk with her dad. Despite everything, a sense of happiness glowed around her. It was May, and she was home. There would be bee orchids up on the ridgeway. Cowslips and cuckooflower down in the water meadows. So many beautiful places to go, on limited time.

'I don't want to come back to London,' she told Starlinda, 'but I must.'

'Yes. Yes, you must come back. It's your karma,' Starlinda said. 'Your job, and your marriage are a sustaining base camp for your true work. I think you know that, Tessa. You are needed here. We are starting the mediumship course at the end of next week, and you MUST be there.'

'Yeah – I know. It's just so difficult with Paul.'

'Paul will apologise. He doesn't want to lose you, Tessa.'

'But the violence has to stop,' Tessa said, quietly, keeping an eye on Kate who was carrying Benita round the garden. She didn't want her mother to hear the conversation she was having with Starlinda.

'Maybe you can't stop him, Tessa, but you can leave him, before it escalates.'

'I don't feel strong enough to just leave.'

'You are strong. My God, girl, you are an earth angel! A magnificent being of love and light.'

'It's hard to remember that.'

'No, darling. It's easy. Let your heart remember.'

'Keep reminding me,' Tessa mumbled, watching Kate walk past with a slitty-eyed, purring Benita in her arms.

'Who just walked past the phone?' asked Starlinda sharply.

'Mum.'

Starlinda went quiet.

'She's carrying Benita around,' Tessa added.

Silence.

'Are you still there? Starlinda?'

'Yes, darling. I'm tuning into your mum's energy. It's

remarkably low for such a feisty lady. There's something she
needs to tell you.'

'Right – I'll ask her.'

'She won't tell you today. Wild horses wouldn't drag it out
of her. Your mum is a VERY determined lady. She'll tell you
when the time is right. Be ready for change, Tessa. It's a time
of transition for your family.'

'So what do I have to do?'

'You know the answer to that, darling. Stay in the heart.
The heart has all the answers to all the questions. Promise
me you will listen to your heart.'

'Okay.'

'You will be back in London tomorrow night,' Starlinda
continued. 'Ring me – and there's a special place down
there in Somerset that you need to visit, today if you can. Is
there an ancient Holy Well nearby? I'm sensing it – a long-
forgotten sacred spring. I see bubbling rings of water, and a
tree laden with blossom. It's crying out to you – if you listen.
Take care, honeychild.' Starlinda put the phone down.

Intrigued, Tessa closed her eyes and put her hand on her
heart. A shaft of light beamed in as if she had opened the curtains. She gasped in astonishment. Her field. The source of
the spring with its bubbling rings of water. A mirror-bright
vision. Could the spring have been a Holy Well? She knew
instantly that it had.

Another surprise flared into life. Someone was waiting for
her at the source of the stream. Who? A feeling flickered low
down in her stomach. Nervous hope, a candle flickering in

a stormy window. She tried to see who it might be. It wasn't a shadow, it wasn't solid, but more like a patch of radiance, a light, a shape of someone sitting under the hawthorn tree. An aura without a body. A shining person. Sitting so still, waiting so confidently – for her. *And what if she didn't go?* Tessa asked herself. She put both hands on her heart.

'Are you all right, dear?' Kate popped out of the kitchen and Tessa glimpsed Benita busily eating from a saucer on the floor. 'I opened a tin of salmon,' Kate said. 'Spoiling her. And I've de-flead her. We'll have her plump and glossy in no time.'

The spell was broken. Tessa blinked. 'I'm going to walk up to the field, Mum. I won't be long.'

'You'll see such a difference in the landscape,' Kate said. 'The elms are gone. It's terrible. Shall I come with you?'

'No thanks, Mum. You look after Benita. I'll be fine.'

Even without the elm trees, Monterose seemed to be a place of lush abundance, surrounded by meadows of buttercups and sorrel. Tessa walked quickly, looking for the patches of dog violets along the verges, remembering the oval-shaped mats of springy little violets in every shade of pink, white and purple. Now they had gone, and so had the clumps of yellow cowslips. Grass and clover, and dead grass lying around, carelessly mown, and the tops of hedges savagely mangled by the flail-cutter.

I used to be a Rainbow Warrior, Tessa thought. Where were they now, those tribes of hippies and flower children who had passionately tried to raise awareness? Had they given up? Were they all, like Lou and Clare, in squats in London, working only to feed their addictions? Did no one care about *Silent Spring*? Tessa paused in the lane, remembering the awful sight of her car burning. The exultant scarlet energy of the flames felt personal. Hungry fire stripping her of material wealth, down to the bone. Lying there in the road she'd felt even her bones were burning. And yet the one sound in her memory, above the crackle of the flames, was the song of a skylark high in the blue air, like her, an endangered species with nothing left but the power of a song.

She walked on, the image of the burning car floating in her mind. Freddie and Herbie had gone off in Herbie's truck to salvage the shell, and she imagined how bad Freddie would feel seeing it. Like a kick in the teeth.

Guilt scorched her mind and, like the car, it wouldn't stop burning. *I haven't been good to my parents*, she thought, *or to Lucy. I've been nothing but trouble since I was born, and they have LOVED me, awesomely*. She thought of Benita tenderly licking the tear from Kate's cheek. *I never loved Mum like that*, she reflected; *why does it take a scraggy little cat to show me how to love?*

Driven along, blindly, by the turmoil of emotion, Tessa suddenly found herself at the gate of the field. Years had rolled by and she hadn't been there. Not since Art.

The stream still gurgled tunefully, emerging from under the hedge in a gully overhung with hart's-tongue ferns and globules of moss. A heavy padlock clunked against the gate and a white board gleamed there, with Freddie's beautiful script painted in black gloss paint.

NO FLAIL-CUTTING

It had worked. The whole hedge hummed with bees and hoverflies like a great white ocean liner in full sail, the blossom like sea foam brushing the waves of grass. Majestic and vibrant with an inner life where nesting birds were raising families, tiny blue eggshells cracking open, tiny wet beaks and secret voices.

The soporific perfume of the hawthorn flowers filled the air. Tessa inhaled the scent, letting it cleanse the smoke from her mind. Starlinda's encouraging words sang in her heart. 'My God, girl, you're an earth angel.'

She climbed over the gate and picked her way through ant hills and years of uncut grass. The turf was cushiony under her feet, and amongst the tussocks of couch and ryegrass, the natural hillside grasses and wild flowers were glowing brightly. Speedwell and scarlet pimpernel, shackle-grass and sheep sorrel. The bright flake of a blue butterfly.

Tessa's spirits lifted. While she'd been suffering in London, a miracle had been painting itself here, in her field. It was humbling. At first she avoided the source of the spring, and walked up the other side, following a winding rabbit path. She was thrilled to discover Freddie's lime trees, now about ten feet tall, their buds breaking into pillow-soft leaves of lemon-green. He'd planted bushy young oaks, and silver-stemmed ash trees, their new leaves wine-coloured and vibrant.

Tessa walked on to the top boundary to inspect the new fence Freddie had told her about. It looked like something from a warzone. Whoever had bought those acres of woodland clearly wanted to keep the world out. A robin was flying ahead of her, pausing in obvious places to wait for her to catch up. *Like the robin in* The Secret Garden, Tessa thought, *he's leading me. He wants me to go in the wood*. She followed him to the wire gate and he perched on it, chirruping at her. She touched the padlock. It was locked, but well used and bright. The strange flutter of nerves in the pit of her stomach started again. Something about the feel of the padlock in her hand. Who had touched it? Who was using the meandering path to the spring? A ghost of a feeling fled through her heart and left as quickly as it had come. Something lost. Forbidden. Forbidden fruit – that was it.

The robin opened his beak and gave her some serious advice. He flew towards the spring and sang in the elder tree, watching her. Lou had once told her robins were messengers from spirits. Tessa believed her. This robin was telling her she could no longer put off visiting the source of the spring. A spirit was waiting. A light shone through the elder tree, a silent light, with a shape.

Why am I scared? Tessa thought. She quietened her footsteps on the hush of the turf until they were whispers on the well-trodden path to the spring. The branches of the elder tree squeaked as she parted them and crept in. She no longer saw the light. She was in it, as if she had stepped inside an angel. A sense of belonging filled her and she found herself doing as Starlinda had taught her. Focusing on the heart.

She wanted answers.

She closed her eyes, put her hand on her heart, and listened.

The listening had incandescence and colour. Like a sea-pearl. She was within the colour of the listening.

Dazed, she sat down under the elder tree, in dappled sunlight. Bees hummed on the nectar-rich umbels of elder-flower. She heard the eternal burble of the rising water. 'Allow yourself' was something Starlinda constantly said to her. 'Allow yourself the heaven that is there for you.' She relaxed and drifted into trance, into another dimension, and it was then that she heard the singing.

It wasn't close. It wasn't by the spring. It was somewhere up in the wood, behind the forbidding fence. The twang of a guitar. The tune. And the words, sung softly, deeply, by a voice that seemed part of the wood, a voice that whispered through time like the wind in the cornfields.

> *Whisper words of wisdom, let it be.*
> *Let it be,*
> *Let it be,*
> *Let it be, let it be.*
> *There will be an answer,*
> *Let it be.*

Hours later Tessa walked back to The Pines in the golden evening. At first she floated along, amazed at what she had done, the ambience of the magic carrying her in her body of light. *I am myself*, she kept thinking, *I am that shining being.* But as the hedges changed to the wreckage left by flail-cutters, and the stumps of dead elm trees, she felt herself going down and down, re-entering the atmosphere of a troubled world. Sadness billowed behind her like a dark flag. She felt doomed. She had to go back. There was work to do, commitments to honour, and Paul. It was exactly as Starlinda said. Karma. The price she must pay. The life she must live in order to get where she wanted to go. It was cumbersome compared to the spiritual joy of being her true self.

'I need to talk to you, Dad,' she said urgently when she arrived home to find Freddie gloomily contemplating the burnt-out shell of her car.

'Can't do nothing with it,' he lamented. ''Tis scrap. No use to anyone. 'Tis a shame.'

Tessa made him look at her. 'I need to talk, Dad.'

His eyes lit up with understanding. 'It's been a long time – since we talked. Too long.' Freddie led her to the bench outside his workshop. 'Kate's in the kitchen boiling fish,' he said, and his eyes twinkled, 'for Her Majesty.'

'Her Majesty?'

'The cat.'

'Do you like Benita too, Dad?'

'Course I do. I love all animals, you know that. It'll be good for Kate to have a cat to pamper.'

'I'm so glad. At least it's a happy ending for Benita.' Tessa picked a stalk of grass and began to pull the seed head apart. 'Lucy and I used to make little baskets from the grass. Do you think she'll ever come home, Dad?'

Freddie's face hardened. "Tis up to her.'

'Couldn't you forgive her, Dad?' Tessa searched his eyes, past the pain to the redundant spark of love he still had for Lucy. She longed to talk him through the heart meditation, but he shook his head and gazed at the sky, effectively closing the door on the subject of Lucy.

'But what if my life doesn't work out the way you and Mum want for me?'

Freddie looked at her eyes again. 'Ah – I know that already, Tessa. I knew that the day you were born.'

'How? How did you know that?'

'I had – a vision.'

'Tell me – please, Dad – it matters to me right now.'

'Why's that?'

'Because I have visions too, Dad, like when I saw the angel. And my life is going to change. I'm already working and learning how – but I need your support, your blessing on what I'm going to do.'

'What are you going to do?'

Freddie was looking at her so intensely that Tessa wondered if she ought to risk telling him. He was still in shock from the burning car, more so than she was. Everything had happened so fast and she was on the rollercoaster, about to plunge over another precipice.

'I'm studying astrology at night school,' Tessa said, taking a deep breath. 'It's brilliant. I love it, and I intend to be an astrologer – that's just for starters, Dad. Astrology is a doorway for me, and it will help me too.'

'Astrology!' he gasped. 'What the blimin' heck is that?'

'It's to do with the alignment of the planets when you were born and how it influences your whole life.'

'Ah – planets – like Patrick Moore sort of stuff? I like his programmes – *The Sky at Night* – and the music's lovely.'

'No, Dad. That's astronomy. This is astrology – the ancient science of using planetary alignments to predict trends in people's lives, warn them, help them understand and plan.'

Freddie looked flummoxed. 'And you study THAT at night school?'

'Yes.'

'Well – I'm telling you – you aren't gonna earn a living doing that. Don't even think about doing such a thing. You're heading for trouble.'

The conversation ground to a halt. Tessa bit back the words she wanted to say. Instead, she asked, 'Is that what Granny Annie said to you when you bought the lorry?'

'Ah – well – yes. But it turned out she was wrong.'

'But – don't you believe in destiny, Dad?'

'Destiny?' Freddie's eyes rounded. 'Destiny.' He repeated the word in a different tone of voice. His eyes deepened into storytelling mode. 'The last time I heard that word was from a Romany Gypsy, a fortune-teller. On the day you were born.'

A cloak of resignation settled around Tessa. She had always relied on being able to share spiritual stuff with her dad. It was disappointing to find him critical of her treasured

313

dreams. A mask of denial hung between them, and Tessa felt suddenly more alone than ever in her life. She'd always loved Freddie's stories, but now she listened dutifully, sensing their precious time together pouring away like sand through her fingers. What if she could never share her dreams with him? What if she had to achieve it alone, in Monterose, with everyone criticising and ridiculing her? *Everyone is against me. No one understands*, she thought. *Even Dad has abandoned me. I can't do this, I can't.*

Gremlins of doubt and depression paraded through her mind all night, like a protest march with banners bobbing. *DON'T BE SO SILLY* and *YOU CAN'T DO THAT* and *YOU'RE HEADING FOR TROUBLE*, painted in red, white and blue letters. Closely followed by another batch: *STAY ON THE STRAIGHT AND NARROW* and *BE BRITISH* and *BE SENSIBLE.*

When morning came, with leaden skies, she felt drained and overwhelmed. She didn't want to get up. Ever. The heavy rain clouds seemed to be in the house, searching for her mind. She worried all night, then slept through the morning, comforted only by Benita who cuddled into her shoulder, purring, and pouring love into Tessa as if she knew they must say goodbye. At least the little cat would be safe and happy with Kate.

Pale faced and switched off, Tessa managed to chat pleasantly and eat lunch with her parents.

'You don't want to go back, do you?' Kate said kindly.

'No. But I must.'

'I hope you don't mind, but I rang Paul,' Kate admitted. 'I thought he ought to know about the car catching fire. He was—'

'Angry?'

'No, dear. He was upset. He didn't know what to say to me. That's because he feels guilty, and he knows I know he's not treating you right. Anyway, he said he'd borrow his dad's car and come to fetch you.'

Tessa sighed. She wanted to tell her mum how that made her feel. How the curtains of mist were drawing in, hanging veils around her heart. But Kate wouldn't understand, she felt, and kept quiet.

When the moment came, and the white Mercedes turned into the drive with Paul at the wheel, Tessa felt as if a ball and chain had arrived. Visions were all very well, but she was chained to reality. *Please God, not for much longer*, she prayed.

Predictably, Paul arrived shamefaced. Kate and Tessa watched him from the kitchen window as he got out of the car, armed with roses and chocolates.

'You should hang on to him, dear,' Kate said. 'You'll have a good life and a solid marriage.'

Tessa gave her a withering look. *If only she knew*, she thought. A solid marriage? *Solid steel*, she thought. *Ball and chain, here I come.*

But Kate was in 'look on the bright side' mode. 'I know you've had a bit of a row,' she said, 'but you're both under pressure, aren't you? It will come right, dear. You must just keep on keeping on, if you know what I mean. And – look at him! He's bought you roses – and fetching you home in a lovely car. What more do you want?'

Tessa felt the gulf widening. Or had it always been there? A gulf between souls. From the moment of her birth. The thought triggered a memory of her talk with her dad on the previous evening. Freddie had been trying to tell her something about her birth, and she hadn't listened!

Paul was standing by the burned out shell of the Morris Minor, staring at it.

'Where's Dad?' Tessa asked.

'In the back garden.'

'You talk to Paul. I need to ask Dad something.'

'Oh – all right, dear.' Kate wiped her hands on her apron and sailed out to make a fuss of Paul, as she always did.

Tessa slipped out of the back door, and found Freddie setting up wigwams of hazel sticks for his runner bean plants.

'Dad! I've only got a few minutes – Paul is here. Dad, I didn't listen properly. I switched off. What were you trying to tell me yesterday, about the Romany Gypsy? It's important, isn't it?'

Freddie's eyes looked at her with a mysterious twinkle. 'Could be,' he said, and went on tying string around the hazel sticks. 'But if he's here, 'tis not the time, is it? For a serious talk.'

'Mum will keep him talking,' Tessa said. 'Please, Dad. There's so much I didn't tell you last night – and we won't get the chance again. It's important, I know it is.'

Freddie went on tying the bean sticks, his cheek twitching the way it did when he was stressed.

'Dad?'

'I dunno,' he said, and turned to face her, the string trailing from his big hands. 'I dunno if I ought to tell you it. You got enough on your plate, Tessa. I don't want to worry you.'

'Why? Is it something bad? I HAVE to know, Dad, please.'

He sighed and stuffed the ball of string into his jacket pocket. 'I swore I never would,' he said, 'but I want you to promise me you won't go doing anything stupid. You hang on to what you've got.'

Tessa's heart started to thump as she followed him into the house and up the stairs to the box room. She sensed they were not alone. Walking beside them were two shining spirits, the blue-eyed lady, and a tiny, bird-like woman with mischievous eyes. Granny Barcussy!

''Tis stuffy in here.' Freddie paused to open the small window. 'Look at that!' he whispered, craning his neck to look out at the cluster of globular nests under the eaves of the roof. 'House martins. Look, you can see the babies peeping out of the nest!'

Tessa leaned against him to look out, feeling like a child again, as they shared a moment of magic. 'They're so CUTE,' she whispered, watching the bracelet of tiny faces peeping over the rim of one of the nests.

'Wonderful birds.' Freddie's eyes shone. 'So small, yet they make these clumps of nests, so perfectly round, out of mud and stuck to the wall. I couldn't make that.'

Entranced, they watched the adult house martin arrive in a flash of black and white wings, deliver a beakful of flies

317

to the row of waiting beaks, and fly off again, all in one graceful arc.

'Wonderful birds,' said Freddie, again.

'Dad – you were going to tell me about the gypsy,' Tessa reminded him.

'Ah.'

'Paul is downstairs.'

Freddie hesitated, his eyes slowly losing the twinkle of magic, his cheek twitching again. He searched his daughter's eyes. 'We've always been close, haven't we? You remember that, Tessa – and remember I love you very much – and so does Kate.'

Tessa nodded. 'Thanks.' She had a feeling he was going to share something bad with her, something from the box of secrets marked 'Family Shame'. It wasn't a real box, but an image she had created to help her and Lucy to cope with the way Kate insisted on keeping their mistakes and shortcomings hidden from the neighbours, the aunties, and the world.

Still he hovered in the light of the small window, his eyes questioning hers.

'Dad – please – we won't get the chance again. If it's life-changing, I need to know.'

'Right.' As if she had flicked a switch in his mind, Freddie crossed the room to the bureau, a dark oak, creaking thing, always open and covered in piles of receipts, notebooks and drawing pads. It had belonged to Granny Barcussy, and Tessa could see the smiling spirit of her, gently pushing him towards it. 'There's a secret drawer,' Freddie said. 'You never knew that, did you?'

'No.'

He moved some papers and opened the middle drawer of the three tiny ones. He pulled it right out. ''Tis full of old three-penny bits and sixpences,' he said. 'Thought I ought to keep 'em. Might be valuable one day.' Then he reached his hand into the hole and extracted the secret drawer from the back. It slid out with a whiff of old sage leaves. 'My granny used to keep dried herbs in here in muslin bags tied up with raffia.'

Tessa was running out of patience, but she knew Freddie could not be rushed. With her nerves twanging she watched his large red hand extract a fusty envelope. He brushed the dust from it and gave it to her.

Tessa stared at her date of birth written on it in Freddie's copperplate script. She turned it over and touched the hard seal. 'Shall I open it?'

'Yes,' Freddie said heavily. 'It's the words of the Romany Gypsy, Madame Eltura. Like I told you, she sat me in front of a crystal ball. She didn't know me, and she didn't know you'd been born the same day – early morning, you were born.'

It felt wrong to tear the ancient envelope. Tessa took the silver paperknife from a jam jar and neatly slit the top. She sat down on the deep window sill, her eyes racing over the words Freddie had written so long ago.

'I don't want it to – to unsettle you,' he said anxiously.

Tessa read both sides of the paper. Her spine shivered like it had done at Stonehenge when she'd felt the Kundalini.

THE WORDS OF MADAME ELTURA

*A baby has been born to you, and her name begins with a
T. She is no ordinary child. Indeed she is a star-child, and
she is destined to be a spiritual healer and medium. She
has a great gift. But, I must warn you; this child will have
a difficult life with many troubles. She will try to take her
life, for she will be misunderstood, misjudged and blamed by
those who think her gifts are evil. You must guard and guide
her as best you can, for when she is a young woman there
will come a time of sorrow for you all, and it will begin with
a fire. I see a fire. Take care. Take great care and allow this
child to always listen to spirit. You, and she, are one of us —
no, I don't mean Romany Gypsies, but psychic clairvoyants.
The gift has been in your family for generations, and you
have repressed it because you were told it is evil. Am I right?
(She was right!) This child has been born to finally bring
that gift into use, into the light. Don't try to stop her, for she
is unstoppable, and her gift will help you through the time of
sorrow I have mentioned. For her it will be the dawning of a
New Age where she will be one of many Earth Angels who
have incarnated at this time.*

Tessa felt a smile opening up her face. She wanted to jump
up and down with excitement. 'But Dad! This is totally me.
Absolutely who I am. Why did you hide it away like that?
It's not BAD.'

Freddie dragged the desk chair over to the window and

sat close to her. 'I didn't want you to go through what I did, Tessa. I was called a liar – my father got in such a temper over it, smashed every cup and plate in the kitchen. And me brother threw me against a wall for saying I'd seen an angel. And it HURT, Tessa. It still does.' He was close to tears. Tessa reached out and held his hand while he continued. 'And what hurt the most was that – the angel I saw, it was MARVELLOUS, it was the best, most beautiful, inspiring thing that ever happened to me, and to be ridiculed and punished for it, in front of all the family, felt like the end of my life, as if my soul had been driven out of my body – beaten and driven out. I never got over it – turned it into anger, and anger into fear, and loneliness – you know, loneliness of the soul.'

'I do know.' Tessa couldn't bear it. She hugged him close, her arms wrapped around his head, and she sensed the pain in him, the wound never healed. 'It's all right, Dad. It will come right, especially now you've got me. You've helped me all my life, Dad, and now I'm going to help you.'

She felt him breathing against her, and his steady old heartbeat. She sent him silent, caring love, the way he had so often done for her, and when he could speak again, he said, 'Then – when I met Kate – she became my shining angel, and she encouraged me with everything I wanted to do. She's made me, Kate has, made me live again. And you – and Lucy.' He was silent again for a few minutes. 'But – those words, Tessa – the fire Madame Eltura said – well, that's happened, hasn't it?'

'And we've got over it,' Tessa said.

He looked up at her, gratefully. 'Sometimes you sound just like Kate.'

She smiled. 'It will be okay, Dad. I can handle all the spiritual stuff. I love it, and I've got Starlinda to help me.'

'But what about the *time of sorrow*?' Freddie asked. 'What's going to happen?'

CHAPTER 18

Oriole Kate

A few months' later, on a crisp autumn day, Kate stood on Paddington Station feeling bewildered. She had never been in such a crowd of hurrying people in her life. *None of them look happy*, she thought, studying the faces. No one looked at her. No one smiled. *Is this where Tessa lives?* she thought. *How can she bear it?*

She'd caught the train from Castle Cary, leaving Freddie standing on the platform gazing after the departing train, his eyes glistening with worry. He didn't want her to go, but Kate was determined. She needed to see Tessa, and for once she wasn't looking forward to it.

They'd agreed to meet at WH Smith, but the station was huge and echoing. Kate couldn't even see the bookstall.

'Mum!'

She was relieved to see Tessa's chestnut hair bobbing as she ran across the station, and glad to see her daughter's welcoming smile. 'Ooh – aren't I pleased to see you, dear. I was feeling like a proper country bumpkin. All these people. I've never been in such a place. Thank you for coming to meet me. I enjoyed my trip on the train. The autumn colours are so lovely this year.'

'You look different, Mum,' Tessa said. 'You've lost weight.'

'Yes, dear. I'm having to take my skirts in, or they'll be falling down.' She laughed cheerfully.

'Even your legs have gone thin, Mum. Are you on a diet?'

'No, dear.' Kate met her daughter's questioning eyes. *She's too young to have this happen to her,* she thought, and swallowed, trying not to cry, not yet. They'd have fun first, go on a boat down the Thames. Eat lunch. Stroll around Westminster Abbey. Five hours before the train would take her home. *Supposing this is the last time I ever see Tessa?* Kate thought. She made herself smile. 'Where shall we go first? I can't wait to see London.'

'Something's wrong, Mum, isn't it?' Tessa's eyes were serious, and very adult, Kate thought. She nodded silently.

'Let's get a coffee.' Tessa picked up Kate's bag. 'We can do the sightseeing after we've talked. I've got lots to tell you.' She steered Kate across Paddington Station and out into Praed Street. 'This is a good place. We can be quiet in here,' she said, and they sat in the far corner of a coffee bar with high-backed red seats. A sort of cubby hole from the turmoil of London.

'Goodness me!' Kate looked in astonishment at the shallow glass cups of expresso coffee Tessa brought her on a tray.

'What a lot of froth. What do you do with it? I mean – how do you get to the coffee underneath?'

Tessa giggled. 'You just go for a frothy moustache, Mum.'

Kate's eyes twinkled with amusement. She took a tea-spoon and spooned the offending froth into her saucer. 'Is this the way Londoners take their coffee? What WOULD Freddie think?'

'They make scrumptious pancakes in here if you feel like one, smothered in whipped cream and maple syrup.'

'But it's not Pancake Day, dear,' Kate said. 'That's Shrove Tuesday.'

'No one cares about Shrove Tuesday in London. You can have a Morello cherry one too. Dad would love it.'

'It's a different world from our little Monterose,' Kate said, sipping her coffee. 'Now, I want to hear all your news, Tessa. How's Paul?'

'He's okay – a bit stressed by auditions. He's applying for jobs now. He wants to get into a good orchestra.'

'And – how's married life?'

'It's not brilliant,' Tessa said. 'But I don't want to talk about it, Mum.'

Kate knew better than to push Tessa for answers, but it saddened her. 'Freddie and I were always so happy. Don't you find London difficult?'

'In some ways. But London's exciting too.' Tessa's eyes brightened. 'I'm studying astrology now at night school. And I go every week to a psychic development circle with Starlinda. I'm learning so much about healing and mediumship.'

'TESSA!' Kate looked shocked. 'Mediumship?'

'I've got a gift, Mum, and I intend to use it. Isn't that what gifts are for? Don't look so alarmed. I'm not doing anything wrong!'

'But – Tessa . . .' Kate was speechless.

'Don't worry, Mum. I'm in charge of my life now.'

'You certainly are. What does Paul think about it?'

'He doesn't know.'

'Why? Why not?'

'He'd disapprove – and so would his family – well, his mum would anyway. Their minds are closed. It's so sad.'

Kate stared hard at the confident young woman in front of her. *Is this really our daughter?* she thought, remembering the troubled little girl Tessa had been. 'We tried so hard to guide you – and Lucy,' she said, bewildered.

'You can't guide another soul,' Tessa said. 'I didn't feel guided. I felt repressed.'

'Repressed? Surely not'

Tessa reached across the table and took her mother's hand. Kate noticed Violetta's ring sparkling very brightly. 'Sorry, Mum, I didn't mean to hurt you. I love you and Dad so much – but I've needed to detach, and to find myself.'

Kate nodded. 'I'm proud of you, Tessa. I love you, and I want this to be a happy meeting – it could be . . .' Again she felt the words rise and fall back, like something knocking on a door, persistently.

'What is it, Mum?' Tessa looked at her with a steady, knowing gaze. *Like Freddie*, Kate thought, overwhelmed by Tessa seeming older than her, not just a few years, but centuries older.

'Mum?'

Kate took a deep, shaky breath. 'I'm not too well, dear. And I want you to promise me that what I tell you now is strictly between us. Freddie must not know.'

'Okay.' Tessa waited, listening intently.

'He MUST NOT KNOW,' repeated Kate. 'But I know, because I was a nurse, you see. I have cancer. Do you know what that is?'

'I'm not sure.'

Kate immediately noticed Tessa going pale. She remembered how sensitive she'd been as a child, how terrified of illness or injury. 'I need you to be strong for me, Tessa. Can you?'

Time stood still as Tessa nodded silently. The sound of traffic faded, and it was just the two of them, in a bubble of pain, in a corner of a café, somewhere in London. Kate started to cry, and Tessa got up, swiftly, and moved around the table to sit beside her mum and put her arm around her shoulders.

'It's in my blood, and in my lymph glands,' Kate said in a quiet, rasping voice, her eyes darkening. 'It started in my ovaries, and now it's everywhere.'

'Can they cure it?' Tessa asked.

'No. I – need you to understand that, dear, please. But of course I'm trying and hoping to get better. What I don't understand, and can't accept, is WHY? Why me?'

Tessa shut her eyes and held her mother tightly, remembering how she herself had sat with Dorothy in the crypt of St Stephen's, asking the same question, *Why? Why me?*

'Don't torment yourself with WHY, Mum,' Tessa said. 'And don't give up hope. You could get better, surely?'

Kate tried to salvage her remaining shreds of courage. 'No, we won't give up hope. I feel better already, for telling you.'

'Does Lucy know?'

'No. How could I tell Lucy in an airmail letter? She's so far away. I made up my mind to tell only you. I trust you not to tell Freddie. It's best for him, I know it is.'

'I want to spend time with you, Mum. I want that so much. I feel as if I've only just begun to appreciate you,' Tessa said.

Kate brightened. 'Well – we've got today. It's a lovely day. Let's not waste it.' She dried her eyes with an embroidered hanky. Then she managed a smile and wagged her finger at Tessa. 'I want you to understand this,' she said, with conviction. 'If I do get better, everything will be all right, and if I don't get better, it will still be all right.'

Christmas came and the rift with Paul deepened when Tessa refused to spend it with his family. She honoured the promise she'd made to Kate, and told no one about the cancer. But it was constantly in her mind, and she felt Christmas was now a bittersweet time. It could be Kate's last Christmas, and only Tessa was allowed to know. She went down to Monterose on her own, in the car, a Ford Anglia, bought with the insurance money from the fire. Another bone of contention with Paul. She was glad he didn't go with her.

She spent as much time as possible with her mum, helping her decorate the tree, going to the carol singing in the market square, cooking Christmas dinner and pulling crackers. Tessa found it unbearably poignant and stressful. She longed to go to the field and see the spring, but instead she drove Kate up to the ridgeway in the frost, and they strolled together looking at frosted grasses and the blue hills in the distance. Kate talked and talked, about her early life at Hilbegut, about the wartime years and about happy childhood times with her and Lucy. She didn't once mention the sad times, and she kept hope alive, popping in comments like, 'I might get better, when the spring comes,' or 'The doctor's trying some new pills on me'. She joked about her regular hospital visits. 'I count my blessings,' she said, often, 'and you are one of them, Tessa – and so is the little cat. She's been such a comfort to me.'

Freddie stayed by the fire, roasting chestnuts and reading, with Benita stretched blissfully on the warm hearth rug. When Kate and Tessa returned, he showed Tessa a heavy old book with gold-rimmed pages. 'This is Granny Barcussy's history book – it's a rare book on Somerset – and it mentions your spring, Tessa. Here – you read it.'

'Thanks, Dad.' Tessa squealed with excitement as she read the page he'd marked. 'This is awesome.'

'Ah – I remembered what your friend – Starlinda – said about a Holy Well, and I reckoned it could be the source of the Mill Stream in your field.'

'It definitely was!' Tessa cried. 'There's a map – look – and a drawing of how it looked. Wow! It was built and used by the Romans – and then the Victorians used it for medicinal purposes. The water has a high mineral content and people used it for healing – wow!' Her eyes shone with excitement. 'I dream of restoring it, Dad, and using it again.'

'You can't do that,' Freddie warned. 'Cost a fortune, it would – and nobody's going to go up there for healing in this day and age.'

'Well, that went down like a lead balloon,' Kate joked, and threw a piece of orange peel at Freddie. 'You're being negative, dear.'

'I'll be earning a lot of money when I'm a practising clairvoyant medium,' Tessa said, and the atmosphere changed immediately. She saw a look pass between her parents. 'I hope you'll support me,' she added, but there was a silence. *I'm alone*, she thought, *even my parents don't believe me.*

'Do we HAVE to go down there again?' Paul asked. 'We saw your mum last weekend.'

Tessa swung her legs out of bed and buried her toes in the flokati rug. As usual Paul had rolled away from her after sex (she didn't call it love-making) leaving her feeling used and frustrated.

'Don't get huffy,' Paul said.

'I'm not getting huffy, as you put it,' Tessa said carefully.

'Mum has got cancer, Paul. I want to spend as much time with her as I can. Wouldn't you, if it was your mum?'

'No. But my mum doesn't mother me the way your mum mothers you. Smother love, I'd call it, not mother love.'

'Don't criticise Mum. Especially not now she's ill.'

'You think she's so wonderful. But she's manipulative, Tessa. She tries to manipulate me, but I'm not having it.'

'No she doesn't.'

'Yes she does. She's always trying to buy my love with cakes and pots of marmalade. One day I shall tell her to back off. I can't be bought.'

'She is NOT trying to buy you! She's just a naturally kind, loving person. And don't you dare even think about being nasty to her when she's ill.'

'I'm not being nasty. I'm being discerning. That's your immature little girl attitude.'

'That's not fair.'

'Aw – it's not fair! There you go.' Paul was sitting up in bed now, his shoulders brick hard, his eyes small and suspicious, his mouth stretched into a judgemental smirk. A stance Tessa knew well by now.

She quickly pulled her clothes on. Black flared trousers, a polo-necked jumper, and a Laura Ashley smock.

'Don't clam up on me, Tessa.'

'I wasn't. Paul, I keep telling you, Mum is seriously ill. Why can't you try to understand? I need to go down there. I would understand if YOUR mum was ill. I'm trying to do the right thing.'

'That's where we disagree,' Paul said. 'You're supposed to be my WIFE, Tessa, and it seems I come last on your list of priorities, not first.'

'You don't put me first. If you did you'd understand. I'm not being a bad wife – I'm being a dutiful daughter. You should be proud of me, and supportive, not try to DICTATE. I've supported you enough times, going to concerts when I'd rather be doing something else.'

'Like spending time with that Starlinda woman. What good is that doing?'

'I'm following MY career.'

'Oh, and what's that? Witchy stuff? Mumbo jumbo? You know I don't approve, Tessa, yet you insist on doing it – it's not the kind of thing I want my wife involved in.'

'You don't KNOW what it is. I can't talk to you about it because your mind is closed.'

'Dead right it is. Closed to your fantasy world.' Paul dragged the bedclothes over his head. 'Piss off to Somerset then and leave me in peace.'

It stung, but Tessa was too worried about her mum to fight with Paul. Yesterday she'd phoned Lexi who had been helping to care for Kate. She'd told Tessa how, suddenly, Kate had taken to her bed and was drifting between waking and sleeping. The doctor had given her morphine, and a Marie Curie nurse was coming in every night. It was a big change, and a shock, Lexi said, for Freddie who couldn't seem to understand how ill Kate was. There'd never been a time when Kate hadn't got up in the morning, got dressed and tried to run the home even though she was ill.

Tessa picked up her key and ran down to the pay phone. Freddie was awkward on the phone. If the pips sounded to prompt her to insert more coins, Freddie would panic and hang up. So she made a reversed charge call to give them uninterrupted talking time.

The phone rang and rang and when he answered he was out of breath.

'What were you doing, Dad?' Tessa asked.

'Hoeing me onion bed,' he said. 'I ran up the garden.'

Tessa imagined him running up the path with money jingling in his pockets. It made her smile. And it made her homesick.

'How's Mum?'

His voice went down an octave. 'Ah – she's bad. Really bad this week. Taken to her bed. I've never seen her like this, Tessa. 'Tis hard.'

'Oh Dad.' Tessa empathised with his feelings of confusion, injustice and anxiety. And something else. 'You feel power-less, don't you?' she asked, guessing.

He struggled to speak. 'You're right, Tessa.'

'But Mum needs you – just having you there is the best help, Dad. Love is better than any medical stuff.'

'Ah.'

'Don't give up, Dad. You're doing so well – I'm proud of you.'

'Ah – well – I'm doing me best. But Kate is on morphine

now, and sometimes she can hardly open her eyes – but when she does, and she sees me there, her eyes light up and she smiles so brightly. Melt a battleship she would, with that smile. It breaks my heart.'

'Aw, Dad – I wish I was there to give you a hug.'

'She'll get weaker, see, if she lies in bed, and she's gone so thin. Like a shadow of how she was – and yet, it's odd, but when she is awake she's more radiant than I've ever seen her, Tessa. She – shines like an angel.'

Tessa nodded slowly. Being so far away from her parents felt wrong. Paul was hunched on the stairs, listening. Beyond the veneer of scepticism in his eyes, beyond the hunger for control, was the endless shadow of the rejected child he had been. The compassion Tessa had once felt for him had hardened into a knot she couldn't unravel. He'd taken her love, her money and her energy and twisted it into bitterness. She needed to detach from him. Live on her own. Or find the man who loved her the way Freddie loved Kate.

She wondered if Freddie now knew the truth about Kate's illness. Kate had willed herself to get well. She'd hung on to the threads of her life, each time setting herself goals. Things she didn't want to miss. 'I love my life so much,' she said constantly. First she'd hung on for Christmas. Then she'd wanted to see the snowdrops come up under the apple tree in late January. Then the crocuses, the primroses, the daffodils, the first blackbird singing. Everything was precious to her. Each flower a jewel not to be missed, each day a new gift.

'I was going to come down again this weekend,' Tessa said. 'What do you think, Dad? Do you need me?'

'Kate does. She'd love to see you. You come, Tessa, but . . .' Freddie hesitated. He and Tessa still picked up each other's thoughts. 'What about Paul? He won't want to keep coming down here. Could you come on your own?'

He knows, Tessa thought. She was desperately tired on that Friday, from trying to cope with her job, her astrology course, the weekly mediumship training, and the weekend chores of shopping and housework. The shadow of Kate's illness had flooded the spaces in her life. Lexi's voice had been so urgent, like a warning bell, and Freddie's silences ached with pain. Kate's bright brown eyes shone in her mind. She had to go.

And be strong.

For one last time.

On the Wednesday before Easter, at twenty past three in the morning, Tessa woke up with a jump. The chilling sound of the hall telephone echoed through the block of flats, making the stair rods and the lampshades tremble.

Paul didn't wake. He slept deeply, needily, curled up on his side. The bell went on ringing, relentlessly. *Mum*, Tessa thought. She rolled out of bed, ran downstairs and grabbed the ringing telephone.

'Hello.'

'Tessa? – It's Lexi.'

'Lexi! What is it? What's wrong?'

'I'm so sorry, Tessa. I had to ring you. There's no easy way to say this, dear, but your mum died about an hour ago. I was with her, and your dad, and the Marie Curie nurse. We held her hands until her pulse stopped beating. She went peacefully – without pain.'

Tessa's aura turned to ice. Hot tears ran down her cheeks. She couldn't move.

'Tessa? Are you there? Can you hear me?'

'Yes – yes, I heard you – Lexi – I'm just – stunned. I didn't believe she was going to die. I hoped she was getting better. I was there with her on Sunday. She – she gave me her ring, and – oh God – I should have stayed, Lexi. But Mum told me to go – she said she'd be fine – she understood I had to go to work – and said she was proud of me, told me she loved me.'

'I'm so sorry,' Lexi said. 'Look – Tessa – it's a hell of a shock, losing your mum. Are you going to be all right? Is Paul there with you?'

'He's asleep.'

'Wake him up,' Lexi said in her fierce voice. 'You can't face this alone in the middle of the night, Tessa. Promise me you'll wake him up.'

'Okay,' Tessa said, and realised she was shivering violently. She had an absurd memory of shivering like that on Weymouth Sands as a small child. She'd been in the sea too long, a cold east wind was blowing, and Kate had wrapped her in an orange beach towel. She could feel it now. The welcome. The comfort.

Gone.

Forever.

'You must make yourself a hot, sweet drink,' Lexi said, 'and get back into bed, Tessa. Don't jump in the car and drive down here when you're upset. There's nothing you can do right now. Are you listening?'

'Yes – but – Lexi – what about Dad?'

'Well – he's devastated, of course,' Lexi said. 'It was so sad. He just sat there for a long time, looking at her, then he got up and stared out of the window at the moonlight, and he said, "That's the end of my world".'

'Oh God, Lexi. I don't know how Dad is going to cope.'

'He will – in time – but you concentrate on YOU, Tessa. You've had a bad shock, haven't you?'

'Yes.'

'Then you need to take extra, EXTRA care of yourself. Are you hearing me?'

'Yes.'

'Your dad said he'd ring you in the morning – he didn't want me to disturb you, but I felt you should know. Now will you do as I say – go and put the kettle on. Will you? Promise?'

'Okay.'

'I'll do what I can to help Freddie in the morning,' Lexi said. 'He's too upset to drive. I'll take him to register the death and cope with the formal stuff that has to be done.'

'Thanks, Lexi.'

Tessa put the phone down and plodded upstairs. She wasn't going to wake Paul. She needed time alone.

She made herself a mug of Ovaltine and sat in the lounge, by the window. She pulled the curtains back to see the night sky. The city sky. Dark orange and humming. She opened the window to the haze of night in London, and was overwhelmed by an intense longing for the sweet air of home, the scent of primroses and apple blossom. *Mum died at home,* she thought, *in the place she loved. Where are you now, Mum? Where are you?*

As she sipped the comforting Ovaltine, a stillness came. The shivering stopped and she sat motionless in the red tub chair they had chosen from Habitat. Between the plane trees and the rooftops of London, the moon flushed pink as it sank into the west. Tessa watched it fade into a bank of cloud. Soon it would be morning. *Where are you, Mum?* She entered a mystic hour before dawn, a brightening twilight experience that opened her eyes and coloured her mind forever.

She saw her mum instantly and with breathtaking clarity. Kate's brown eyes were alive with wonder and joy. Tessa saw only her head and shoulders in a sort of cameo, a bubble of light. There was a rushing sound, like an eternal wind, and a sensation of speed, faster than anyone could ever travel on earth. The speed of light shone in Tessa's mind, as if her mind had become the universe. She kept her eyes fixed on Kate's eyes, and travelled with her. They shared the journey, over a vast celestial archway, shaped like the top half of a clock. Speeding, speeding onwards, until her mum's bright image reached a point on the archway that would be about two o'clock.

Something changed. The head and shoulders cameo of Kate entered a golden web that sparkled like fireworks. The gold was pure, mysterious and glistening with energy. Then ecstasy as Kate's beautiful smile broke through the sparkling web.

Tessa knew her mum had arrived. She heard cheers of celebration. She felt the warm welcome, and saw the radiant people of light who stretched out their arms to embrace Kate.

But Tessa couldn't follow.

She was earthbound.

The music vanished like wind chimes in the still of the night. Her mum's face turned away into the light and she was gone, into the essence of divine joy. The golden web dimmed and closed its network of brilliance. The archway melted into the sky over London, and the dawn chorus began with the shrill cries of swifts and swallows. On the highest building, a song thrush flooded the city with his endless song. Tessa could see his tiny silhouette, his breast faintly gold in the rising sun.

Oriole Kate, she thought, *my mum, named after a golden bird. Gone now, into the light.*

And how will we live, without her? Without Mum?

CHAPTER 19

A Black Dog

Freddie stood in the kitchen looking at the egg in his hand. Kate had always made his breakfast, nicely arranged on willow-patterned china with silver cutlery and a hand-knitted cosy to keep the egg hot. She'd cut his toast into fingers, the way he liked it, and it was always perfect. Crisp and warm with the butter just melting. The pepper and salt, porcelain models of a cockerel and a hen, were always there, and the square glass bottle of Daddies Sauce. Sometimes she'd give him half a grapefruit, lusciously juicy, cut into convenient chunks and glazed with white sugar. And the teapot would be basking under its knitted cosy, a reassuring curl of steam wafting from the spout.

He looked down at the bare table, brushed away a few crumbs from his last hasty meal, and the task of getting breakfast seemed impossible. All those things Kate had done, and he'd taken it for granted. How did you boil an egg? For how long? And should he try to lay the table first? Make the tea? Put the toast under the grill? So many decisions. About things that didn't matter, or hadn't mattered before.

There were lambs bleating out in the meadows. Blackbirds singing and bees humming. But Freddie heard none of it. To him, The Pines was silent and gloomy, the voices of his children long gone, the chicken run empty, and the vibrant presence of Kate gone forever. There was only Benita looking up at him, meowing for her breakfast. His body ached to sit down at the table and cry. Grief seemed to have a gravity of its own, pulling him down towards benches, chairs and beds, towards the hopelessness of sleep, and down even deeper into the living earth and the need to burrow and hide like an animal.

Freddie fed Benita and then made himself open the cupboard. He took down the biggest saucepan he could find and filled it with cold water. He put it on the electric hotplate and gingerly lowered the egg into the deep water. He looked at the clock. About half an hour, he reckoned, to boil an egg. He waited impatiently by the saucepan for the ten minutes it took to boil the water and for the egg to be afloat on furiously boiling bubbles. Thinking it might get ejected from the saucepan and broken, he turned the heat down and went to find himself a plate and an egg cup.

Just touching the china Kate had used made him even sadder, and he found himself holding the tea cosy to his face for a moment, knowing Kate had knitted it; every coloured strand of wool had passed through her hands, and picked up

341

her happiness. He stared into the garden, and listened for her laughter, her quick footsteps on the path, but heard nothing. Nothingness was his whole life now. A time capsule adrift in the universe. The birds, the scent of roses, the sound of rain, the bees in the lime trees, all that he loved was gone, banished, outside his capsule of nothing.

It was as if he was suddenly deaf, blind and stupid. Humiliating. But did humiliation matter when there was no one in his life or in his home to witness it? Freddie had never felt stupid. He could make intricate models, he could carve angels and owls, he could mend complicated engines, and grow prize-winning vegetables. But he couldn't cook himself a simple meal. Alongside the unspeakable sorrow of bereavement was the shock of having normal home comforts removed. Living basic. Like a hermit.

While the egg went on boiling he wandered around their home, touching things, wondering how he would keep them clean. He opened the airing cupboard and gazed at the stacks of pure white neatly folded linen, beautifully scented from the homemade lavender bags Kate kept in there. It made him nervous. How would he know which sheet to put on his bed? And if he dared to unfold one, could he ever fold it up again? Kate had been proud of her airing cupboard. He could keep it undisturbed like a museum, or try to use it and let it turn into a heap. Ashamed, he closed the door, and something made him open the coat cupboard. He switched on the light and looked up at the metallic glint of a gun hanging on the wall, a twelve-bore shotgun which had belonged to Kate's father, Bertie. She'd kept it polished all these years. Freddie had handled it and examined the mechanism as he did with any gadget, curious to know how it worked. But he'd never used it and never wanted to. The thought of killing a wild creature sickened him.

But now?

Freddie imagined himself in the woods, holding that gleaming gun to his head. He relived how he felt when Tessa had tried to take her life at fourteen. Sick, and profoundly shocked.

Then he remembered how closely Tessa had walked beside him at the funeral. She needed him. It was a reason to stop looking at the gun, shut the cupboard door and go back to the kitchen.

The egg had now been boiling for forty minutes. He ate it miserably. The yolk had turned black around the edges and most of the white had bubbled out through a crack in the shell. It tasted leathery and sour. Freddie wondered what kind of a chicken could have laid such an egg. He didn't bother with toast but cut a hunk of bread and struggled to butter it from the hard yellow brick he took from the fridge. Exasperated, he dumped lumps of the impossible butter on the bread, feeling more and more like giving up as he tried to swallow his lonely meal.

The church clock struck eight, each chime a sharp reminder of the interminably empty hours before him. Freddie got up to wind the mantelpiece clock, another lonely sound he'd have to listen to. He began to sink into a negative spiral, and would have ended up in a dark well of depression when he heard Kate's voice clearly. 'Answer the door, dear,' she said, and he was jolted awake by the sound of knocking. Benita was on the window sill, her fur bushed out with fright.

'You there, Freddie? Come on, answer the door, man, or have I gotta break in?'

Herbie stood there in dust-caked overalls, his eyes unusually serious and full of concern. Freddie opened the door, pleased to see Herbie's dog come running in, eager for a stroke. 'Hello, Jilly girl.' Freddie picked up the squirming bundle of dog and allowed Jilly to make a fuss of him and gaze into his eyes as if she understood everything. 'And who's this?' he asked, looking at the black Labrador Herbie was dragging into the kitchen. 'I didn't know you had two dogs.'

'This one's for you,' Herbie said.

Freddie threw him a look of disbelief. The Labrador was quivering. His tail was down and so was his head.

'He's called Tarka – after Tarka the otter,' Herbie said. 'And he's a bundle of nerves. I can't do anything with him.'

'Where did he come from?' Freddie asked. He put his hand out to stroke the silky black head, but Tarka backed away.

'If you don't have him, he'll have to be put down,' said Herbie. 'Rory O'Sullivan had him – paid a lot of money for him – tried to train him as a gun dog, but Tarka wasn't having it. Useless, he was. Got no heart. Scared witless if he hears a gunshot. Hypersensitive he is, or something. Goes under the table if I even strike a match.'

'Aw.' Freddie's heart went out to the shivering dog. 'My Tessa would love you. Pity she's not here. She's got a way with animals.'

'So have you,' Herbie said. 'And you could do with a dog right now. For company.'

'The only company I need is my Kate,' said Freddie bitterly.

'I know – but 'tis no good talking like that,' Herbie said. 'You gotta let love into your life, even if 'tis only a dog.'

Freddie was silent. He tried again to hold out his hand to Tarka, but the big dog ignored him and crept behind the sofa, taking no notice of Benita who was hissing at him from the top shelf of the dresser.

'I got work to do,' Herbie said, looking at the clock. 'What if I leave the dog with you for today? I'll come back at tea time and if you don't want him, I'll take him away. But don't let him loose. He'll run away and end up goodness knows where.'

Herbie gave Freddie an understanding pat on the shoulder. 'You know where I am, if you need a friend.' He left, with Jilly trotting happily beside him. Freddie stared after him. Gratitude and annoyance jostled in his mind. He thought of Jonti's bright friendly face. This miserable Labrador couldn't have been more different from the confident little terrier.

He padded round the sofa to look at Tarka who was crouching there, trembling, his body pressed against the upholstery. 'I won't hurt you,' he said, and the dog looked hard at him, as if he'd heard it all before. Freddie thought of the outside jobs he'd planned to do, in his first week without Kate. A vague, subconscious list, separate from his grief, a work-list from another lifetime. As he looked down at the terrified dog, a startling thought came to him: *In this moment your job is to love.*

The thought triggered an intense ache in his heart. 'You gotta sort yourself out,' he said to Tarka. 'I'll be upstairs if you need me.'

He trudged upstairs, and stood by the bed he had shared with Kate. Instead of the smooth, orderly bedspread, it looked like a crumpled heap. He found himself doing something he'd never done in his life. Crawling back into bed after breakfast, seeking the comfort of pillows and the oblivion of sleep.

He dozed, half listening to the sound of Tarka walking around downstairs, his nails clicking on the linoleum floor. Left alone, the dog had found confidence to explore. *He needs peace*, Freddie thought. *I must leave him be. Let him settle.*

About an hour later, he heard Tarka coming upstairs. Freddie pretended to be asleep. He kept still as the dog slunk into the bedroom. Freddie felt the weight of him as he put two cumbersome paws on the bed. He felt the dog's whiskers and his warm breath coming close, smelling his hand, making a decision about whether this sleeping human could be trusted.

Moments later, Freddie sensed a smile deep in his heart as Tarka jumped right onto the bed. He didn't dare to move but let the dog settle, turn around a few times with his heavy paws sinking into the mattress, and finally Tarka lay down with a gargantuan sigh. As if he'd come home. *And he has*, Freddie thought. *He's come home. To me. He's chosen me.*

Tessa drove back to London in a daze. The thought of going back to work the next morning, as if nothing had happened, was daunting. Only a few months of the school year remained, and she planned to resign in July, and try to work full time as a clairvoyant medium and astrologer. A scary decision that Paul wasn't going to like.

As she drove the now familiar route, she relived the funeral over and over in her mind. The red roses on the coffin, one for every year Freddie had known Kate. Red roses and white chrysanthemums, and the sunlight shining on them through the stained glass window of the church. The rim-lit petals cruelly bright, as if infused with the pain she had felt at having to follow the coffin into church. She and Lucy, one each side of Freddie, holding on to each other so tightly.

Lucy had flown over from Australia, on her own, and Tessa had met her at the airport, hardly recognising the suntanned young woman. Jetlagged and distraught, Lucy had wept bitterly. She couldn't believe her mum had died. She hadn't said goodbye. She hadn't told Kate how much she missed her. At the funeral Lucy had cried and cried, as if she cried for all of them, when Tessa and Freddie had been stoically silent.

The church had been full of friends and neighbours who

knew and loved Kate. It made the singing robust and earthy, the vicar's voice melancholy, the black clothes gloomy. None of it was what Tessa would have chosen for her mother's bright spirit. She felt isolated, driven into silence, the way it had always been for her in her home town. She longed to step into the centre and share the beauty of what she was seeing, but Freddie's story about seeing the angel had touched her deeply, and given her a warning. *Monterose is not ready for this*, she told herself, and kept quiet, glancing occasionally at Freddie's stone-like expression.

Tessa saw her mother's spirit throughout the service, her bright brown eyes still full of life, her smile radiant. Kate drifted around the church, visiting everyone, looking into their faces with warmth and compassion for their earthbound, physical state, and wanting to say she still loved them. She spent a long time with Lucy, enfolding her in layers of light, as if light was a soft, translucent fabric. Tessa watched Lucy, detecting a momentary aura of calm, before the crying relentlessly continued. Then she watched Freddie as Kate wrapped cloaks of love around him and looked into his face with that searching, caring gaze he had loved so much. Surely he saw her? Still he was rigid with grief, unresponsive, numb. It bothered Tessa deeply. What had happened to his gift?

Her own special moment came at the church door when they all filed out. Kate was there, waiting for Tessa. It was her turn to receive the searching, caring gaze, and the words that gave her courage and joy.

'Use your gift, dear,' Kate said.

Four words that changed her life. Permission to spread her wings and fly.

Now she drove on, over Salisbury Plain, secretly empowered, but confused by the conflicting demands on her time. She didn't want to go home. It felt wrong to leave her dad at The Pines, alone for the first time in his life. She was worried for him, and her mind kept going to the shotgun in the cupboard. Before leaving she had picked Benita up for a cuddle and looked into the little cat's attentive golden eyes. 'You must look after my dad. Stay with him, please, Benita, and give him lots of love and purring.'

She felt drawn to stop at Stonehenge and stroll up to the stones, muffled in a coat and scarf in the crisp easterly wind. The skylarks were singing, high in the blue air, and the wind whipped through the expanse of grasses, turning them to a glistening weave of patterns in the light.

Tessa sat down with her back against one of the stones. Ignoring the tourists wandering about with cameras, she closed her eyes and remembered something Starlinda had told her, a precious nugget of spiritual truth. 'Closing your eyes is like opening them to another dimension. When you close your eyes with intention, you can go through the point of infinity and go home, to your true home in the world of spirit.'

Tessa wanted answers to the problems bugging her life. She wanted a break from the people-pleasing altruism she had got herself into. Pleasing Paul. Pleasing the children she worked with. Pleasing her family. Trying to heal broken hearts. She was constantly striving to do the impossible. Yet still the impossibles queued up in her mind. Why was her life so difficult? Why did this moment of sitting alone at Stonehenge feel exactly the same as that long ago time on the Ridgeway when she had tried to take her life? Why was it the same when it was different?

And why, why, why was she still obsessed with finding Art?

I've made no progress at all, she thought, devastated, and Paul's eyes danced in her mind, mockingly, possessively. *He thinks he owns me. I have to leave him. I have to get away, and begin to LIVE.*

It took Tarka a week to settle down at The Pines.

'I've never seen such a joyless dog,' Freddie told Herbie. 'I've had him a week, and he hasn't wagged his tail once.'

'What about the cat?' Herbie asked. 'Is he all right with her?'

'Benita soon sorted him out.' Freddie couldn't help smiling. 'She hissed and spat, and scratched his nose a few times – made him yelp like a puppy. Now she's curling up with him. Tarka seems to like her company. It's me he doesn't like.'

It was depressing, as if he and the dog were locked together in some kind of emotional prison. Freddie tried to take Tarka for a walk on the lead, but the dog wouldn't go. He dug his paws in at the gate, lay on the path and refused to move. He whined pitifully and Freddie wondered if he was in pain. He got down on the ground with him and ran his hands over the dog's heavy coat. It felt harsh and unloved. Unresponsive and numb. 'Will you walk round the garden with me?' Freddie asked, and Tarka got up obligingly and they did two circuits of the garden, including the Anderson hollow where Tarka wanted to linger and sniff around close to Jonti's grave. Still with his tail down and his eyes dull with gloom.

At night he slept on the bed, and Freddie found his weight and presence comforting. But the dog's behaviour in the house was puzzling. He followed Freddie around, but he wouldn't go in the kitchen, even for his meal. It was weird. Freddie wished Tessa was there. She would know the reason. He stood looking at the phone and decided to ring her.

'Hello, Dad!' She sounded surprised, but then he didn't often pick up the phone. 'Are you all right?'

'Ah – well – it's been a miserable week,' he said, 'on me own. And 'tis hard. I miss Kate. I never realised how much she did for me – little things I never noticed. Are you all right?'

'Just about,' Tessa said.

'Back at work, I suppose?'

'Yes. The children take my mind off things, Dad. I go into work feeling terrible and they lift my spirits.'

'Ah – well – I got something to tell you, Tessa.'

'What's that?'

'I got a dog. A black Labrador. Tarka.'

Tessa's voice brightened and there was a smile in her voice. 'That's great, Dad! What's he like?'

'He's a bundle of nerves. Herbie got him for me – well –

351

no – he dumped him on me. I wish you were here. You'd soon figure out what's the matter with him.'

'What is he scared of?'

'The kitchen. He won't go in there even for his tea.'

Tessa was quiet for a moment, and Freddie could hear a crackling sound.

''Tis a windy night,' he said, 'branches hitting the telephone wires – makes the phone crackle.'

'It's not the kitchen, Dad. It's something in the hall – on the way to the kitchen,' Tessa said, 'or in the coat cupboard. Maybe you should open the cupboard door and let him look inside.'

Freddie was astonished at her insight. Not for the first time he thought, *I hope Paul appreciates her.* 'Right,' he said, 'thanks, I'll try it.'

'Where's the dog now?' Tessa asked.

'Behind the sofa. He always goes behind the sofa when I'm using the phone.'

'Yes – well, the phone is close to the coat cupboard,' Tessa said. 'And he thinks your life is in danger, Dad. He's a highly sensitive dog.'

Freddie was silent. It was making sense.

'And he wants you to brush him, Dad. He hasn't been loved and cared for. His coat is bad – and brushing him will help him relax, and bond with you.'

'You're right,' Freddie said, a lump in his throat. 'How can you be so sure? You've never even seen the dog.'

'It's easy. As easy as breathing.'

Freddie felt choked with emotion. It was all coming true. The words of the Romany Gypsy, given to him the day of Tessa's birth. He was glad he'd shared them with her, and they were crystal clear in his memory. 'This child has a special gift.' He couldn't think beyond that point. It was too overwhelming. Especially now, when he was so vulnerable, so lost without Kate.

'Dad?'

He wanted to tell Tessa she was wasting her life up there in London with a bunch of kids. He wanted to say she was too good for Paul. But he couldn't find the words.

'Are you okay, Dad? I know you're there. I can hear you breathing!'

'Yeah – I'm all right, love, just a bit emotional. But I'll give it a try. Brush the dog – and show him what's in the coat cupboard. And – by the way, Tessa,' his voice brightened a little, 'how long do you boil an egg for?'

'Four minutes.'

'Oh dear – I boiled mine for forty minutes and it was awful. Like the inside of me shoe.'

Tessa screamed with laughter, and he felt better immediately, as if a breath of Kate's irrepressible humour had come bubbling down the phone. He felt a smile warming his face, and his heart. He had a daughter. And a dog. He heard a whine and saw Tarka watching him from the doorway and, for the first time, the tip of his thick tail was twitching as if it wanted to wag.

*

Tessa put the phone down and stood in the hall, feeling locked like a padlock with two chains pulling in opposite directions. It was Friday, six days after the funeral, and she sensed how badly her dad needed her. But Paul needed her too. This weekend she'd planned to catch up on the housework. The place was a mess, the laundry basket overflowing, the fridge empty; whichever way she turned there was clutter. Depressing – and daunting when her energy was low. She needed to rest, to sleep through the weekend, walk under green trees, sit on a bench by the river. 'I need a weekend here in London, Dad,' she said, but his response conveyed a desperation deeper than he would admit. His voice shook with disappointment. Despite the new dog, he wasn't coping. Emotional support was thin on the ground in Monterose. Bereaved people seemed to fade into a thick mist of grief where no one could reach them. She saw her father's spirit shrivelling into a hard knot, and unless it could be unravelled it would destroy his will to live. Freddie didn't talk easily to strangers; he wouldn't phone The Samaritans and find a listening, caring angel like Dorothy, as she had done. The sustaining sparkle had gone from his eyes. Tessa found it distressing. She felt she must deal with her dad's grief as well as her own.

Tessa was still standing, undecided, with one hand on the phone when Paul came home, his hair falling over his brow, his lips white around the edges. He looked at her with tormented eyes. 'I've had a hellish day.' He dragged his jacket, briefcase and violin case through the door and up the stairs in a disorganised tangle. At the top, he turned and glared down at her. 'I'm boiling hot and bloody tired. Are you going to stand there looking like a miserable cow or are you going to get my tea? I need my migraine pills and an ice pack.'

Tessa bit back her retort. She wanted to tell him her mum had just died and she was entitled to be miserable. She wanted to remind him she was exhausted and overwhelmed. But what was the use of trying to tell Paul anything when he was in one of his ugly moods?

Halfway up the stairs, she made a decision. From the heart. Paul had left the door open and she guessed he had gone to the bathroom. She took her bag, car keys and coat from the kitchen, shut the flat door with a quiet click and hurried downstairs, praying the car would start, and praying she'd get there in time to stop Freddie doing what she knew he was thinking about.

CHAPTER 20

A Taste of Glory

The night was starry and mystic as Freddie padded down the
lane, the air cool and still, the luminous faces of primroses
staring from the deep grasses. The dead elms loomed, bone-
pale like driftwood, but the hedges bristled with white sloe
blossom.

Freddie saw none of it. He saw Kate. Only Kate.
Unreachable. Gone. He felt none of the magic, none of the
joy in the night. He didn't listen to the owls. He heard only
the harrowing sound of Tarka howling. It sounded like a
pack of long-ago wolves, filling the night, filling his heart
with a sense of doom.

In one hand he carried an old rubber torch with a fading
battery. He didn't use it. A lifetime of watching badgers in
the night woods had given Freddie a unique ability to see
his way in the dark.

Tucked under his arm was something he had removed

from the coat cupboard. Bertie's gun. He felt guilty carrying it through the night, as if Bertie was watching to see what he would do with the gun.

Tessa was right, he thought. Tarka had backed away, his eyes glittering with terror when Freddie took the gun from the cupboard. The big dog had gone behind the sofa and cowered there, whimpering. The springs of the sofa twanged as he pressed his shaking body against the fabric. No amount of coaxing, reassurance or biscuits would tempt him to come out. So Freddie had locked the door and left him to howl.

He walked on, past the derelict station which still had a lingering whiff of coal and soot. Piles of rusting metal and ballast were softened by the graceful panicles of buddleia which had seeded itself in every available crack, growing with purpose like the forest in *Sleeping Beauty*. Freddie paused to watch a train hammering through, relentless and brightly lit, as if the station had never existed.

'Off shooting rabbits are you, Freddie?'

Charlie's voice startled him in the quiet of the night. Charlie had been the stationmaster ever since Freddie had been a boy earning pennies by carrying luggage over the bridge. He still lived in the cottage below the disused signal box.

'Ah – might be.' Freddie didn't want to say yes, or no. And he didn't want to explain his doom–laden mindset to Charlie.

'All right, are you, Freddie?'

'Fair to middling.'

''Tis sad seeing the old station,' Charlie said. 'And – I'm sorry, so sorry, about your missus. Lovely girl she was. Lovely. I knew her when she were a little girl with plaits. Always a smile she had – always.'

Freddie struggled to breathe normally, look as if he was coping. *Funny*, he thought, *after all the sadness, 'tis a drop of kindness that makes me want to cry.*

'You can come in if you like – have a tot of brandy with me,' Charlie offered, 'or a cup of tea.'

'Thanks – but – not right now. I'll go on me way, Charlie. Left me dog shut in and howling.'

'I can hear him,' Charlie said. 'I reckon dogs still believe they're wolves.'

Freddie headed for the river, a new, hotter pain in his throat. Would he feel like this forever? Was this how it would be now? His life savagely stitched with the fibres of grief. The silence deepened as he plodded downhill. The Somerset Levels had once been an ocean, and he felt its enveloping tide, the sound of Tarka's howling now a lost cry from a distant shore.

He was aware of Benita following him, a velvet shadow with big lamp eyes trying to engage with him. She stayed with him, sometimes dashing ahead, then hiding and popping out as he strode past. The little cat was out of her comfort zone but determined, it seemed, to keep him company. Would she find her way home? He didn't want to lose her.

The river bridge loomed, the water a silent slipstream

weaving between reeds. Freddie shone his torch on the marsh-marigold, their golden flowers closed for the night. He leaned over the parapet, still faintly warm from a day of sunshine. He dropped a stone into the pool below. The torchlight gilded the circular ripples. A huge carp rose momentarily to the surface and he saw the sheen of its gaping lips, the iridescence of its eye. The fish was legendary, eluding all attempts to catch it. Freddie thought it had been in the pool since he was a boy.

There was no doubt that the pool was deep enough, and so was the mud below, deep enough to swallow a cow.

Freddie lifted the gun down from his shoulder. He rested it on the uneven stone of the bridge, his heartbeat pounding through his body. His hands shook. He scanned the diamond night, listened for footsteps or voices. No one was there. Except Kate. He felt her strongly, sensed her watching him, and felt the touch of her hand waft over the gun, as if giving it a final polish.

He hesitated. Kate would know. She wouldn't be happy with what he was about to do. But what was left of his life now? What use was he? A man alone in an echoing house? A man disempowered by grief. A half-person. A nobody.

Benita appeared, meowing, walking purposefully along the stone parapet, her big lamp eyes shining in the dark. 'You miss Kate, don't you?' Freddie mumbled, and the cat rubbed herself against him, walking to and fro, her fur cool and lustrous. *Kate's pride and joy*, he thought, a lump in his throat as he remembered how lovingly Kate had restored the little cat to health, the hours Benita had spent lying on the bed with her, purring.

It only took Freddie an instant to make a decision. He lifted the gun with both hands and held it over the water, reaching out as far as he could. *Let go*, he thought, and Kate's voice spoke brightly into the silence of his grief. 'Let go of it, dear.' It was something she often said to people if they were worrying about a problem or a responsibility. 'Let go of it, dear. Let go.'

Freddie opened his hands and dropped the gun into the river with a satisfying splash which sent Benita scurrying into the dark. The splash was somehow cathartic. Freddie watched the ripples race outwards until the black water was smooth as glass. He watched a water vole glide out from the reeds, and saw the shadow of the huge carp cross the pool with a flick of its tail. Planet Earth had swallowed the gun in one gulp, and healed the scar, effortlessly. All he had to do now was go home to Tarka.

'Maybe I can survive,' he said aloud, and Benita ran to him with her tail up. He picked her up and put her on his shoulder. 'God knows how, but we gotta try.'

Paul banged his fist on the roof of Tessa's blue Ford Anglia. She wound the window down, glaring at him. 'Don't try to stop me, Paul. I've got a right to go and see Dad.'

'Why don't you LISTEN?' he yelled. 'You're wanted on the phone. It's that bloody woman. She said it's urgent.'

'Starlinda?'

'Whatever her stupid name is.'

'You'd better not be kidding.' Tessa switched off the engine and got out, thinking Paul might be tricking her into staying. 'And I've told Dad I'm going down there.'

'Who cares?'

'You obviously don't.' Tessa tucked her car key safely into her jeans and went inside. Paul had left the wall telephone dangling on its cable. She picked it up. 'Hi.'

'Oh, Tessa – thank God I've caught you.' Starlinda's voice sounded faint and stressed.

'What's the matter?' Tessa asked, surprised.

'Take a deep breath,' Starlinda said in her normal confident tone. 'I'm dropping you in the deep end, darling.'

'What do you mean?'

'I am booked to do a public meeting as a clairvoyant medium, at 7.30 in that lovely hall in Pimlico – you know the one I mean? You came with me last time.'

'Yes.'

'Well – deep breath, Tessa – I am sick, with a tummy bug, and I can't possibly do it. I've promised to find a gifted young psychic to replace me – and it has to be you. Will you be there?'

'ME! But but . . .'

Paul was standing close, listening, his arms folded over his chest, shaking his head and looking sceptical.

'Yes, you, Tessa. There's no one else I trust to stand in for me.'

'But I don't feel ready.'

361

'Yes, you do, and you are ready. I've got total confidence in you. It's a golden opportunity, darling – it won't come again.'

Tessa was speechless. She wished Paul would go away. Having him looming there, putting pressure on her to say no, and Starlinda pouring flattery into the phone to persuade her, felt like being torn apart.

'People who stand in your way are needy souls who want a slice of your light, Tessa. Isn't this what you wanted to do? Then go for it, girl, I'm handing it to you on a plate.'

'But what am I going to WEAR?' Tessa asked. She covered the mouthpiece and hissed at Paul. 'This is a private conversation – will you please BACK OFF.'

'I can lend you something stunning – but you must get over here quickly.'

Tessa felt as if bells were ringing all around her, inside her aura; tambourine bells and fairy bells, brass hand bells and a church tower bell, its vibration reaching her from far away, from Monterose. She felt entangled in webs of resonance.

'You look shocked,' Paul said, frowning. 'What's going on, Tessa? What does that woman want?'

'Nothing much. She's sick.' Tessa heard her own voice calmly being economical with the truth. 'I'm going over there now. Then I shall come home and drive down to Dad's place, no matter how late, and whether you like it or not, Paul.'

'What about my supper?' Paul said petulantly.

Tessa smiled sweetly. 'You're a big boy now. Make yourself

a sandwich, or go to the chippie.' She twirled around and back to the car, leaving him open-mouthed. *I am powerful*, she thought joyfully. The long years of studying astrology, the meditations and spiritual training came together in one illuminating moment, like the brilliance of stepping into her own light by the spring in Monterose. Calmly she pulled out and drove down the tree-lined street, seeing Paul in her driving mirror, in his white shirt and tie, his image shrinking to a matchstick. A thought butted in. *I'm being arrogant*, closely followed by *No, I'm not. I'm reclaiming my soul.*

Hours later, dressed in Starlinda's sequinned turquoise kaftan, silver stilettos and a white faux-fur cape, Tessa swanned in to the familiar hall in Pimlico. She'd always loved going there with Starlinda for life-changing workshops on crystal healing and colour therapy, psychometry and a range of spiritual development. The hall itself was special, aligned on one of London's powerful ley lines. She felt good there. It couldn't have been a better place to make her debut.

She'd had no time to prepare. But that, Starlinda said, was the way of the spirit. You didn't write speeches or read from a book. You opened your heart and listened, and the words would come. They always did.

The rows of chairs were full. Heads turned and a hush fell like stardust as Tessa swept down the central gangway to the front where a man called Ross with white hair and an even whiter jacket was setting up a table for her. She saw a velvet cloth, a glass of water and a candle flickering in a pink glass lantern.

Her heart was beating with fierce energy, as if she'd never before been so alive. Ross introduced her simply as 'Tessa, a new, young talent, trained by Starlinda. We are honoured to have you, Tessa.'

She began with a smile so radiant that she felt her mum was actually inside her infusing her with warmth and energy. 'I'm Tessa,' she said, beaming, 'and this is the work I was born to do.' She scanned the blur of watching faces, and immediately a few individuals caught her attention. 'Let's begin by being quiet together'

A ripple of anticipation spread through the audience. There were about a hundred people, she guessed, and the hall was filled with the scent of shower gel and shoe polish, and a sense of repressed emotions. Sorrow, anger, jealousy, scepticism and fear. *Don't go there*, she thought, remembering her training, *rise above the emotional body into the pure light of spirit*. In those first few moments it could go badly wrong if she allowed her own emotions to bubble up through the tiniest crack in her confidence. It was like walking a tightrope, believing you could do it. Not looking down.

Using her healing voice, Tessa talked them through the heart meditation and sensed the room slowly infusing with light. When she opened her eyes, the faces were gazing raptly at her. 'There are always a few sceptics,' Starlinda had warned her. 'Just carry them kindly, like passengers on a bus; don't focus on them.'

Tessa waited for the words and they came instantly. 'There are no limitations. This room has become an arena of celestial light, and it is full of dear friends who have passed into spirit. There are hundreds. Some have come simply to sit with you, to reassure and love you, to wrap you in the softest blanket of comforting light. And some have come to do what they have longed to do – to talk to you. If you listen, from the heart, perhaps you will hear the precious words they will whisper to you, and some will need my help to reach you.'

She paused, and her gaze was drawn to an elderly woman sitting in the front row with desperate eyes set in her well-dressed, well-permed, well-powdered image. Tessa asked her name and she said it was Louise.

'I see a young man standing by your left shoulder,' Tessa said, speaking directly to her. 'And he is pure gold. He is giving me the name, Martin, shortened to Marty.'

Louise gave a cry of joy. 'My son!' she cried. 'Marty – oh Marty! You can see him, Tessa?'

'Oh yes,' Tessa said, in a smooth, confident voice. 'He is very powerful, as if he might have been an athlete in his time on earth. He's showing me the sea – was he a swimmer?'

'A lifeguard,' Louise said, dabbing at her powdered cheeks with an embroidered hanky. 'A beach lifeguard in Cornwall.'

Tessa swallowed. Don't go back. Go forward. Stay in the heart. 'He still loves you,' she said, 'and he is with you more than you know. He wants me to say thank you for the dog made of flowers '

Again, Louise cried out with amazement. 'How did you know that? He loved our Scottie dog, Jethro, and I did have a wreath made in the shape of a dog, in red and white chry-santhemums. How wonderful.'

Encouraged, Tessa continued listening to Marty. 'He tells me his death was an accident but he doesn't want you to think of it like that. He says he came to you as a golden gift, for a short time, and he was more than a son – he was your teacher.'

Louise was nodding, tears running freely, her eyes hungry for every last crumb of information. 'He was my teacher – it's true,' she wept. 'He taught me how to love.'

'He's got one more message for you, Louise. He's showing me an airport, and a big passenger plane with a red maple leaf on it. He says it will take you safely to Canada. He wants you to go, and see the Rockies. You will be quite all right, and you have nothing to fear.'

Louise reached up with frail arms and gave Tessa a hug. 'How did you know? It's exactly what I want to do, so much. You've made me so happy. Thank you. Thank you, Tessa.'

'You're welcome – and you've done brilliantly,' Tessa smiled at Louise, and moved on, her eyes drawn to another spirit who was looking at her intently like someone waiting in a queue, this time a spirit child with understanding, loving eyes. 'I have a little girl with me, aged about ten, with long dark wavy hair. Her name begins with an M, and she wants to contact her grandad.' Tessa scanned the faces and found the grandad, hunched and flinty-eyed, on a chair close to the door. 'Is it you, sir?' she asked gently.

The man looked petrified. He covered his eyes with

shaking hands. 'Mandy,' he whispered. 'My little Mandy. I – I adored her. She was taken from us so young – it was so cruel.' He looked up at Tessa in wordless grief.

'What's your name?'

'Terry.'

Tessa sat down on the empty chair next to him. 'It's okay, Terry. Mandy wants me to tell you how much she loved the tree house. Did you build it for her? I'm seeing an oak tree in a big garden, with a round lily pool.'

Terry gasped in surprise. 'That's right – I did.'

'Mandy says you must use it. Climb up there and write the poems she loved to hear. She wants to see them published in a book.'

Terry's thin face was getting wider and wider with smiling. He clasped his hands together and looked at Tessa in awe. 'Are you sure you're not an angel? You've given me HOPE, my dear. It's a dream of mine, to publish a book of poetry.'

Tessa brushed her hand across his shaking shoulders, and moved on again, to the next waiting spirit. It was easy. The two hours flew by, golden hours of effortlessly doing what she now knew she was born to do. She wasn't even tired. And at the end, when Ross declared it was time to close the meeting, there was a standing ovation. People didn't want to leave, but queued to talk to her and congratulate her. Some asked for private sittings with her, wanted her phone number, her business card. Tessa thought quickly. She couldn't give her home contact because of Paul – so she asked for theirs and promised to ring them.

When everyone had gone, Ross handed her a remarkably fat envelope. 'You've done well, Tessa,' he enthused. 'There's a few donations in there as well as the entry fees.'

Tessa felt her eyes popping at the bundle of cash. *Better pretend I'm used to it*, she thought, accepting it graciously and tucking it into her bag.

'How are you getting home, my dear?' Ross asked. 'I don't think you should be alone in London at this time of night with that kind of cash.'

He walked her back to her car.

'I feel like Cinderella getting home from the ball,' she joked, unlocking the door of her scruffy Ford Anglia.

'You don't look like Cinderella. You look like a film star,' Ross said. 'I hope we'll see you again.'

She sat in the car, watching him walk away. *I can't go home*, she thought. *Paul will destroy everything I've done tonight.*

'What the hell's going on?'

Freddie was jolted awake by Tarka's thunderous barking. He switched on the light and saw the dog at the window, his hackles up like a porcupine, and each reverberating bark lifting the front half of the dog up in the air, his ears flying up wildly. A fearsome sight. Freddie seized the cricket bat from under the bed and crept to the open window with it, ready to crack the burglar on the head.

He peered out. The back garden was tranquil with pools of moonlight on a wet lawn, and the girls' old swing hanging motionless.

'What's the matter with you?' he asked Tarka. 'You nearly gave me a heart attack. I never heard a dog bark so loud. Wake the blimin' dead, you would.'

Tarka had the grace to look ashamed.

''Tis three o'clock in the morning,' Freddie told him.

But Tarka continued to growl. He ran to the bedroom door and listened, his head on one side. It spooked Freddie more than the thunderous barking. Silence was definitely worse. Especially when it creaked. At times like this he missed Kate terribly. She would have looked at him with those bright brown eyes and giggled.

He opened the bedroom door and let Tarka go skidding downstairs. Freddie followed him down, cautiously on his bare feet. The dog was quiet again, doing the stiff listening act, sensing someone standing on the doorstep. A key turned in the lock, the door was pushed open, and Tarka chickened and disappeared behind the sofa.

'Dad! It's me.' Tessa switched on the hall light and Freddie immediately noticed the excitement in her pale blue eyes. 'What are you doing standing on the stairs with a cricket bat, Dad?' she joked.

'I thought it was a burglar.' Freddie put the bat down. He'd been so vulnerable since Kate had died. Tides of emotion ebbed and flowed and he no longer felt in control. He didn't feel like a man, more like a piece of wreckage flung onto an alien shore. Seeing his daughter was overwhelming. He didn't speak, in case he cried.

'Are you okay, Dad?' Tessa took off her wet mac and hung

it up. She guided him to the sofa and sat down with him. 'Shall I make some cocoa?'

Freddie shook his head, wanting only to sit close to Tessa and recapture a sense of belonging. Benita jumped down from Kate's chair and ran to Tessa, doing funny little mewling sounds. She climbed onto her lap and made a welcoming fuss, purring and reaching up to pat Tessa's face with a silky paw. The three of them sat wordlessly, listening to the night rain pouring down the windows.

'Where's the dog?' Tessa asked.

'Oh – he's gone behind the sofa. He's terrified of anyone new. He'll come creeping out in a minute. But didn't he bark! I never heard a dog bark so loud. Shook the blimin' bulbs out of the lights. He makes the noise and tries to be a dog, then he chickens. I dunno what's wrong with him, Tessa. He's a lovely dog.'

'Did you let him look in the cupboard?' Tessa asked.

'Ah – I did more than that. I took Bertie's gun out, and, well to tell you the truth, I felt like shooting meself.'

'Dad!' Tessa looked horrified.

'I took it down and dropped it in the river. 'Tis gone, and I reckon that dog saved my life, Tessa, in a way. And when I got back he went straight into the kitchen, no problem – he knew what I'd done. Dogs are so wise. I've only had him a week, but I wouldn't be without him now – and Benita – she ran with me all the way to the river, looking at me with big black eyes. I wouldn't be without her either, she was so attached to Kate.' Freddie paused, aware of his new tendency to talk too much. Once he started, he couldn't seem to stop. He looked at Tessa and noticed raindrops on her face and hair. 'You're soaking wet. And cold.' He touched her hand.

'I ran out of petrol a mile from home. I left the car in a layby up on the hill, and walked. It was VERY dark.'

'Oh dear – I've got a can of petrol – we'll fetch the car in the morning,' Freddie said, looking at his daughter with more awareness of how she might be feeling. He hadn't welcomed her the way Kate would have done. Tessa had always been so sensitive. He looked at her eyes. They were like the night outside, alternating between the silver of moonlight and the jet blackness of night rain. 'Has something happened?' he asked.

'Everything has happened,' she said, 'in one incredible evening. I did my first solo meeting as a clairvoyant medium, with about a hundred people,' her eyes brightened, 'and I LOVED it, Dad. It's the best, best thing I've ever done – and when I'd finished they gave me a standing ovation.'

At the sound of her voice, Tarka crept out on his belly and sidled up to Tessa, the tip of his tail wagging. He gazed up at her adoringly. 'He's wonderful,' she breathed. 'I love him already. So much love. There's just – so much love here, Dad, in this house. I need it. I really need it.'

'Don't you feel loved with Paul?' Freddie asked.

Tessa shook her head wildly. 'No. Emphatically – NO.'

'So what happened?'

She sighed and looked at him with that blend of night rain and moonlight in her eyes. She spoke slowly, in a different, hurting voice. 'Tonight, when I got home, I was so happy, and all dressed up in Starlinda's clothes. I felt wonderful. But Paul threw me out. He'd packed my bag and he flung it down the stairs at me, and said he never wanted to see me again. It's over, Dad, and I'm hurt – but I don't care. I feel liberated.'

CHAPTER 21

Kate's Red Ribbon

'I'm no use to anyone,' Freddie declared, staring into the fire. One year on from losing Kate, Freddie had lost himself as well, Tessa thought, looking at the shell of a man he had become. His skin looked blotchy, his ankles swollen from endless hours of sitting in a chair, his eyes had lost the sparkle Tessa remembered, the deep blues and the twinkle of light so like the Cornish sea, the mystery in them, the curiosity, the empathy. All gone. He was caught in a negative spiral, resisting attempts to help him, even hers. He just sat and stared at nothing, his hand caressing Tarka who had become a devoted companion dog, glossy and contented.

'What were your dreams, Dad, when you were young?' Tessa asked. She had a plan. Something she would do first and tell him afterwards.

He shrugged. 'It doesn't matter now.'

'I remember you as a creative artist,' Tessa said. 'You were always carving something, or drawing.'

'Ah – I were. 'Tis no good thinking about it now.' His eyes didn't change, didn't look at her.

'I'm trying to help you, Dad.'

'I know you are – and it's good of you – but don't waste your time. There's nothing you can do.'

Tessa picked up her car keys from the table. 'Oh, but there is, Dad. There IS something I can do, and I'm going to do it. I'll be back later, about tea time.'

'No – don't you go bothering about me. Where are you going?'

'Wait and see,' Tessa said brightly, 'and you'll like it.' She kissed his grey-looking cheek and swept out, twiddling the keys.

'Just like her mother she is, my Tessa,' she heard him say to Tarka, but he made no attempt to stop her.

Her brand new white Capri was parked in the drive. It still gave her a buzz, seeing it, getting in and driving away smoothly, purring, not popping and rattling like her previous cars had done. She opened the boot and checked the papers she needed were in there, a neat bundle tied together with a red ribbon. She'd touched the ribbon and felt her mother's vibes on it – one of Kate's hair ribbons from her childhood.

If Mum could see me now, Tessa thought as she drove on, over the Polden Hills, through Ashcott, and out across the Somerset Levels. It was March and some of the fields were still flooded, a vast expanse of mirror-like water, reflecting the sky. There were wheeling flocks of lapwing and many pairs of nesting swans. She passed Burrow Mump, a steep green hill with a ruined church on top, and on towards Taunton.

Tessa was proud of the way she'd rebuilt her life after Paul. She'd stayed in London, found herself a flat with a telephone, and begun to work as a clairvoyant medium. At first she'd kept her job with the children. They were good for her, and it paid the rent while she was building her client list. After her successful debut in Pimlico she was in demand, for public meetings and for private sittings. Money rolled in to her bank account and soon she was able to buy herself a few exotic clothes, and the new car.

She spent much of her free time at The Pines, striving to help Freddie out of his paralysing grief. It was hard slog, doing washing, ironing and shopping, and patiently teaching him how to cook simple meals. It left little time for visits to the field. She'd been there with Freddie in the autumn to plant more young trees, and at the winter solstice she'd made him go to the source of the spring with her. A snowy wind howled through the bare trees, and the water steamed gently as it bubbled up from the earth. Tessa tried to share her dream of restoring the well, planting a magical garden, and starting a healing centre. But Freddie wanted to go home to the cosy fire, and he'd said bluntly, 'You can't do that in Monterose.' Disappointed, Tessa followed him down to the car, their feet crunching the frosted grass. She tried to understand and forgive, but it stung. *Mum would have told him off for being negative*, she thought, and her own grief hurt like never before.

Today as she drove to Taunton she sensed Kate beside her, encouraging her and celebrating her success. She found Elrose College of Art, drove into the car park, and took the bundle out of the boot. Tucking it under her arm, she walked into the entrance, feeling good in the 'flowing robe' she had chosen to wear. It was one she used for her meetings, and the colours were arty, subtle abstracts of pink and mellow orange on a cream background. She looked, and felt like an artist.

'I'm Tessa Barcussy,' she told the receptionist, with a disarming smile. 'I have an interview with the principal.'

He turned out to be fortyish, and hippyish, with a ponytail and discerning eyes. He looked her up and down with approval and more than a hint of sexuality. 'Great to meet you, Tessa. I'm Oliver Portwell. It's an interesting idea you have – I hope we can sort something out.'

Oliver led her into a studio with two white cane chairs. 'I'm keen to see what you've brought me,' he said, eyeing the bundle, and his eyes lit up. 'I can smell talent – and it smells musty – goodness, those do look old!'

'They are.' Tessa gave him one of her bewitching smiles. Her pale blue eyes shone with mystery as she undid the red ribbon and handed Freddie's sketchbooks, dated 1930–1950, to the principal of Elrose College of Art.

*

It would be hard to resist telling Freddie where she had been, but Tessa wanted a positive result before revealing her plan to him.

She hurried back to Monterose for another meeting she had secretly arranged, this time in her field. A slow tractor on the narrow road over the Poldens made her late, and she felt flustered when she needed to be calm. There was no time to change into her jeans as she'd intended, and the flowing robe would look inappropriate, even silly, in the field.

A few shiny cars were parked in the lane and five men in suits were there, looking over the gate and brandishing clipboards. Tessa parked on the grass verge. She took her amethyst crystal from the dashboard cubby hole and put it into the pocket of her aquamarine cape coat. She and Starlinda had programmed the crystal with a special prayer of intention, and Tessa wanted to be able to touch it discreetly while she was talking. The five men turned to stare at her arriving, the key to the road gate hooked over her finger.

Tessa was used to walking into meetings looking like a Goddess, her hair and clothes shimmering, her eyes alive and powerful. *It's who I am*, she reminded herself now, facing these five local men who were trying to look important. She smiled into the eyes of the man who held out his hand to her. 'Hello. I'm Tessa Barcussy. Thanks for coming.'

'I'm John Whitsby, chairman of Monterose District Council,' he said, and his eyes looked into her soul in a friendly way. 'I understand what you want to do here, Tessa.' He held on to her hand long enough for her to get the feeling he was sending her. *He's spiritual*, she thought immediately, *but he's in chains.* She gave him a secret smile. *He's already said yes*, she thought.

John Whitsby introduced the other four, and Tessa's heart sank. One looked bored, two looked sceptical, and the fourth was a young man, Mick Tucker, who Tessa remembered from primary school. He had bullied her, and the old hostility still brooded in his peat-dark eyes, an 'us and them' kind of smirk, now disguised as a district councillor in a suit. *Don't engage with him*, Tessa thought, but in that moment she felt like the loneliest person on the planet.

Her fingers shook as she unlocked the heavy padlock and let the men strut into her precious field. Right on cue, an orange-tip butterfly went bobbing over the wild flowers and grasses.

'As you can see, this land is a sanctuary for wild flowers and butterflies,' she said, hoping they would appreciate the violets and primroses, the patches of wild thyme and mosses.

'Looks a proper mess to me,' Mick Tucker said, with relish.

'Don't take any notice of him – he's a farmer,' said John Whitsby pleasantly. 'You're not getting your tractor in here, Mick.'

There was laughter and a bit of banter. Tessa led them up to the source of the spring, and they stood in a bored semi-circle, not even looking at the miracle of the bubbling water. *They're out of the body*, Tessa thought, and she longed to say something outrageous. Instead she spoke to John Whitsby, directly into the sparkle of his eyes. 'I have done some research,' she told him, 'and this used to be a Holy Well. It was used by the Romans, and by the Victorians who used it as a spa. It had an exquisite well-house building around it, with a circular stone seat, and of course the Romans had a beautiful mosaic floor.'

'How fascinating.' John Whitsby was looking at her eagerly.

'What I'd like to do is restore it very beautifully, plant a woodland garden around it, and re-open it as a sacred spring, a place where people can come for healing. Like Chalice Well in Glastonbury.'

'Yes – yes, I know Chalice Well,' John Whitsby said, but no one else spoke, except with looks of derision which passed between them.

'That ain't gonna work in Monterose,' Mick Tucker announced. 'I'm tellin' you now. This is a good, down to earth farming community. People don't want Glastonbury stuff here – hippie stuff.'

Tessa made her voice smooth and quiet. 'We have to ask ourselves what kind of a world we want our children to inherit,' she said. 'Do we want them to have beautiful places with wildflower meadows and butterflies, places where they can feel peaceful, and joyful? What kind of a world would it be without joy?' She turned her sparkling blue eyes on the dumpy hostility of Mick Tucker, and raised her eyebrows enquiringly. He fidgeted and looked down at his feet. 'I grew up here in Monterose,' she continued, 'and I played in those wildflower meadows, I listened to the nightingales singing under the stars. It filled me with beauty and happiness, and I carry that with me in my heart. I want to give back. I want to do something to restore this special place. I think it matters. Don't you?'

No one answered, and no one seemed aware of the shimmering light weaving itself around them. No one else saw the shining people who came gliding through the trees to offer their loving support. A silent moment, a 'between place', a moment where time expanded and magic was allowed a voice. And there was a voice, a real voice, singing in the wood.

There will be an answer

Let it be

Tessa froze. The voice from the wood shocked her and she felt close to panic. It was the second time she'd heard it, and what touched her so deeply was the earthiness of it, and the way it reached her with such perfect timing, clarity, and disturbing familiarity. It wasn't a spirit voice. It was a real voice, low-toned and breathy, targeting her like a storm blowing under a door, a door she thought she had closed long ago.

John Whitsby was looking intently at her. 'Are you all right, Tessa?' he asked.

'Yes. Yes, I'm fine,' she answered him but he didn't look convinced.

'Well, I expect you have to get back to London, don't you?' he said. 'I think we've seen enough, and we should draw this meeting to a close. We will look very seriously at your application in the next planning meeting.' He turned to the four men. 'Thank you, gentlemen, you can go now.'

He lingered, obviously wanting a private chat with Tessa.

'Of course, I can't predict the outcome of this meeting,' he said, 'but I myself will recommend it, so let's hope they vote yes.'

Tessa re-focused her attention on John Whitsby, and the sudden brilliance of his aura. She felt compelled to tell him about it. 'You have an extraordinary light around you – and with you.'

He smiled as if he had emerged from a tunnel into the sunshine. 'Tell me more – please.'

Tessa hesitated, waiting for the spirit to materialise, and it did. 'Well – there's a lady with you who looks like an angel, but she's not, she tells me – she's shaking her head – but she loves to walk beside you. She's showing me a garden with white and purple irises just coming into bloom, and she's showing me a rocking horse which is being restored. I think she wants you to finish it.'

John Whitsby looked stunned, and delighted. 'I knew it,' he said. 'I knew the minute I saw you, Tessa – you're a medium – aren't you?'

'Yes.'

'So was my wife – the lady you saw. She did look like an angel – to me anyway. And before she passed over, I was restoring a rocking horse for our granddaughter. But I'm afraid I became gloomy and depressed after my wife had gone, and I'm only just beginning to live again. You've given me hope, Tessa, real hope, and motivation. I shall go home and get on with painting that dappled grey horse now. I can't thank you enough.'

'You're welcome. It's something I love to do.'

'Are you a practising medium?'

'Yes, in London. I do private sittings, and meetings.'

'That's marvellous!' John Whitsby said. 'I do wish you luck.'

'Thanks – I usually have to keep the lid on it, especially around here.'

'Well – my wife and I were both members of a healing circle. If you do move back here, Tessa, please get in touch. Maybe you could do a session for us?'

'I'd love to.'

'Wonderful, I'll look forward to that. Now I really must go, I've got another meeting.'

Left alone by the spring, Tessa felt encouraged by what had happened. She listened to the sounds from the wood, but the singing didn't come again. There was only the laughing call of the green woodpecker and the rustle of leaves in the breeze. She looked at the path made by whoever was fetching water from the spring. Last time it had been well trodden. Now the grasses were growing over it again as if no one used it. She looked up at the fence and the gate was still shut, the padlock a glint of grey on its chain.

When the time is right, she thought, *I must go up there, get close to the wood, and listen, and find out who is in there. Who is watching me? – and singing!*

'Dad, will you PLEASE get in the car?' Tessa said in exasperation the following morning. 'You won't come to any harm.

I'm a careful driver – I drive round London, for goodness' sake.'

'I know,' Freddie said. 'It isn't that.'

'So what is it then?'

'Well – I don't like mystery trips.' Freddie stood on the doorstep, looking out at the sky with his eyes dull and sad. 'You promise me you're not taking me to see some quack of a doctor.'

'No. I promise.'

Freddie put on his cap and tweed jacket. 'And it better not be a vicar either.'

'Dad! You KNOW I wouldn't do that.'

'And I don't want to leave Tarka on his own. He digs holes in the carpet. I only left him once when I did a job with the lorry, and when I came back he'd eaten the rug in the hall – my mother's rug – and in two hours that dog reduced it to a ball of string and a heap of fluff. He panics, see, if he's left alone.'

'Well, bring him,' Tessa said when she'd finished laughing. 'He can lie on the back seat.'

'He might be sick.'

'Well – bring him anyway.'

Tessa clipped Tarka onto his lead. 'You want to come in Tessa's car, don't you?' she said, and Tarka squirmed with excitement. He went willingly with Tessa and jumped into the car. 'He thinks he's going to the river,' she said. 'Shall we take him on the way back? Let him have a swim?'

Freddie's eyes brightened, and to Tessa's relief he finally

got in the car. 'We could get fish and chips too,' he said, patting his wallet.

'Good idea.' Tessa started the car.

'I'm sorry, dear,' Freddie said. 'I'm a miserable old sod. I don't mean to be. Kate wouldn't want me to be like this. "Don't be so morbid, dear," she'd say!'

'She wants you to be happy,' Tessa said.

Freddie put his hand on her arm. 'Stop a minute. Stop.'

She'd been about to pull out into the lane. She braked. 'What is it, Dad?'

He looked at her, and the consciousness which had disappeared from his eyes flooded back momentarily. 'Do – do you see her?' he asked. 'My Kate. Do you see her?'

'Often,' Tessa said. 'I did try to tell you, but you've been too upset to listen.'

He nodded. 'I've been in a very dark place.'

'Grief is a terrible dark place to be,' agreed Tessa, 'but – please trust me, Dad. All you have to do is sit in the car for twenty minutes, and when we arrive you'll see it's something you want – but if you decide you don't want it, then we'll still get our fish and chips and come home – and everything will be all right.'

Freddie stared at her with mixed emotions flickering through his eyes. 'All right – go on then – take me there,' he said resignedly, and added brightly, 'and I do believe Kate put you up to this.'

'She kind of did.' Tessa flashed him a smile, and drove on towards Taunton with Freddie giving her a running commentary on the birdlife as they drove across the Levels. Tarka sat up on the back seat with his head out of the window.

'Elrose College of Art?' Freddie said in surprise as they turned into the car park. 'What the hell do I want to come here for? Eh? Or are you going back to college? Is that it? I always hoped you would. We were so sad when you dropped out all 'cause of that blimin' hippie. And look what he did.'

Tessa kept quiet. She locked the car and put Tarka on his lead. The dog was confident now. He would go anywhere with Tessa, or with Freddie. Now he pulled Freddie along as if he wanted him to go into this strange building.

Oliver was waiting for them, dressed in a brown velvet jacket with a coffee-coloured shirt and a fat tie covered in calligraphy. 'Pleased to meet you, Mr Barcussy. I'm Oliver Portwell, and I'm the principal of Elrose College of Art.'

Freddie looked gobsmacked, but he shook Oliver's hand, and glanced at Tessa with his eyes open very wide.

'Come this way.'

They followed Oliver into the studio, with Tarka skidding on the shiny floor. On a low glass-topped table Freddie's sketch books were laid out, along with a set of photographs Tessa had done of his carvings. In the centre, neatly folded, was Kate's red hair ribbon.

Freddie's eyes rounded. 'Oh my God,' he said, after a silence, and Tessa thought she'd never, ever heard him say that before. 'How – how did these get here?'

'Ask your wonderful daughter.'

'Don't be cross with me, Dad,' pleaded Tessa.

'Would you mind sitting down?' Oliver waved an arm at an enormous white sofa.

'Cor, this is low, too near the floor for me,' Freddie said, but he sat down next to Tessa, his knees hunched. His eyes looked piercingly at Oliver who sat on one of the cane chairs. 'So what's this about?'

'May I call you Freddie?' Oliver asked.

'Ah – okay,' Freddie said, 'and this is Tarka.'

'He's lovely,' Oliver said, admiringly. He reached over and smoothed Tarka's head.

Tessa thought she could hear Freddie's heart thumping. He looked apprehensive, and his cheek was twitching.

'Well, Freddie,' Oliver began. 'We – that is me and two of the tutors here – have looked at your work and we're impressed, very impressed indeed. Especially, as Tessa tells me, you had no art training. Is that right?'

'Ah – that's right. All I ever had was one pencil, and a weekly art lesson in school. We had to sit there and copy something, copy a picture or draw an apple or a blimin' teapot. It was boring, and we never were allowed to keep our pictures. Only once in my life, the day the 1914–18 war ended, the teacher Mr Price – oh, I hated him – he hated me too! – on that day he said we could draw anything we liked – and I did a shire horse with a little girl on it – Kate.'

'This one.' Tessa held up the old picture which Freddie's mum had proudly kept in a frame.

386

'And when the teacher tried to take it off me (I were nine years old) I grabbed it and ran away. I folded it into eight and stuffed it in me pocket and ran two miles across the fields in the pouring rain to me granny's place. She lived in a cottage in the middle of a wood with her chickens – but when I got there, soaking wet, with me picture, I found her dead on the floor. Dead as a stone. Terrible it was.'

Oliver was listening, fascinated. 'So how did you start the stone carving?'

'Ah – well, that's another story. A stonemason, Herbie, used to ask me to haul stone for him, and one day he bet me a pound that I couldn't carve an angel out of a stone gatepost. Well, I knew I could. I could already see the angel inside the stone, looking out.'

'This one.' Tessa held up the photo of the stone angel.

'Then, once I started, I couldn't stop,' Freddie continued. 'I had a queue of ideas on me mind – things I wanted to carve.'

Oliver listened patiently as Freddie told him about his first commission, about the alabaster quarry, and about his more recent wood carving. Tessa sat there smiling. She hadn't seen him so animated for years. It felt good to see him sitting there, coming alive, his eyes twinkling with untold secrets. She sensed him warming to Oliver who was giving his whole self to listening, with empathy, and with obvious enjoyment.

Freddie would have gone on talking for hours if Oliver hadn't intervened neatly in the gap between two stories.

'You did most of your work in pencil?'

'Ah – I had one pencil to last about three years – sharpened it down to a stub. Precious, it was, that stub of pencil.'

'We particularly admired your detailed drawings of machinery.' Oliver turned the pages of one of the sketch books. 'What kind of machines were they? Like this one, for example?'

'I used to invent things,' Freddie said. 'The one you've got there was a steam powered heli-bus.'

'A steam powered heli-bus. I LOVE it!' Oliver's eyes lit up. He looked at Tessa. 'I think your father is like Leonardo.'

'Leonardo?' Freddie looked bewildered.

'Leonardo da Vinci, Dad,' Tessa said. 'He painted the *Mona Lisa.*'

'Ah – well, I never studied art. Wish I'd had the chance,' Freddie said wistfully.

It was the cue Oliver was waiting for. 'Well, Freddie, Elrose College of Art is keen to offer places to mature students now – we feel so much talent went undiscovered through the wartime years, and mature students have a high work ethic, and life experience to share. So – we'd like to offer you a place here on our three year Bachelor of Arts course, from this coming September.'

Freddie looked at Tessa. 'You mean my daughter, surely, not me.'

'No. We mean you, Freddie. We'd like to offer you a bursary.'

'A bursary?'

'It's like a scholarship, Dad – a free place,' Tessa said.

'Me? You want ME? At my age?'

'Yes, we do. I hope you'll accept.'

'Would I have to come here every day?'

'Four days a week, in term time.'

Tarka sat up and put a large paw on Freddie's knee, gazing at him. Freddie fondled the dog's large head. Finally he said, 'I can't leave me dog.'

'You can bring him with you,' Oliver said. 'He's a good dog, and some of the students will like to draw him.'

Freddie retreated into a transitional silence. Oliver handed him a folder. 'It's set out in there,' he explained. 'The offer of a bursary, and the information about Elrose College, the tutors you'll be working with, and the choices you can make. You'll see there's a Sculpture option, and Calligraphy which seems to be another of your gifts.'

Freddie looked at Tessa. 'Calligraphy?'

'Lettering, Dad.'

'Will you think it over?' Oliver said. 'It's a golden opportunity.'

'It could be,' Freddie said. 'But I will think about it.'

'You can come back and see me, or phone if you've got any questions – anything you want to know.' Oliver stood up and stretched. Tessa helped him to gather up the sketch books and photographs. She took Kate's red ribbon and lovingly tied it around the bundle, aware of Freddie watching her with a poignant expression.

The two men shook hands, with eye contact sparking between them. Freddie managed to say thank you, and then he disappeared into an even deeper silence. It lasted all the way home, even when they stopped by the river, and stopped for fish and chips.

Back at home, with the bundle of sketch books on the dresser, Freddie made just one comment. 'So that's what you were up to.'

Later, Tessa sat cuddling Benita, and observed Freddie studying the folder.

In the morning he was still quiet, reading the information over and over, and staring at buzzards circling in the sky. He seemed emotional, but didn't communicate until lunchtime when he picked a bunch of daffodils from the garden. 'These are for you, dear, to take back to London,' he said, 'and, you know, I've thought long and hard about this bursary. Been awake all night. 'Tis a dream, you see, a dream I had all me life. And I appreciate what you've done. But, honestly, I can't do it. I've got to say no.'

'Aw, Dad – I'm disappointed, for you,' Tessa said. 'Why don't you take your time and think about it a bit longer? There's no pressure.'

But Freddie shook his head.

'What's stopping you?' Tessa asked, but he wouldn't tell her. His eyes took on a glaze of secrecy. She felt powerless and bitterly disappointed. Privately, she feared Freddie was on the edge of a breakdown.

'Now, don't you worry about me,' he said. 'I know you gotta go back to London – and I want you to follow your own dreams, not mine.'

*

A few days later, when Tessa was back in London, Dr Jarvis walked up the path to The Pines, past the empty chicken run with its rusting wire, through the wreckage of Freddie's vegetable garden, which had become a patch of tall thistles, dandelion and rosebay willow herb. He paused to look at the stone carvings in the yard, some of them overgrown with moss and bindweed. The door to Freddie's workshop had always been open and throbbing with the sound of chiselling, the hum of the lathe, and Freddie's whistling. Today it was closed, and ivy fanned across it from the wall.

Benita was on the doorstep, apparently waiting for him, and she escorted him inside, rubbing around his ankles as he pushed the door open.

He found Freddie in his chair by the window, staring into space, with Tarka leaning adoringly against his legs. Freddie looked at him with startled eyes. 'Who called you, Doc?' he asked.

'Lexi.' Dr Jarvis sat down in Kate's chair. He didn't open his brown leather doctor's case, but put it on the floor, and looked at Freddie with knowing eyes. 'Well, the dog and cat look bonny. What about you?'

Freddie struggled to speak. His hands gripped the threadbare arms of his chair.

'Take your time.'

'Ah – Lexi.' Freddie said finally. 'I asked her to go to the Post Office for me, and she said no. She said – "Come on, Freddie, you can do that yourself." Then – I – I couldn't help it, I broke down and told her.'

'Told her what?'

'What I'm gonna tell you now,' Freddie said, his voice gathered strength. 'BUT . . .' His eyes were fierce with terror. 'I want you to promise me that you won't lock me up in one of those places – even though I'm past caring. My life couldn't be much worse, Doc. I know, you're gonna tell me to get up and go out – but I can't, see? I can't. Only if I've got me dog with me. And those beggars in the Post Office, they don't like dogs, they won't let me bring him in. 'Tis like a warzone, that blimin' Post Office.'

'So what exactly is the problem? I need to understand, Freddie, if I'm going to help you.'

Freddie struggled to get the words out.

'I know you're still grieving for Kate,' Dr Jarvis said.

'Ah – but it's not that, Doc. Now, I've never told this to anyone, not even Kate when she was here, not even Tessa.' He stared at Dr Jarvis with desperate eyes. 'I'm like me mother was. Scared to go out – it's an irrational fear, I know that, but she drummed it into me, all my life, that I wasn't to tell anyone in case she got sent to the mad house.'

'We don't have mad houses now,' Dr Jarvis said. 'I understand your fear very well – and it can be treated quite simply with some tablets, and a few sessions of talking to a specialist doctor who will come to see you here in your own home.'

Freddie looked at him in astonishment.

'I promise you, no one is going to lock you up,' Dr Jarvis continued, 'and you don't have to accept the treatment I'm offering. You can go on as you are, if you like.'

'No.' Freddie shook his head. ''Tis ruining my life. It's got worse, see, since Kate died, and my daughter Tessa wants me to go out and about – she even tried to get me into art college, would you believe? At my age!'

'You're not old. You're a spring chicken,' Dr Jarvis said. 'Look at me – in my seventies and still working, still playing golf and doing the garden.'

'How long will this treatment take to work?'

'It depends on how determined you are – but the tablets will make a difference immediately, the talking will take longer, but it's worth doing in the long term.'

'Then – let's give it a go,' Freddie said. 'And I'm glad you came, Doc – I feel ten ton lighter now I've told you.'

CHAPTER 22

There Will be an Answer

A robin was the first bird to investigate the brightly painted bus in a secluded part of the wood. It had been parked there for longer than the robin could remember. No one came out or went in to it. The robin assumed it had been abandoned and was now part of the wood. The door was open, and at first it had banged to and fro on windy nights, keeping the wild creatures away. But over the years tenacious vines of ivy, bindweed and wild clematis had crept over it, immobilising the door, twining in through the open windows. Brambles arched right over the roof with strong thorny stems, some even touching the woodland floor on the other side, sending eager roots fanning out into the rich leaf mould, making a new thicket. An elder tree seeded itself and grew vigorously from behind the front wheel, its sharply scented branches pushing into the driver's window, through the steering wheel and over the red leather seat.

In early March, the robin dared to fly in through an open window. First he checked that he could fly out again and not be trapped, then he fetched his mate from the curly oak tree where she was waiting, fluttering her wings impatiently. Together they explored the interior of the bus, the moss-covered table and chairs, the rusting Queenie stove, the shelves of mouldering books. They found the right spot between an *Oxford Dictionary* and the *Penguin Modern Poets* which were leaning against each other creating a robin-sized wigwam. Perfect! The robins set about building a nest in there, flying in and out from the wood, their beaks bursting with twigs and straw. They lined the nest with sheep's wool and moss.

In April when the robins were busy feeding a family of five, the wild bees found the pencil hole in the bodywork, the hole that Tessa had skilfully camouflaged as the centre of a marigold. With much humming and dancing in the air, the wild bees crawled in and set up home for their queen, building a golden dome of hexagonal cells. They worked the elderflowers and the pale green flowers of the lime trees, and made honey in such abundance that it oozed out of the pencil hole and poured down the side of the bus, attracting more wild creatures, the badgers, ants and foxes.

A family of wood mice moved in, exquisitely beautiful and sensitive with their jet black eyes and shell-like ears. They chewed the pages of an orange and white Penguin classic, *For Whom the Bell Tolls* by Ernest Hemingway, and made a soft white mansion of a nest for their children and grandchildren. Below the bus was a haven of dry leaf litter where hedgehogs hibernated and families of copper-skinned slowworms set up home. Ferns, mosses and fungi colonised the wheels and the steps.

Like a sunken ship becoming a reef, the bus became one with the wood, completely covered in summer by leaves and blossom. Only in winter did the colours glow between the lattice of bare branches, like stained glass. Over time, the bus itself would become organic, a rusting, flaking relic returning its timber, paper and metal to the earth.

The track through the woods became narrower from never being used. The old wheel-ruts filled with leaves; the wood irises, hemp-agrimony and tough grasses made clumps along the edges, and blackthorn bushes seeded themselves. What had once been a wide path for horses, tractors and carts became a rabbit path, used by the creatures of the wood.

Tessa pounced on the white envelope with Somerset County Council along the top. Standing in the kitchen window of her flat in London, she unfolded the letter eagerly, unprepared for the cold wave of rejection rushing into her life. No. They had said no. No, she couldn't restore the Holy Well. She couldn't build a barn and open a healing centre. Not in Monterose.

To add insult to injury, John Whitsby's signature was at the bottom.

Furious and hurt, Tessa screwed the letter into a ball and hurled it into the bin. 'Pompous bunch of bureaucrats,' she ranted, and slumped into a chair, staring out of the window at rooftops and chimneys, everything terracotta and grey in the heat-haze of early summer. *I'm stuck in London. Forever and bloody ever*, she thought, and felt the longing dragging her down. The blue-green landscapes of Somerset burned in her mind. *Not another summer. Not another summer in London.*

When the first surge of anger had passed, she retrieved the letter from the bin and smoothed it out again. John Whitsby had added a handwritten note, commiserating, and advising her to appeal.

'Bring it over here, Tessa,' Starlinda said, on the phone. 'I need to touch this man's signature. Something's going on. I've got an hour now, before my next client.'

The two women sat in Starlinda's rooftop garden, under a potted palm tree, with the letter on the coffee table, weighted down with a chunk of rose quartz. 'It's not John Whitsby's fault – he's okay, he's a kindred spirit,' Starlinda said. 'It's something else – some missing ingredient, Tessa. What's missing from your life?'

Tessa hesitated.

'Close your eyes, and put your hand on your heart,' Starlinda said, patiently. 'What is missing from your life?'

Tessa knew the answer, but it stuck in her throat.

'What is missing from your life?' Starlinda repeated quietly. 'Let it speak, and if it can only speak in tears, then let the tears flow. Tears were given to us for cleansing and healing.'

Tessa felt herself collapsing. 'Art,' she gasped, and

yesterday's pain engulfed her in what felt like the final letting-go.

Starlinda sat with her in an oasis of calm. 'So where is Art?'

'No one knows,' Tessa said. 'No one even knows if he – if he's alive. Lou said he'd gone to Findhorn, and someone else said he was in Nepal. But even if I found him, Starlinda, he's with Rowan and their child.'

'He may not be. Have you looked at his star-chart, Tessa?'

'I have – and it does prove we've got a strong link.'

'I'd call it an unbreakable bond,' Starlinda said.

'But what if—'

'No – you must ride over the what-ifs to get to the truth. You have to find him, Tessa. I think you know that – don't you?'

Tessa nodded dumbly.

'Nothing will happen until you take the first step. This letter, this decision, has been sent to challenge you, to make you go beyond the fear, beyond the pain, and find the blessing.' She handed the letter back to Tessa. 'This letter is a signpost. Darling, you have to do something bold – a leap of faith. And the time is NOW.'

Tessa stared at her, frightened by what she knew she must do.

'You're an awesome friend. Thanks.' She gave Starlinda a hug. 'I'll go now. I know you've got a client.'

Starlinda's extraordinary eyes smiled into hers, for an expanding moment. *She's saying goodbye*, Tessa thought. But Starlinda never used cut-off words like 'goodbye'. She lived in the now. Her smile was bright and encouraging. 'Good luck, darling. I'll send you love and light.'

Tessa went home and packed. Jeans, tops, and one exotic outfit, her favourite, a full-length dress in a soft, sparkly fabric. She loved the way it glittered with greens of the forest, the flared sleeves flowing as she lifted her slim arms. She packed her crystal bracelets, silver stilettos, and a white mohair bolero. She added rose and sandalwood incense sticks, shampoo and conditioner, and her makeup bag. Then she took out the box of posters she'd had printed, and put them in before zipping up her light blue case.

She locked the flat, and drove out of London.

It was the time of the harvest moon. Late August, when sunset over the Somerset Levels was mirrored in the eastern sky by a huge, coral-coloured moon.

Tessa had deliberately chosen the night of the full moon to do her first big event in Somerset. She'd booked Glastonbury Town Hall, and advertised widely, in the newspapers and by distributing the posters herself. She was more nervous about working in her own home area than she'd ever been in London. Old demons from childhood stalked her, no matter how she tried to ignore them. Memories of being bullied at school, being labelled a troublemaker. Old attitudes and prejudices. In London she always had support from Starlinda, or Ross, or whoever had booked her. It felt scary to do a meeting totally on her own.

She passionately wanted her dad to go with her. 'I really

want you to experience what I do, Dad,' she said. 'I've worked so hard at it, and this meeting is important – it could make or break my chance of living and working down here in Somerset.'

She was disappointed when Freddie consistently refused to go, his excuses ranging from 'I can't leave me dog' to 'I never did like Glastonbury'. Even when she'd said, 'Mum would have made you go,' he stubbornly refused, and wouldn't discuss it with her. Tessa wanted to scream at him. Instead, she quietly picked up Benita and carried her into the sunlit garden. She sat in the Anderson Hollow, talking to the little cat's attentive golden eyes.

'I feel like packing it in, Benita,' she said. 'Dad is impossible – just impossible. And I miss Mum so much.' She paused and took some deep breaths. In the hours before her meeting she didn't want to be crying, and arriving with swollen red eyes. She must look joyful and confident. Extra, extra confident as this was Somerset, not London. 'London EXPECTS me to be brilliant and successful,' she told Benita, 'but Somerset expects me to fail. WHY?' It was like being a child again, kicking the earth and sulking out in the garden. She felt that same endemic loneliness of being different. Benita stretched a velvet paw and patted her cheek, purring and rubbing her head against Tessa's heart. 'You're a darling,' Tessa said, and sighed. 'Maybe I should quit and go back to London, forget trying to move back home.' She looked at her watch. Three o'clock. Her Glastonbury meeting was at 7:30, and she'd planned to have a bath and change, then leave at 6:45.

At the moment when the Monterose church clock chimed three, she had a flash of inspiration. There was just time for her to go to the field, sit by the spring, and try to recharge.

She took Benita indoors; Freddie was still in his chair, and he was actually asleep, his head sagging sideways. Tessa looked at him sadly, and decided not to wake him. She left a note on the kitchen table, and set off, feeling inconspicuously at home in her jeans, denim shirt, and with her hair tied back in a loose ponytail.

Mellow sunlight coloured the apple orchards, the trees laden to the ground with fruit. Tessa walked slowly through the balmy afternoon, wondering why she felt so tired. The last six weeks had been hard, dashing to and fro between London and Somerset, trying to honour her commitments. Ironically she'd had hardly any time to visit the spring, which was her main reason for wanting to move back home.

She climbed over the gate and immediately sensed that something had changed. Half walking, half meditating, she followed the stream up to the source. She sat under the elder tree's drooping fronds of purple berries, and closed her eyes. She listened. Subconsciously, she was listening for the singing, but it was silent up in the wood. In her meditation she asked for help with tonight's meeting, clarity of insight and nerves of steel. Detachment from the bonds of her earth life. She'd tried so hard to explain her work to Freddie, and there had been an occasional glimmer of interest in his still grieving eyes. 'It's not about me showing off my clairvoyance, Dad,' she'd said. 'My passion is to use it to help people, and it does. I know it does. It helps them to climb out of their grief and their scepticism, brings them into the light and proves their loved ones are still alive, still close enough to care. They can't get that kind of help anywhere else – and I love to do it, Dad.'

The way the water bubbled up from the earth was calming, like a song with the background music of grasshoppers and swallows. The robin appeared just when it was time to go.

Tessa got up and stretched. The robin chattered from a branch, looking at her with unfathomable knowing. She watched him fly towards the wood, and what she saw sent a chilling tingle around her bare neck and into her hair. Goosebumps prickled along her arms. And time stood still.

The gate in the new fence, which had always been locked, was swinging open, the emerald light of the woodland path calling to her – calling. And she couldn't go – not NOW.

Freddie felt as if he'd been asleep for a hundred years and was suddenly shocked into life. He stared, open-mouthed, at the young woman drifting down the stairs. Her dress swished seductively as she walked into the room where he was sitting. Freddie had never seen, or imagined, such a dress. It glistened with all the greens of the forest, a soft, hazy jacket whiter than the morning mist over the Levels. A pair of graceful young arms with crystal bangles. A mane of chestnut hair, caught back with a slide of rhinestones and pearl.

A bewitching smile, like Kate's smile, and THOSE EYES, pale blue eyes with a core of gold, eyes so full of light. It took his breath away.

'Wish me luck, Dad.' Tessa bent over to kiss him, her car keys hooked around a slender finger. 'I'll be back about ten thirtyish.'

Freddie got to his feet. He touched the softness of the white jacket covering her shoulders. 'You look – beautiful – stunning.'

'Thanks, Dad. Are you sure you won't come?'

Freddie felt the encrypted power of the word NO clamping his heart. He heard Tarka's tail thumping against the chair. He knew from Tessa's expression that she'd seen the light die in his eyes. He didn't need to say it.

'Okay,' she said pleasantly. 'I'll see you later, Dad.'

She swanned out, briskly. Like Kate.

Freddie went to the window and watched her get into the car in the golden evening. *Whatever happened to our little girl with plaits?* he thought, shocked. *I can't let her go to GLASTONBURY to some meeting, all alone, looking like THAT.*

He strode to the front door and out into the drive, only to see Tessa's car disappearing down the lane. 'Hang on a minute,' he shouted, 'I've changed me mind.'

Too late. Tessa had gone, in her dazzling dress, her aura shining with the radiance he needed.

Freddie looked down at Tarka. 'I gotta go,' he said and noticed his scruffy trousers and slippers. He bounded upstairs

403

with money jingling in his pockets, tore a suit from the wardrobe, and a shirt and tie he hadn't worn for years. It still fitted. He combed his hair and eased his feet into a creaking pair of shoes, glanced at his frightened eyes in the mirror, and ran downstairs.

Benita had got Tarka onto the sofa and was curled up, blissfully, under his chin. She gazed at Freddie with confident eyes, as if to say she'd keep an eye on the big dog and not let him howl or eat the hearth rug.

Freddie started the Morris Traveller and headed for Glastonbury with the sun setting out west over the Levels and the harvest moon rising over the wooded hills.

'We can just squeeze you in, sir,' John Whitsby greeted Freddie at the door and found him a chair. 'I'm John Whitsby, by the way – you're Tessa's father, aren't you?'

Freddie nodded, breathing hard from running up the steps of Glastonbury Town Hall. Inside it was buzzing with excitement. He looked at the sea of heads in front of him, and couldn't see Tessa anywhere. Had he come to the right place?

'I offered to be the doorman for Tessa,' John Whitsby whispered to him, 'when I saw she was on her own.'

At seven thirty, the audience fell silent, and there was only the swish of Tessa's dress and the tap of her shoes as she walked down the gangway. Freddie reached out and touched her, a lump in his throat, wanting her to know he was there. She did more than smile in surprise. She paused and hugged him. 'Thanks, Dad,' she whispered, and it meant the world to Freddie. He sat, on the shoreline of tears, and watched her in awe.

She began with the heart meditation, something she had offered to do for him many times, and he'd said no. Now he closed his eyes with everyone else, amazed at how easy and right it felt to open his heart like a flower and feel his spirit coming in, coming home. He felt alive and awake for the first time since Kate had passed.

Two hours flew by as he watched and listened, entranced by the way Tessa seemed to mesmerise the audience as she picked out people who had visitors and messages from spirit. Her voice was firm and gentle, her eyes bewitching, her confidence unwavering. There were tears of joy, and hugs and spontaneous applause. And gratitude. It was huge. Freddie began to feel himself changing inside, as if a pathway to heaven opened in his heart. He never wanted it to end, and when Tessa closed the meeting by asking everyone to reach out and hold hands with the person next to them, Freddie was overwhelmed. For the first time, ever in his life, he felt that every single person in the hall was his friend.

'We are one,' Tessa said. 'We are all on a journey, a journey home to our true spiritual selves. The loved ones who have visited you tonight are not just here, in this hall, on this day. They are with you always. Trust and go forward. You are not alone.'

She sat down to thunderous applause and a few wolf whistles. Someone at the back shouted 'Awesome!' and Freddie swung round to see a man with a black hat pulled over his eyes. An oddly familiar figure, who quickly got up and left the hall before anyone else.

Freddie stayed in his seat as people filed out, some of them lingering, crowding around Tessa to thank her and ask her questions. Freddie's vision cleared and he saw Kate, radiant and bright-eyed, standing next to Tessa. *I can still do it*, he thought, wanting to laugh and cry at the same time, *and maybe I can begin to live again*.

Tessa slept late into the following morning, emerging at ten o'clock, to find Freddie standing in the hall, his hand on the telephone. All night her mind had been on the open gate to the wood, the way it called to her, the robin enticing her in. Would it be wise to go in there on her own? Should she ask her dad to go with her? Or borrow Tarka? Consistently her inner guidance said she must go alone. Today. At noon.

Freddie was looking at her strangely as she came downstairs, carrying Benita on one shoulder. 'Now I'm gonna tell you something,' he began, and led her to the kitchen table, his eyes like they used to be, twinkling with some untold secret.

'You look different, Dad,' she said, sitting down at the old kitchen table.

'Ah – I am different.' Freddie sat down, looking into her eyes. 'You inspired me last night, love. You were wonderful. I were proud of you – and surprised. I never realised you'd done all that training and achieved so much – you were such a troubled little girl – and now people love you, I can see that. It woke me up, I can tell you – I've been in the fog ever since Kate died. I'd given up. I really had.'

'You were grieving,' Tessa said kindly.

'Well – that's not what I wanted to tell you,' Freddie said, his eyes even brighter. 'You inspired me so much, I thought I'd make a phone call.'

'Go on.'

'I rang Oliver Portwell, and asked him if his offer was still open, and he said yes – said they'd be glad to have me. So I told him I'd go. I start at Elrose College of Art in September.'

'Oh Dad!' Tessa squealed with joy. 'That's fantastic! Wow. I'm proud of you too. You've been the best dad on the planet, and you deserve a chance like this. Wow! If Mum was here she'd be dancing round the kitchen.'

Freddie beamed, and his face ached from smiling, the way it used to when Kate was there.

'Where are you going now?' he asked.

'Up to the field,' Tessa said, not wanting to worry him with talk about the gate being open. 'What are you going to do?'

'Open up me workshop and think about carving another angel,' he said, 'and this time, she'll look like you.'

CHAPTER 23

The Singer in the Wood

The robin was waiting on top of the spindle tree as Tessa arrived at the field. She saw him immediately, his red breast glowing amongst the pink and orange spindleberries.

This time she'd brought the car, and backed it into the gateway, in case she needed to escape. She wore her favourite jeans, flared and frayed around the ankles, her *Friends of the Earth* t-shirt and stone-washed denim jacket. She fished in the innermost pocket of her bag and found her velvet pouch of crystals. Closing her eyes, she touched each one, and chose the amber bead Art had given her long ago. She threaded it into a strand of her hair, and got out of the car. With her eyes fixed nervously on the open gate in the far corner, she followed the robin along the hedge.

She tried to remember if she'd ever been in that part of the wood in her childhood, before it was divided up and sold. It had been part of the six miles of ancient woodland on the southern slopes of the Polden Hills. There was a memory of an enchanted glade where she and Lucy had played, and a mossy bank overhung with giant beeches, and the wood of coppiced hazel where the nightingales sang.

At the gate she stood touching the padlock which had been left, unlocked, hooked into the wire. She listened, tense and alert. Deep in the leaf-layers of time she could hear the true song of the wood, the fairy harps, the Pan Pipes. She felt free now to hear their music, free to learn the secrets of this special grove.

Tingling from head to toe, Tessa followed the robin from tree to tree, her shoes soundless on the path. The noon-time light cascaded over the canopy of beech and oak, sharpening the outlines of the dark spaces. The deeper she ventured into the wood, the more the light burned silver, the greens more vivid, the branches more indigo like veins and arteries carrying pulses of life to the far edges of sky.

Each time she paused to listen, the robin scolded her and led her on. The sounds of the outside world had gone. Tessa felt she floated in a bubble of translucence. Yet she was increasingly afraid. To go back was no longer an option. There was something she had to find. Something waiting. She sensed the leaves closing behind her, like a conspiracy, the trees growing older, more gnarled with faces, with lips, and eyes, and breath.

She stopped to admire a raindrop caught in the palm of a sycamore leaf. The robin had vanished. She heard him deep inside a thicket of arching bramble and the trumpet flowers of bindweed, shockingly white, like flowers piled on top of a hearse.

A chill crawled over Tessa, an unexpected doom-laden shudder of fear. With cold, unsteady hands she parted the foliage in front of her. She reached through a tangle of stems and touched something rubbery. A tyre, an old tyre someone had dumped in the wood. Why did it spook her? She tugged the tendrils of creeper apart, and saw colours. Colours she knew well. Colours she had once painted. Her mind flashed back to a scorching day in St Ives, a happy day when she'd been free and in love, painting marigolds on Art's bus, with the ocean surf foaming and sparkling. Now she was seeing those painted marigolds, rusting, covered in moss.

The bus. She'd found the bus.

Abandoned.

She screamed. 'NO. NO. Oh God!' and her scream pierced the canopy of leaves and fractured the sky into flakes of blue glass. Birds flew up, out of the wood, screaming with her, their wings beating like the panic in her heart.

He's dead, she thought, and stumbled across the path, and collapsed against the trunk of a beech tree, her hands clutched against her temples. *I can't face this. Surely he didn't die, all alone in the bus?*

It might have gone on, and on, hauling her into the deepest grief she could possibly imagine. But as the echo of her scream reverberated into the hills, she heard the singing. The earthy twang of an acoustic guitar, the husky voice, the same old Beatles song, now close, the words distinctly reaching her.

When I find myself in times of trouble
Mother Mary comes to me
Speaking words of wisdom, let it be.
And in my hour of darkness
She is standing right in front of me
Speaking words of wisdom, let it be.

Tessa hesitated, her nerves on thin ice as her eyes searched the spaces between the trees. She noticed the path was wider, the light more luminous, the air seasoned with a tang of wood smoke. She tiptoed over the beech leaves, while the song gathered a magnetic power that rang through the wood.

And when the broken-hearted people
Living in the world agree
There will be an answer, let it be.
For though they may be parted
There is still a chance that they will see
There will be an answer, let it be.

And then she saw him. The singer in the wood. Standing against an oak tree, singing his heart out, a black hat pulled down over his brow. The man in the hat who had been there at her meeting! She'd heard his voice shout 'AWESOME' at the end. She'd seen him slip away, out of the door before anyone could see the face below the hat.

She stood there looking at him.

And suddenly he couldn't sing any more. The guitar slid

down to the earth. The hat came off. The dear, beloved smile lit his face, reached his intense grey eyes.

'Tessa.'

His voice was tender. Loving.

They ran towards each other.

'Art!' she breathed, and ribbons of joy seemed to swirl around them as they hugged in the silence of the wood. Hugged, as if they'd never been apart.

Hand in hand they climbed the path through the ancient woodland, where ferns grew along the branches, and creepers, centuries old, hung down from the tallest trees. Alongside the path were clouds of hemp-agrimony, alive with butterflies, and clumps of wood irises with seed pods crammed with orange berries. At the top of the wood was a grove of mature pine trees, and beyond them, a sense of a light, a new world to be discovered.

Tessa floated, in a bubble of dreams. Was she really walking hand in hand with Art? Going with him so trustingly as he led her, with light in his eyes, to the other side of the wood. It seemed symbolic, as if the dark wood was her life, and now she was going to arrive into the shimmering light. Into the future.

They emerged from the pine wood into warm, grass-scented sunshine. The Vale of Avalon stretched out before them, like a smile. Peaceful fields and cottages, the green Levels dusted gold by the sun, the velvet slopes of Glastonbury Tor, and the blue hills of Mendip beyond.

An afternoon place. Like heaven, where the embers of day burned on forever.

'This is where I live now.' Art waved his hand at the margin of grassland on the edge of the wood. At the far end was an expertly made bender, with a VW camper van parked nearby. A wooden gate led into a lane.

Tessa was holding back, expecting Rowan to appear and shatter her glimpse of paradise. Someone was there, she was sure, and it was a woman, a bright, bird-like face that bobbed out of the trees and beckoned to her.

'I bought this section of the wood when the forest along the Poldens was split up,' Art told her, obviously enjoying the look of surprise on her face. 'I spent every last bean of my trust fund which Grandad left me. I fenced it off to protect the wildlife. It was my ambition, to do something like this for the planet.'

'That's brilliant,' Tessa said, but still she waited for the woman to appear. She fixed her eyes on a tall lime tree which had the feeling of being a guardian, a sentinel, an entrance to some magical place. And the woman was behind it. Waiting.

'When I first bought it,' Art continued, 'I drove the bus in along the old cart track. It was muddy, and the wheels sank in and got horribly stuck. I bust a gut trying to get her out, but she was leaning sideways, and I had to leave her there. I went off to Nepal for a couple of years – that was awesome. Then I stayed with my folks while I studied Ecology at college. By then the bus was so overgrown, and birds were nesting in there, so it felt right to let her become part of the wood.'

Tessa was only half listening. She could see the aura of the woman waiting behind the lime tree.

'I've been studying sustainable forestry,' Art said, his voice warm with enthusiasm. 'I intend to manage the wood sympathetically, and I really hope that one day the nightingales will come back. I know how much you love them.' He looked puzzled when Tessa didn't respond. 'What are you looking at?'

'So – where's Rowan?' she asked.

'Aw – that only lasted a few months.' Art looked sad, and serious. He took Tessa's hands. 'It was a big lesson for me. Rowan's in Crete now, with Willow, living in a commune – and – I'm so sorry, Tessa, for hurting you like that.'

Tessa's spirits lifted. Rowan was gone! So who was the woman behind the lime tree?

'Actually it kick-started me into doing something with my life,' she said. 'I had a job I loved in London, with special needs children. But I made a terrible mistake in marrying Paul. We've split up now. I've still got a flat in London, but I'm trying to move back here.'

'I know your mum died,' Art said. 'I'm so sorry.'

Tessa shrugged. 'I miss her – a lot – and Dad is ...' she paused, distracted by the bright face of the woman who darted out from behind the lime tree and beckoned mischievously. *Art would have someone else*, she thought, *so what am I doing here? I should go.*

'Tessa?'

She felt the love from his intense, enquiring gaze. 'But there's someone here with you,' she asked, 'isn't there?'

'No. Nobody.'

'Okay. Hang on a minute.' Tessa needed to tune in to spirit. It wasn't the first time she'd been confused by seeing a spirit person so clearly. Was this a spirit? Or was she real?

Art waited, respectfully.

'I'm seeing a woman – a vibrant, happy little person,' Tessa said, and then she smiled with relief. 'Oh, I know who it is – I've seen her before. It's my dad's granny. Granny Barcussy! She keeps popping out from behind that big lime tree, as if she wants to show me something.'

Art smiled. 'Wow! I've sensed her around, often, Tessa. It's good to know who she is – or was.'

'Is,' Tessa said.

'And she does want to show you something – come this way.' Art looked excited now. He led her to the lime tree. 'Da da!' He waved his arm proudly and Tessa stared, open-mouthed into the glade.

A ruined cottage stood there, partly covered in ivy. The walls, door and windows were still intact, and rays of sunlight beamed in, illuminating an inglenook fireplace and a floor of blue-lias flagstones. Scarlet rosehips and trails of bryony grew around the porch, and a Red Admiral butterfly was sunning itself on the silver-white stones.

'What is it? What's the matter,' Art asked, as tears poured down Tessa's cheeks.

'It's okay – I'm not sad.' She brushed the tears away. 'I'm just – overwhelmed, Art – this is Granny Barcussy's cottage. It's where she lived. Dad used to bring us up here sometimes to see it, and he was always upset because it was a ruin. But we'd sit inside, Lucy and I, and he'd tell us stories.'

'That's awesome,' Art said. 'Well, I'm restoring it. I've just started the roof – hopefully I can get it up before the winter, then I can move in.'

'Dad will be thrilled,' Tessa said. 'And I'm – over the moon – Did she lead you here? Granny Barcussy?'

'Maybe – she kind of did.'

'I'm overwhelmed,' Tessa said, again. 'So much happiness in one day.'

But Art looked serious. 'I thought you'd never forgive me. So I didn't hassle you. I watched you from afar.'

'The black hat?' she said, grinning.

'Yeah, the black hat,' he confirmed. 'I watched your wedding, from a distance and I felt – gutted – absolutely gutted – and angry with myself. That's why I went off to Nepal. The truth is, Tessa – I've never stopped loving you.'

Tessa couldn't speak. She let him hold her. She felt the longing in him and she sensed him holding back.

'It's awesome to be with you again,' he murmured. 'Even to spend five minutes with you, Tessa. I realise I'm not good enough for you now – you're so accomplished and you're not a lost little girl any more. You're a beautiful, shining soul. I'd love to be part of your life, if you'll have me. I'll do anything I can to help you.'

Tessa closed her eyes. She became aware of an auspicious gathering of spirit friends around them both. Kate was there, and Bertie, and Granny Barcussy. The tiny spirits of the wood were there, and a tall angel of light. *It's like a wedding,* she thought, *they have come to witness and wish us luck.*

'I really wanted to do that project we dreamed of together,' Art said. 'Restoring the Holy Well and building a healing centre. I read the piece you wrote for the *Gazette* – about the history of it – and it inspired me. It's important for us to do it.'

Tessa opened her eyes to the intensity of his gaze. She felt his soul merging into hers, like two colours of paint, making a new colour, never seen on earth before. And she wanted it with the whole of her being. *The marriage is now. In spirit,* she thought, *here in Granny Barcussy's cottage.*

'Do you still have the dream?' he asked. 'I watched you one day, with those men with clipboards. Planners? I knew they voted no – I saw that in the *Gazette* too.'

He was still holding her hands. Tessa took a breath. She wanted to scream with joy, but she lowered her voice and talked to him quietly. 'Art – I never stopped loving you either. I searched for you. Every hippie in the distance was you. I've carried you in my heart. I will never let you go, even if you walk away from me now. We are soulmates, lovers across time, through many lifetimes.' She paused, letting the stardust settle between them. 'And when soulmates come together, their auras merge and create a unique flame of light, a flame that kindles dreams.'

'Aw, Tessa,' Art seemed overwhelmed, 'I hardly dared to hope we could be together again.'

'It was meant to happen,' Tessa said, 'and we're both stronger for having been apart. I was in denial for years, until

I met Starlinda and she believed in me. I owe her everything. She led me home to who I am. When the planners said no, I was furious, but she helped me to see the spiritual reason. It made me take a leap of faith, and look what's happened – I found the singer in the wood!'

Art grinned. 'I was singing that song for you, every time. I knew you loved it. And next time the planners will say yes. We have to begin – that's the secret.' He took a dog-eared postcard from the inner pocket of his jacket. 'I carry this with me, Tessa. It's like a mantra!'

With their heads close, they read the words of Goethe, printed on a photo of a rainbow:

> *Whatever you dream, or dream you can do, begin it.*
> *Boldness has genius, power and magic. Begin it now!*

'I love it,' Tessa said, and her eyes shone, pale blue with flecks of gold.

Art smiled into her soul. He drew her slowly towards him, and they kissed for a burning moment. In the hot silence of reunion, the dream they had once shared came drifting in through the veils of spirit light, like a crystal gifted from the aeons of time. The ultimate jewel of creativity and love.

ACKNOWLEDGEMENTS

Thank you to our Tuesday Meditation Group for their love and encouragement.

Thank you to my family – Jade, Pete and sister June for your kindness and support, and to my husband, Ted, for his endless patience. Thank you to my agent, Judith Murdoch, my editor Jo, and to Beth Emanuel for her dedicated typing and technical support.

THE SAMARITANS, founded by Chad Varah in 1953 at St Stephen's, Walbrook, is still alive and well, offering help, listening and anonymity to anyone who is desperate, suicidal, or in need of help.

Find them online at www.samaritans.org, or via their helpline 116123 from UK mobiles and landlines.

The Boy with no Boots

Sheila Jeffries

Freddie Barcussy knows hardship and pain.
His parents Annie and Levi are struggling to make
ends meet, both suffering with illness and poverty.
Freddie is an outsider at school, misunderstood
and angry. They need their luck to change.

Unbeknown to his parents, Freddie holds the key to their
future. He has a gift, a gift he has told no one about. If
he can learn how to overcome his fears, he could use it to
change all their lives for ever . . . Searching to overcome
hardship and prejudice, can Freddie find love and
happiness or will mistrust ruin his life?

For fans of nostalgic saga, this is a gripping saga
from the bestselling author of *Solomon's Tale*.

Paperback: 978-1-4711-3765-5
eBook: 978-1-4711-3766-2

The Girl by the River

Sheila Jeffries

Moments after she is born, Tessa Barcussy is
branded as 'trouble'. On the same day, her father
Freddie encounters a Romany Gypsy who makes a
chilling prediction about Tessa's destiny. Freddie finds it
so disturbing that he writes it down and hides it in a
sealed envelope – never to be opened, he hopes.
Yet the gypsy's words haunt him as he bonds
with his new baby daughter.

Hyper-sensitive and rebellious, Tessa grows up a misfit,
difficult to handle and disruptive. Freddie and his wife
Kate struggle to raise this challenging child and nurture
her creative gifts. Tessa feels that her path to happiness is
chequered, growing up in the shadow of her sister, golden-
child Lucy, and hiding a dark secret from everyone?

Will the words of the Romany Gypsy come true?
Or will they empower Tessa to finally become
the person she was born to be?

Paperback: 978-1-4711-5492-8
eBook: 978-1-4711-5493-5

to him saying that. He wore his hatred like a hat turned backwards, a badge of rebellion.

'I want to play you something I've been working on. Will you listen?'

'Sure,' Tessa said. 'You know I love to hear you play.'

She sank into the beanbag chair in Paul's attic study. His parents were in Italy, and they had the big house to themselves on a winter Saturday. Tessa gazed down at the rose garden below the window, its bare brown twigs still dusted with frost. Her eyes were drawn to the archway in the box hedge, half-hoping to see the mysterious Violetta again.

'Are you listening or not?'

'I'm listening.'

'No you're not. You're more interested in the garden.'

'So you want me to look at you as well as listen?' Tessa said. 'You don't own me, Paul. Wait and see if your music grabs my attention.'

'It will,' he predicted, tuning the violin. 'It's the Bruch violin concerto. It begins like the sea, with the wind blowing and the waves curling higher and higher. You'll like it. But look at me, please – PLEASE!' he snapped with sudden intensity. 'I can't bear to play to someone who is staring out of the window. That's exactly what my mother used to do – but if Amelia was doing it, even badly, she'd sit there looking besotted.'

Tessa swallowed the words she wanted to say about why Paul was punishing her for Penelope's past crimes. 'I'm listening,' she repeated patiently. Understanding Paul was like a project to Tessa. He was challenging, like Selwyn had been, but he was like that because he needed her to give him something he'd never had. Healing love. Nurturing praise. Part of her was flattered that he thought of her as some kind of mothering angel, and part of her was nervous about his intensity and whether she could handle it.

Paul began to play, a deep frown over his brow, his eyes closed, his body swaying with the haunting music. It was indeed like the waves of the sea, and technically difficult. Tessa held her breath, praying he wouldn't make a mistake, lose his temper and smash things. But he played perfectly, and with passion, his eyes alight with a kind of love different from human love. Music was his true language, his only language, and no one except Tessa understood that. What she was hearing, and seeing, was the transformation of an angry young man into a loving, eloquent being: a being striving for perfection.

Having witnessed his fury at failure, Tessa was thrilled to hear him playing so well, to see the frown soften into joy as he played the last note with a flourish.

'Fantastic! Fabulous – I LOVED it,' she smiled and jumped up to give him a hug.

'Thanks.' Paul gazed at her radiant face. Then he did something surprising. He put the violin down on the table and reached into his bureau, taking out something small enough to conceal in his hand. He came towards her, hesitantly, with strange excitement in his hazel eyes.

'I've wanted to play you that music ever since I first saw